VARIANT LOST

The Evelyn Maynard Trilogy
Part One

KAYDENCE SNOW

Cover design by Mila Book Covers
Book design by Inkstain Design Studio
Editing by Kirstin Andrews

www.kaydencesnow.com

To John.

For believing in me, even when I didn't.

VARIANT
LOST

ONE

I looked down at my watch: two minutes past midnight. It was officially my seventeenth birthday.

In the uncomfortable plastic seat next to me, my mother, Joyce, saw me checking the time. She kept her voice low as she reached for my arm. "Happy birthday, Evie."

"Don't," I grumbled and pulled my arm out of her reach.

She sighed and sat up straighter. To the casual observer she looked completely calm, sitting in the departures lounge at gate twelve at Melbourne Airport, her hands folded gently in her lap. It was a well-practiced mask—she was on high alert. We were sitting in seats with a wall at our backs as she scanned the airport every few seconds. Her oversized handbag was still slung over her shoulder, just like mine, in case we needed to move fast.

I bit down on my tongue to stop myself from crying. I was trying to be as alert as she was, but I kept thinking about the reason *why* we were at the airport, waiting to board a flight to Los Angeles with tickets purchased only hours before and new counterfeit passports tucked into our bags. I had committed a cardinal sin in my mother's eyes: I had made friends and got myself a boyfriend.

Naturally, we had to change our names and leave the country.

Ever since I could remember, my mother and I had been running, never staying in one place for longer than a few months, never getting close to other people. I was used to this routine, but this time I was more than just frustrated with having to start at another new school and memorize another new name. This time, for the first time, I was actually leaving something behind.

A flash of movement caught my attention and my mother stiffened, but she relaxed when she realized it was just a Variant, rushing through the airport at superhuman speed. The man in a suit had a panicked look on his face as he used his ability to get to his gate on time.

He was one of the approximately 18 percent of the world's population lucky enough to have Variant DNA, but his ability was a common one. I was just a boring human, a fact my mother was eternally grateful for, as it made it easier for us to blend in.

A painfully polite female voice came through the speakers: "Ladies and gentlemen, Qantas flight QF83 to Los Angeles will begin boarding shortly."

I tuned her out. I had taken more flights in my seventeen years than most people did their entire lives. I knew the boarding procedures better than half the ground staff.

I knew many things your average teenager didn't.

Instead of explaining the reasons behind our nomadic lifestyle, my mother had taught me how to be invisible. I knew to place myself near an exit in every building. I knew how to spot a person or vehicle that was following me and how to lose them. I knew how to completely wipe the memory of any electronic device. I knew how to forge official documents.

I knew everything except what I actually wanted to know—*why?*

I *didn't* know why my mother chose the places we went to over the years, zigzagging from one continent to the next. Until now, whenever I'd suggested America, she'd shut me down with a firm "no," but all of a sudden we were on our way to LA, and from there to Nampa, Idaho—a very specific location that I suspected was chosen very randomly.

Whatever the reason Joyce had chosen Nampa, the first leg of our journey was about to begin. Boarding had started.

With another surreptitious look around the airport, my mother placed herself behind me as we joined the line, shielding me from some unspoken potential threat. I rolled my eyes at her and faced the front as her dark blue eyes narrowed in exasperation.

I had the same eyes—dark blue—and just like her, you could see the blue in them only in natural light. I had her thick chocolate-brown hair too, but hers was cut short, and mine reached the middle of my back, falling in soft waves.

I was also just as stubborn. In a display of this trait, I crossed my arms over my chest and stared at my feet, concentrating on the swirls of little double helixes that littered my DNA socks. The machine ahead beeped rhythmically as the attendants scanned boarding passes, and I shuffled forward, wondering how such a great day had managed to turn to absolute shit in a matter of hours.

We had lived in Fitzroy, one of the most hipster suburbs of Melbourne, Australia, for almost eight months. Our moves hadn't been quite as frequent for the past few years. I was a teenager—moody, hormonal, and antisocial—which made it easier for my mother to prevent me from getting too close to anyone.

It's so much easier to make a friend at six than it is at sixteen. *Want to be my friend? OK!*—done deal. By the time you're in your teens, people

3

have established friendships and years of shared experiences, and you're more aware of what others think of you. No one wants to disturb the delicate balance of their already angst-ridden existence by befriending the new girl.

Also, I had given up. With our next move always around the corner, I'd learned to make superficial conversation, seem friendly with a few people, but never truly get to know anyone.

Imagine my surprise when I not only made friends in Fitzroy but also got a boyfriend.

Somehow, Harvey Blackburn and his sister managed to weave their way into my solitary life. It happened slowly, over many weeks—sitting together in class, then at lunch, then chatting online. Then, somehow, Harvey and I were "a thing." I'd been on a few secret dates before, but none had gotten as close as Harvey. Harvey was the first of many things for me.

But even with the very first friends I'd ever made, I never spoke about our strange lifestyle in any detail, and I changed the topic when asked directly. I never invited them over. I rarely met with them outside of school, and then only when I was sure my mother was at work. I had to be careful. I burned to tell my mom about my first boyfriend, but I kept my mouth shut.

I'd been good at keeping my two lives separate, until earlier today.

Harvey, knowing he wouldn't be seeing me on my actual birthday, had pulled me around the corner of the English classroom and presented me with a small gift box, his warm chocolate eyes sparkling with excitement. Inside was a charm bracelet with a heart charm attached.

I had never been given a gift from anyone but my mother. I was elated, and I slipped.

I forgot to take the bracelet off and hide it before going home. As if she was looking for evidence of my treachery, my mother spotted it as soon as I walked into the house. She came out of the kitchen, her eyes homing in on the offending jewelry.

I replayed the scene in my mind—my mother wiping her hands on a tea towel, her greeting catching in her throat as the smile fell from her face, the cold look in her eyes, the fear in her voice as she quietly asked, "What have you done, Evelyn?"

"*Miss?*"

We'd reached the front of the line. The attendant was looking at me expectantly, her palm outstretched. My mom nudged me.

I shook her hand off my shoulder and darted forward, passport and boarding pass in hand. "Sorry," I muttered.

The lady gave me a tight smile, scanned the boarding pass, and checked my fake passport with the efficiency of an often-repeated task. She didn't even hesitate before handing them back, and my heart sank yet again. A big part of me had hoped she would notice it was a fake and we would be forced to stay. The forgery was very good though; she had no idea. No one ever did.

I didn't return her smile as I moved past. Pausing as she repeated the process with my mother, I looked longingly back in the direction of the exit. I imagined myself pushing past the remaining passengers waiting to board and making a run for it, catching a taxi straight to Harvey's house.

It was a stupid fantasy.

With a shuddering breath, I followed my mother as she took the lead up the narrow corridor toward the aircraft. There was no going back for us—we never returned to any place we had previously lived in.

When I was younger, I used to cry and ask why I didn't have friends and why I didn't have a dad. As I got older, my questions became more specific. I asked why we couldn't stay anywhere for longer than a few months, why we couldn't use our real names, what or who we were running from in the first place.

My mother did her best to explain things to me without actually giving me any answers. It always came back to her fervent declarations that everything she ever did was for me. Her vague explanations just weren't enough for me anymore.

We trudged up the narrow aisle of the plane to our seats. I settled into the window seat, buckled my seatbelt, and turned away as my mother lowered herself into the seat beside me.

She sighed deeply and leaned over me, but she didn't touch me. "I'm so sorry, Evie . . ."

At least, for once, she wasn't making excuses. I glued my attention to the people in safety vests bustling about on the ground below. She had said those same words, but with a decidedly less gentle tone, only hours before.

We had spent the evening fighting, crying, and packing. As she'd yanked open drawers and shoved clothes into a bag, my mother had admonished me again. "How could you be so careless, Evelyn?"

"Careless?" I was sitting in the middle of the bed, refusing to participate in the packing. "I made some friends and got a boyfriend. And I didn't tell them anything!" I almost screeched in frustration, angry tears rolling down my red cheeks.

"I'm sorry, but that's just not good enough," she spat, not sounding sorry at all. She held her hands out, a bundle of clothing in each one, before letting them flop to her sides. "It would only be a matter of time before you slipped. That's what getting close to people does—it makes you let your guard down, and you tell them things about yourself. Deep, important things."

"What things?" I yelled as she resumed stuffing our belongings haphazardly into bags. "How could I tell them anything when I don't *know* anything?"

"We do not have time to have this argument again. We're leaving in twenty minutes. Anything you don't pack will be left behind."

We stared each other down, both of us breathing hard, both of us stubborn in our silence.

Finally, her shoulders slumped. "Please, Evie," she said quietly. Her wide eyes were pleading, and her hands had begun to shake. She was no longer mad at me; now she was just scared.

I was still mad at *her*, but I caved in and reluctantly got ready to leave. Again.

I didn't even get to say goodbye to my friends, to hug them tightly and say I'd never forget them. I'd tried to send a quick message to Harvey before my mother had burst into the room and confiscated my phone, wiping it clean and destroying the sim card.

The pilot's voice coming through the intercom as we taxied snapped me back into the present. "Welcome aboard flight QF83. My name is Bob Wheeler, and I'll be your captain today. Sitting next to me is Andy Cox, your copilot. Andy is a Variant with an ability to control the weather, so I'm pleased to let you know that we can guarantee a turbulence-free flight tonight."

He continued to deliver the usual speech introducing the flight crew, but my mind was momentarily distracted, even from my ire at my mom. I had never met a Variant with an ability to control the weather, and I itched to research the science behind how it was possible, the impact it might have on weather patterns, the physics behind it all.

Science still didn't fully understand the Light—the energy that fueled Variant abilities and made it possible for people to control the weather, run faster than a Maserati, or read minds. It was a fascinating area of study. All sense of social propriety went out the window whenever I realized I was speaking to a Variant, and I would start firing all kinds of inappropriate and intrusive questions, my curiosity getting the better of me. I burned to ask the copilot how his ability worked, but I was strapped into an economy seat and had no way of making that happen. My mind returned to my previous miserable thoughts, and I slumped back with a sigh.

"That's an interesting Variant ability," Joyce piped up beside me.

I grunted and went back to looking out the window. She was making an effort, but I wasn't ready to let go of my resentment.

The plane took off, and everyone settled into the routine of a long-haul flight. My mother attempted to make conversation with me a few more times before finally giving up with a frustrated huff. I was determined to maintain my simmering outrage at how she had ruined my life, and I sulked, staring out at the pitch-black sky, forty thousand feet above the ground.

We were halfway across the Pacific Ocean when the plane crashed.

There was no warning—no time for anyone to wonder what was happening, get scared, hold each other. One minute we were gliding through the air, the next there was a loud *bang*, the plane lurched sideways, and we were plummeting.

I reached for my mother at the same time she reached for me, and we grasped each other's hands as our eyes met, wide with fear. There was no opportunity to say anything. No time to tell her the two simple things that actually needed to be said—*I'm sorry. I love you.*

A terrible metallic sound scraped against my ears, and then her hand was violently ripped out of mine, her mouth forming an O as she disappeared into darkness. The back of the plane had completely separated from the rest of it, as if a giant had torn it apart like a loaf of bread.

I stared at the emptiness next to my seat. There was the floor of the plane, there was my foot in my DNA sock (the shoe was gone), and there was the jagged line where the metal and wires and fabric had come apart, right between her seat and mine.

Beyond that there was nothing. Darkness.

We were still falling. People were screaming over the deafening whistle of rushing air as various items flew by me and out of the gaping hole through which my mother had disappeared. I focused on the jagged, torn edge of the plane, a piece of the carpet flapping furiously in the wind. My mother, my only family, was gone—probably dead. My mind couldn't process it, so instead, it helpfully supplied relevant statistics.

Statistically speaking, flying is the safest mode of transport.

The odds of a plane crashing are one in 1.2 million.

The odds of actually dying in a plane crash are closer to one in eleven million.

By comparison, the odds of dying in a car accident are about one in five thousand.

Just my luck that I would be on that one in 1.2 million flights.

As we plunged through the dark, I considered another number—2,130. The last time I had checked the in-flight information screen, that's about how many miles we were from Hawaii. I had calculated the distance, as it was the nearest land with things like hospitals and emergency response teams. Assuming the pilot had sent a distress call, it would be hours before anyone could get to us—if I even survived the crash in the first place.

I don't remember hitting the water. I remember the flapping piece of carpet by my feet, and I remember that useless information running through my head, but I have no recollection of the impact. After that is just disjointed flashes of memory.

The water was freezing cold. It felt like spikes of ice, all piercing my skin at the same time in a million different spots. People were shouting. Not many—nowhere near as many as were on the plane. I wore a life jacket. When had I put that on? Something was burning furious and bright nearby. I wanted to go closer to the heat, but I couldn't move. I couldn't do anything but shiver.

The fire was still there, but it had calmed down significantly. Like the embers of a campfire. No one was shouting anymore. The water rippled gently in front of me, calm and black like tar—impenetrable. I couldn't see even an inch past its surface. I couldn't feel my arms or my legs.

A light. Was it the fire? No, that had gone out a long time ago. It tinged the darkness. Violet. Dawn was coming. But that wasn't right either. This light was sharp, focused, and moving. There was a sound too—a loud whooshing from above. The water in front of my face rippled from the wind created by the helicopter blades. Helicopter! I had to look up, shout, wave, do something so they didn't leave.

I was being lifted into the light, but I was still cold and wet and I still couldn't feel my legs. The light wasn't warm and welcoming. It was harsh and bright, and the loud whooshing overwhelmed me. Someone lifted me from behind. An arm wrapped around my middle, holding me steady. The water seemed really far away now.

It was loud inside the helicopter. I was being jostled where I lay, tied down with something over my chest and hips. I couldn't see. My eyes were closed, and I didn't know how to open them. Voices shouted over the helicopter engine, only snippets of conversation.

"... only survivors? Are you positive?"

"Yes." A firm "yes." His voice was clear, close. Strong and masculine, but smooth like warm honey. "We searched the whole area. Only her and the copilot. I don't know how she even survived. She was in the water so long."

Then a sliding sound and a third voice, farther away. "... in touch with her people ... never got on the flight ... last minute change of schedule ... good intel, but can't predict ..."

A hand landed on my calf. The man with the honey voice. I knew it belonged *to him, but I didn't know how. It was good that I could feel my legs again.*

When I woke up in the hospital, I had been asleep for nearly two days, but I didn't know it at the time. They told me all of it later. Nurses and doctors piled into my room, marveling at the lack of permanent injury and my fast recovery. Variants were more resilient against injury and faster to recover, but I, as someone who was only human, was lucky to have survived, or so the doctors kept saying. I didn't feel lucky.

No. When I first woke up, it was only for a few moments. The sounds came first: the soft thrum of machines, a quiet beeping, muffled voices. Then I felt the soft blankets and pillows under me.

I managed to lift my heavy eyelids and found myself looking up at those corkboard squares that make up the ceilings of hospitals and office buildings. The fluorescent light was off, but it was still very bright in the room. It must have been morning.

I angled my head down and scanned the space. There was a door on my left and a window on my right, a hospital tray on wheels under it. In the corner, next to the window, was a chair. A man was sitting in it.

I could tell it was a man by the broad set of his shoulders, the muscles in his tattooed forearms. His elbows rested on his knees, and his head was in his hands. He had dark hair and a buzz cut. His fingers were digging into his scalp; I had a feeling that if he had more hair, he would be pulling at it. He was dressed in black: black boots planted firmly on the floor, black pants, and a black T-shirt.

I tried to speak, but all I managed was a straggled inhale. It was enough to get his attention anyway. His head snapped up. He looked young, maybe in his twenties, but the look in his intense eyes gave me the impression that he had lived a thousand lifetimes while he'd sat in that ugly hospital chair. He had a five o'clock shadow covering his strong jaw and shocking ice-blue eyes. They pierced me, as the frigid water had pierced me.

"You're awake." I don't think he meant to say it out loud. It just came out on a breath. And then he was on his feet and next to my bed, leaning over me.

He reached a hand out as if to touch me and then pulled it back sharply. "I'll get a doctor." It was the man with the honey voice.

I was asleep again before he'd even left the room. The ice in his eyes was making me remember, and I couldn't handle it yet.

The next time I woke up, it didn't take me as long to gain consciousness.

I opened my eyes and lifted myself into a more comfortable position. I felt so much stronger than the first time, as if I didn't need to be in the hospital at all. It was dusk, the window on the right still letting in the fading light.

My eyes immediately went to the chair in the corner, but the room was empty, and for a second I wondered if I had hallucinated the man with the ice-blue eyes. Then I heard the tap turn on in the bathroom, and a moment later he walked out of it. He was still dressed in all black, but this time he wore a long-sleeved T-shirt, fitted enough to hint at the strong torso underneath. He was tall, his head nearly reaching the top of the doorframe.

As he turned, closing the door behind him, our eyes met. He paused for a second and then stepped up to the foot of my bed, resting one hand on the railing. He watched me with a neutral expression on his face. I watched him back, not feeling at all awkward about maintaining eye contact with a complete stranger for so long. A scar cut through the middle of his right eyebrow, and a black-and-gray tattoo was peeking out of the black fabric at his neck.

"How you feeling?" His voice was firm, forceful, but it still felt like honey washing over me.

My own voice was groggy, though clear enough in the silent room. "You pulled me out of the water." I didn't bother answering his question. It wasn't important at that moment.

"No. My colleague did. I pulled you into the chopper."

He wasn't going to insist I focus on my health, on getting better, on getting my strength up—all those empty things people insisted when they were trying to avoid speaking about the difficult things. The important things. *Good.*

"You sat with me. I could hear your voice. Even over the engine."

"Yes . . ." He looked away briefly before meeting my gaze again, letting the word trail off. As if he was going to add more but decided not to.

"Only the copilot and I made it. There were no other survivors?" I had to be sure. I had to hear someone say it.

"No." His answer was definitive, but his eyes narrowed slightly, wondering whom I was asking about. Whom I had lost.

I screwed my eyes shut, fisting the hospital sheets in my weak fingers.

My mother . . .

My mother was on the plane with me.

There were no other survivors.

She was not a survivor. She was . . . she . . .

"My mother." I opened my eyes as I said it.

His face fell when the two words left my mouth. He lifted his other hand to the railing of my bed and leaned heavily on the utilitarian gray plastic, hanging his head. He swore under his breath and started breathing hard.

Why was he so upset?

I had so many questions. *What happened? Why did the plane crash? How did no one else survive? Why did I make it? Why not her? How did you know where to search? Where am I? What's going to happen now? Who are you? Why are you still here? Why do you care?*

But I couldn't find it in me to care about the answers.

No. That one little word had confirmed what I had suspected since I'd first woken up, with a stranger sitting in the chair at my bedside instead of my mother.

I'd felt strong when I'd woken up a few moments earlier, but now I felt weak again. An awful pressure built in my chest, and a lump formed in my throat.

She was gone. Forever. I would never see my mother again. Never speak to her, hug her, argue with her. *Argue.* That was the last thing we'd done. She died thinking I was mad at her.

I was alone in the world. I was motherless. An orphan. I had felt lonely for much of my life, but whatever my mother's reasons were for keeping us distant from other people, she had always been there for me. She was the one constant in my life, the one person I could always rely on.

Yes, I had felt lonely in the past, but lying in that hospital bed with a stranger at my bedside, I truly knew what it meant to feel *alone.*

I'm alone.

Fat tears finally overflowed, and I wrapped my arms around my torso. I began to sob as I rolled onto my side toward the window, every muscle in my body taut with despair.

Boots squeaked across the linoleum, and then the thin hospital blanket was pulled over my shoulder. The bed behind me dipped, and his body pressed into mine from behind, his arm snaking around my front. He held me tight and I heard his voice, close to my ear.

"You are not alone."

I must have said that out loud. His declaration made me cry harder—ugly, unrestrained tears. Sobs wracked my body as I curled into a ball.

He held on to me through it all. We didn't touch, nowhere did our skin make contact, but he held me tight until my crying calmed down to soft sobs. He held me tight as the sobs gave way to silent tears pooling on the pillow. He held me tight as I drifted off into blissful unconsciousness again.

When I woke up the next morning, there was a nurse at the foot of my bed, writing something on a clipboard, and the stranger really was gone.

TWO

On the morning of my eighteenth birthday, I woke up half an hour before my alarm in a bed that didn't feel like mine. In a room that belonged to me but held none of my personality. In the life I had been living for the past year but still didn't fit into.

I didn't have that moment of bliss, those hazy few seconds when you don't know what day it is or what's going on. I opened my eyes and immediately knew it was my birthday; it had been exactly one year since my mother died.

I lay on my back and stared at the ceiling.

Swallowing hard around the thick lump in my throat, I just managed to stop myself from falling apart first thing in the morning. I had to keep going, be strong. It's what my mom would have wanted.

I tried to concentrate on something else, running through what my day looked like, but other than a chemistry quiz, there wasn't much noteworthy. My thoughts kept turning back to the moment my world had come crashing down as hard as the plane we were on. I rolled onto my side. Instead of getting lost in the memory of when I'd realized I was alone in the world, I forced myself to focus on what had happened *after*.

When the hospital in Hawaii released me, social services had decided it was best to send me on to the destination my mother had chosen for us. They couldn't have known she had randomly opened a map and pointed.

After a long boat ride and several trains and buses—because I refused to get on a plane—it was the Idaho social services who placed me in Nampa with Martha and Barry, or Marty and Baz, as they liked to be called. They were a nice enough couple in their fifties, semiretired and a little bored. Why not get a foster kid to spice things up a little? Unfortunately, I wasn't that exciting.

I had my own room, and as much as they encouraged me to make it mine, I couldn't bring myself to do it. I looked around at the twin bed, desk, and mostly empty wardrobe as I pulled the blanket tighter around my shoulders. I was still stuck in my old ways—not getting too comfortable, the next move always around the corner.

Marty and Baz made an effort to get to know me, to make me feel like part of the family. It wasn't their fault I didn't know how to be part of a family.

The alarm I hadn't needed went off, filling the impersonal room with a high-pitched beeping. I reached for my smartphone and turned it off. Sitting on the edge of my bed, I scratched at the tingling sensation at my wrists, willing my body to catch up with my mind and get moving.

I had bought the smartphone myself after selling some fake IDs, feeling too awkward to accept anything other than the basics—food and clothing—from my would-be parental figures. Marty and Baz had repeatedly offered to buy me more clothes, books, makeup, and other "normal teenage girl stuff." I refused, but one indulgence I did allow them to provide was journal subscriptions. I devoured scientific literature the way most teenage girls went through fashion magazines. I was top of my class in all my science and most of my math classes at school. I had subscriptions to *The American Statistician*, *Advances in Physics*, *New Scientist*, and a few others.

I got up from the bed only to sit back down at my desk, pushing an old issue of *New Scientist* out of the way. I turned on the ancient computer running Windows XP and waited impatiently for it to wake up. We both struggled a little to get going in the mornings.

While I waited for the geriatric tech to boot up, I stood and reached into the half-empty closet for an outfit. My eye caught on my mother's sundress with the big poppy flower print, and the lump in my throat reappeared.

If all it took to push me over the edge today was a glimpse of fabric, maybe I needed to skip school.

Not much had survived the plane crash. The crash investigation team had managed to recover some luggage, and the only salvageable items were a few photos and some clothes, including my mother's favorite summer dress. None of our documents were found. My mother's body, along with more than two hundred others, was also never found.

I got dressed in jeans and a loose sweater, consciously training my mind on how the cotton-poly blend aggravated the persistent itch at my wrists. The lump had receded, and I planted myself in front of the computer once again, giving my mind another distraction.

There were only two constants in my life now—science and my bordering-on-obsessive search for the honey-voiced stranger who had saved me in more ways than I could articulate.

I opened Tor—I only ever used the secure browser—and logged in to some of the forums I frequented, as well as checked a few non-mainstream sites for any news.

I hadn't even learned his name before he'd disappeared. I had tried asking the nurses and doctors when I woke up, but they couldn't give me any information on his identity. They just said he was part of the Melior Group rescue team who had brought me in. He had not spoken much to anyone but had been very interested in my progress and test results, ensuring I had the best care possible.

I didn't know much about the Melior Group at the time. I had heard of them, of course—the elite private security firm that employed Variants with rare abilities almost exclusively, had ties to Variant communities as well as mainstream law enforcement, and operated all over the world. Every high-profile Variant had a Melior Group bodyguard on the payroll, and governments often employed them to aid in peacekeeping, rescue missions, and other shadier things, I was sure. Things with words like *intelligence* and *dark ops* involved.

When the air crash investigators interviewed me, I did my best to get them to shed light on my stranger's identity. They wouldn't elaborate on why a Melior Group team had been sent out on a simple rescue mission for a civilian plane crash. The word *classified* was thrown around more than once.

I tried contacting Melior Group directly once I was settled in Nampa, but I hit a brick wall and more *classified*s. That's when I'd powered up the ancient computer and put my research skills to use. Unfortunately that wasn't getting me anywhere either. I was really getting sick of the word *classified*.

I was no closer to finding him now than I had been that first day in the hospital, but it had become a bit of an obsession. At some point I turned to shadier corners of the Internet, posting to forums, detailing my experience, and chatting to other people who'd had run-ins with Melior Group special teams. I was trying to find any link, no matter how tenuous, to someone else who may have crossed paths with him.

As with a complex mathematical problem or opaque scientific theory, the harder it was to puzzle out, the more determined I became to solve it.

But it wasn't just the challenge of it. The fact that the word *classified* had come up so often told me there was more than just a simple engine failure to blame for my mother's death. I had made it my mission to find out *why* my mom had lost her life. The stranger was my closest link to that information.

On a more emotional level, I *needed* to find him. The strength of my inexplicable pull to this man who had held me in my darkest hour frightened me a little. His team had saved me—they had pulled me out of the icy water and provided first aid—but my honey-voiced stranger had saved me on a much deeper level. He had stayed with me, cared for me, held me as I completely fell apart. Had I been alone when I woke up in that hospital, I don't think I would have had the strength to get better, to keep living my empty life. I was too emotionally wrecked to realize it at the time, but his presence had given me a tiny scrap to hold on to—a glimmer of hope that maybe I didn't have to be alone in the world.

Yes, I wanted to find the answers to all my questions surrounding my mom's death, but I also needed to look into his ice-blue eyes one more time and thank him for saving me.

The itching, which was spreading up my forearms, reminded me I needed to get to school, so I logged out and headed into the kitchen.

Marty was bustling about near the stove, her gray hair perfectly combed into a "fashionable" bob.

"Good morning!" She beamed at me over her shoulder, rushing to turn knobs and juggle pans. "You're up a little early, but it's good timing."

Marty was a morning person, always full of positive energy. I was not a morning person. Coffee would have helped, but even after living in the States for a whole year, I still couldn't get used to the filtered crap they drank.

I rubbed my temple and went to extract the milk from the fridge, trying to decide if Cap'n Crunch or Wheaties was a more anniversary-of-mother's-death kind of breakfast cereal. Marty stepped in front of me and smiled, holding a plate of pancakes in front of her.

"Happy birthday, kiddo," she said, much softer than I was used to hearing her speak. "I know this day is bittersweet for you, but hopefully this will help to make it just a little sweeter."

"Oh." I hadn't realized we were on birthday pancakes terms. "Thank you." My own voice was soft and, I hoped, genuine.

She gave me a little squeeze just above my elbow. Marty and Baz were not huggers, and for that at least, I was grateful.

I sat at the breakfast bar and ate my pancakes, Marty next to me with a large mug of American pond sludge coffee. They were delicious—Marty was a great cook—but they weren't my mom's.

Once again, grief threatened to pull me under. I choked down a mouthful of pancakes, eyes stinging as I stared down at the countertop.

Marty chatted about pointless things while I ate and tried really hard to stop myself from crying, then she left for work. Once I was alone, I took a few deep breaths, unable to finish the food.

I put the dishes in the dishwasher, slung my bag over my shoulder, and walked to school. It was the same route I had taken every day for the last year. The same boring suburban streets, the same cars, the same trees.

It took me a lazy twenty minutes to walk to Nampa High School. Students were milling about, trying to squeeze in every last second of free time before the first class. As I approached the low brick building, a brown-haired boy wearing a bomber jacket jogged over the grass to me.

"Hey, Eve!" He smiled. I had a feeling he was on the football team, but I couldn't remember his name. "Happy birthday."

How did he know? I wasn't exactly friends with anyone.

I didn't reply to his birthday wish. I simply stood there with a confused look on my face, so he filled the silence with his own voice. "Can I take you out for your birthday tonight? Or maybe tomorrow? Whenever you're free, really. I have the game next week, but other than that . . ." He looked at me expectantly.

Nameless football guy didn't actually want to take me out. He just wanted to get lucky.

When I'd first arrived in Nampa, I went through a brief promiscuous phase. I was doing whatever I could to ignore that my mother had died, so I fully embraced everything about high school life I couldn't have embraced with her around. I dated a lot, no one exclusively, and gained a bit of a reputation. On top of that, I could make *really* good fake IDs, and I suddenly had a whole crowd of people to distract myself with.

My sudden popularity didn't last long. Just as I couldn't settle into my new "home," I also couldn't find it in me to try to make friends. I had attempted to embrace my new freedom, but that was just it—this so-called freedom existed because my mother wasn't around anymore. I couldn't make myself give a shit about any of the trivial things I'd so desperately cared about before she died. Who cares about making friends when you've lost the only family you ever had?

I became a loner and only made time for my science and my mysterious stranger. Every once in a while, one of the boys would try to ask me out on another date. I always said no.

Football guy was still waiting for my response, but thinking about my rebellious months made me think about how my mother would have lost her shit if she'd known how careless I'd been. I didn't know what was more distracting or unwanted—the unbidden emotion or the persistent itchiness on my arms. I needed to get away from the linebacker before I had a very public emotional meltdown.

"My mother died one year ago today," I deadpanned.

22

I hadn't intended to say that, but the boy's reaction was proving enough of a distraction. He looked equal parts horrified and uncomfortable. As he opened his mouth to say something, I blinked once and walked past him into the school building. I preferred to let him think I was rude and odd than to have him see me cry.

The rest of the day passed without incident. With my mother's face constantly at the forefront of my mind, the sensation of her hand sliding out of mine achingly present on my skin, I went through the motions. I went to classes, ate lunch, aced the chemistry quiz, and did my best to avoid the other students. Word of my strange declaration to football guy spread, and before second period was over, I started getting weird looks. Thankfully, everyone gave me a wide berth.

By the end of the day, I was sick of all the passive attention, tired from constantly being on the lookout for the overwhelming grief that was becoming impossible to ignore. I just wanted to get back to Marty and Baz's and lose myself in an article or a school assignment.

The day had turned out to be beautiful, the afternoon sun warm enough that I could take my sweater off and walk home in just a tank top, but my foul mood wouldn't allow me to appreciate it. The itchy, tingly sensation had spread up my arms to my chest and was making itself infuriatingly known nearly all the way up my legs too. With a grunt of frustration, I picked up my pace and scratched at my arms, hoping I could stop myself from ripping the tank top off or sticking my hand down my pants in public.

This new development—bursts of itching—had started not long after I was settled with Marty and Baz, and it came with insane amounts of energy. Every week or two I would have more physical energy and more mental energy for study and reading. Occasionally I would stay awake all night, not feeling tired at all the next day. I took up running to try to manage it, pushing myself until I struggled to breathe. It was never painful, more like a persistent hum. A harmless kind of vibration throughout my body that made me insanely itchy and feel as if I were on cocaine. No biggie.

It always started out faint, as it had that morning—a tickle at my wrists and ankles—but if I ignored it for too long, the infuriating itchiness all over my body would have me removing layers of clothing, which would begin to feel like burlap.

I never mentioned this to Marty or Baz. I didn't want further inconvenience them, and I really couldn't complain about the extra study time. I read up on the symptoms, learning many new, very long words, and did my best to self-diagnose, monitoring my symptoms and vital signs closely. My extensive research suggested the extra energy was neither a symptom nor a cause of anything of concern.

Across the street, a girl in jogging gear was walking her Labradoodle, her face in her phone, reminding me that I was outside where anyone could see me scratching like a maniac. I extracted my hand from the waistband of my pants, where it was dangerously close to reaching a particularly itchy spot on my ass, and picked up my pace.

It made sense that the odd humming energy would rear its unpleasant head today. It wasn't as if anything good ever happened on my birthdays.

I used to think birthdays were special. Like any child, I used to look forward to the presents, the fuss, the cake. My mom had done her best to make it special, even if it was just the two of us celebrating. No matter what day of the week it fell on, she would call in sick for both of us, and we would spend the morning in bed watching TV and eating birthday pancakes. In the afternoon, we always went out and did something fun.

We used to pick up and move just before or after my birthdays too.

When I turned eight, we had just moved to Tokyo. We were in high spirits that afternoon. It was a new place, new streets to explore, exciting new food to try.

As we wandered around Shibuya intersection, the world exploded into chaos. People screaming and running, a loud *boom*, the smell of burning—something acrid with a harsh chemical smell to it. Mostly I remember the shared terror of everyone out on the street that day, so clear it was almost palpable.

Many people died. It made the news all over the world. My mother and I got away unscathed, but we left Tokyo that same afternoon. We didn't leave the country, but we went to another part of Japan—a smaller, quieter part. News of the tragedy in Tokyo made it there before we did.

That must have been the record. We were in Tokyo for five days before my mother decided it was time to leave. On my birthday.

That was one of the worst birthday incidents, last year notwithstanding, but there were other things.

Like the flood two days before my ninth birthday, when we were living in Vietnam, destroying most of our possessions. Or my mother getting mugged on the way to her night shift on my twelfth birthday, when we were living in Turkey. Or when we were living on the coast of Croatia and my mother woke me in the middle of the night, three days after my fourteenth birthday, whispering frantically to me that "they found us," sending a jolt of terror down my spine and spurring me into action.

It was after that birthday that I started paying more attention to the things she'd been teaching me, like digital footprints and falsifying documents.

I managed to make it to Marty and Baz's without scratching too much out in public, but I knew I was in for a sleepless night. When I walked into the house and shut the door, I breathed a big sigh of relief, scratching indulgently at my forearms, but I stopped quickly at the sound of movement in the living room. I'd been hoping to head straight to my room so I could change and go for a run, but I'd forgotten that Baz would be home.

"Hey, kiddo!" he boomed as I came around the corner. I didn't know why they both liked calling me "kiddo." It was as if they'd huddled together, deciding that a nickname would bring us closer, and chose "kiddo."

My real full name was Evelyn Maynard. That much, at least, my mother made sure I always knew. But I couldn't use that name. What would be the point of disappearing constantly if you kept popping up with the exact same name? Every time we had moved, we'd created documentation with new names. The last name would be completely new, but my first name was always some variation of a name beginning with E—Emma, Elle, Ebony, sometimes even Evelyn. That way, I could just tell kids my nickname was E, and it would be less confusing for me, easier to remember.

While living in Melbourne, we had created some new identification (we always had fresh identities ready to go), and I'd given myself the name Eve Blackburn. Harvey and I hadn't started dating yet, but I had a pretty big crush on him, so I created an identity with his last name.

It was the name I boarded the plane with, the name that was on the passenger manifest, the name that everyone in Nampa knew me by. It was the name that had followed me into my current life. That was Eve Blackburn's bed, Eve's room, Eve's house, her school and her life. No wonder Evelyn Maynard felt out of place there.

"Hey, Baz." I tried to smile at him, but even I could feel that it didn't reach my eyes.

"Happy birthday." Baz's smile was genuine, unlike mine, as he got out of his favorite chair. Baz was as gray as Marty and had sported an impressive handlebar mustache the entire time I'd known him.

"Thank you," I said to his back as he made his way into the kitchen.

"Want a snack?"

"No thanks. I'm just going to go for a run."

"Okie dokie."

I'd made it past the kitchen and into the hallway, dying to have another scratch, when he called out again. "Oh, by the way, you got a letter. Left it on your bed. Looks fancy." He smiled at me before his head disappeared behind the fridge door.

"OK. Thanks," I mumbled, confused. I never got mail. Who would be sending me letters? Who would be sending me *fancy* letters?

I softly closed the bedroom door. I couldn't help but be suspicious as I stared at the envelope. The fact that it had arrived on my birthday was enough to make me wary. Was this it? Was this the awful thing that would happen this year? What horrible news was within? Maybe there was anthrax inside?

I lowered myself to my knees, facing the bed, and dragged the envelope to the edge of the mattress, pinching one corner. It was A4 size, and the pale gray paper was thick under my fingers. It felt expensive. My current name, Eve Blackburn, and the address were printed in the middle, and there was a logo in the top corner, *BHI* in a distinctive font. I flipped it, but there was no return address.

Having gleaned all I could from examining the outside, I had no choice but to open it. Taking the Band-Aid approach, I tore it open as fast as I could. Inside were several booklets printed on glossy paper, and on top a letter addressed to me. The letterhead had the same logo and an elaboration of what the letters stood for—Bradford Hills Institute.

I read through the letter twice, reading slowly the second time to make sure I didn't miss anything or misconstrue the meaning. Bradford Hills Institute— the most exclusive educational facility in the country—was offering me a full scholarship to study any scientific field of my choosing at a tertiary level. The school year was not finished yet—I still had a few months of high school to go—but because of their unique approach to learning, they weren't concerned with a high school diploma and wanted me to start classes as soon as possible. A spot had recently opened up, and they were offering it to me.

Apparently they had been keeping an eye on me and were impressed with my grades and my approach to study. I had no idea they had even been speaking to my teachers.

I sat on the floor and stared at the letter for several minutes. Less than half an hour ago, I'd been walking back from school thinking about how awful things always happened around my birthday, yet there I was—holding in my hands something that made me so excited I almost forgot what day it was. It was an opportunity to start yet another new life. In New York, no less!

Maybe it was my own morbid curiosity, a need to see what the universe had in store for my birthday this year, or maybe I'd simply gotten used to moving, and some subconscious, impatient part of me was nudging me to move on, but I knew I wanted to go.

After the shock wore off, I called the number at the bottom of the letter and said yes to Bradford Hills.

I spoke for about an hour to Stacey from admissions, and she explained how it would all work, answered the few questions my frazzled mind remembered to ask, and told me she could book my plane ticket the very next day if I was ready. I said yes. I was saying yes to everything, and it had my heart hammering a million miles an hour.

Marty got home from water aerobics as I was finishing my phone call, and I sat her and Baz down to tell them the news. They were both very excited for me and very impressed. Bradford Hills Institute was exclusive, but it was well-known. Apart from being an educational institute, they did research in many fields, especially around Variants, and they specialized in teaching young Variants to control and manage their abilities. As a result, Bradford Hills had a higher population of students with Variant DNA. For a human to be accepted, their academic performance had to be exceptional. I had no idea what they had seen in me, but I wasn't about to question them on it.

After an intense run, I spent the rest of the night packing and researching Bradford Hills on the Internet. I barely noticed the itchiness as I crawled into bed around three in the morning, hoping the excitement had allowed me to expel enough energy to get a few hours' sleep before my flight.

What I didn't count on was the overwhelming wave of emotions I'd been avoiding all day hitting me as soon as I turned the light out. The grief and pain I had worked so hard to push down finally washed over me as I lay in the bed that, come tomorrow, I would no longer need to pretend was mine.

Nothing could remind me of my mother as much as packing up and starting over. There were no fake passports or rushed dashes to the airport, but I was moving on nonetheless. I was about to do something we had been doing together my whole life, and for the first time, I would be doing it without her.

Tears rushed down my cheeks and into my hair as I struggled to take a breath against the crushing pressure on my chest. With a broken sob, I rolled onto my side and buried my face in the pillow, letting the emotion course through me as violently as it had that day in the hospital. Only this time, I didn't have a mysterious stranger with intense eyes to curl around me and comfort me.

I didn't have my mother by my side as I prepared to start yet another new life, and I didn't have *him* to comfort me through the knowledge that I didn't have *her*.

I was all alone. Again.

THREE

I checked my seatbelt one last time as the distinctively mechanical clicks and hums started up beneath my seat. While the pretty flight attendant delivered her practiced instructions, I swallowed around the lump in my throat and murmured along.

My mom and I had taken so many flights that we didn't even bother listening to the safety information. While most of the other passengers learned how to inflate the life jacket, my mom would be absorbed in some novel as I devoured a journal article. Sometimes we would whisper along with them, reciting the instructions word for word, making each other giggle like schoolgirls.

Halfway through, I gave up and stared out the window, watching Nampa, Idaho, disappear below me. I knew I would never go back. My meager possessions were stuffed into a duffel bag in the overhead compartment, not even enough to fill a bag that needed to be checked.

Bradford Hills Institute paid for my ticket to New York. Within two hours of my phone call with Stacey from admissions, I'd received an email with a ridiculous number of attachments, flight details.

It was the first flight I'd taken since the one that literally crashed and burned. I should have been scared, traumatized, upset.

I wasn't.

I had cried it all into my pillow the night before, and the statistics hadn't changed. A car accident was still more likely.

When I landed at LaGuardia, Bradford Hills had a car waiting for me, complete with a smartly dressed driver holding a sign with my name on it.

I was driven past Manhattan into Upstate New York, the concrete and steel giving way to tall trees and wide roads. The Institute was in the town of Bradford Hills and took up half its surface area. Its reputation as a hub of Variant research, education, and training preceded it. Bradford Hills Institute was to Variant studies what Harvard was to law—internationally renowned and notoriously exclusive.

I tried not to dwell on it too much as I took in the campus. We drove through the main gates and up a wide, curving, tree-lined avenue. Signs posted at regular intervals had arrows pointing in various directions, toward this building or that. We seemed to be following the ones that said "Administration and Reception Building."

Vast green lawns, dotted with people strolling around or sitting in groups, rolled out beyond the trees. The layout and buildings were not designed to be utilitarian—not harshly jutting out of the earth or bunched together. Rather, buildings throughout the massive campus blended seamlessly into their natural surroundings, hugging the gentle slopes of the hills and nestling between ancient oak trees, some of them covered in vines, none of them obnoxiously tall. They were old red-and-black brick structures, with ornate windows and wide doorways, oozing history and tradition.

The administration building was in the middle of it all. As we pulled up, it was plain to see this structure was not old and historic like the others, but the contrast to its elderly companions wasn't jarring.

I was too busy staring at the perfectly manicured grounds to notice my driver had exited the car, and I was a little startled when he opened my door for me. He stood back and waited for me to exit.

I timidly crawled out of the spacious back seat and just stood there, unsure what to do.

He saved me from having to figure out what to say. "Shall I have your bag delivered to your residence hall, miss?"

"Oh, no, thank you." Bag. Singular. Overhead compartment compliant. "I'll just hold on to it. Thank you." I spoke too fast as I dragged the item in question from its spot on the back seat. I was out of my element. There is no scientific journal dedicated to the social nuances of interaction with posh, rich people—and their drivers.

There was a pause. Neither one of us quite knew how to proceed. "Thank you for picking me up from the airport . . . and driving me here. Um . . . am I supposed to check in with someone, or . . . ?"

"You are most welcome, miss." Was that a hint of a smile on his serious face? "Please make your way to the main reception area, and they will take care of you from there."

"Great! Thank you." That was the third time I'd thanked the man in less than five minutes, and I internally rolled my eyes at my own awkwardness.

He inclined his head in that subtle way posh people have, walked around to the driver's side, and left me there.

I took a deep breath and walked up the stairs and through the front door.

The cavernous reception area was so spacious I was confident Marty and Baz's three-bedroom house could fit into it three times over. Warm natural light flooded in through the floor-to-ceiling windows that made up three of the walls, and a long reception desk with several people behind it was situated straight ahead. My sneakers squeaked obnoxiously on the polished gray concrete floor as I made my way up to it.

I counted five receptionists, three women and two men, all in matching navy-blue collared shirts, all perched on high office chairs, and all on the phone. They spoke in quiet, efficient voices, their posture as impeccable as their clean-cut appearance.

I stopped in front of the desk and stood awkwardly, trying to tuck back some of the loose strands of hair that had fallen out of my messy bun. When was the last time I'd washed it? Two days ago? Three?

"You're welcome, ma'am. Have a nice day." The receptionist closest to me, a young woman with blonde hair pulled into a tight bun, ended a call. As I opened my mouth to say who I was, she pressed a series of buttons on the phone in front of her and continued speaking into her headset, not even acknowledging my presence.

"Bradford Hills Institute. Please hold the line," she said politely to three callers in a row before finally looking up at me expectantly, a perfectly pleasant smile on her face. I guess it was my turn to speak.

"Hi. I'm Eve Blackburn." I gave myself a silent pat on the back for not accidentally saying Evelyn Maynard. Even after living as Eve for a whole year, I still tripped up on the last name. "Um, I was told to come in here. To report to someone, or . . ." Stacey from admissions hadn't actually told me what to do when I got here, despite the pages and pages of information she had sent in her email.

"OK." The receptionist kept the smile plastered on her face as she ticked away at her computer for a few seconds. "Ah, here we are." She turned back to me. "New student. Welcome to Bradford Hills. You're scheduled to meet with someone from admissions at ten, but you're a little early. Please take a seat and I'll let him know you're here." She gestured to one of two seating areas I had walked past on my trek from the front doors. The seating areas were mirror images of each other, settled on either side of the reception desk and consisting of low leather couches around low glass tables.

I smiled politely and squeaked over to the nearest couch, dropping my duffel bag on the floor and sitting in a spot with a clear view of the elevators. There were two on either side of the reception desk. Everything in this building was very symmetrical.

Once again, Bradford Hills had planned everything perfectly. Had I needed to collect checked luggage, I would have arrived at the exact scheduled time. They couldn't have known I owned next to nothing and would be out of the airport so fast—and therefore early for the appointment I hadn't known had been made for me.

After a few minutes of trying to breathe quietly so I wouldn't disturb the receptionists, I looked around for a distraction from how awkward I felt in this world of full scholarships, personal drivers, and neat buns. From the pile of magazines in front of me, I grabbed the latest edition of *Modern Variant*—a glossy monthly publication that printed human interest stories about high-profile Variants and goings-on in Variant society. It wasn't exactly the kind of thing I usually picked up. I loved learning about Variant abilities and the scientific explanations behind them, but I had little interest in the social and political drama of a world I had never dreamed I would get near. Still, since I was about to be thrust into a school where most of the staff and students were Variant, it couldn't hurt to read up on current affairs.

On the front cover was a photo of a smiling brunette, her hair pulled back into a tasteful style, her perfect teeth gleaming. She looked to be in her late forties or early fifties, the laugh lines around her eyes prominent. The headline read "Senator Christine Anderson on her Crusade to Bring Variant Issues to the Forefront of Political Debate."

I had seen this woman pop up in the news lately, giving passionate speeches about equality between humans and Variants and legislating for equal rights. I got a sense she was making a roundabout argument that Variants were hard-done-by or disadvantaged. I guess you could argue that, to a point—humans made up the majority of the population, and majority usually rules. If you asked me, Variants had all kinds of advantages when you considered the supernatural abilities and stronger resistance to injury or illness. But what did I know?

I skimmed the main article about the senator, but I soon lost interest and closed the magazine, returning it to the pile.

Just as I dropped it down on the massive coffee table with a *flap*, the elevators pinged and opened. A man wearing dress pants and a dark blue shirt stepped out slowly. His clothing was immaculate—pleats in correct places, and tailored perfectly—but he wore no tie, and his shirtsleeves were rolled up to the elbow. He was tapping very fast at his phone, and his messy brown hair, cut short at the sides, had fallen over his face, in defiance of the neat and ironed look of his clothing.

When he finished typing his message, he slid the phone into his left pocket and reached up to swipe his hair back, his rolled-up shirtsleeve tightening around his defined forearm as he did so. He turned and looked straight at me with a polite smile.

His eyes were gray. For a second I thought they were blue, but that was just the color of his shirt and the reflection of the bright blue sky through the window he was facing.

"Eve." He didn't say it like a question: *Are you Eve?* He said it like a statement. He knew who I was.

Despite his defiant hair, his effortlessly polished look left me feeling self-conscious. I was in jeans, ripped at the right knee, and a plain white T-shirt with an oversized black cardigan over the top. I should have made more of an effort. For the third time that day, I felt as if I had no business being there.

I rose from my seat slowly, pulling the cardigan sleeves over my hands. "Yes. Hi." Eloquent. It was the best I could manage at the time.

"I'm Tyler Gabriel. I work in administration. Stacey, who you spoke with yesterday, has updated me on your file. You've been assigned to me for orientation. Let's go to my office and have a chat. Get you settled in." He had put his hands in his pockets and almost imperceptibly relaxed his stance. Was he trying to make me more comfortable with his body language? I liked him already.

"OK. Great. I actually have a lot of questions. This happened so fast." I reached down for my duffel bag while slipping my satchel over my shoulder.

He swiped my duffel off the floor before I could and straightened, chuckling. "Of course. You wouldn't have been admitted here if you didn't have a curious mind. I hope I can answer them all."

I followed him to the elevators, my eyes level with the collar of his shirt. As he reached over to press the button, the muscles in his back tightened beneath the dark blue fabric, and I realized I'd been staring. *Crap! Don't get a crush on the fancy school's fancy admissions guy.*

I stepped to the side so I wouldn't be standing behind him like a creep and averted my eyes, letting them roll over to the reception desk again. All three of the perfectly coiffed women were looking at Tyler Gabriel with secretive smiles and shy looks.

The elevator pinged, and we stepped inside.

"How was your flight, Eve? You've come from Idaho somewhere, yes?"

"Yes, Idaho. The flight was fine. Uneventful." Which was a nice change from the last one I'd taken. I pushed that thought to the back of my mind, swallowing the lump in my throat, and tried to focus on the present moment.

In the reflection of the mirrored doors, Mr. Gabriel was staring at me intently, concern written all over his face. He took a breath as though to say something, but then the elevator lurched to a stop and the doors opened. He cleared his throat and stepped out, turning left.

We were on the fifth floor, the top of the building. Voices and the occasional phone ringing hummed through the air as we walked past rows of offices. We stopped at a door halfway down the corridor, "Mr. T. Gabriel" written in neat gold print on the panel next to it. He stepped in and held the door open for me.

Inside, directly opposite the door, a large desk housed a computer monitor and various other items, including several newspapers stacked haphazardly on top of one another. Two tub chairs were positioned invitingly in front of the desk. To my right, a large window spanning the width of the wall looked out onto the avenue I'd been driven up earlier and, in the distance, the front gates. On the left, a shelf stacked with books, folders, and a few knickknacks was making its best attempt—but failing—to be as neat and proper as the institution it was in.

I could relate to that shelf.

"Please have a seat." He gestured to the tub chairs as he lowered my duffel to the floor.

As I walked farther into the room, four wall-mounted TVs across from the desk—all on different channels, all muted—blinked off. I recognized CNN and CSpan before the screens went black.

I turned back to the desk to see Mr. Gabriel pointing a remote.

"Sorry. Forgot to turn them off." He shrugged and dropped the remote on top of the newspapers. As if it was normal to have four televisions in your office.

"Why do you have four televisions in your office?" I sat down in the chair closest to the window. *Shit! That was inappropriate and nosy!* I was too relaxed with this man, his casual shirtsleeves and carefully relaxed posture had put me at ease better than I'd thought. He was that coveted thing that all school administrators, counselors, and teachers strove for—*approachable.*

Before I could cringe and apologize, he answered, "I like to keep an eye on what's happening in the world."

"Oh . . . OK." *Why though?* I really wanted to prod further, but I kept my mouth shut.

He sat in the chair next to me instead of behind his big desk, crossed his legs, and angled his body toward mine. *We're on the same side, you can talk to me,* his posture was saying.

"Welcome to Bradford Hills." He looked me right in the eyes with a relaxed kind of intensity, as if he was studying me. That I could understand—the need to study something, to know it in order to understand it.

"Thank you, Mr. Gabriel."

"Please, call me Tyler, or if you prefer, Gabe—that's what some of the other students and staff like to call me. We are not strict with titles and labels here. We like to create a more relaxed, fluid learning environment. For example, my role sits somewhere between admissions counselor and academic advisor—among other things."

So the relaxed vibe was intentional. I nodded, not sure what to say to that. I wasn't expecting a place as exclusive and old as Bradford Hills to have such a relaxed approach.

"Before we go any further, I am obliged to tell you something about myself." His tone didn't suggest that he resented this rule; it was the same as it had been thus far—relaxed and easy.

"OK." I sat up a little straighter.

"As you probably know, many of the staff and students here are Variants, myself included. I have an uncommon ability, and I find that most people are more at ease if they know what it is and how it works."

I leaned toward him a little, intrigued. The few Variants I'd met before mostly had common abilities—a woman with enhanced strength carrying four bulky suitcases through the airport, a kid with enhanced speed flying past me in the corridor on his way to class. Enhanced strength, speed, hearing, and sight were the most common.

"I have the ability to tell when someone is lying to me. Don't worry, I can't read your mind or anything so invasive as that. It's more like a mental alarm system that alerts me when someone is being untruthful."

"Really?" I could feel the smile spreading over my face, my eyes widening, while he carefully monitored my expression. My mind raced with a million questions about whether his DNA differed from that of Variants with more physical manifestations of power. "That is so cool!"

His eyebrows raised in surprise, but he reined it in quickly, arranging his features into a neutral expression. He did smile though, a pleasant, easy smile. "I have to say, I was not expecting that response. Most people are uneasy when I first tell them. They immediately start worrying about what they might've lied about recently, paranoid that I'm about to expose their deepest secrets."

"Yes, I suppose that would be worrying . . . now that I think about it. Should I be worried?" I still wasn't really freaked out by his ability—I had nothing to hide. I'm fairly certain my mother did, but I had no idea what it was, so there was no way for me to be evasive about it. I was more concerned that my response was abnormal.

His smile spread wider, the gray in his eyes becoming lighter. "Not at all. And don't stress that you didn't react how most others do. It's a good thing. It tells me you're more concerned with matters that are of far greater importance than my ability."

He had leaned toward me too at some point, and his compliment made me suddenly aware of how close we were sitting, our elbows on the arms of our chairs, heads bent toward each other. Like two friends having an intimate conversation, rather than a student and administrator who had just met. He must have realized the same thing, because we looked away and straightened up in our chairs at the same time.

He cleared his throat. "Right. Now, you'll need to fill out these forms and return them to reception." He grabbed an envelope off his desk and handed it to me. "And it's standard protocol for all our students to have a blood test to screen for the Variant genetic markers."

"Oh, that won't be necessary." A particular protein was present in the blood of Variants—it was the most accurate indicator there was Variant DNA present. I had been put through all kinds of tests in the hospital after the crash, and nothing had come up then. "I had a battery of tests about a year ago, and they didn't find anything."

"I'm afraid we insist on running our own tests." He smiled politely, a little apologetic. "It's a requirement for all students. Do you understand why?"

"Yeah." I nodded. A big part of the work Bradford Hills did was helping young Variants learn how to manage their abilities; knowing which students may present with an ability at any moment would be incredibly useful.

Tyler (I had, without thinking about it, decided to call him Tyler—Gabe was too casual somehow) gave me a satisfied nod, and I remembered his ability. He knew I was telling the truth when I said I understood.

"The information is all in the envelope. Just go down to the clinic on campus, and I'll call you in for a meeting when the results come through."

He spent the next half hour patiently explaining how Bradford Hills

Institute operates and answering all my questions. He helped me choose my subjects, steering me toward some specialized Variant studies units.

"Correct me if I'm wrong, but I think you have a keen interest in Variant abilities." He had worked me out pretty quickly, but I guess that was his job. "Some of these introductory Variant units, combined with your other science studies, will give you a good foundation for delving further into that area of research if you decide you like it. Plus, it gives you an excuse to be as curious and nosy about people's abilities as you want."

He had *really* worked me out. I laughed out loud, and he grinned, a mischievous look in his eyes.

He sent me on my way with the fat envelope, my class schedule, my residence hall assignment, and a *giant* map of the campus. The thing was seriously like one of those folding maps you get at truck stops—the ones that are bigger than a newspaper when spread out completely.

I stuffed all the papers except the map into my handbag, jostling my duffel on my other shoulder as I rode the elevator back down.

In the lobby, the reception lady I had spoken to was on the phone and didn't notice my polite smile—which lingered as I thought about the last hour. It was clear why all the reception girls had googly eyes for Tyler. He was smart, easy to talk to, made you feel comfortable in his presence—and he was gorgeous. Those searching gray eyes and the messy hair that kept falling over his forehead . . .

Crap! I'd told myself not to get a crush on him, and there I was, not even an hour later, having failed miserably.

FOUR

Outside, I stopped at the top of the stairs and unfolded the giant map, the sun pleasant on my face. The weather was warming up; T-shirts-and-shorts season couldn't come too soon.

The admin building was near the edge of the curving maze of lines and markers; Res Hall K was much farther in. I took off, the strap of my duffel bag digging into my shoulder.

After a few minutes of walking down the curved, tree-lined paths, I reached a neat three-story building. About a dozen stairs led up to double doors, which opened into a cool foyer. I made my way over to a small elevator on the left and pressed the button. My every step echoed up past the stairs twisting through the center of the building, reaching all the way to the third floor.

The elevator was quiet and smooth—it must have been a recent addition to the obviously older building. I double-checked my messy scrawl at the top of the map—*room 308*—before following the signs to the right.

I paused when I reached the door, key in hand. I was sharing the room with two other girls—a Zara Adams and a Beth Knox—and I didn't want to just barge in on them. After a few moments of awkward indecision, I knocked.

A moment later, a girl with brown eyes and short, silky red hair cracked open the door. "What?"

She obviously wasn't in the mood for visitors, but I wasn't a visitor, so I couldn't just go away. I shuffled my feet. "Uh . . . hi . . . um . . . I'm Eve. I live here?" It came out as a question.

"*What?*" This time there was confusion mixed in with the annoyance. Shuffling and other voices came from inside the room. Someone was crying softly.

I took a deep breath and forced myself to speak clearly. "Sorry. I just arrived today. I've been assigned to this room. Are you Beth? Or Zara?"

She sighed and rolled her eyes. "Right. Of course. Your timing is fucking great." The sarcasm rolling off her was almost visible. "You might as well come in." She opened the door wide.

Gripping the strap of my duffel tighter in some desperate attempt to have something to hold on to, I stepped inside.

Red—she still hadn't told me her name—closed the door just a little too forcefully and turned her back to me, walking over to a couch where two other girls were sitting.

The room was small but comfortable looking. Most of it was taken up by the three-seater couch pushed up against the wall to my left. A TV stand with a flat screen on top of it, a coffee table littered with tissues, and a round dining table surrounded by three mismatched chairs filled the rest of the space. A door to the right led into the bathroom—I could just make out the edge of the sink through the crack—and on the opposite wall were three evenly spaced doors: the bedrooms.

As I opened my mouth to ask which room was mine, I realized no one was speaking. I looked over to the couch and met three sets of eyes staring at me.

The redhead was sitting on the arm of the couch. In the middle was a blonde girl, her long platinum locks unbrushed and her eyes red and puffy. On her other side was another redhead. Her hair was lighter, longer, and had more orange in it than the first girl's, and freckles sprinkled her nose and cheeks. She was the only one with a small smile on her face.

"Hi. I'm Beth. That's Zara." The freckled redhead pointed to the girl who had answered the door.

So I would be sharing with two redheads. What were the statistical probabilities of that? Only 2 percent of people had red hair. Were they related? I dismissed the thought immediately. Their features were too different despite the color of their hair—also two very different shades of red.

I half raised my hand in a little wave and was about to introduce myself, but the blonde on the couch cut across me.

"So you're my replacement then." It wasn't a question. It was a statement, delivered with bitterness and anger. I had no idea why this girl thought I was replacing her, but I didn't want to be on the other end of her death stare.

"Umm . . ."

"Oh, forget it. It's got nothing to do with you anyway." The end of her sentence morphed into a wail, and she started sobbing again, dropping her head into her hands, which were clutching a bunch of tissues. "I can't believe they're actually kicking me out. 3.8! 3.8 GPA because of that one stupid paper, and I'm out. My parents are fuming! They spent all this money to send me here, and now I'll have to go to Yale or something. Ugh!" A disgusted look crossed her features, as if the word *Yale* personally offended her.

"Holy shit. They're that strict?" The words were out of my mouth before I could stop them. If they were throwing out people who were paying tuition, they definitely wouldn't hesitate to get rid of someone on a scholarship. I had better keep my grades up. *No pressure.*

All three sets of eyes flew back to me. Beth was rubbing soothing circles over her friend's back, while Zara sat with her arms crossed over her black T-shirt.

"You're still here?" Zara gave me a flat look and then rolled her eyes. "Yes. And it's not like a 'three strikes and you're out' thing. You don't get a warning. As soon as you slip, they throw you out on your ass. And it's not just grades either. Since this isn't just a college and not everyone is just a student, there are other factors. Like if you're spending some of your time studying and some working for one of the departments, you have to show that you're continuing to be an asset to the Institute."

She got up and grabbed the strap of my duffel, yanking it unceremoniously off my shoulder. "Anna has been attending here since she was sixteen, and now she's out. As you can imagine, it's a stressful situation." She made her way to the middle door and tossed my bag in without looking where it landed. "This used to be her room. Guess it's yours now. Mind giving us a minute?"

The last bit was delivered with less sarcasm, and I could appreciate that I was intruding on a private situation. Even though I didn't mean to. Even though this was technically my home now.

I nodded and walked into my new room. Zara nodded back as I passed—a quick nod that seemed to say "thanks"—and I gave her a small smile in return.

I closed the door softly and took a look around. Directly opposite the door was a window with a wide sill and thick timber frame, typical of these older buildings. A desk and chair, nightstand, and stripped twin bed composed the room's only furniture. It was small and basic, but it was also clean and light and cozy. It already felt more *mine* than my bedroom in Nampa ever had.

Most importantly it was private. I wouldn't have to share sleeping quarters with anyone. After a lifetime of never getting past superficial friendship, I preferred to be alone.

It took me twenty minutes to unpack my clothing, a few notebooks, and the one framed picture I had of my mother. I left my toiletries sitting on the desk, as I didn't want to walk through the common area while Anna was still out there.

After I'd carefully refolded my T-shirts and arranged the hangers in color-coded order, I flopped down on the bed, no idea what to do with myself. It was around midday, and using my trusty campus map to go in search of the cafeteria seemed like an excellent idea. But I was trapped by the crying blonde on the other side of the door.

Instead I spent five minutes making a list of all the things I needed to buy with my fancy new scholarship allowance money—like sheets for the bare bed I was lying on, towels, shampoo, and conditioner. Everything study related, such as textbooks, pens, and notebooks, would be provided by the Institute. I was expecting a package by the end of the day.

An hour later, my new roommates knocked on my door and let themselves in. They found me lying across my bed, legs up on the wall, head hanging off the edge.

"Hi. Eve, right?" Beth's simple blue skirt swished around her knees as she came in, a more reluctant Zara following behind.

I scrambled up into a sitting position and tried to look casual. "Yes. Hi. Nice to meet you properly, Beth. Is your friend going to be OK?"

"Oh, yeah. She'll be fine. She tends to be a little dramatic, and it all happened so fast. Her parents picked her up. Sorry you walked right into the middle of that."

"That's OK." I wasn't sure what else to say.

"So, Zara and I were just heading to the caf for some lunch. You wanna come with? It would be nice to get to know you."

Zara was picking at her nails in the doorway. She looked up at me, her expression completely blank.

I was just about to decline—Beth seemed nice enough, but I wasn't going to spend time with someone who clearly wanted nothing to do with me—when Zara straightened up, dropping her arms to her sides.

"It's fine. You can come. Whatever."

"Well, gee, with an invitation like that, how could I possibly refuse?" Two could play at the sarcasm game.

She stared me down for a moment, then smiled wide. "Well, all right then. I guess we'll get along just fine. Let's go, ladies."

I followed the Reds—as I had taken to calling them in my head—out of the building and through the grounds, listening to their chatter but not contributing much. Honestly, I would have preferred to go to lunch on my own, but since these girls were going to be my roommates, possibly for the next few years, a good relationship with them was probably worth a little effort.

A few years.

The concept of staying anywhere longer than a year was foreign to me, but I could do this—embrace it, buckle down, study hard. I might even make some friends. Might as well start with my roomies.

The cafeteria was an *entire building*. It was a flat, one-story structure, one of the smallest on campus, but it stretched wide. Picnic tables were scattered across the lawn, stretching toward the front doors and a paved, covered area with café tables. Clusters of people were eating outside, taking advantage of the sunshine.

As we made our way toward the entrance, a brightness to my right caught my eye. A group of people were milling around a picnic table, on top of which sat a boy, his feet on the bench.

Boy was probably the wrong word. He was . . . big. Big arms, big chest, big tall body, big booming laugh. A white T-shirt stretched over his defined chest. The only reason I hadn't mistaken him for a hulking man was his

47

face—too youthful and carefree to belong to anyone much past my own age.

The brightness was coming from his big hands. Which were on fire. I stopped, fascinated. This was the second uncommon and very impressive Variant ability I had encountered since getting here, and it had only been a few hours.

The Reds must have noticed I'd stopped walking. They'd doubled back to stand beside me.

"That's Kid," Beth said.

I watched the guy in question lazily wave his hand in front of his torso, the flame coming off his fingers dancing languorously along with his movements.

"He has a fire ability, as you can see, and he's fond of showing it off. Not that anyone minds. It's pretty cool. Or . . . hot, I guess. In more ways than one." A smile had crept into Beth's voice.

"Kid?" I asked without taking my eyes off him. "What kind of name is that?"

"His name is actually Ethan Paul. Everyone just calls him Kid. I don't actually know why."

As if he could hear us talking, he looked up from his spot on the bench, and our eyes met. He held my gaze as he curled his fingers and threw a ball of fire the size of a baseball right at me. I gasped in surprised delight, a smile pulling at my lips, but before it even got halfway, it fizzled out into a puff of smoke.

A wide grin spread over Kid's face, and he leaned back onto the table, his hands behind him.

Zara chuckled. "That's one of his favorite tricks, but his fire isn't really dangerous. I mean, he could start a fire if he sparked up while holding a piece of wood or something but not, like, remotely. He doesn't have a Vital, so there are limits to what he can do. They keep a pretty close eye on him though, because if he were to meet his Vital, he could be seriously dangerous."

About 10 percent of Variants were Vitals, people who didn't have abilities themselves but had direct access to the Light and the capability to channel it. I had never met a Vital, and Zara's mention of them made we wonder how many there were at Bradford Hills. Their direct link to the Light—the energy that made abilities possible in the first place—fascinated me. Vitals were a kind of conduit; they could draw Light into themselves and pass it on to Variants through skin-on-skin contact, basically giving the Variant a power boost.

All Vitals eventually found a Variant, or two or three, that was meant for them—if they didn't already know each other. They were drawn together. The Light flowed through a Vital into their Bonded Variant easier than water through a sieve. Science was still working on understanding Variant abilities, and one of the least understood aspects of it was the Light and how Vitals accessed it.

If someone like Kid found his Vital, he would have access to unlimited power. Theoretically, he could raze entire towns, even cities, to the ground. No wonder Bradford Hills Institute was watching him closely.

Kid was still looking at me, but the grin had fallen away, replaced by a more serious face. My own expression must have been curious. I was studying him.

I had to stop doing that—looking at people like puzzles to solve or experiments to complete. It would not help my chances of making friends.

I turned away to resume our walk. My heart was racing, but not from fear. I had been surprised, sure, and a little excited to see another cool ability close up, but at no point had I felt fear. That wasn't normal. Any normal person with functioning survival instincts would have been scared of a ball of fire flying at their face, right?

I was probably overthinking it. As we entered the cafeteria, I focused back on the Reds.

"He's obviously noticed you, so here's your first piece of Bradford

Hills insider advice: stay the hell away from Ethan Paul. His power may be harmless, but he is dangerous to the female student population." Zara delivered this in what I was quickly learning was her default voice—flat and slightly disinterested. As if she had explained this a million times and was over it.

"He's actually kind of a nice guy if you speak to him for longer than a few minutes . . . and don't mind the whole throwing balls of fire at your face thing." Beth moved toward a very long buffet display at the back of the room. At least I wouldn't have to worry about where my meals were coming from—once again, part of the full scholarship.

"So is he going to roofie me, or is he a nice guy?" I asked.

Zara snorted as she helped herself to some pasta.

Beth giggled. "She didn't mean it like that. It's more like . . . he's a distraction. I mean, he's hot, a natural at most sports, and throws these amazing parties at his uncle's house where he lives, just up the road from here, but he's never had a girlfriend. He seems to fixate on a girl and then get bored with her quickly. Meanwhile, the girls get distracted from their study or work, and their contribution slips. Sometimes that can get them kicked out. It's partly what happened with Anna. She was seeing Kid a lot the last few weeks, and she wasn't spending enough time focusing on her studies."

Zara carried our trays to a free table near a window. "Yeah, and the thing is, because he's Variant, they're more lenient. You hardly ever see Variant kids getting kicked out."

"What do you mean?" One minute they were telling me the school was really strict, no second chances, and now they were telling me it was lenient.

Zara rolled her eyes and started eating her pasta while Beth elaborated: "There are no second chances if you're a human. But because this is one of only a few schools in the country that specializes in helping Variants learn

VARIANT LOST

how to control their—sometimes dangerous—abilities, they tend to be more forgiving. They can't have someone like Kid never learning how to properly control his power out in the world. It could be disastrous."

"You mean it would be bad press. Especially with these Variant Valor dickheads spouting their superior race bullshit lately. They can't afford to look bad or dangerous right now. So yeah, the Variants pretty much get away with everything, while we Dimes have to bust our asses." Zara slapped her fork down on her tray and pushed it away, her pasta half-eaten, and stared out the window.

I cringed at her casual use of the word *Dimes*—a derogatory slang term for humans. There were simply more of us—we were a dime a dozen. *Dimes* for short.

The extremist group Variant Valor was rather fond of the term. They saw all humans as Dimes—common, unremarkable, inferior. Those nuts believed that Variants were superior in every way and should therefore rule the humans. They were completely unhinged, staging protests, posting elitist propaganda all over the Internet, and occasionally causing violent incidents. They were shit-stirrers of the worst kind—dogmatic.

"So I'm guessing you're both human then?" I hedged, unsure how safe this topic was but curious nonetheless.

"Yes," Beth answered for both of them. Zara was still looking out the window. "My blood tests returned a clear human result. Zara's tested positive for Variant DNA, but—"

"But I'm defective," Zara cut across her, leaning forward on the table. "I've never manifested an ability or made a connection with a Variant who has one, so I'm not a Vital either."

"Oh. OK." Not all people who tested positive for Variant DNA had abilities—the gene could be dormant. Some people went their whole lives

51

without knowing they had it. Why did Zara resent it so much?

Beth cleared her throat. "So, Eve, where are you from?"

It was a common enough question that I was prepared for. I gave them a vague answer about moving around a lot, and they both commented on how that explained my indistinct accent. Then I put the focus back on them. It was easy. If you asked people enough questions, they wouldn't notice you weren't sharing much about yourself.

We spent the rest of the hour chatting. Beth was from Atlanta and studying literature and journalism. Zara was from Anaheim and studying political science and Variant studies. They had both been attending and sharing the same dorm in Bradford Hills since they were sixteen. The Institute wasn't concerned with age—any given class could have kids as young as twelve along with adults studying for their third degree. They told me more about how the Institute worked; we discussed movies and favorite foods.

For a while, I actually felt normal.

By the time we left, full on pasta, I was beginning to feel more comfortable with the Reds. Beth was lovely and friendly; Zara clearly had a chip on her shoulder, but her sarcasm and ire were not directed at me. I didn't know what her beef with the world was, but I could understand it. I had my own beef with the world. Being less than impressed with what life had thrown at us so far was one thing we had in common.

When we got back to our res hall, three boxes were waiting for me at our door. Two had the Bradford Hills logo on the side, and one was just a plain box with a note taped to the top:

Eve,

These are the supplies BHI provides to all its full scholarship students. The last box is a care package from me. I noticed you arrived without certain essentials that BHI does not provide, so I took the liberty of arranging them for you. I hope you don't mind. Have a good first day of classes tomorrow, and again, please don't hesitate to come see me if you need to.

Best,

Tyler Gabriel

It was handwritten on a piece of notebook paper. Had he delivered these himself? How thoughtful.

"You got Gabe as your admin?" Zara was reading over my shoulder. "Nice."

"Very nice!" Beth leaned over my other shoulder to get a look herself. "He's scrumptious. Never dates students though."

I was beginning to think Beth was a little boy obsessed. "Um ... wouldn't that be illegal or whatever?"

"Between students and anyone on the teaching staff, yeah. But Gabe doesn't teach. It's frowned on, but there aren't any rules against it exactly. The student body varies in age so much, plus many of the older students work for the Institute in some capacity too, so the lines are kind of blurred. It's a moot point anyway. Many have tried and failed."

She sighed as she picked up one of the boxes and carried it into my room, and I had a sneaking suspicion she was speaking from experience. Zara grabbed one too, and I picked up the last one, kicking the door shut behind us.

"Thanks guys." I couldn't decide if it felt nice to have them helping or intrusive to have them touching my stuff.

Thankfully, they left me alone to unpack and set up my room. After unpacking the extra box Tyler had sent, I scrunched up the list of things I needed to buy and threw it away. He had thought of everything, down to new sheets.

When I came out later in the evening, the Reds suggested we order a pizza, sparking a brief argument about whether to get pineapple as a topping—Zara was pro, but Beth was firmly against. They turned to me.

"You're the decider, Eve." Beth smiled, and Zara raised her eyebrows expectantly.

I didn't want to get on either of their bad sides this early on, but I had to make a stand. I gave Zara an apologetic look. "I love pineapple, but it does *not* belong on pizza."

Zara huffed, and Beth did a fist pump before picking up the phone to order. "Anna loved it too, and I could never get those two to let me order a good, pineapple-free pizza. Looks like the tables have turned."

"Whatever." Zara tried to keep the annoyed look on her face but couldn't contain her laughter in the end.

I laughed along with them, wishing I had these kinds of silly memories with lifelong friends.

As the Reds continued to reminisce, I did my best to push out the longing for what I'd never had. What mattered was what was *ahead* of me. Soon, Zara and Beth and I would make our own memories together.

I had a feeling they would be good friends to have.

FIVE

After doing a little research on fire abilities during one of my sleepless nights, I didn't see the guy who'd thrown a ball of fire at me as a welcome to Bradford Hills for a while. Then on my third day of classes, I had the same lecture as Zara in Variant Abilities 101, and there he was.

He was chatting with a guy with dirty blond hair who was impeccably dressed in chinos and a gray shirt. When Kid saw us come in, he slapped his friend on the shoulder and came right over.

Zara immediately rolled her eyes and crossed her hands over her chest.

"Hey, Zee." He grinned, looking between us and smiling widely. I was mesmerized by his light amber eyes, a sharp contrast to his coal-black hair, cut short at the sides. "Are you going to introduce me to your new friend?"

"Don't call me that, *Kid*," she spat. "And no, I'm not. She just got here. I'd like her not to get expelled."

"What?" He chuckled, looking at her as if she were a little batty. "Who got expelled?"

"Anna, you dick. Her parents picked her up three days ago."

"Shit. Are you serious?" His playful demeanor dropped and he focused all his attention on Zara, giving me a chance to study him further. He was built like an athlete. Even standing one step below us in the aisle of the lecture theater, he was a little taller than me, and his V-neck T-shirt, pulled tight over his chest, accentuated his broad shoulders. A tattoo peaked out from under his left sleeve, but I was a little distracted by the curves of his defined biceps and didn't get a good look at it.

The lecturer walked in, and we all had to get to our seats.

Even though I hadn't said a word to Kid, I couldn't help but be intrigued, but my new friend's warning to stay away from him was hard to ignore. If anything, my instant attraction was warning enough to keep my distance. I didn't need any distractions here. I couldn't afford to get sidetracked by a beautiful, very muscly, annoyingly confident boy.

Over the next week and a half, Kid tried to get close to me at every opportunity. Once, he came into class late and spent an inappropriate amount of time looking around the half-full lecture theater before zeroing in on me and sitting in the seat right next to mine. Even though half the row was empty.

I focused hard on the lecture and my notes and made a conscious effort not to look in his direction, but about halfway through, a flash of light caught my attention. I looked over to see several tiny scraps of paper on fire and floating above his desk. I watched, transfixed, as the little flickers danced around, my note taking frozen in midsentence.

Just as they were getting too big to go unnoticed by other people, he made a subtle motion with his hand, and they spluttered out, little bits of ash floating down to the table and the floor.

I smiled despite myself and looked up at him. He was watching the front of the room intently, as though none of it had happened. Then one side of his mouth lifted into a smirk.

Self-satisfied show-off. He knew he had my attention, and that was apparently enough.

Another time he saw me come into the cafeteria. He took a step toward me, but a girl with shiny auburn hair sidled up to him and pressed herself against his side, whispering something in his ear.

I shook my head and headed toward the food, ignoring him once again.

Every other time he'd tried to approach me, he'd been thwarted either by Zara's sarcastic quips and raised brows or my own evasion tactics.

I didn't think I was likely to run into him on the other side of campus though, so when it finally came time to get the Variant DNA test Tyler had insisted on, it was a relief to stop worrying about dodging Kid for a while.

After putting the test off for two weeks, sure it would come back negative, I'd received a stern text message from Tyler (*Why are your blood test results not on my desk yet?*), caved, and made an appointment. On my way, I'd also caved by stepping foot inside a Starbucks for the first time in months. This one was on campus, conveniently located near the medical buildings, where my appointment would take place.

My first two weeks at Bradford Hills had allowed me to start falling into a routine, which consisted mostly of classes, study, and hanging out with the Reds. I hadn't had a chance to explore much past the confines of the campus—the campus itself was so huge that I still hadn't seen it all, sticking to the buildings that contained my classes, my food, and my bed. Unfortunately, that meant I hadn't had a chance to find a coffee shop with a decent latte. Starbucks would never compare to the amazing Melbourne coffee that had been my introduction to the black gold, but at least it provided something other than that American filtered crap.

I was relieved to find the Starbucks mostly empty. Only five or six people were milling about, waiting on orders and seated at tables. Just to be safe, I checked the time before ordering. Still twenty minutes until my appointment with the campus nurse.

Stepping up to the counter, I ordered my latte in the smallest size possible, moved along, and took my phone from my back pocket. I was dressed casually, as usual. Sticking to campus didn't really require anything dressier than jeans, flats, and a warm sweater. Even though the sun was out, there was still a chill on the breeze.

I scrolled through my schedule and to-do list as I waited. The massive campus was still a pain to navigate, but at least catching up in the coursework was proving relatively easy. Tyler had not exaggerated when he said that Bradford had a different approach to education. It really wasn't a problem that I was joining classes so late in the year. They worked at a different pace and with a different structure.

Even so, the amount of reading that piled up after my first meetings with all my professors had been overwhelming, but once again, my weird spurts of energy had saved me. An episode a few days after arriving—three nights without sleep—gave me plenty of extra time to read up on the study materials and even do some extra research, in between several vigorous workouts. It had been a productive few days.

I was on top of everything. The only reason I was checking my schedule was to fill time while I waited for my latte. After all, it wasn't as if I had any friends to message.

As I put my phone away, I sensed someone behind me, standing a little too close. I turned my head to find Kid craning over my shoulder. So much for not running into him on the other side of campus.

"Damn." He leaned away to a more comfortable distance and grinned at me. "I was hoping to see who you were texting. So I could tell him to back off."

"That's a bit presumptuous." I faced the counter again, giving him my back. "You don't even know my name."

"You're right." He chuckled, stepping up next to me and reaching his hand out as if to shake mine. "I'm Ethan Paul, and you are . . ." He raised his brows expectantly, his amber eyes shining with mirth.

"On my way to an appointment and don't have time for this," I deadpanned, forcing myself to look away from those eyes.

He laughed. "Oh, come on. You won't even tell me your name? What have I done to deserve such suspicion?"

I sighed and rolled my eyes, willing the barista to hurry with my latte. When the young guy behind the counter finally pushed the beverage toward me, I realized the flaw in my getaway plan.

"Tall latte for Eve," the barista announced before turning away to make the next coffee.

"Shit," I muttered under my breath, taking a sideways glance at Kid.

He was looking right at me, grinning. Deep dimples gave him a very innocent look, which the sparkle in his eyes elevated to an infectious kind of glee. It was a stark contrast to his large, intimidating frame. He towered over me, once again dressed in jeans and a tight white T-shirt. How was he not cold? Despite a string of cool spring days, I hadn't seen him in a jacket or sweater once.

With another eye-roll (my new roommate was rubbing off on me—Zara was a pro eye-roller), I jammed a lid on my latte and rushed toward the exit as the barista called out behind me, "Venti dark roast for Ethan."

Of course his order only took seconds to fill. All they had to do was pour the stale filtered excuse for coffee into a giant cup and hand it over.

"Hey, *Eve!*" he called after me, emphasizing my name, as I stepped outside. "Wait!"

I didn't slow down, but he caught up to me anyway.

"Hey, come on. All I'm trying to do is introduce myself. You're new around here. You could use some friends."

I pulled up short and faced him. "I have plenty of friends, thank you very much," I lied, crossing my arms over my chest. He had hit a sore spot.

He loudly gulped his sip of coffee before lowering the cup, the easy expression on his face gone. "Of course. I didn't mean anything by it."

Realizing I may have overreacted a little, I made a conscious effort to relax my stance and tried giving him a small smile. "I really do have to go."

"Wait." The sudden seriousness of his tone made me stop. "Look, I don't know what Zara has told you about me, but all I'm saying is maybe you could get to know me a little before making up your own mind."

Dammit. He had a point. His cocky and boisterous behavior had been in line with Zara and Beth's description of his womanizing ways and careless attitude toward school, but Beth *had* defended him a few times. I hadn't seen him be mean or intentionally rude to anyone since he'd thrown the fireball at me on my first day.

Now he was standing right in front of me, and I wasn't entirely sure I still wanted to avoid him.

"So, can we start again?" He rubbed the back of his neck, and I tried not to stare at the way his arm muscles popped out in that position.

"Yes. OK." I nodded, extending my hand. "My name is Eve."

He wrapped his hand around mine firmly but gently. "Hi, Eve. I'm Ethan, but my friends call me Kid." He flashed me his brilliant smile with a side of dimples, and I did my best to focus on the word *friend*. That's all we would be—friends. I could handle that.

But even as I was trying to convince myself I wasn't attracted to him, I was noticing how warm his hand felt wrapped around mine, which looked tiny by comparison. Neither one of us was pulling away, which left us standing there, holding each other's hands and staring at each other. I wondered if his palm felt tingly too.

I pulled my hand out of his and stepped back, taking a sip of my mediocre latte. He glanced down at his palm, looking bewildered for a second, before shoving it into his pocket.

"So, *Eve*." He smiled widely, obviously still happy to finally know my name. "Where are you off to?"

"I have an appointment with the campus nurse. Apparently it's school policy to run a full blood workup on new students. Seems a little intrusive if you ask me, but my admissions guy, Tyler, is insisting."

"Oh, Gabe is your admin guy? Sweet!"

"You know him?" I guess it wasn't much of stretch. The Variant community here seemed tight-knit and well established.

"Yeah. We live together."

"Oh!" I fixed him with a very surprised look. Maybe Zara had read him *way* wrong.

He tossed his head back and laughed loudly. "Not like that, *Eve*. We grew up together."

"Oh. Sorry. So you're related?"

"Nah, not really."

My curiosity was piqued, but I was making an effort to curb that in social situations, so I didn't ask for more information. Realizing we had been talking for some time, I checked my phone and saw I only had five minutes to find the correct building, then the correct room, for my appointment.

Cursing, I started walking in what I hoped was the right direction. "I'm going to be late for my appointment. Nice to meet you, Kid. Bye!"

He grabbed me by the back of my sweater, stopping me in my tracks, and chuckled. When I looked over my shoulder, he pointed at a low ivy-covered building next to the one that housed the Starbucks. "You want to go there."

"Right," I breathed, embarrassed. "Of course. Thanks. See ya!" I took off in my new direction.

"You're welcome, *Eve!*" he yelled after me. "Nice to meet you, *Eve!* See you later, *Eve!*"

I couldn't contain my smile as I lifted my hand over my head to wave, rushing to my appointment.

Twenty minutes later, I walked back out, my coffee long gone, my right elbow bandaged where the nurse had inserted the needle. After I'd signed some paperwork, the young nurse had taken several vials of my blood with gentle fingers and practiced movements and told me the results would be ready in two weeks.

Emerging into the fresh air, I paused. I wasn't due to meet the Reds for lunch for another hour, and I had nothing to do until then. Was trying to explore this end of campus worth the risk of getting completely lost? I had stupidly left my trusty giant map behind in my room. I may have had the table of elements memorized, but my sense of direction was seriously awful.

As I looked around this quieter part of campus—the buildings just as old and impressive as all the others, the oak trees swaying in the light spring breeze—I spotted someone familiar.

My new friend was hard to miss, his big frame towering over everyone else in the vicinity. Kid was standing near the entrance to the Starbucks, talking to the blond, well-dressed boy I had seen him with several times. They were standing close, their heads bent together, their faces serious.

I knew I shouldn't be staring—I had vowed to treat people like people, not puzzles—but my indecision about what to do with my free hour was completely forgotten. All I could do was watch and wonder what Kid and his friend were discussing so intently.

As he replied to something Kid had said with a wave of his hand, the blond looked in my direction. Our eyes met, his gaze rooting me to the spot. Kid soon turned to look at me too, and I finally snapped myself out of it and glanced around the square, struggling to remember which direction I had come from to get there. I headed for the main path, hoping to find one of those signposts with the arrows.

Eyes downcast, embarrassed for getting caught staring, I nearly barreled into Kid when he stepped into my path.

"Oh shit." I jumped, my heart flying into my throat, my hand clutching at my chest.

"Hey, Eve." He sounded relaxed. "How was the blood test?"

"Um." I looked up at him. He was just standing there casually, his hands in his pockets, his face as relaxed as his voice sounded. I looked back toward the Starbucks, but his friend had disappeared. "It was fine. Didn't hurt at all."

"That's good. What are you up to now?"

"Did you wait for me?" I was relieved he didn't seem worried about my awkward staring, but it had suddenly occurred to me that his behavior was beginning to border on stalkerish.

"What?" He chuckled, flashing his dimples. "I bumped into my friend and we got talking. I think you saw me standing with him . . ." There was a hint of humor in his voice—so, he'd noticed me staring after all.

"Right. Sorry. Um, I'm meeting some friends for lunch soon, so . . ." I was ready to be away from this whole awkward encounter.

"OK, OK." He chuckled again but stepped out of my path. "I won't keep you from your super early lunch. I just wanted to invite you to my party. It's next weekend."

"I don't know . . ." I hadn't been to a party since my wild streak in Nampa. Considering I was here on a scholarship, my focus should probably be on my studies, not getting drunk with frat boys. Not that there were any fraternities or sororities at Bradford Hills Institute.

"It's just a party at my place, and it will mostly just be Bradford students. You can bring your friends too, if you want." He pulled his phone out of his pocket and handed it to me, my fingers closing around the sleek black rectangle reflexively. "Put your number in there, and I'll send you the details."

I watched him for a moment, standing there with his mischievous eyes and his big arms and his confident personality. I quickly put my number in his phone, muttering as I typed, "I'll think about it."

"Sweet!" He put the phone back in his pocket and beamed at me. "See you there."

"I said I'd think about it, Kid." I laughed despite myself.

"What? Can't hear you!" He started to walk away in the opposite direction. Apparently he had somewhere to be, now that he'd completed his mission of inserting himself into my life. "I'll see you at my party! Bye!"

I caught one more glimpse of his brilliant smile before turning away, shaking my head.

I decided to risk getting lost after all and took a walk around campus, sending a message to Tyler to let him know I had done the blood test. His reply was almost instant.

Tyler: Finally! That was slower than a reaction between covalent compounds.

I snorted at the lame joke before replying.

Me: Chemistry humor. Really?
Tyler: Be thankful it wasn't a pun.

Me: Haha! Good point.

Tyler: I'll let you know when the results arrive and we can set a meeting to discuss.

It would be a boring meeting with *nothing* to discuss, but I wasn't going to pass up an opportunity to spend some time with Tyler Gabriel. I put my phone away and headed to the cafeteria.

Halfway through our tacos, as Zara and Beth were chatting about their morning classes, my phone went off. Before I could wipe the salsa off my fingers, Beth unashamedly leaned over to read what the message said.

"Party next Sat at 1175 Oakwood Cres. Bring your friends! Hope to . . . Hey! I was reading that." Beth sounded outraged as I swiped the phone away, but there was a big smile on her face.

"God, you two have no boundaries." They really didn't. They were constantly walking into my room without knocking, barging into the bathroom to ask me things while I was in the shower, reading my messages, borrowing my things, and just generally getting all up in my business. They acted the same way with each other. I guess it was nice that they were treating me like one of their own, but it was taking some getting used to.

"Who needs boundaries when you have friends like us?" Beth tried to grab the phone, but I held it out at arm's length. Of course, that put it in Zara's range, and she yanked it right out of my hand.

"Hope to see you there." She picked up where Beth had left off, tucking her sleek red hair behind her ear. "Winky face." Her face scrunched up in disgust as I flopped back in my chair, giving up.

"Who's inviting you to a party?" Beth asked at the same time Zara demanded in much growlier voice, "Why is Ethan Paul inviting you to a party?"

"Kid invited you to his party?" Beth bounced in her seat, but this time I was the one who spoke over her.

"How do you know it's from him?"

Zara rolled her eyes, crossing her arms over her chest. "I know his address. We're not going."

"Oh my god, can we please go?" Beth pleaded, hanging off my arm and leaning into me. "Zara never wants to go to these things, and I never get invited. Please!"

"Look, I only just met him properly this morning, and he invited me. I haven't decided if I'm going yet."

"These elitist things are just another excuse for that crowd to reinforce their own inflated sense of importance. Beth never gets invited because she's a Dime. I *always* get invited because technically I have Variant DNA and my parents run in these god-awful Variant society circles. You're invited because they're not sure what you are yet, and they want to keep you on their side in case your blood test comes back positive."

Beth groaned as Zara completed her diatribe, and I stared at her, stunned. Here I was thinking it was just a party.

"Or maybe I don't get invited because I don't know Kid or his friends, and Eve got invited because he likes her?" Beth was clearly trying to sound firm, but she always seemed to come across as gentle and polite. "Please, Eve, can we go?"

She gave me her puppy dog eyes, the freckles on her nose only adding to the innocent act. I rolled my eyes, and before I could even voice my agreement, she was thanking me and hugging me from the side.

"I've lost my appetite. I'll see you guys later." Zara didn't wait for a response before scraping her chair back and hurrying out of the building.

Beth and I shared a look, and then she leaned forward. "Bradford Hills Institute and other Variant-affiliated organizations hold regular events. Things like luncheons, fundraising balls, and socials. The goal is to facilitate as many

66

Variant introductions as possible in the hopes of finding a Variant-Vital match. Zara grew up going to these things, and she used to enjoy them, but as time went on and her ability never manifested, she felt more and more pressure from her parents, and she started to resent even being invited anymore. She's just over it."

Beth really cared deeply for Zara. She sighed before continuing. "Most abilities manifest by age thirteen. Zara's nineteen and still nothing. It's likely she has the dormant gene and her parents are real assholes about it. They make her feel like a disappointment over something she has no control over."

"OK. I can understand that. But what does it have to do with Kid's party? It's not like it's an official Bradford Hills event."

"Yeah, it is, but a lot of younger people use parties—especially Kid's parties, because they're legendary—as an informal way of doing the same thing, trying to find a Vital. All it really means is that people there are more likely to talk to someone they don't know than they are at a regular party, but for Zara it just turns the knife—reminds her that she's a failure in her parents' eyes."

"Well, if it means so much to her, we don't have to go. I'm not huge on parties anyway."

"Oh, we are going to this party. You already agreed. It's happening!" The excited smile was back. "Don't worry about Zara. She just needs to cool off. She'll be fine."

I reluctantly agreed, figuring Beth knew Zara better than I did, and allowed myself to get a little excited about the prospect of a party. Plus it was making Beth ridiculously happy.

True to Beth's word, when we all got back to our res hall after classes, Zara apologized for how she'd reacted at lunch and seemed to be in a much better mood. I breathed a sigh of relief as Beth pulled me into a lengthy conversation about what to wear, while Zara rolled her eyes at us and shut herself in her bedroom.

SIX

P eople streamed past me in every direction as I stood in front of the admin building, looking up and down between my trusty map and what felt like an infinite number of possible paths to take. Several lanes wide enough to accommodate two cars, as well branching veins of narrower walkways, wound away from me on all sides.

My destination was the Variant History Museum on the other side of campus, but I had seriously underestimated my bad sense of direction. While most of the lecture halls and study rooms were grouped at the east end of campus, near the residential buildings, the rest of campus was an unfamiliar maze of various office buildings, research labs, and three separate libraries. Three!

I took a deep breath of fresh air, fighting back frustration.

My only lecture had been canceled, and I had the morning off. With nowhere to be until lunch with the Reds, I'd ventured out into the sunshine in nothing more than leggings and a long T-shirt, loose around my hips, hoping to explore my new home a little bit.

The enormous campus was just one of a million things I still needed to figure out in this crazy elite world. Still, there were many things I was enjoying.

The Reds topped the list. Yes, Zara had her moments, but she was the most honest and open person I had ever met. Beth was the perfect counterbalance, always giving people the benefit of the doubt, effortlessly caring and thoughtful, though never hesitating to call Zara out on her shit. Those two had clearly been friends for a long time, and although that should have left me feeling left out, it didn't. I was already beginning to feel as if I belonged with them.

It was an odd feeling—*belonging*. Even when I'd made friends with Harvey and his sister in Australia, it hadn't happened this fast or this effortlessly.

I was really enjoying my classes too. Chemistry was my favorite by far, and I was even considering applying for a lab assistant position with the research lab on campus. It would allow me to earn some extra cash, and I would be making even more of a contribution to Bradford Hills, cementing my place here.

I was turning my map every which way, trying to figure out which path was correct, when Tyler stepped into my field of vision.

"Lost?" he asked with a soft smile on his face. He was dressed similarly to when I'd first met him—gray pants and a navy shirt, sleeves rolled up to the elbows. He slung his messenger bag over his shoulder, then had to swipe his messy hair out of his eyes.

So adorable!

"Nope! I'm all good." I didn't want to admit I couldn't read a simple campus map, so I tucked the offending piece of paper into my bag.

"Liar." He chuckled and then raised his eyebrows, waiting for something.

How could I have forgotten his ability?

"Right. Human lie detector." I wasn't sure if I was more embarrassed about being lost or lying to him about it. "That's really not fair, you know. I'm so embarrassed. Give me a partial differential equation and I'm all over it. Ask me to read a map . . . Well, just don't ask me to read maps, OK?"

"Fairness is subjective, and I can't turn my ability off, so that's a moot point. But don't be embarrassed about being lost. This campus is massive, and it can be confusing. Where are you going?"

I was grateful he didn't tease me and glad to have someone point me in the right direction. I was doubly glad it was Tyler. This was only the second time I'd met him. The first time he'd encouraged my curiosity, and now he was quickly dispelling my embarrassment over not being able to do a simple task. Trying to resist liking this guy was beginning to feel futile.

"I was trying to get to the Variant Museum."

His face brightened and he smiled wider. "Great! I can guide you there myself. I'm heading that way."

He gestured to a path leading in the complete opposite direction I was going to take and took off at a leisurely pace.

"Right. This is the way I was going to go too." I stepped up next to him, matching his slow pace.

"Liar!" This time he did laugh, but it wasn't mocking—more amused and lighthearted.

"Dammit!" I laughed too, letting the ease of his presence and the warm sun melt my embarrassment away.

The occasional tree provided shade as we walked down the narrow, fern-lined path, chatting easily. He asked about how I was settling in, and I thanked him profusely for his care package. He waved it off as nothing and asked about my classes; I was loving them all. He seemed pleased to hear that and began recommending articles I might find interesting.

"It was written in the mid-nineties, but it's still widely regarded as the beginning of serious Variant genetics research. It's a good starting point for the basics if you want to know more."

Tyler was telling me about an old research paper when we emerged into another bustling square. It was nowhere near as busy as the area around the admin building, but there were plenty of people milling about—albeit more suits and high heels than T-shirts and backpacks. Three low buildings edged the sides of the square, and at the base of the one directly opposite us was a café, outdoor seating scattered around its doors.

Standing near the café, facing us, was a man dressed in all black—long-sleeved top, pants, and boots. He was with a short girl with long black hair and a tall boy with short black hair.

I watched him closely as we emerged from the path.

Tyler pulled up short. "Oh, whoops. We've actually gone past where you need to turn off for the museum, but if you just—"

"Holy shit!" I cut him off midsentence as realization hit me. I couldn't believe my widening eyes.

I knew that man. I had been looking for that man for over a year.

That was my honey-voiced stranger.

"Eve?" I could feel Tyler watching me, concern leaking into his voice, but I had no attention to spare for him. I couldn't take my eyes off the stranger. Maybe he wasn't really there, and if I looked away, he would disappear again. Just as he'd done in the hospital.

He looked up, his eyes landing on Tyler first, his hand raising in greeting. Then his focus shifted to me, and a look of pure shock crossed his face.

He was real!

I launched myself across the square and straight for him. His eyes widened, the shock replaced by horror.

I didn't stop to contemplate his reaction, or the alarm in Tyler's voice as he called my name again, or all the people who were no doubt giving me strange looks as I barreled through their quiet day.

I pulled up right in front of him, staring into his face to make sure it was really him. Ice-blue eyes stared back. There was the strong jaw, the scar through the right eyebrow, the closely cropped hair.

"Holy shit, it's really you!" I declared at an inappropriate volume as I wrapped my arms around his middle, pressing my cheek to his firm chest.

He froze, holding his arms out and going stiff. Several people gasped, and the level of background noise considerably lessened. Was that me drowning out the noise, completely in the moment, overjoyed at finally finding my stranger? Or had everything really gone silent?

"Eve." This time there was a hint of panic in Tyler's voice when he said my name. He placed a firm hand on my shoulder, and I let him pull me backward. The stranger was not returning my hug. I looked around slowly at the silent onlookers' faces—at the looks of shock, worry, or amazement.

My stranger just looked pissed off.

Did they frown on hugging here? I could have sworn I had seen people hug.

"I can't believe you're really here," I said at a more normal volume.

The stranger spoke at the same time, his hushed tone discernible only to our weird little group. "How the hell did you find me? I've been blocking your annoyingly persistent attempts for over a year."

Life was resuming its regular rhythm around us—general chitchat, footsteps, chairs scraping on concrete. Whatever the crowd had poised itself to witness hadn't happened, and they were all moving on with their day.

"Wait. What? You knew I was looking for you?"

"Looking" was an understatement. I had called Melior Group repeatedly, even though they never gave me any new information. I had trawled the Internet, read through pages and pages of redacted documents released under the Freedom of Information Act, sifted through paranoid conspiracy theories on forums, frequented some of the darkest corners online. I had done all I could think to do for a whole year to find any scrap of information that would lead me to him.

And there he stood, telling me he knew I'd been looking for him and had actively blocked me.

He pressed his lips together and crossed his arms over his chest, taking a step back. "It's kind of my job to know things."

"What?" None of this was making sense. "Why? I just wanted to thank you." To begin with. I wanted to thank him profusely, and then I wanted to ask a million questions. Perhaps I had been naive to think someone who worked for Melior Group would be willing to answer them.

The two people he had been standing with, who looked like brother and sister, started laughing softly. As if it were absurd that anyone would want to thank him for anything.

"Do you two *know* each other?" Tyler cut into our conversation, sounding incredulous, but we both ignored him.

"There's no need to thank me. I was just doing my job."

"That's not your decision to make. Whether or not I *need* something is my business." I matched his stance, crossing my arms over my chest in defiance. I had been overjoyed when I first saw him standing across the square, but that had quickly turned to frustration. What was his problem?

"Answer the question. How did you find me?" We were standing off against each other, him determined to get answers to his paranoid question, me getting more and more angry as he ruined a moment I'd been thinking about for more than a year.

"Self-absorbed much?" This meeting had gone so wrong so fast. "I was offered a scholarship, and I took it. Nothing to do with you and your snarky ass. I've been so preoccupied with this move for the last month I haven't even looked for you."

He turned his attention to Tyler, ignoring me completely. "You know this . . . girl? Has she asked you about me?"

Before Tyler had a chance to answer, I jumped in. "Hey! Asshole! *The girl is standing right here.*" Fists clenched, I stepped back into his personal space. I had just as much right to be here as he did. "What the hell is your problem?"

He didn't flinch, but his breathing became labored as I got in his face. He looked as angry as I felt.

Before our bizarre standoff could escalate any further, three distinct groans came from behind me. I turned to see Tyler and the brother and sister clutching their heads in pain.

"Man. Rein it in, would you?" Tyler spoke directly to the stranger, visibly making an effort not to double over.

Confused, I looked back at the stranger to see a horrified expression on his face. He met my eyes, his features hardening into anger, before he turned on his heel and stalked away.

I wanted to run after him—after all that, I still hadn't actually thanked him—but I found myself rooted to the spot.

What the hell had just happened?

I turned around, the question on my lips, to see my three companions all staring at me, no longer holding their heads.

Tyler was the first to spring into action, throwing me one last perplexed glance before hurrying off after the stranger. "Dot, interference please," he yelled over his shoulder as he broke into a run.

"I got this, Gabe," the black-haired girl yelled after him. She turned to face me fully, a wide smile spread over her face as she looked me up and down. "I don't know who you are, girlie, but you've got some serious balls, accosting the 'Master of Pain' like that. I'm Dot. That's my brother, Charlie"—the boy behind her lifted his hand in a lazy wave—"and I can't wait to hear *this* story. Charles, coffee."

Charlie rolled his eyes and walked off in the direction of the café while Dot linked her arm through mine, guiding me toward one of the alfresco tables.

Up close, I could see her heavily made-up eyes were green, like moss, and her long black hair was perfectly straight. She was wearing a blouse, buttoned to the neck, and wide skirt that gave off the vibe of a fifties housewife, but she'd paired them with a studded leather jacket and hazardous-looking six-inch heels that only just put her at eye level with me. Her outfit seemed to say, "Yeah, I'm short—I dare you to point it out to me."

I wasn't about to point it out to her. It was an adorably deadly ensemble. Or maybe it was dangerously cute.

We sat down, but as soon as my butt hit the seat, I was up again. I had come *this close* to finally being able to get some answers, and now, once more, he had disappeared. I should have been chasing after him, like Tyler. I should never have let him walk away in the first place.

I didn't get very far. Dot grabbed my wrist and, with surprising strength, pulled me back down into my seat.

"Let go! I have to go after them." There may have been a hint of hysteria in my voice.

"Yeah, no. That's a bad idea, cowboy."

"Cowboy? Who . . . What? Please let go! I have to find him and . . ."

"Thank him," she finished for me.

"Yes." I met her eyes, the fight draining out of me.

She smiled back reassuringly and released my wrist. "Why is that exactly? What did he do to have you searching for him for a whole year for a simple thank you?"

"He saved my life." It was so much more complicated than that, but it was the truth.

Charlie returned just in time to hear my response. He joined his sister in regarding me with confusion.

"Huh," he muttered as he sat down between us, lowering a tray with three giant cups and assorted muffins onto the table. He was much taller than Dot, but they had the same dark green eyes and black hair, his cut short and a little messy. In complete contrast with the outrageous outfit his sister was sporting, he was dressed in simple dark clothing.

"And how did he save your life?" Dot asked as they both lifted their giant cups to their lips and took a sip.

Stalling, I reached for my own cup and had a taste. Scrunching my face up in disgust at the pure American pond sludge within, I placed it back on the table and pushed it away.

These two seemed to know both the stranger and Tyler. They had to have at least some of the answers I needed. Whether or not I could trust them was a whole other question. I would have to take a gamble—give something to get something back.

"Just over a year ago, I was on a plane that crashed over the Atlantic. That . . ." Asshole? Jerk? Angel? ". . . *man* saved me. He was part of the team that pulled me out of the freezing water, performed first aid, and got me to a hospital. The copilot and I were the only survivors. Two hundred and twenty-eight people died, and I lived. I'm pretty sure it was because of him."

I reached for a blueberry muffin to mask the foul taste in my mouth. I'd left out the fact that my mother had died and the fact that my stranger had been there for me at the lowest point in my life. I hadn't talked about those two things with anyone; I wasn't about to start with these two.

"Heavy." Charlie leaned back in his seat, sipping his coffee.

"And you've been trying to find him to thank him?" Dot asked.

"Yeah." It wasn't a lie. I really did want to thank him. They didn't need to know that I also wanted to grill him with questions—such as why a special ops team was sent out to a civilian crash site, or how they even knew where to search, or even what brought the plane down. I was so close to being able to ask those questions. I had to be careful.

"Look, I don't really know you guys, but I'm happy to tell you more about it if you answer some of my questions. Quid pro quo."

"Deal." Dot leaned forward on the table, all business. "Did you know he was Variant?"

"Hey, you already got two. It's my turn. What's his name?"

"Alec Zacarias. Did you know he was Variant?"

"Not on the night of the crash. After, when I woke up in the hospital and was told I was rescued by a Melior Group team, I put two and two together. What's his ability?"

"Pain."

Pain? The sudden headaches that had come over them earlier made more sense now, as did the crowd's bated breath when I'd caused a scene. He was dangerous. Or at least, the people of Bradford Hills thought he was dangerous.

"Pain? Elaborate."

She didn't argue that it was her turn to ask the question. "He can cause pain by skin-on-skin contact. He's very good at controlling it—he has to be—but sometimes, when he's highly emotional, it kind of bleeds out of him and can give people around him headaches, or sometimes it makes them feel sick. He's spent a lot of time learning to manage his ability, but it doesn't make any difference to people who don't know him. They avoid him like the plague because they think getting anywhere near him could hurt them."

"That's why you were so surprised that I was touching him so easily."

"Yes. And now that you know . . ." A sad, resigned look fell over her face.

"Now that I know, it changes nothing. He still saved my life. And if what you say about his control of his ability is true, then I'm not afraid of him. I've given him no reason to want to harm me."

She looked a little surprised, but a small smile had wiped the sad look off her face. "Well, all right then."

That acceptance sounded loaded—as if it was for more than just my previous statements. She had observed me, questioned me, and now was accepting me in some way.

"All right indeed." Charlie was a man of few words, but his emphatic agreement with his sister made me feel as if something had been decided. "But you should still be careful."

"Yeah." Dot elaborated, "Alec is mostly just . . . misunderstood, but he can still be dangerous, and he doesn't know you, so proceed with caution. OK?"

"Noted." I gave them a firm nod. I wasn't an idiot. Someone with an ability to cause excruciating pain was dangerous; I just wasn't scared of him. Kind of like I wasn't scared of Kid when he threw that ball of fire at my head. Maybe I was turning into some kind of adrenaline junkie. "So, how do you two know Alec then? And how does Tyler fit into it?"

"Charlie and I are cousins with Alec. And Tyler . . . they've known each other since a very early age, and they went through some difficult things together some years back. They're family too, if not technically related by blood. They live together with . . . It's kind of complicated."

They lived with Kid? Kid had told me himself just a week ago that he lived with Tyler. Dot was being as cagey about the situation as Kid had been, and my curiosity was piqued, but I could only focus on one mystery at a time.

Dot waved her hand dismissively. "I'm sure you'll meet them all eventually anyway, now that we're friends."

VARIANT LOST

"Friends?" I raised my eyebrows but couldn't help the smile pulling at my lips.

"Of course! What's your name, by the way?"

I laughed, amused at how she could be so sure of our friendship without even knowing my name. "Eve Blackburn."

Even though the circumstances of our meeting had been a bit strange, I genuinely liked Dot and Charlie and wanted to get to know them more. If they could help me pin Alec down, that was a bonus.

"Listen, thank you for explaining some things to me, and thank you for the coffee and muffin, but I'm serious about delivering this thanks. Can you point me in his direction? Please?"

"Oh, Eve, honey, no." It was Dot's turn to laugh, and Charlie joined her. "We'll help, I promise, but not today. When he's that pissed off, Tyler is just about the only person he'll allow in the same room as him. And anyway, I have no idea where he went. When he doesn't want to be found, you won't find him."

"Don't I know it." I had been *not finding* him for a year.

"Another day. I promise. He has to stick around for the next few weeks anyway—official Melior Group business." She gave me an exaggerated wink. Charlie shook his head at her, but he was smiling too.

Dot kept firing questions at me and sharing about herself and her brother. I found out Dot was the same age as me, and Charlie was only a year older. The conversation flowed so seamlessly that my plan to visit the museum was completely abandoned, and my mission to track down Alec almost forgotten. Almost.

Charlie mostly just watched us with his intelligent eyes, only occasionally throwing in a word or two. When he formed another complete sentence, it took me a little by surprise.

79

"Are you Variant, Eve?"

Dot and I both looked at him as he casually finished off his coffee, waiting for me to answer.

I found my voice. "No. I mean, I'm still waiting for my blood test results, but I've had tests before, and they came back negative, so . . . Um, are you guys?"

In answer, they shared a look, and a small gray blur came darting out of nowhere—startling me—climbed up Dot's voluminous skirt, and perched itself on her shoulder. Once it stopped moving, I could see it was a ferret.

"This is Squiggles." Dot scratched it under the neck and smiled wide at me. "My ability allows me to communicate with animals. It's referred to as 'control' of animals, but it's not a master-subject kind of dynamic. I simply ask them to do things, and they're almost always happy to oblige."

"Wow! That's amazing!"

All of a sudden, I was the one firing questions. During my interrogation, I found out we were in some of the same classes. Dot was taking some science units in preparation for a career as a vet.

"Naturally, I'll already know what's wrong with the animals—I can just ask them—but I need to learn how to actually heal them."

When she casually mentioned that Charlie was her Vital, the intensity of my interest and the speed at which I was firing questions doubled. Charlie was the first Vital I had ever met, and I wanted to know everything.

They were more than happy to explain things to me patiently. I knew that Bonds could form between any connected people—siblings, lovers, friends— but friendship Bonds were rare. There was a direct correlation between the strength of the Bond and the strength of the relationship between Variant and Vital, so the Bond sometimes pulled people who were not related by blood closer together, turning friendships into something more.

I had started reading an article about it the other night. The only relationship that never presented Variant-Vital Bonds was parent-child, and often the people in the Bond were close in age. Research had yet to determine why this was exactly.

He was only a year older, but Charlie had the protective big brother thing down pat. Apparently being Dot's Vital only heightened the dynamic, bringing a supernatural element into his instinct to protect his sister. She said it could be overbearing at times, but they were so close it was hard to stay mad at each other.

"I'm sorry, Eve," Charlie cut me off midsentence as I was trying to ask another question, "but I have to get to my Variant Abilities lecture."

"Oh, of course. Sorry." I checked the time on my phone, swearing under my breath. I had to get to the same lecture. We had been talking for hours, and I'd completely missed lunch with the Reds. "I'm in that class too actually."

I laughed nervously, worried that I had bored them with my overbearing questions, but they both smiled, the resemblance clear in the curve of their mouths.

"I'll see you soon." Dot hugged me goodbye and turned in the opposite direction. "Give our new friend our numbers, Charles," she called over her shoulder, her big skirt swishing around her calves as the sharp black heels clicked on the concrete. Squiggles settled in around her neck like a live scarf.

"Have a good afternoon, Dorothy!" he called after her, and she made a gagging sound.

"Neither of us likes our full name much. So naturally we use them all the time." Charlie chuckled. As we walked to class together, he followed his sister's instructions, putting both their numbers in my phone.

Zara walked up to the lecture theater at the same moment we did. "What happened to you at lunch?"

I was relieved she didn't sound upset I'd stood them up. Before I had a chance to answer, she spotted Charlie next to me. Her sarcastic mask fell over her face, and she crossed her arms over her chest.

"Charles," she deadpanned, arching one eyebrow in a decidedly hostile way. I had no idea eyebrows *could* be hostile.

"Zara." He smiled, unaffected by the dangerous eyebrow or her use of his full name. "See you later, Eve." He gave me a friendly wave and went in search of a seat.

"What was that about?" I asked as we made our way to our own seats.

"You should be careful with that one. He's his sister's Vital, and she gets a little protective. If you're not careful, you could get your eyes gouged out. By a bear."

I laughed, a little too loudly, my voice carrying through the massive lecture hall. "You mean a ferret? I met Dot this morning. She seems really nice actually."

"What is it with you and that family?" Zara grumbled, pulling her books out of her bag.

"What?"

"Dot and Charlie are Kid's cousins."

"Wait, does that mean that Kid and Alec Zacarias are brothers?" If Dot and Charlie were cousins with both Alec and Kid, it made sense. I just wasn't sure how Tyler fit into it.

"No, they're cousins too. It's a big family. Wait"—her voice rose in pitch—"how do you know *Alec?*"

"I met him this morning too."

"What do you mean *met him?*" She turned on me, her eyes wide. "One does not simply *meet* the 'Master of Pain.'"

I rolled my eyes at what was obviously a common yet twisted nickname. "We'll talk about it later," I whispered back to her. The lecturer had arrived, and the rest of the room was falling into silence.

I ignored her huff of frustration. Her problem with Dot and Charlie probably had to do with her aversion to all things related to the Variant community in New York. I felt a little sad for her—she had so much anger about her situation—but at the same time, I just couldn't feel bad about having made more friends.

Plus, I had finally, *finally* found my stranger. Even though I hadn't been able to speak to him properly, at least now I knew his name. I knew who he was. Not only that, but Dot had promised to help me deliver my thanks.

I did my best to focus on the lesson, but I kept smiling to myself, practically giddy. The scholarship letter that had brought me to Bradford Hills had also delivered me to something I had been chasing for a whole year; it had thrown me directly into the path of Alec Zacarias.

Maybe my bad birthday luck was finally running out.

SEVEN

Beth's cute red heels clicked on the smooth footpath as we walked past the grand front gates of Bradford Hills Institute. It was a mild spring evening, and Zara, Beth, and I were on our way to Ethan Paul's party.

Beth was beside herself with excitement, her freshly curled hair bouncing around her shoulders. Zara had illustrated her lack of enthusiasm by waiting until the last minute to get ready and putting in almost no effort, although she still looked fierce in her black jeans and gray jacket, her short silky red hair and simple black eyeliner completing the look.

I'd opted for jeans too, paired with a long-sleeved black top I'd borrowed from Beth. It was cut low in the front, showing more cleavage than I was used to, but she'd gotten so much joy from getting ready together that I couldn't be mad about it.

Kid's house was just off campus on a wide, leafy street. Half the walk there seemed to be devoted to reaching the end of his ridiculous driveway—

clearly, his family had money.

We'd passed the intimidating iron gates and were making our way up the tree-lined gravel drive when my curious mind popped up again. Maybe the Reds knew more about why Kid, Alec, and Tyler all lived together. "So, how many people actually live here?"

"Including the army of servants?"

I had a feeling Zara's sarcasm was going to be in overdrive tonight. Beth just laughed lightly. Nothing was going to ruin *her* good mood.

"I'm just curious about . . ." I wasn't sure how to finish that without sounding really nosy.

"About why Kid doesn't live with his parents?" Zara finished for me.

"Something like that," I mumbled.

"It's because they're dead."

I stopped in my tracks and turned to look at her.

"Zara!" Beth had pulled up too, her lacy skirt swinging around her knees. She fixed Zara with a stern look and looped her arm through mine in an explicit show of solidarity. I had told the Reds about never knowing my father and losing my mother. It had come up one night while we were sitting around in our pajamas, watching episodes of *Cosmos*—it had been my turn to pick the TV show.

Realization crossed Zara's face, wiping the sarcastic mask away.

"It's OK." I gave them both a smile. "I just wasn't expecting that."

"I didn't mean to be an insensitive douche." Zara was defensive most of the time, so it was easy to see when she was being sincere.

"Guys, I'm fine. Really." I extracted my arm from Beth's death grip. "What happened to Kid's parents?"

Beth gave me a weak smile and shrugged her delicate shoulders, but Zara tried to explain.

"I don't know the full story. It happened before I started at Bradford, so I've only heard what other people have told me. Basically, when he was little, Kid's parents were on some trip overseas, and they died in this massive accident. Alec's, Tyler's, and Josh's parents were all there too."

"Who's Josh?"

"Oh, he lives here too. He's Kid's friend."

Josh had to be the preppy blond guy I had seen Kid with.

"Anyway, this is Ethan and Alec's uncle's house. He took them in after . . . you know. He's high up in Melior Group management, so he's never around. Those guys basically raised themselves. I'm not sure why the other two ended up here as well. I guess traumatic shit tends to make people close."

"Right." I didn't really know what to say to that. I was taking Zara's account with a grain of salt—it had mostly been pieced together from gossip. I was curious about the truth, of course, but mostly I just felt sad for Kid. And Tyler, even though I didn't know him that well. And Alec, even though he had been a jerk to me. And the Josh guy too, even though I hadn't even met him.

I knew what it was like to lose a parent.

"OK. Enough depressing shit." Beth waved her hands between us maniacally. "We have a party to get to."

As if to illustrate her point, the low thud of music reverberated from the house, beckoning us to finish our trek up the obscenely long driveway.

As we continued our walk, I tried to put the new information out of my mind. A party was no place to be asking a guy I'd only met a few times about how his parents died.

The house had *presence*. As we rounded the curved driveway and it came into view past the oak trees, I slowed a little to take it in. It was huge but not obnoxiously hulking—classy—and screamed sophisticated opulence.

A few people were milling about the front, chatting on the stairs leading up to the front door.

"What do we do?" Beth asked, a tremble in her voice.

"What do you mean? It's a party. We go inside, have a drink, make meaningless chitchat." Why was she so confused?

"No, as in, should we be checking in with someone? What if you need an invitation to go in?"

"We have an invitation. Kid invited us."

"No, like a proper physical one."

"What?" I laughed a little.

Zara just stood there with an amused smirk on her face, not helping at all as I tried to talk sense into Beth.

"I'm going in. You two can stand around and"—I waved a hand in their general direction—"do whatever this is, or you can come with."

I turned and walked toward the front door, exchanging polite smiles with the half-drunk people on the stairs. Behind me, two sets of heels crunched along the gravel. They caught up to me as I reached the door.

What we found inside was just like any other house party. Just bigger. Much, much bigger and more over-the-top.

The foyer was massive, immediately dragging your eye up to what felt like an abyss but was actually three floors of staircases with an extravagant chandelier at the top. We headed toward the music, which was coming from the back of the house.

After walking down a cavernous hallway, we emerged into a large open-planned area with floor-to-ceiling windows along the back wall. Giant speakers in the back corner of the room looked as if they belonged onstage at a rock concert, and a DJ with a professional setup was whipping the crowd into a frenzy. At least a hundred people were writhing and contorting in a drunken dance in front of the speakers, where I guess the living room furniture usually was.

In an enormous kitchen on the right, plastic cups and liquor bottles littered the surfaces of stone benchtops. On the left, a dining table, which looked as if it could seat twenty, hosted a group of guys playing an intense-looking card game; a bunch of drunk people were playing a much rowdier drinking game at the table's other end.

In the five short minutes we'd been there, at least three people in various states of drunkenness had come up to Zara to say "hi." She'd tolerated the first, ignored the second, and flat out told the third to "fuck off." She seemed to know a lot of people here, and even Beth waved to a few friendly faces. I knew no one, so when I saw Dot marching in my direction, a big smile plastered on her face, I returned it enthusiastically.

She closed the distance between us and wrapped me up in a big hug. "You made it!" she half yelled before turning to Zara. "Hey, Zee!"

Zara's face scrunched up, but before she had a chance to tell my new friend to fuck off, Dot turned to Beth.

"Hi, I'm Dot. You must be Beth. Love your skirt!"

Beth returned her greeting and gushed about Dot's unique outfit: a bright pink skintight dress with rips in the fabric—strategically placed so they weren't revealing anything outrageous—black fishnets, pink Mary Jane heels, and an actual candy necklace.

Dot and Beth chatted as our little group made its way through the crowd toward the back of the room. Half of the window wall was opened onto the outdoor area.

As we passed the threshold into the backyard, Charlie appeared, heading in the opposite direction. He was dressed simply in black jeans and a blue T-shirt, and he had a guy with brown hair pulled into a bun on his arm.

When he spotted me, he made his way over with a big smile and dropped a kiss on my cheek.

"Hey Eve." He spoke close to my ear. "I'll catch up with you later. I'm a little busy right now." He winked and gave me a cheeky grin.

I hadn't seen Dot much in the few days since we first met, but Charlie and I had gotten into a few lengthy, nerdy conversations after our Variant studies lectures. We'd really clicked, and I soon realized Zara's warning to stay away from him was moot—he wasn't interested in me. He wasn't interested in anyone with boobs.

I laughed and nudged him in the direction of his date. "Have fun. I'll see you later."

The two of them disappeared into the throng inside as I turned to join the girls.

People in various stages of undress were milling about the pool—the clear centerpiece of the sprawling backyard—drinking, dancing, and jumping into the water. A girl with a water ability was sitting in a lounger by the pool, waving her hands in lazy, elegant movements that alternated between creating elaborate, fountain-like shapes and crashing water down on her swimming friends, all of them laughing uncontrollably.

A more chilled out crowd was chatting around a fire pit surrounded by comfy-looking chairs—maybe a little *too* chilled out, judging by the heady scent of weed wafting from that direction.

A canopy of string lights provided the only illumination and, if it weren't for all the drunken idiots, would have actually set a charming mood over the whole setting. They extended as far as the tables and chairs on the other side of the pool. The rest of the yard—and I had a feeling there was quite a bit more of it—was cast into darkness.

To the left was a fully stocked bar complete with stools and four frantic waiters serving all manner of drinks. One of them had super speed and was mixing cocktails so fast that the cocktail shaker in his hands turned to a blur.

"Uh, how are they getting away with that?" I gestured to the bar, frowning, surprised to see alcohol being served so freely to people under twenty-one.

"Oh, thank god!" Instead of answering me, Zara headed toward the bar without waiting to see if we were following.

"Ooh! Great idea! Let's have cocktails." Dot grabbed me with one hand and Beth with the other, answering my question as she walked. "The staff are paid very well to not check IDs."

Beth bounced rather than walked beside her. "This is the best party I've ever been to!"

I smiled, glad she was having fun and glad I'd somehow made that possible. I knew Zara didn't want to be here, but I was touched she'd come along with the sole intention of protecting me and Beth from whatever exaggerated threat she thought the Variants of Bradford Hills posed. She was a hard-ass, but with a gooey center.

The fire pit had reminded me of Kid's ability and the persistent guy it belonged to. I still hadn't seen him. I let Dot order our drinks as I leaned back on the bar and looked around.

The reflection of the string lights on the pool's surface were keeping me mesmerized when Dot pushed a bright green concoction in a tall glass into my face.

I gave her a worried look. "Do I want to know what's in this?"

"Probably not!" She grinned at me as the Reds joined us, and we all clinked glasses and took a sip. The drink was fruity but potent—definitely not something I should drink too fast.

As I took my second sip, Beth lost her footing and bumped into me, both of us spilling some of our drinks in the process. I steadied her, then my spine went rigid as I realized what had caused her to stumble.

A girl in a white one-piece bathing suit, her wet hair still plastered to her head, had shoved my new friend as she walked past with two other bikini-clad girls.

"Hey, watch it," I called out, letting a little bit of ire enter my tone.

The girl completely ignored me, speaking to her friends in a voice that was intentionally loud. "Who invited the Dimes?"

Every muscle in Zara's body stiffened, and she slammed her drink down on the bar, turning her blazing eyes on the mean girl. Dot stepped into her path, preventing her from going after the bitch, and I briefly considered going after her myself—*who the fuck did she think she was?*

"She's not worth it, Zara." Dot kept her hands on Zara's shoulders.

"She's right," Beth piped in, and Zara started to relax. "It's no worse than the hateful things humans say about Variants—calling you guys freaks of nature and a danger to society. She's just showing off to her friends."

"Doesn't make it right," I grumbled, passing Zara her drink so she would have something else to focus on.

"No, it doesn't, but I'm not letting this ruin my night!" Beth took a sip of her drink and smiled.

I took her lead and tried to steer the conversation onto other topics. After a while, even Zara joined in.

After a few minutes of chatting, Dot suddenly turned to me. "Oh, by the way, you're not gonna believe this! Alec is here."

I laughed. "Doesn't he live here?"

"Yes, but he never comes to these things. He's either away or he hides up in his room, glaring at the crowd from his window." She gestured to a spot high up on the house behind us, and we all turned to look. All the windows on the two top floors were dark.

"Maybe you could thank him tonight," Beth interjected.

After I'd mentioned to Zara in class that I'd met him, she'd demanded to know everything, so I'd told the Reds that evening about Alec saving my life. It was a bit of a relief to finally tell someone the full story. I'd gone a year without even mentioning my mother's death, and after only knowing them for a few weeks, the Reds had made me feel comfortable enough to want to spill it all—all except how Alec had been there for me in the hospital. I didn't want to tell anyone about that; it felt too private. I just wasn't sure if it was my privacy or his that I was protecting.

Dot agreed with Beth. "I promised I would help you pin him down, and tonight might be a good opportunity. He must be in one hell of a good mood to be down here with all these people."

"Right." I squared my shoulders and slammed the rest of my drink back, abandoning the empty glass on the bar behind me. "Where is he?"

All three of them laughed.

After her giggles subsided, Dot held up one finger and closed her eyes, taking a deep breath. Then she opened them again and just stood there, smiling at me serenely. Beth and I exchanged a confused look, but Zara had a small, knowing smile on her face.

Just as I was about to ask what the hell we were doing, Squiggles climbed up Zara's leg and perched on her shoulder. I was expecting Zara to make a derisive comment about "vermin" and throw the little ferret into the pool, but she surprised me by smiling wider and giving it a scratch on the head.

"I missed you too, girl." Her voice was so low I almost hadn't heard.

Zara and Dot clearly had more history than I'd thought, but that was a conversation for another day. I had a moody man to find.

Dot smiled at her furry friend and turned to me. "Squiggles says he's in the living room, by the dining table." Apparently, Squiggles had a knack for reconnaissance.

I turned around and headed back inside.

He was leaning on the wall near the card-game end of the table, dressed in all black again—jeans and a T-shirt. Everyone was giving him a wide berth, shrinking away and staying well out of Alec's reach if they had to walk past.

As he lifted his beer to his mouth, he spotted me. I smiled, going for a friendly approach, but he looked away as he finished the last few drops of his drink, ignoring me. He leaned over a girl with dreadlocks to set his empty bottle on the table, and she visibly jumped in her seat.

He was unaffected by it, returning to his spot against the wall and crossing his arms over his chest.

I waded through the crowd until I was right in front of him, looking him square in his ice-blue eyes. He just stood there, silent. The black-and-gray tattoos completely covering his right arm and peeking out of the left sleeve of his T-shirt did nothing to make him seem more approachable. The small frown line that had appeared on his forehead wasn't helping either.

Refusing to wither under his stare, I made myself speak: "Look, I know we got off on the wrong foot the other day, and I'm sorry about the part I played in that, so can we start again? Please?"

His frown only deepened.

I extended my hand and forged on. "I'm Eve. It's nice to finally meet you properly."

A few people laughed, and some others gasped in shock. He chose to side with the amused group, chuckling softly, a cruel smirk on his face. I was trying really hard not to let his mocking attitude get to me, but the tension in my shoulders was building.

When it became clear he wasn't going to shake my hand, I dropped it and stepped a little closer to him, trying to make this conversation as private as possible.

"I just want to thank you, OK?" I kept my voice low, despite the blaring music. "Can I have five minutes of—"

"Not this shit again." He uncrossed his arms and pushed off the wall, standing at his full, intimidating height. "I already told you. I was just doing my job. Leave me alone."

"Yes, well, speaking of your job"—if he wouldn't let me thank him for saving my life, at least I could try getting some answers—"maybe you could explain to me exactly what made the plane crash? Or how you guys knew where—"

"Shut the fuck up," he growled, stepping farther into my personal space while still being careful not to touch me. "We can't talk about this here."

I'd spoken as quietly as I could in a room full of partying people, and his growly response had been even quieter, so I doubted anyone had heard our exchange. Still, it was clear he wasn't willing to speak to me about any of it. Not in a room full of people. Considering the secretive nature of his job, it made sense, but would he ever allow me to say my piece or give me any answers?

I had been nothing but nice, but he was being downright hostile. It meant a lot to me that I say these things to him, that I ask some questions, but the asshole couldn't take five minutes out of his busy scowling-and-intimidation schedule.

"What the fuck is your—"

"Go away."

This time a woman had interrupted me. She'd appeared next to Alec, handing him another beer and taking a sip of her own, watching me with narrowed eyes. Her blonde hair was pulled back into a messy bun, and she was wearing skintight jeans and a top that was little more than a scrap of fabric. She oozed a confidence I'd only ever come close to in a chemistry lab.

Pressing her amazing body up against Alec, she draped one elegant hand over his shoulder, then smiled widely at me and fluttered her lashes.

"What the fuck is *your* problem?" *Who just walks up to a person and tells them to "go away"?*

The smile fell from her face, replaced by something much more malevolent, and I suddenly regretted my outburst.

Before the situation could escalate, Alec wrapped his arm around her middle and pulled her in close, stepping between us and giving me his back—a wordless dismissal after he'd barely acknowledged my presence.

My blood boiled.

Zara appeared at my side, slinging an arm over my shoulder and turning me in the opposite direction. "That went well," she mumbled, bugging her eyes out at me as Dot pushed a drink into my hand with a commiserating look.

"Maybe we could try to forget all the drama and go have a dance?" Beth was trying to salvage the night again, and I couldn't blame her.

"Stellar idea, Beth!" Dot led the way to the dance floor.

The girls—and the cocktail in my hands—slowly coaxed me out of my shitty mood. We danced and joked together, jumping around to pop music until we were panting and sweaty, but my eyes kept wandering over to where Alec was still standing with the snide girl. I couldn't help it; the situation felt so unresolved. Plus I was curious about this woman who could touch Alec so casually when everyone else avoided him like the plague. Zara was dancing closest to me, so I asked her.

"Ah, yeah, that's Dana. Her ability is to block other abilities."

"That's interesting." I hadn't heard of that one before, and I wondered how it worked. Did it have something to do with blocking access to the Light? It made sense, though, why she was unafraid to touch Alec. His ability couldn't hurt her.

"Yeah, it's unique." Zara followed my gaze, so we both ended up watching

Dana push Alec up against the wall and kiss him, his hands gripping her hips, as we talked. "But it makes her as much of a pariah as him."

"Why?"

"Variants love their abilities. Having a connection to the Light, even a small one without a Vital to amplify it, is revered. Would you want to be around someone whose mere presence takes away what's special about you?"

Of course. No one would want their ability stripped away. Except Alec. Alec seemed happy to be rid of his ability. He was embracing being powerless as enthusiastically as he was embracing Dana.

I felt a little voyeuristic watching them as they shared such an intimate moment, but they were the ones making out in the middle of a party. My gaze felt locked on his hand as it trailed lower, gripping her firmly by the ass.

As if he could feel my eyes on him, he opened his and looked directly at me. I should have looked away, but I couldn't, and he held my stare as he continued to kiss the girl in his arms.

I was so focused on my stare-off with Alec that I didn't notice someone coming up behind me until a warm, sweaty body pressed against my back.

"You like to watch, huh?" The guy's breath reeked of beer as it washed over my cheek. "Do you like to *be watched* too? I can help you put on a show."

His hand landed on my hip, and my face scrunched up in disgust. "Eew! No chance in hell!" I spoke loudly, getting the attention of my friends, and the relaxed smiles fell from their faces.

I tried to step out of his grasp, but his grip on my hip tightened, and his other arm wrapped around my shoulders. My instinct was to elbow him in the stomach—all the paranoid advice my mother had given me about avoiding abduction flashing through my mind—but before I had the chance, Zara and Dot stepped up, each taking a sweaty arm, and shoved the drunk away from me.

"She said *no*, asshole!" Dot yelled as Zara stared daggers.

Beth gently wrapped her hand around mine and tugged me backward, and I turned around to get a good look at the guy. Between Zara and Dot's defensive stances, I glimpsed him swaying just a little where he stood, eyes glazed. He was a little older than us, wearing jeans, a tank top, and a backward baseball cap.

"Why don't you crawl back into whatever hole you came out of, Franklyn, and leave our friend alone?" Dot was doing all the talking while Zara just stood there, looking intimidating.

The guy laughed, as if it were all a big joke, and walked off, waving his hands in the universal "yeah, yeah" gesture.

My new friends surrounded me.

"Are you OK, Eve?" Beth put a hand on my shoulder.

"I'm . . ." My eyes were flying about the room, my brain trying to take in as much information as possible in its heightened state. Once again, my attention snagged on Alec. Dana was still pressed up against him, but she was in a conversation with some other girl. Alec was staring right at me. His expression was completely blank, but his eyes held a perplexing intensity that was evident even from across the room.

I couldn't stand the scrutiny and looked away, giving my friends a smile. "I'm fine, guys. Really."

They looked skeptical.

"I might get some water or something." I really was OK. My brain had processed the fact that the immediate danger had passed, but the oppressive crowd and loud music had become a little overwhelming. My friends all offered to go with me, but I insisted they stay. I didn't want to ruin their night any further, and honestly, a moment alone was exactly what I needed.

I managed to squeeze my way off the dance floor and picked up my pace as soon as I was free of the throng. As I passed the kitchen, focused on the foyer ahead, I barreled into someone.

The guy had come from around the huge kitchen island, shouting to someone behind him and not looking where he was going. As we crashed into each other, the beer he'd been holding, filling two red cups to the brim, ended up all over his very neat outfit. Only a few drops had landed on my sleeve, but his pale green Oxford shirt and beige chinos were dripping.

I stepped back, my hands out in front of me, eyes going wide in shock. His perfectly smooth dirty blond hair fell over his forehead as he surveyed the mess down his front. He looked vaguely familiar, and my brain got stuck on trying to place him, completely forgetting that I should be apologizing.

"Shit," he muttered. He glanced at me, then dropped his arms by his sides, resigned, before turning around and disappearing toward the front of the house.

As he walked away, I finally realized who he was: Kid's friend—the one I'd seen him hanging out with around campus and the one the Reds had said lived here. I couldn't remember his name though.

I stood there stunned for all of three seconds before another familiar guy stepped into my field of vision. The drunk from the dance floor was back.

"Hey! There you are!" He spoke as if we were old friends, not as if he had accosted me on the dance floor.

He started moving toward me, arms wide as if to give me a hug. I held both hands in front of me and started backing away.

Naturally, I ended up bumping into another person.

Big, warm hands landed on my shoulders, steadying me, followed by Kid's booming voice. "Franklyn, leave the lady alone." There wasn't an ounce of humor in his tone. It was serious and firm, but the drunk guy laughed anyway and started slurring about what a great party this was.

I half turned to look at Kid, craning my neck to meet his eyes.

"Thanks." Just having his strength at my back made me feel calmer. We smiled at each other, but the moment didn't last long. I still wanted to get out of there, and he still had a drunk dickhead to deal with.

"Anytime. Excuse me while I . . ." He gestured to our "friend."

I nodded and walked toward the foyer, immediately missing the steadying weight of Kid's hands on my shoulders.

EIGHT

I speed-walked toward the front of the house, trying to look casual, but the whole thing had shaken me up. I wanted nothing more to do with that drunk guy. Thank god Kid had been around to step in.

When I got to the giant staircase at the front of the house, I sprinted up it, desperate for a moment away from the party and the craziness of it all. I was out of breath by the time I reached the landing, my heart beating fast inside my chest—whether from residual fright or from the run up the million-step staircase, I wasn't sure. I needed to sit, calm myself, but I couldn't just plonk down in the middle of the corridor.

Voices drifted up from below, and I groaned—I hadn't gotten far enough away.

The drunk guy slurred something unintelligible while laughing boisterously. Kid's booming voice, talking over the top of him, carried up the stairs.

"Dude! Not cool. You need to leave."

It didn't sound as if drunk guy was going to go without a fight, and I didn't envy Kid his task of trying to get a wasted person to do—well, pretty much anything.

Not wanting to get caught between them again, I rounded the corner and made my way, much more slowly and quietly, up the second flight of stairs. Convinced no one would be up in this part of the house, I walked to the first door on my left and let myself in, turning immediately and pressing my ear to the wood.

Nothing. Even the booming music from the giant speakers was muffled to a distant rhythmic thud. I relaxed my shoulders and turned to check out where I was, only to find myself staring into a pair of amused green eyes.

I jumped, startled by the guy standing in the middle of the room. He was taller than me, not by much but enough that I needed to angle my head up to look him in the eye. He wasn't as tall as Kid and nowhere near as wide—no one was quite as big as Kid—but he had presence

"Jeez!" My hand flew up to my throat, trying to calm my panic. "You scared the crap out of me! What the hell, man?"

He chuckled, crossing his arms over his chest loosely. "You're the one that barged into *my* bedroom without knocking, *and* you made me spill beer all over myself."

It was the guy I'd run into downstairs. He'd changed out of his beer-soaked shirt and into a grungy Metallica T-shirt. Combined with his now mussed hair, it was such a contrast to the polished look of his original outfit that he almost looked like a new person.

His eyes were the same though. A rich green, almost emerald, muted in the dim light of his bedroom.

"Right. Fair point. Sorry about that. I didn't know there was anyone in here. And sorry about before . . ." I made a waving gesture at his chest, indicating where the beer had soaked him. He had the build of a soccer player, lithe and defined, his biceps not bulging out of the T-shirt sleeves but still making themselves known. ". . . with the beer and all that."

As I spoke, I took in the room. The tall ceilings, wood paneling, and heavy drapes over the window were in line with the opulence of the home, as was the sheer size of the space—yet the room was filled with personality. Opposite the neatly made king-size bed, a leather couch faced a large fireplace in the left-hand wall. Surrounding the fireplace and curving around the two adjoining walls were floor-to-ceiling bookshelves bursting with books, records, CDs, and even tapes. In one section of the shelf sat an impressive-looking stereo system.

"I didn't like that shirt anyway." His voice dragged my gaze away from the bookshelf and back to him. "Hiding from someone?"

"Ah, yeah. Some drunk guy—Freddy? Frankie? Something."

His face got serious. "Franklyn? Are you all right?" He took a step toward me, his eyes running over me from head to toe. "You need me to go take care of it?"

"No! No, it's fine. Kid's already kicking him out, I think." The last thing I wanted was more drama, and Kid seemed as though he had it under control.

"Right. OK." He visibly relaxed. "I'm Josh Mason, by the way."

I made a mental note to remember his name. Zara had mentioned it in the driveway earlier, but I'd forgotten it.

"I'm Eve Blackburn. I'm kind of new here." The shelf was drawing my attention again, and I found myself drifting toward it. "So, you're not related to Ethan and Alec, are you? You don't look alike." I couldn't help digging for some information—something to confirm or deny the facts of the tragic story Zara had told.

"No. I just live with them. We grew up together." He didn't seem inclined to elaborate.

I was wary of being too nosy, and besides, the bookshelf now had me thoroughly distracted. "You must read a lot."

Obvious, but I was so occupied with scanning the sea of titles that I wasn't really paying attention to what I was saying. Some familiar ones jumped out at me. He had the classics—Dickens, Bronte, Austen, Tolstoy—but also some modern literature and, in among those, some nonfiction too—philosophy, history, and a bit of politics.

His chuckle came from close behind me. He had followed me over, his movements completely silent on the soft carpet. "Yeah, I like to read. Do you read?"

"Yes. More like *devour* the words."

He laughed, a soft, contained sound.

"Although I don't read as much fiction as you," I continued. "I don't mind philosophy and politics, but there's still too much subjectivity. Give me an edition of *New Scientist* any day. Even textbooks . . ." I trailed off—I was sounding like a total nerd and maybe a bit of a show-off. *I, an intellectual, read scientific journals and textbooks for fun.* I groaned internally, afraid to look at him. Maybe it was time to slowly back out of the room and leave the gorgeous boy with the full lips and kind eyes alone.

He stepped up next to me and leaned one shoulder on the shelf to my right. "As interesting as I find science, I struggle with the journals. Too much jargon."

We were looking at each other now, him casually leaning on the shelf, arms crossed, me with my arm still resting on the spine of the book I'd been looking at, my mouth slightly parted in shock. He wasn't freaked out or put off.

Then I remembered where I was. Of course everyone here would be intelligent and well-read. Bradford Hills Institute was the most exclusive school in the country.

"You must be studying some science subjects then?" he asked. "Are you taking any of the Variant studies units?"

I quickly did my best to cover my astonishment and tried to act naturally, pushing my sleeves up to my elbows to give my hands something to do. *Natural*, however, was becoming increasingly difficult to pull off; I was speaking to a guy that was not only ridiculously good looking and intelligent but also actually interested in speaking to *me*.

We chatted briefly about which classes we were both taking. He was twenty, a bit older than me, but due to Bradford Hills' unique way of structuring classes, we had a few in common. When I made an intentionally cheesy joke about how organic chemistry is difficult because those who study it have "alkynes" of trouble, Josh laughed and leaned forward, lightly touching my forearm where it rested on the shelf. His warm hand felt soft on my bare skin.

A tingling warmth at the point of contact reminded me of when Kid and I first shook hands. We both stopped laughing, and the air became heavier around us. I looked down at where we were connected, marveling at the sensation. He must have mistaken it for discomfort, because he withdrew his hand and rubbed the back of his neck, looking a bit uncomfortable.

"So . . ." My voice sounded shaky even to myself. That buzzing energy was starting up again. It had been nearly a week since my last stretch of sleeplessness, and it was choosing this particular moment to rear its head. *Great.* "What kind of music do you like? By the look of your shelves . . . all of it." I laughed lightly. There were easily just as many records, CDs, and tapes jammed onto the shelves as there were books.

He laughed and looked at me with a sparkle in his green eyes, the awkwardness gone. "I don't mind most music, but what I really love is rock."

"So all these are . . ."

"Yep. Everything from AC/DC to ZZ Top. From Foo Fighters to Linkin Park to Marilyn Manson to . . . well, you get the idea. There's such a variety in sound and style and so many subgenres. So much to listen to, and real artistry in the way the music is made. These guys really play their instruments, you know?"

His enthusiasm was downright adorable, and I smiled wide, equally amused at his excitement and impressed with his knowledge.

He returned my smile and crouched down, flipping through some records stacked along the bottom shelf. "You wanna hear something?"

"Sure." I could watch Josh geek out over rock music for the rest of the evening. I didn't even need to go back to the party. What party?

He plucked out a record and walked over to the stereo system, lifted the flap, extracted the record from its sleeve, and placed it gently on the turntable.

As a slow, moody guitar filled the space, he walked back over to me, eyes never leaving mine. "This is Led Zeppelin. It's one of their less well-known songs, but I love it. Rock doesn't have to be all high energy and loud banging. There's real emotion in music like this."

He stopped right in front of me.

The itching, as hard as I tried to ignore it, was burning at my wrists. It was torture not to reach up and scratch my arms, but Josh's eyes had pinned me to my spot.

He gently laid his hand on my waist, and I reacted instantly, placing my hand on his bicep. We leaned into each other slowly, keeping eye contact until our faces were so close that I could see how dilated his pupils were, the green around them almost pulsing.

Our lips met softly at first, in a gentle kiss that felt like a sigh. I'd only met him twenty minutes ago, but kissing him felt like a much-anticipated reunion after a long absence, as if I'd been waiting for him for years. We moved into each other simultaneously. His arms wrapped around my middle, pressing me into his chest as I lifted my own arms around his neck, one hand twisting into his hair.

The kiss was soft, but also intense and warm. Comforting and firm. Our breathing deepened as our lips moved against each other. It felt so natural. It felt like home.

That warm tingly feeling was back but so much *stronger*. It was everywhere, bleeding in and out of me. His touch felt like liquid gold. The sensation was present wherever our skin touched, but my whole body felt connected to him. I was acutely aware of his every movement, every twitch of his fingers against my spine, every breath that pressed his chest impossibly closer to mine.

When he pulled away, the lights seemed to dim. I leaned forward, moving with him, a snake leaning toward the snake charmer. He had broken the kiss but didn't let me go. We stood there, holding each other, looking into each other's eyes as a look of shock spread over his face.

The kiss had been nothing short of spectacular—I'd never been kissed like that before. Judging by his speechlessness and the way his hands were flexing against my back, bunching the fabric of my shirt, I had a feeling he'd liked it too.

So why had he broken it?

As if coming out of a fog, the details of our surroundings drifted back into focus, and movement to my right caught my attention. I immediately tensed up, assuming someone was in the room with us. Then the whole picture became clear, and shock and a hint of fear rushed down my spine.

A book was floating in midair above the couch. And it wasn't the only one. Books, records, CDs, clothes, and other various inanimate objects were floating all around the room. Even the heavy drapes were lifting off the ground, as if they were the softest sheer curtains caught in a breeze.

I glanced back into Josh's face, and his expression matched mine, his gaze trained behind me. We still held each other, frozen to the spot, both of us trying to process what we were seeing.

Had I done this? Would my blood test come back positive? Was I somehow a Variant? *Oh my Stephen Hawking!* How was I supposed to make it stop? I had no idea how I'd even done it. What if all this crap came tumbling down and knocked us both out?

Before I could descend into full-blown panic, Josh spoke distractedly. "Did I mention I'm a Variant?" He looked back at me, the shock on his face mixing with wonder. "Telekinetic ability."

His last word trailed off as his shell-shocked expression morphed into a wide, almost manic smile. He was looking at me like a kid who'd woken up on Christmas morning to find a puppy under the tree.

A frown pulled at my brows. This was getting weird. The fact that Josh had such a unique power came as a surprise, and part of me wanted to ask a million questions, but his strange behavior was putting me off. Add to that the fear that I might die under a stampede of inanimate objects, and the whole situation was getting pretty overwhelming.

He seemed to realize the oddity of it then, and a horrified expression melted the smile off his face.

"Holy shit!" He dropped his arms and stepped away from me lightning fast. Immediately, all the crap floating eerily about the room thudded to the ground.

I shrieked and covered my head with my hands while lifting one knee up and huddling against the bookshelf. Miraculously, nothing hit me. Not a single item even grazed me on its way down.

"It's OK. You're safe." There was a tinge of panic in his voice as his hand landed gently on my shoulder. "It could never hurt you . . . I would never . . . that is to say . . . it's impossible for my ability . . . Shit!"

As I straightened, he snapped his hand back.

I finally found my voice. "What the hell is happening?"

"How is this possible?" he was mumbling to himself. "I thought Kid . . ." He swallowed audibly and looked at me again, eyes wide, a mixture of incomprehensible emotions written all over his face. After a moment, he managed to pull a coldly neutral expression down over it all.

"You need to leave." He spoke evenly, but with hardness to his tone.

"What? Why?" Was he somehow blaming me for this? And why did he mention Kid? I had maybe met the guy two times—it wasn't as if we were dating. Josh and I had just shared an incredible kiss, and now he was throwing me out? Although he hadn't said it in so many words, I was 60 percent sure Josh had enjoyed the kiss too. *Right?* Shit.

"It's complicated. I can't really explain . . . Look, you just need to go before someone sees . . . Please." His mask of calm was slipping, and a hint of frantic energy was coming through in his voice and posture. He raised a hand, palm upturned, and gestured toward the door.

I hung my head, unable to look at him. Refusing to let him see me upset, I turned and forced myself to walk at a steady pace to the door, letting my features crumble into a pained expression now that he couldn't see my face.

Kid chose that moment to swing the door open, without knocking, two meters in front of me, sweeping aside all the debris that had fallen to the ground.

"Dude! Where have you been? I can't find . . ." His booming voice stopped midsentence when he saw my face, his brow creasing in confusion. Or maybe it was concern. I couldn't be sure. My ability to read what people were feeling through simple body language was obviously on the fritz.

"Hey, Eve." His voice was much softer now. "You OK?" Then his eyes scanned the room, taking in the chaos. "Whoa! What the hell happened in here?"

I was done. I was *so* done with this party and this house and these people. Maybe Zara had been right about avoiding them. Once again something wonderful was being ripped away from me.

Anger settled in the pit of my stomach. That was good. I could use anger to propel me out of this room, out of this house, and away from this whole messed-up situation.

"Whatever," I ground out between gritted teeth, squaring my shoulders and pushing past Kid and out the door. To be fair, I didn't push past Kid—no one could really push past Kid if he didn't want them to—but he stepped out of my way as I pretended I was pushing past him, and for that one small concession, I was glad.

I stormed down the corridor and flew down the two flights of stairs. At the bottom, I nearly barreled into the Reds, who were just coming around the corner.

"Oh my, Eve, are you OK?" Beth had concern written all over her face.

"Would everyone stop asking me that?" I snapped at her.

Sweet, lovely Beth didn't deserve that. I was being a jerk. As much of a jerk as Josh had been. The anger drained out of me. "I'm sorry. I didn't mean that."

"That's OK. What happened?" My rude outburst was already forgotten. That's just the kind of person Beth was.

"Nothing. I'm all right. Really." I forced a smile in response to the skepticism on both their faces. "I'm just over this party. Going to head home. Can you tell Dot and Charlie goodbye for me?"

I was already on the move again before I'd finished speaking.

"Want us to go with you?" Zara asked.

I was touched by their concern, but it only added to the emotional turmoil already whipping around inside of me. Tears pricked at my eyes as I kept going. "No, no. All good. You guys have fun. I'm fine. Promise!" I managed to make my voice sound even. Just.

Despite the fact that I had shared some of my deeply personal history with them already, my instinct in my current emotional state was still to run away from the Reds. I wanted someone to comfort me. To help me make sense of what had just happened. But I hadn't been that close to anyone since my mother died. Maybe I just didn't *know* how to get close to someone. Maybe the distance my mother had devoted herself to establishing between us and the rest of the world was permanent.

Maybe I would never have true friends that I could talk to. Maybe I would never have a boyfriend to share my life with. Maybe that's what Josh had picked up on in his bedroom when he'd shut off from me—that it was impossible to get close to me. He was Variant, after all; maybe his superhuman senses allowed him to sense these things.

The tears spilled over in earnest as I reached the end of the long driveway. Thankfully, there was no one around to see. At the gates, I broke into a run and I didn't stop until I reached the front door of our residence hall.

I was so focused on the pit of negative emotions writhing inside me I didn't even register that the tingling, itching sensation had completely left my wrists.

NINE

I pulled my knee-length jacket tighter over my chest as I walked to class, regretting my decision to wear flats instead of boots. The warm weekend had given way to a chilly Monday morning. The sun was hidden behind fat clouds threatening to burst with rain.

I had gone straight to bed after the party, welcoming the oblivion of sleep, and spent all of Sunday holed up in my room, reading and studying, trying to distract myself from the feelings of rejection and self-consciousness. When the Reds had invited me to lunch, I told them I just wanted to read. Later, Beth had come in on her own, brow creased with worry. I'd been so close to telling her the whole story, but I hadn't wanted to relive it all, so I'd convinced her I was just tired, and she left me alone.

As I approached the building where my first lecture was due to start soon, I was hunching my shoulders against the cold, my gaze turned down.

I didn't see them until it was too late.

"Eve." Ethan's booming voice was unmistakable.

I looked up, my steps faltering. He was standing with Josh at the door to the building, students streaming past them. Ethan was in his usual white T-shirt and jeans, apparently not bothered by the cold at all, and Josh was back to his preppy, polished look, the collar of a neat shirt peeking out underneath a cashmere sweater.

I did *not* want to see them. I was mostly over what had happened at the party on Saturday. Mostly. But I wanted nothing more to do with them. I was heeding the Reds' warning about Kid and extending it to Josh.

Squaring my shoulders and narrowing my eyes, I marched past them and into the building.

"I need to speak to you," Josh said from behind me. They were following me.

"That's funny," I threw over my shoulder as I kept walking. "You had nothing to say to me on Saturday night. Couldn't wait to get me out of your room, as I recall." OK, so maybe I wasn't as over it as I'd thought.

"Yes, I was a jerk. Will you please stop so I can explain?" He was keeping his voice low. The corridor was teeming with people. I couldn't decide if I was grateful no one would overhear us talking about my embarrassing encounter or if I was further insulted he didn't want anyone to hear us speaking to each other.

"Just leave me alone." Frustration leaked into my voice as I sped up.

"Where are you going?" Ethan chuckled.

I stopped—I had no idea. I'd been so busy trying to get away from them that I hadn't paid any attention to where I was going. Unfamiliar rooms lined up on either side of the unfamiliar hallway. We appeared to be at the back of the building somewhere, standing next to a narrow stairway.

"Shit!" I turned around, figuring it was best to get this out of the way so I could get to class. "What do you want?"

In perfect synchronicity, they each looked down an opposite length of hallway, checking for prying eyes. Their movements made me acutely aware there was no one else around in this part of the building. I was alone with two guys I didn't really know, and not only were they bigger and stronger than me, they also had rare and dangerous Variant abilities.

They stepped closer, and I retreated instinctively, my back pressing against the railing of the staircase.

Josh leaned forward, his voice low. "Look, I just need to know if you told anyone about the . . . what happened at the party."

He wanted to make sure I would keep my mouth shut?

"Oh my god!" My voice was much louder than his, echoing up the stairs behind me. "Do you have a girlfriend? You're an even bigger asshole than I thought."

"Shh!" Ethan craned his neck around the corner.

Josh's lips pursed in annoyance. "What? No, I don't have a girlfriend. That's not what this is about."

"What then?" I refused to lower my voice, raising it a notch just to spite them. "You don't want anyone to know that you got it on with the new girl, who's here on scholarship and is probably a Dime? Don't want to damage your reputation? You only date Variant bitches, is that it?"

"Variant bitches! Hah!" Ethan laughed, trying hard to do it quietly and mostly failing. Ethan didn't do anything quietly.

Josh just looked even more irritated. "Would you please lower your voice?" he whisper-yelled at me, stepping even farther into my personal space. "This has nothing to do with any other girls or anything as petty as reputation. Look, I know you're new here and you still don't understand how the Variant world works, but if anyone knew what happened the other night, we could all be in danger. Including you."

His words sent a chill down my spine, making me acutely aware of how close he was to my vital organs. I swallowed audibly and looked away from his intense stare.

"Are you threatening me?" I meant for it to sound outraged, as though I wouldn't stand for this, but it came out sounding weak and quiet.

Immediately Josh stepped away, and the amusement disappeared from Ethan's face.

"No! I am so sorry." His green eyes looked sincere. "We didn't mean to . . . I'm not trying to scare you."

He sighed and flopped down onto the stairs. "Maybe I should just—"

"No," Ethan cut him off midsentence. "It's safer this way. You know it." He crossed his arms over his chest and leaned on the wall opposite the stairs.

The path down the corridor was clear again, but I stayed put. Even though they'd been a little intense, they hadn't actually threatened me—and they were being just cryptic enough that my stupid curiosity was piqued.

"Why am I in danger?" It seemed like the most pertinent question to ask.

Josh looked up at me from his spot on the stairs, his intense green eyes reminding me of the way those eyes had taken me in just before we'd kissed. I looked away quickly. I didn't want to be reminded of that. Mostly because I wanted it to happen again. Why did he have to be so damn hot and mysterious?

"It's a dangerous time to be a . . . Variant. The government is tightening regulation on the use of our abilities—all you need to do is pick up a newspaper to know that. People like Ethan and I are closely monitored. We're left alone for now mostly because our abilities haven't grown too far past what they were when they manifested. When we . . . when you were over the other night, I realized that my ability is much stronger than I originally thought because—"

Ethan cleared his throat and threw Josh a pointed look.

". . . because of . . . reasons," he finished lamely, looking away from me, and I rolled my eyes. "I'm sorry. The less you know the safer it is. If anyone found out about how strong my ability was and it got back to certain people, . . . it just wouldn't be good for me, OK? And anyone close to me, like Ethan, would immediately fall under suspicion, and it wouldn't be good for them either. You were right in the thick of it when it happened. So that's not good for *you*."

"Right." I looked from one to the other, barely containing my skepticism. "So for reasons that you can't explain, your powers are suddenly stronger, and for more vague reasons, that puts you in danger, and I happened to stumble into this mess, so now I'm up shit creek too? That about cover it?"

Josh pulled himself back into a standing position. "Yes?" It came out as a question.

"OK. Well, I have no interest in sharing that particular embarrassment with anyone anyway, so your secret is safe with me. Now can we just pretend like none of this ever happened and go to class?"

Both of them sighed in relief and nodded. I gave a single nod and took off in what I hoped was the direction of my lecture hall.

I wasn't entirely buying their "we're all in danger" spiel, but pretending the incident with Josh never happened was fine by me. My ego and confidence were bruised enough.

The next day was even colder, made worse by the steady rain that had started overnight and seemed to intensify as I got ready for the day. Staying in bed and listening to the rain was tempting, but there was no way I was going to miss chemistry lab.

I trudged to the science building, already getting excited about which experiments we might be running. Not one to make the same mistake twice, I wore the boots I had wished for the previous day and a jacket with a hood pulled low. Luckily, the science building was one of the closer ones to my res hall, and it only took me five minutes to walk there.

Head down, I ran the last few meters—just as a particularly nasty gust of wind sent the rain flying sideways—and came to a stop under the cover of the front of the building. Lifting my head and pulling the hood off, I came face to face with the intense blue-eyed stare of Alec Zacarias.

I stood there, stunned, as other students filed into the building, desperate to get out of the rain.

Alec had his hands stuffed into the pockets of his black coat, the collar turned up against the wind, as he alternated watching me and scanning the area around us. When the last student entered the building, he took a step in my direction.

"I know those two spoke to you yesterday"—his voice was low, muffled by the sound of the rain, but loud enough that I could hear him clearly—"but I need to make sure you understand the gravity of the situation."

"Well, hello to you too," I huffed. Who accosts someone in the morning—before they've even had their coffee—and starts talking *at* them without even saying hello? "Wait . . ." His words registered, and my skin prickled with embarrassment. "They told you about that?"

I averted my gaze, the embarrassment giving way to a spike of outrage. So I was supposed to keep it a secret, and they could tell whomever they wanted?

"They trust me. And they were right to keep it quiet. No one can know what happened, do you understand? This is not something you gossip with your girlfriends about before you have a pillow fight. When we say tell no one, we mean tell *no one.*"

"Pillow fight?" I chuckled—this had to be one of the strangest conversations I'd ever had. And my mother and I'd had some doozies. "You don't spend much time with women, do you?"

He leaned down so our faces were closer together, his shoulders hunching, the hard set of his features laced with frustration.

"I don't spend a lot of time with anyone, *precious*." He spat the last word out like an insult. "Now, start taking this seriously. Those two dickheads are my family, and I will do whatever it takes to protect them. They can't . . . they're too young to get dragged into . . ."

The frustration in his eyes had melted into a desperate kind of pleading, the eyebrow scar becoming more pronounced as he raised both brows slightly. He couldn't seem to bring himself to speak the words, to actually plead with me, but it was written all over his face. "And *you* . . . you definitely shouldn't be anywhere near *any* . . ."

His shoulders sagged—his voice had turned to honey.

It was the first time I'd heard that voice since the hospital, and it broke something inside me. My insides twisted into a knot under my warm coat. I knew I was seeing the real Alec for the first time since that night.

Without thinking about it, I reached out and placed my hand on his shoulder gently. I spoke as quietly as he had, injecting as much sincerity into my voice as I could muster. "I won't say anything. I promise."

The muscles under my touch relaxed a little, and he gave me a nod as he straightened, squaring his shoulders, making my hand fall away.

Encouraged by the calmer, more approachable Alec, I figured I had nothing to lose by trying to bring up the crash and the hospital again. "About the night of the plane crash . . ."

His attention had caught on something behind me, but his eyes flicked back to mine, the frown back in place.

"I don't have time for this." The honey was gone from his voice again. "Make sure you keep your promise."

He adjusted the collar of his coat and rushed into the rain. I turned to watch as he crossed paths with Dot, who was jogging toward the chemistry building.

"Hey, Alec." She greeted him with a little surprise in her voice, her steps faltering.

"Hey, Dot. Get to class. You're late." He didn't slow down at all and soon disappeared around a corner.

Dot joined me under the cover of the entranceway. "What's going on? You OK?"

"Yeah." I tried to give her a smile, but it fell flat. "Um, I just tried to thank him again, and he got all weird about it. Again." It wasn't the whole truth. As much as I wanted to confide in my friend, there was something in me that didn't want to break Alec's confidence. All three of them had been very serious about me keeping my kiss with Josh a secret.

"Damn. Why was he here though? He rarely ventures far from the admin building when he's on campus."

"Beats me." I had become a pretty good liar living with my mother. I shrugged my shoulders and tried to change the topic. "Do you have a class here too?"

"Oh shit! I am so late for my biology lab!"

It worked like a charm. She rushed inside the building and I followed, matching her pace. I was late for my chemistry lab too.

That evening, the itching at my wrists returned again. It briefly reminded me how the beginnings of an episode had come on right before I'd kissed Josh at the party, only to perplexingly disappear. Most likely that had been a milder surge of energy, which my body had expelled immediately as I ran from the Zacarias mansion back to my res hall.

This surge of energy was *not* mild.

The itching spread up my arms and legs quicker than ever before, and I declined the Reds' invitation to watch a movie over hot chocolate—perfect rainy weather activities, according to Beth—so that I could hide in my room, tear my clothing off, and spend the night scratching unashamedly. I alternated doing sit-ups and push-ups with long stretches of study and reading, trying to exhaust my body and my mind.

I had four sleepless nights—more than any episode so far—which worried me a little. But at least it allowed me to get way ahead on all my coursework and read every scientific article on Variant DNA Tyler had recommended. But eventually the tingling, nervous energy left my body.

I spent the week trying to focus on my studies and ignore all the things I was worried about but powerless to deal with. Of course, this turned out to be impossible.

The intensity and length of my latest itchy energy—along with the fact that it had come right after I'd kissed a Variant—was disconcerting. Of course, several previous tests had confirmed my human status, but how could I reconcile that with the odd things I was experiencing? I was suddenly glad Tyler had insisted on the blood test—I need to confirm I was normal, that it was all in my head. Until then, I was doing my best to pretend this problem didn't exist.

The fact that I didn't have the full story behind why Ethan, Josh, and Alec were being so secretive about Josh's ability and our kiss was also driving me insane. But I couldn't pretend *they* didn't exist. In fact, I couldn't seem to get away from them.

It was a classic case of the Baader-Meinhof phenomenon—now that I knew who Ethan and Josh were, I was seeing them everywhere. When I was having coffee with Dot and Charlie or chatting to the Reds after class, one or both of them would join us. They acted perfectly naturally, making conversation and joining in whatever the group was doing, not giving me any more attention than anyone else but not ignoring me either.

They were basically pretending nothing had happened. It was infuriating.

They never spoke to me or approached me when I was alone, never giving me a chance to ask for answers. Not that they weren't around when I was by myself.

When I went for my early morning runs, trying to expel the crazy energy, I would spot Josh sitting under a tree and reading a book or Ethan throwing a football with some friends. One or both of them were in half of my classes, but they never sat next to me. As I walked out of Starbucks, mediocre latte in hand, there was Ethan walking in, giving me a friendly smile and a "hey, Eve" but hurrying past before I could stop him. As I walked into the library to do some research for an assignment, there was Josh, coming in a few minutes after and settling into a chair with a book.

They even crashed a girls' night. The Reds had suggested we go see a movie in Bradford Hills, since I hadn't had a chance to explore the town. We made a night of it, deciding to go for dinner as well. As we reached the gates of the Institute on our way out, Ethan and Josh appeared. They engaged the Reds in conversation, Ethan's easygoing personality putting even Zara at ease after a few minutes, and ended up spending the whole evening with us. Neither of them sat next to me at dinner or in the theater, and they walked us all the way back to our res hall, even though it meant they would have to double back to get home.

I'd seen Alec around as well. Unlike the other two, he made it clear he was watching me. His hard stare would be unashamedly fixed on me, his mere presence reminding me to keep my mouth shut—which I'm sure was his intention. If I stared back at him too long or if I tried to approach him, he would turn around and stalk off.

Even Tyler was popping up where I didn't expect him. Although, to be fair, he did work at Bradford Hills. For all I knew, it was normal for him to be talking to my physics professor as I walked in for class, or to be passing by

120

me in hallways and on the leafy lanes of campus more and more. He would always give me a friendly smile, but he never seemed to have time to stop and chat. I had no idea if Ethan and Josh had told him about the kiss, and I was not about to ask.

I knew they weren't actually stalking me, that it was just the curious state of my mind noticing them more than before. Still, it was getting a little weird how one of them was always around.

But their constant presence and my increasingly suspicious mind were not even remotely as alarming as what happened in the middle of the night, one week after I'd been sworn to secrecy about what I'd seen in the Zacarias mansion.

Nothing was as perplexing as why I found myself racing back there, feeling as if my chest were being torn open.

TEN

When I woke up, it was instant. One second I was asleep, and the next I was sitting up in bed, eyes wide, all senses on alert. Something was wrong. *Really* wrong.

For a second I wondered if I was in pain. What had woken me? Was I in danger? But even before the worry had a chance to take root in my mind, I knew that wasn't it. I was fine. I was warm and safe in my bed.

Yet I *knew* that something was wrong. I could feel it with every fiber of my being. It took only another second of confusion before I threw the sheets off and jumped out of bed. I had to do something. I had to stop it.

Somewhere in the depths of my mind, I knew this wasn't logical. I just had to *go*.

I slipped my feet into flats and grabbed a cardigan off the back of my chair on my way through the door, slipping it over my shoulders as I rushed through the living space.

"What?" Beth shot up into a sitting position on the couch. Zara was out on a date, but Beth had stayed in, binge-watching something. "Where are you going? It's the middle—"

But I was already through the door and running. Halfway down the corridor, I heard the door slam behind me.

My heart was beating frantically against my ribcage. I was running out of time. I was too far away.

What if I don't get there in time? A cry tore itself free from my mouth as I sprinted down the three flights of stairs. I couldn't wait for the elevator.

Beth caught up to me as I burst out of the front doors and flew down the front steps, the cool night air doing nothing to snap me out of my frenzy.

"Wait!" She grabbed my elbow.

I wrenched it out of her grasp and broke into a sprint, darting over the lawns in the most direct path toward the front gates.

Beth managed to keep up with my frantic pace. "Eve, what's going on? You're freaking me out."

"Don't!" I sounded distraught, even to my own ears. "Don't try to stop me. I have to hurry. Before it's too late to save him."

The words had sprung out of my mouth without thought, but they rang true. *I have to save him.*

"Save who? Is someone in trouble?"

I didn't answer. I had no idea who "him" was or where my frantic feet were taking me, only that they were following some inexplicable pull, running on pure instinct and adrenaline.

I passed Bradford Hills Institute's massive front entrance and turned sharply to the left, Beth hot on my heels. Something in my voice, my expression, my frenzied behavior must have convinced her this was serious, and she was sticking to my side like the good friend she was.

My breath was becoming labored and my legs burned, but I was nearly there. I could feel it. The pull was easing the closer I got, yet also somehow becoming more urgent. My heart beat wildly for reasons that had nothing to do with the punishing pace I'd set.

He was fading away. I had to get to him *now* or I would be too late.

I turned right at the next street, dashing across the road, barely checking for cars.

Just a little farther. I grabbed the iron gate of the Zacarias mansion and used my momentum to propel myself around the corner.

My feet crunched on the gravel of their ridiculously long driveway. *Nearly there.* I could feel him even more now, but it was . . . *less.* He was getting weaker.

Beth had begun to fire questions at me again. Questions I had no answers to. "Oh my god, Eve. Why are we here? What the hell is going on?"

At the end of the driveway, where the trees ended, a charred mess resembling a vehicle was sending coils of acrid black smoke into the night sky.

The shock of seeing something so unexpected in the perfectly manicured front yard, combined with my own exhaustion, finally brought me to a stuttering stop. I leaned over, resting my hands on my shaking knees, and struggled to draw oxygen into my lungs, but the terror slamming into me from somewhere deep within wouldn't allow me to pause for long.

This is where it happened.

"Holy shit!" Just as spent as me, Beth continued to ask questions between gasping breaths. "What happened here? Eve, you have to start talking! Please, just . . ."

I ignored her, springing back into action, the urgency of my single-minded task impossibly doubling again. I ran up the front stairs and pushed through the front door, which was already ajar. No hesitation. No wondering where to go, which room to search for. I didn't even think to call out. I just bolted straight through the house, past the kitchen, and out another half-open door.

I *needed* to get to him.

I ran as fast as I could around the pool and to the right, finally sprinting into the pool house.

Josh was pacing the main area inside, barefoot and wearing only a David Bowie T-shirt and boxers, his hands in his hair. Bowie's painted face seemed somehow out of place in a life-and-death situation.

". . . to get him warm. It's the only chance we have." Tyler's voice was coming from the back of the building, along with another deep male voice swearing profusely.

Josh's hands dropped from his hair, a shocked expression falling across his features as I flew past him. "Eve? What . . . ?"

Both he and Beth following me down the short hallway and into a tiled bathroom area. On the left was a wooden door with a small square window—a sauna. On the right, the glass wall of a steam room, steam billowing out of the wide-open door and past the three people huddled around the entrance.

Held between Tyler and Alec, Kid was unconscious, his head lolling to one side, his big body completely limp. He was dressed in only his underwear.

Tyler saw me first, barely sparing me a frown before focusing on his task. He had his hands under Kid's arms and was half carrying, half dragging him into the steam room. Alec had his legs, the muscles in his shoulders bunching with the strain.

As soon as I laid eyes on him I knew. This was why I was here.

He was dying.

I bent over as a sob broke past my lips and fat tears spilled over, running down my cheeks. It felt as if a piece of my soul was being torn away from me, making it hard to will my limbs into moving.

But the tearing pull in my chest was impossible to ignore.

In the moment it had taken me to absorb the scene and fall apart completely, Tyler and Alec had carried Kid into the steam room and lowered him onto the wide bench, his head and shoulders propped up on the adjoining tile wall. They were all speaking over me—frantic, confused voices—but none of it registered. My mind and body had homed in on the reason I'd woken up in a panic and sprinted here like a crazed person.

There was no doubt in my mind that if I could just touch him, everything would be OK.

I stumbled into the steam room, pushing past Alec as he tried to close the door, and fell to my knees next to the bench. At last, my hand reached out to press against Kid's chest.

I took a deep breath. For the first time that night, the sense of hopelessness, the feeling that he was slipping away, ceased. Everyone else in the room had gone quiet. The only sounds were my own breathing, still a bit erratic, and the soft whistle of steam being pumped into the room.

The agonizing pull in my chest had eased, replaced with the instinctual knowledge of what he needed next. I became acutely aware of—and more than a little annoyed by—the wide-open glass door letting all the heat out.

He was too cold.

"Close the door. I . . . I can't . . . I won't be able to . . . He needs to be warm!" My last statement came out as a panicked shout.

It broke the stupefied spell everyone was under, and they all sprang into action. Several voices spoke over one another in the background, becoming muted as someone finally closed the door to the steam room.

He was getting warmer, but he needed . . . *more.*

Urgency not unlike the itchy hyper-energy I'd been experiencing over the last year spread through me. But this felt heavier somehow. *That* feeling was all about me and the need to expel it—whatever *it* was. *This* feeling was

126

about Kid. He needed this. His life depended on it.

I took a deep breath and lifted my hand from his chest. The panic slammed back into me immediately, demanding that I resume contact, but I managed to ignore it for the few seconds it took me to undress.

I kicked my shoes off as I ripped the cardigan away from my body and pulled my oversized T-shirt up and over my head. Feet shuffled and throats cleared behind me, and the realization darted through my mind that I was now standing in nothing more than my underwear and a tank top in a room full of people I barely knew. But I didn't have time to be embarrassed or self-conscious.

The frantic pull toward the fragile boy on the bench had become almost painful yet again. Without further thought, I swung a leg over his slumped form and lifted myself onto the tiled bench over him, my knees pressing into his sides. I swept my messy, tangled hair out of the way before lowering my whole body onto his, my belly and chest resting on his torso as I gently dropped my head onto his chest.

Eyes closed, I gave in to whatever it was that had brought me to his side so swiftly and decidedly. Every point where our skin made contact hummed—a warm, pleasant sensation. Slowly, my breathing began to even out.

After some time—*minutes? hours?*—his chest rose under my cheek in a deep sigh. I slowly lifted my head to look into his face as his eyes cracked open. He shifted under me, and his big hands landed softly on my back as we stared at each other.

After only a moment, his eyelids drooped closed again and his head lolled to the side against the tiles.

I dropped my cheek back down to his chest. His heartbeat was stronger, and his breathing steadier. My skin was still humming wherever it touched his. Gradually, the furious energy of the evening's events drained out of me.

At some point, I passed out.

When I woke up, I was warm, the pleasant humming feeling still flitting over my skin. I opened my eyes slowly, lazily. It must have been around dawn; the dark room had a soft blue tinge to it—the first light of day creeping in. I was bundled into a bed with the softest sheets my skin had ever touched.

My head was resting on his shoulder, my arms tucked in front of me between our chests. He had one arm under my neck and the other slung gently over my waist, his fingers resting on the sliver of exposed skin between my underwear and the bottom of my tank top.

I should have been freaked out. There should have been a million questions going through my mind. Instead, I was still half-asleep and still in the daze that had brought me to him in a panic, only the panic was gone. It just felt right. I was *supposed* to be here in this bed in the arms of Ethan Paul at dawn, hours after he had nearly died. This was where I belonged.

Nothing existed outside the pleasant humming of our touch. Nothing existed past the edge of the bed.

Everything felt sluggish: my mind, my body, the light with its lazy blue hues beckoning me back to sleep. But I needed to check on him. I knew he was alive—I could feel his chest expanding with strong steady breaths, hear his heart beating under my cheek—but I had to look into his face to convince myself.

As I shifted gently in his arms, angling my head to get a better look at him, his body responded immediately. The hand on my waist pressed down ever so slightly—as though to keep me in place but unsure if demanding this halting of movement was permitted.

I dragged my eyes slowly up his chest, over the curve of his neck, past the angle of his jaw, to look into his face.

His eyes opened. They looked as sluggish and relaxed as I felt.

An inexplicable warmth flooded my chest at the sight of him conscious and well, if still a little out of it. I sighed with pleasure, and the corners of my mouth curved up infinitesimally in a lazy smile. He responded with a soft smile of his own.

For a few moments we just stared at each other, as if to make sure the other person was real. I'd never looked someone in the eye for so long before. With anyone else, in any other setting, it would have been too weird, too intimate. One of us would have turned away, cracking a silly joke to dispel the intensity.

Yet staring into Ethan's eyes as we held each other felt perfectly normal and comfortable. It didn't matter that I hardly knew the guy, that we had met only a handful of times. In that moment, I knew *him*. I knew who he was underneath all the bullshit and the secrecy and the big boisterous personality that matched his big boisterous physique.

It felt right to have his hand on my waist—his fingers now flexing just slightly on my bare skin. It felt natural when we both leaned in.

We were on opposite ends of an invisible tether, being tugged toward each other.

It was not a desperate and frenzied embrace—it was slow with inevitability. Our lips met halfway and pressed together softly. Once again moving in tandem, my arm traced his shoulder and landed behind his neck while his hand snaked up from my waist, underneath my tank top, toward the middle of my back.

We pulled each other closer at the same time.

Our chests pressed together as the kiss deepened, still slow and gentle but steadily increasing in intensity.

As naturally as it had started, the kiss came to an end with slow pecks against swollen lips. Our foreheads met, and our noses rubbed gently together.

He extracted his hand from the back of my tank top, and his fingers tangled into my hair, beginning a gentle massage on my scalp.

"Thank you." He whispered it so softly that if my face hadn't been pressed into his, I wouldn't have heard him. I wasn't sure what he was thanking me for, and I couldn't find the energy to think about it. Unconsciousness was tugging at me again.

He rolled onto his back and took me with him, gently cradling my head and settling it into his shoulder. The arm under me curved around, his hand finding the sliver of exposed skin once more. It seemed we both still craved skin contact.

I settled into his side, and we both went back to sleep.

When I woke up the second time, it was broad daylight, made painfully obvious by the sun streaming in through the window in front of my face, blinding me even through my closed lids.

I groaned softly and shifted, intending to roll over and away from the offensive light, but I froze. There was an arm slung over my middle and a warm chest pressed into my back.

Why was someone in my bed?

Even as the thought floated through my mind, I realized it was inaccurate. I couldn't have been in *my* bed. There was no window directly opposite my bed and therefore no way sunlight could be shining on my face.

I was in someone else's bed. With . . . someone?

I was now wide awake, all senses on alert, my heart hammering in my chest.

Forcing myself to take a deep, calming breath, I tried to pinpoint the last thing I could remember, but my train of thought was immediately interrupted by the person behind me, who had responded to my deep breath with a breath of their own and a tightening of their arm around my waist. He—I didn't know any women with arms that wide—snuggled in closer to my back, nuzzling his face into the back of my head.

Did he just smell my hair?

I needed to extract myself from this person and try to figure out where I was.

As slowly as I could, I wrapped my fingers around the wrist resting on top of me and lifted it gingerly, then awkwardly shimmied toward the edge of the bed.

Behind me, the mystery person froze. He cleared his throat and gently extracted his arm from my grip, and the mattress dipped as he shifted farther away from me.

I turned my head to finally find out who had kidnapped me and . . .

"Ethan?" He was propped up on his elbows, mirroring my position, shirtless, the blanket pooling around his hips. He had a wary, slightly shocked look on his face—as if he too was trying to figure out what was going on.

"Uh . . . hey?" His eyes flicked down my body and flew back up to my face.

I looked down at myself—I was wearing only my tank top. The left strap had slipped off my shoulder, pulling the front down to almost reveal my left nipple. I gasped and immediately pulled it back up, suddenly very aware of how *naked* Ethan was in the bed next to me.

My mind warred between dragging the blanket up to cover myself and throwing it off to see exactly how nude we were under it.

I needed all the facts before I could form a conclusion, so, sitting up fully, I lifted the blanket off my lap and peered down. At the sight of my fluro pink underwear, still securely in place, I breathed a sigh of relief.

Ethan chuckled. I turned my head sharply in his direction and glared at him. He was still leaning back on his elbows, his coal-black hair sleep tousled and looking . . . sexy. Dammit! He looked sexy, OK?

But I wasn't going to let his shirtlessness and messy hair distract me from my fact-finding mission. I whipped my hand over to grab the blanket at the base of his stomach, yanking it away so I could look under it.

Ethan chuckled again and asked, "Like what you see?" in his gritty, sexy morning voice just as the door to the room burst open. Josh, Alec, and Tyler spilled inside.

As if the situation weren't ridiculous enough, apparently it was time to throw in the boy I'd recently kissed who'd then rejected me, the man who had saved my life and then actively avoided me for a year, and a staff member at the educational institute I currently attended whom I'd begun to develop a crush on. This was turning into a bad improv comedy show.

We all froze. Me with a handful of blanket held over Kid's crotch, Josh gripping a steaming mug of coffee in each hand, Tyler similarly holding two plates of food, and Alec just watching everything with narrowed eyes.

Ethan was the one to break the silence. He burst out with his booming signature guffaw and flopped back onto the pillows. This snapped us all out of the awkward spell we were under. While Ethan continued to laugh on the bed beside me, Josh and Tyler began to speak over each other, setting the mugs and plates down on the desk near the door.

Alec just crossed his arms over his chest and leaned in the doorway, the slight frown on his face unchanged and directed at me.

I grabbed the blanket and dragged it up to my chin, scooting back until I hit the headboard. The pressure of held-back tears was making my face ache. I pulled my knees up to my chest, unable to look away from Alec's stare, its intensity pinning me there, his eyes accusing.

I had no idea what was going on or how to get myself out of this situation.

I was in a room with four other people, but I felt so alone.

I was still meeting Alec's glare when the tears welled over and my breath started coming in broken pants.

Alec's expression shifted to something incomprehensible—but unnervingly intense. He dropped his arms and took a step into the room before changing his mind, turning on his heel, and stalking out, slamming the door behind him.

That's when the others realized I was crying.

The room fell silent as tears began trailing down my cheeks. I dropped my eyes to focus intently on the blanket covering my knees, tracing the swirly pattern in the fabric. I was hoping everyone would just go away so I could think.

Tyler cursed softly. Next to me, Ethan had begun to fidget, unsure of what to do with the crying girl in his bed.

After the longest and most awkward few moments of my life, Tyler finally decided to take charge.

"Eve." He was using his serious, adult-in-charge voice. "What's wrong?"

Despite how confused and scared I was, I looked up at him—his authoritative tone made me feel as though I had to. My gaze wandered from his neutral, serious expression to Josh's intense, confused eyes and then finally over to Ethan, who looked . . . as if he was in pain?

Something about that seemed familiar. I felt so lost, and I had no idea how to explain it to them.

It must have showed on my face, because Josh explained it for me, his voice quiet but confident. "Oh my god. She doesn't remember."

Ethan's pained expression turned into one of shock, and he stared at me, eyes wide.

It must have dawned on him then what this scenario must look like from my perspective—the girl who found herself half-naked in his bed without any memory of how she got there.

I looked around at them again; they all wore matching horrified expressions.

"No!" Ethan reached for me, then thought better of it and snapped his hand back, completely getting out of the bed.

But that only made it worse. Now he was standing there in nothing but his underwear, and looking at his almost naked body somehow felt *more* intimate than having him lying next to me.

"This is *so* not what it looks like, Eve. Oh god! Why doesn't she remember?" The last bit was aimed at Tyler.

"I'm not sure. This isn't how the connection usually forms. It was a traumatic experience for both of you. Maybe her mind just can't . . ."

As Tyler spoke, Ethan grabbed a T-shirt from a chair by the bed and pulled it over his head. "So, what do we do? Eve, what can we do?"

"I don't know." My voice was shaking. "I need to know . . . I just . . . why am I here? Did we . . . ?"

Tyler attempted to answer my disjointed questions. "You came here last night because Kid was in trouble and you wanted to help. Nothing untoward happened." He looked uncomfortable.

Ethan, his hands in fists, leaned on the bed, putting himself at eye level with me but not getting any closer. "You saved my life." He said it with such intensity, such conviction, that I couldn't suspect he was lying or being dramatic.

I stopped crying and released the death grip I had on my knees, straightening up as the sensation at the back of my mind nudged at me again.

I brought my hand up to my chest, rubbing lightly just below my neck. Lingering remnants of the urgency, the pain I'd felt last night tugged at my memory. I glanced around the room and my eyes caught on Josh. The bright colors of his David Bowie T-shirt served as the anchor my mind needed to put it all together.

It came rushing back—the sudden way I woke up, the overwhelming desperation that had me sprinting all the way here, the pain at seeing Ethan unconscious and vulnerable, the crushing worry that he might die, the unexplainable urge to touch him.

I sprang to my feet, and Ethan straightened. He was so tall that my standing on the bed put me only half a head above him.

"I have a feeling she's remembering it." A tentative smile spread across his face, bringing his dimples out.

He almost died.

The urge to be sure he was all right slammed back into me, and I bounced across the mattress and launched myself at him. He caught me, wrapping his arms around my waist as mine wrapped tightly around his shoulders.

I breathed a sigh of relief and smiled wide as I felt the strength in his grip. He was OK. He had made it.

Our embrace only lasted a moment before two sets of strong hands yanked me back onto the bed. As soon as I was away from Ethan, Tyler and Josh released me and stepped back, though they remained standing close.

"Probably best if we keep the physical contact to a minimum now that you're back to full strength. We wouldn't want to burn down the pool house." Tyler sounded as if he was explaining their weird behavior, but I only had more questions.

"OK, someone better start explaining. Preferably with visual aids. Because I'm no longer worried that you're a bunch of creeps who drugged me and had your way with me, but I am still really confused." I must have looked like a crazed person sitting in the middle of the bed in my underwear, my face tear-streaked but smiling—*because Ethan was OK.*

Instead of answering me, Ethan made a beeline for the plates on the desk and started shoveling food into his mouth. "Man, I'm starving!"

"OK. Fair enough." It was Tyler, once again, who was attempting to answer my questions. "But you both need to eat and ... ah ... get dressed. Why don't we give you some privacy, and then we can talk out in the living room?"

Now that he mentioned it, I *was* pretty hungry. And now that he mentioned it, I *was* sitting in a bed in my underwear. I'd spent a little bit of time with Josh and Ethan, but Tyler was still firmly in the category of "official Bradford Hills representative" in my mind. All my interactions with him had been strictly related to Institute business, despite his laid-back approach. Even though I knew he lived here, it was still a little odd for me to be seeing him off campus. *In my underwear.*

I slowly lifted the blanket back over myself, feeling self-conscious again, and nodded. Tyler grabbed the other plate and walked out of the room, herding Ethan through in front of him.

Josh didn't follow them straight away. He walked around to my side of the bed, a small smile playing at his lips. He leaned down in front of me, just like Ethan had moments earlier, and looked at me with those intense green eyes.

"You're amazing." He raised one hand and brushed my cheek with his knuckles. Instinctively I leaned into the touch, and that tingling feeling spread like warm butter where our skin met. It felt amazing. It felt like ... when I'd touched Ethan last night.

As I grasped at half-understood facts, beginning to *maybe* connect them into a half-comprehensible theory, Josh straightened and walked toward the hall. Grabbing the mugs off the table, he exited the room and turned, smiled at me again, and flicked his eyes to the door. It swung slowly closed at his command.

ELEVEN

As soon as I was alone in the room, I didn't want to be.

I needed answers and knew they had them, but I also just wanted to be around them. The pull I had toward these two guys I hardly knew was beyond anything I could explain. I didn't *feel* as if I hardly knew them. I felt as if we were family who just hadn't seen each other in a really long time. As if there was an established connection regardless of what I knew about their favorite foods and music preferences.

I was relieved to find a bathroom connected to the room I was in and a spare toothbrush left on the counter for me. After a quick freshen up, I got dressed. It felt warm, so I opted not to put the oversized T-shirt or cardigan back on, but I couldn't go out there in just my underwear. I rifled through the items on the chair and decided to borrow the shorts that were obviously intended for Ethan.

By this point, I was so hungry that my stomach was in a constant state of grumbles. I followed the intoxicating smell of bacon down the short hallway.

"...both of you. It's a delicate situation, to say the least."

"What's a delicate situation?" I wasn't eavesdropping; I'd simply walked in while Tyler was speaking. It was odd seeing him outside the confines of Bradford Hills, but at least it wasn't as awkward as him piling into the little bedroom with the other boys when I was half-naked.

I had run through the pool house so fast the previous night that I had no memory of what it actually looked like. Now, walking out from the back of the structure, I saw an open-planned living area. Directly opposite me, a wall of windows looked out onto the yard, the double doors in the middle flung open, letting the breeze in. Alec was leaning in the doorway, looking out at the pool, his back to us all.

To my right was a small kitchen area; on my left, couches and a TV. The whole space was decorated in the Hamptons style—lots of whites and blues with touches of light timber.

Ethan sat at a round dining table under the window facing me, already finishing his first plate of food and loading up his second. Tyler and Josh were situated on either side of him.

All three of them looked up and smiled. "We'll get to that," Tyler assured me. "Have something to eat."

He didn't have to tell me twice. I marched over to the table and sat across from them, snatching up a plate heaped with food. As the bacon and eggs landed on my tongue, I moaned, and my eyes rolled back into my head. I felt as if I hadn't had a meal in days. All my focus was on my plate, until the smell of coffee hit me.

I reached for the steaming mug in front of me but paused with it halfway to my mouth. *American coffee.* I set it back down, a disgusted look on my face. "I don't know how you guys drink this swamp water. I need to find somewhere that does a decent latte around here or I'm going to go nuts.

And don't say Starbucks! Don't get me started—" I looked up. They were all staring at me. "—on Starbucks."

Even Alec had turned around to look at me, an *almost* smile on his face. I didn't have a chance to wonder about this sudden improvement in his mood though. Without so much as a "goodbye" to anyone, he turned around and walked out.

I returned my attention to the three people still present, beginning to feel a bit self-conscious. "What?"

Ethan just chuckled and took a sip of his swamp water.

It was Josh who answered me, leaning on the back of his chair. "We've just never seen someone eat as much as Ethan."

"Oh." I shrugged. I was not about to apologize for a healthy appetite. Although, looking down at my plate, I had eaten a lot more than I usually did. Double the amount of bacon I could normally stomach, and there must have been at least five eggs on the plate, plus the toast, mushrooms, and avocado.

Tyler must have recognized the confused expression on my face, because he leaned forward. "It's natural to be hungry after something like last night."

"Right." It was time for answers. "And what exactly was that?"

Tyler sat up straight. Falling back into more familiar conversation territory for us—facts and information—felt reassuring.

"Eve, you're not human. If there was any doubt over your blood work, it was eliminated last night."

"What?" I spoke around another mouthful of food as I attempted to digest the bombshell Tyler had just dropped. "When did my blood work come back? Are you saying I'm Variant? Do I have a healing power? Wait, but how would I have known that Ethan was in trouble?" My mind was racing with the possibilities.

"Slow down." Tyler chuckled. "Your blood work came in on Friday—a little early. Since you had not presented any powers and I knew you were being truthful when you said you didn't believe you were Variant, I was waiting until Monday to set a meeting. But we've suspected . . ." He threw a meaningful look in Josh's direction.

Josh casually sipped on his own pond sludge, looking completely unfazed by the situation. "Since the night of the party. When we kissed," he finished, his green eyes trained on me the whole time.

I lifted my chin and crossed my arms defiantly, refusing to be embarrassed. He was the one who had made it weird by throwing me out and then practically stalking me.

Ethan had stopped eating too. I shifted my gaze in his direction to find him grinning at me.

And then the memory slammed into my consciousness.

We kissed!

I gasped, my hand shooting to my mouth, my eyes going wide.

"Remembering more from last night?" His grin was mischievous, despite the adorable dimples in his cheeks.

Was he teasing me? I resumed my defiant posture and stared at him.

Tyler was thoroughly confused. "What the hell?"

Again, Josh saved me from having to answer. "They kissed. Last night, or rather early this morning, in bed."

"What?" Tyler and I spoke at the same time. Apparently he didn't know this piece of the story either. How the hell did *Josh* know that?

"I was there. One of us was in the room with you right up until an hour before you woke up. We had to monitor you and make sure you were both OK." A serious expression passed over Josh's face. "Ethan, you came so close . . . and Eve, you passed out and we couldn't wake you. It was scary."

He was worried about us. Both of us. Ethan slapped a big hand on his friend's shoulder and squeezed.

"It's all good bro. I made it. Eve's fine. Everything's totally copacetic." He grinned and went back to eating. Josh rolled his eyes at him, but I caught the affectionate smile on the end of it.

Tyler cleared his throat, ready to steer the conversation back toward a more productive topic. "Well I guess that's natural under the circumstances. But let's focus. We have a lot to cover."

"Right. What exactly are those circumstances?" Even though my brain had begun to piece it together, the logic and evidence undeniable, I still needed to hear it. It didn't feel real.

"You are not only Variant, Eve." Tyler leaned forward, fixing me with his serious look. "You're a Vital. And it would seem you've already found your Bond in Ethan and Josh."

My mind went blank for a moment, struggling to process this information and reconcile it with the fact that I'd grown up believing I was human. I blinked slowly and looked at the three guys sitting across from me, one by one. Tyler's eyes were cautious, assessing my reaction. Next to him, Ethan and Josh were watching me with matching tender looks on their faces. Soft smiles just for me.

I'm a Vital. I tried the label on for size in my mind.

I had unbridled access to limitless power. Two people with some of the rarest and most fascinating abilities I had ever seen were in my Bond.

I have a Bond.

A Bond—a group consisting of at least one Vital and one Variant. A tight, unbreakable connection defined by the Light shared between the people in it, tethering them to each other for the rest of their lives.

I took a deep breath, pushing aside my contradicting feelings of apprehension and excitement, and chose to focus on the more immediate questions.

"So that's why I knew Ethan was hurt? The Light was instinctively drawn to saving him. I couldn't have stopped myself from sprinting here like a maniac if I'd tried. And Josh, when we kissed, that's why all that stuff started flying around the room. It was you doing it, with your ability. But it was me too because I was feeding you more Light."

Now they were all smiling. Tyler looked relieved, probably because I was allowing my curious mind to connect the dots rather than freaking out. I should have been more floored, more surprised. But as soon as the initial shock wore off, it all made perfect sense.

I hate unanswered questions more than anything, and this revelation was allowing so many pieces to fall into place. I felt strangely calm about it. If anything, I was becoming excited. Hungry to learn more about my Light access, about my connection to the boys, my mind had sprung into full curiosity mode.

But before I had a chance to start firing my million questions, Alec walked back into the room. He marched right up to us and set a takeaway coffee cup on the table in front of me. Resting one hand on the back of my chair, he leaned down, careful not to touch me, his intense eyes level with mine.

"Thank you for saving my cousin's life. I don't have a lot of family left. I'm glad we've found . . . their Vital. Ethan and Josh's Vital. You." He frowned at the end, looking a little unsure of what he was saying.

"I couldn't have stayed away if I tried. There's no need to thank me." I bit my lip. I'd unintentionally thrown his words back in his face. After trying to thank him for saving my life several times and being repeatedly dismissed, here I was, doing the same. "You're welcome," I hastened to add, injecting as much sincerity into the words as I could and giving him a smile—despite the fact that he'd been a massive asshole to me.

He nodded once and straightened, walking back to his spot in the doorway, facing us.

"Love you too, bro!" Ethan piped in.

Alec smiled briefly but ignored him otherwise. "The latte is from a café nearby. Best non-American pond sludge coffee in town."

Stunned, I looked down at the little cup in front of me. He'd gone out to get me coffee? How . . . thoughtful. I'd known the kind, gentle stranger who had been there for me in the hospital was in there somewhere. I just wished it hadn't taken someone nearly dying to bring it out of him.

My first tentative sip of the latte got me way more excited than what could be considered normal. It was good. Really good! So good that it made me think of Melbourne—the city that had made me such a coffee snob in the first place.

"What did I miss?" Alec asked.

"Eve and Kid kissed," Josh threw in before anyone else could speak, leaning back, hands crossed behind his head, a teasing smile on his lips. He seemed to be getting an unusual amount of pleasure from sharing that little fact.

Alec looked from me to Ethan and then sighed heavily, pinching the bridge of his nose. "I leave for five minutes . . . This is getting out of hand." He turned to Tyler, speaking to him directly. "The connection is too strong now. Avoidance is futile. We're going to have to start teaching them to control it, or the three of them are screwed and we won't be able to do much to protect them."

His words were heavy with frustration, and I understood why. Josh's power could be incredibly destructive unchecked—as evidenced by the sheer volume of stuff floating around his room after our brief kiss—and Ethan's was even more dangerous.

I sat bolt upright, a new question occurring to me, and I blurted it out without thinking. "How come we didn't light the bed on fire?"

Alec pinched the bridge of his nose again, sighing deeply; Tyler looked up to the ceiling, his expression decidedly uncomfortable; Josh choked on his sip of coffee; and Ethan laughed, loud and from deep in his chest.

"We still can, if that's what you want," he said on the end of his laugh, leaning his elbows on the table and giving me a devilish grin.

I was momentarily embarrassed at my choice of words, not to mention distracted by Ethan's obvious flirting, but I pushed it all aside and rolled my eyes. "You know what I mean. If brief contact with Josh had all his worldly possessions floating around like we were in a scene from *Carrie*, why didn't Ethan's fire ability go haywire when we . . . touched?"

Tyler was quick to explain. "You were both weakened. He had nearly died, and you had completely drained yourself feeding him the power he needed to survive. At that point, almost all the Light was being used to sustain you, Eve, as your levels recovered. Although I suspect that even as your levels of Light rose slowly, you were still channeling small doses into Ethan.

"As soon as we put you two in the bed, you both immediately gravitated to each other, seeking out contact, despite being passed out. Eve, you began to cry in your sleep when we lifted you off Ethan—once we were sure he wouldn't die, of course.

"Ethan wouldn't have been able to muster even a matchstick-sized flame in his state, and you had no energy to spare for his ability. It was all being used to keep you both alive. That's why you were so hungry this morning—your body is craving energy, from all sources. You don't realize you're even doing it, Eve, but right now you're building up your stores, drawing Light into yourself, ready for when it might be needed next."

"So last night we were simply too weak for it to be dangerous. But this morning when I hugged him, that's why you pulled me off?"

"Yes." Tyler nodded, and Josh answered simultaneously with a vague "More or less. Sure. That's why."

Tempting as it was to delve into why the boy who had kissed me had pulled me out of a hug with another boy who had kissed me, I had more pressing concerns. Such as why Ethan had been dying in the first place.

"What exactly happened to Ethan last night? Why didn't you just call an ambulance?"

This time no one jumped in to answer. Silence filled the room as all the boys turned to Tyler.

When Tyler answered, I knew I wouldn't get the full story.

"Basically he used too much of his ability. There was an incident, and he used his fire to . . . help someone. He used too much. We don't have direct access to the Light like you do, Eve. We can use our abilities without a connection to a Vital, but it's limited. If we push it too far, it starts feeding on our life force."

I watched Ethan as Tyler spoke. His face was serious again, piercing me with his amber eyes.

"A hospital wouldn't have been able to help him?"

"There is nothing that modern medicine can do when we overuse our abilities. There have been studies. I'll send you links to some research. When we deplete ourselves like that, our body temperature plummets, like we're going into hypothermia. The hypothesis is that the ability uses every bit of energy available to it—it drains the very life from our veins, the very heat from our flesh. The only chance we have is to warm the body up and hope it can heal itself. It happens so fast that even waiting for an ambulance would have taken too long."

"Of course, having a Vital helps," Josh added. "As you saw last night. If it wasn't for you, Eve, Ethan probably wouldn't have . . . made it."

The room fell silent, everyone looking down at their hands, their mugs, the table.

I began to understand how close these four were. Even though only Alec and Ethan were actually related, it was clear they were all family. The kind that runs deeper than blood.

"The burned-out car." The charred remains of the vehicle I'd encountered on my mad dash here had to connect with what they were telling me. Sort of telling me. Kind of alluding to without *actually* telling me anything.

I looked from one to the other, waiting for confirmation. Ethan and Josh avoided my eyes, and Tyler was staring into space, lost in thought. The only one who returned my gaze was Alec, his blue eyes unwavering. I raised my eyebrows and gave him a "start talking" look.

"Ty?" He surprised me by turning to Tyler, who recovered from his distracted stare and gave Alec a slight nod.

"Yes. That was Ethan," Alec finally confirmed.

"Holy shit! What happened?"

"We can't tell you that. It's classified," Tyler cut in.

"I am so sick of that word." I rolled my eyes, flopping back in my seat. The fact that Tyler had even used that word told me this had something to do with Melior Group and Alec's secretive, dangerous job, but Alec's deferring to Tyler spoke volumes too. "Wait, do you work for Melior Group?" I fired the question at Tyler before he could give me any more evasive talk.

"You're too observant for your own good." He sighed, but it was said with affection, and warmth sparked in my chest at his praising of my intellect. "Yes. I work for Melior Group *and* for Bradford Hills. They're two of the biggest Variant associated institutions in the country—they need to have a collaborative relationship. I act as a sort of liaison. My position isn't a secret, but it's not exactly advertised either." He fixed me with a meaningful look, and I nodded.

"Yeah, and that technically puts Tyler's rank above Alec's, even though

Alec is older by two years." Josh lifted his mug up to his mouth, barely covering a cheeky grin. I was starting to think Josh was a bit of a shit-stirrer. I knew I probably shouldn't encourage him, but the corners of my mouth twitched up involuntarily.

"Man, it's not even funny." The humor in Ethan's voice contradicted his statement. "Ever since he became Alec's boss, he's been even bossier in all other areas of our lives."

"I am not bossy!" Tyler sounded downright outraged.

"And Tyler is not my boss. He just happens to outrank me," Alec finally piped in. "Can we please get this conversation back on track?"

"Look," Tyler said to me. "There are some things happening—things we can't really tell you about yet—but it's a dangerous time to be a Variant. Especially one with an intimidating ability like Ethan's. Things happened last night, and if it wasn't for Ethan, people might have lost their lives."

"Oh my god! Someone tried to kill you guys?"

"Eve, please! We can't tell you more. And you can't tell anyone what happened here. It would put you in danger too. Do you understand?" His gray eyes were fixing me with an intense look.

"Fine." I meant for it to sound sarcastic, but it came out soft and meek.

My brain was running a million miles an hour.

The Reds had said that without his Vital, Ethan's ability was limited to small fire-setting and visually impressive tricks. It would have taken an incredible amount of Light to destroy a car and fight off a bunch of super assassins (OK, so I was filling in some of the blanks with my own version of what happened). Ethan didn't have that kind of power. Not without me around to feed it to him. He had endangered his own life.

Tension filled my muscles as worry and frustration bubbled up within me.

I stood up and leaned my hands on the table, fixing my eyes on the big

147

idiot sitting across from me. Surprised and wary, he leaned away, looking to Tyler and Josh on either side for backup.

"Ethan..." *Dammit.* "What's his middle name?" I stage-whispered to Alec.

"Terrence." He smirked.

"Ethan Terrence Paul." I said with as much force in my voice as I could muster. "What you did last night was reckless and irresponsible. Don't you dare ever do that again. Don't you push your ability past its limits. Don't push it *at all* unless I'm there to give you more juice than you possess in your ... admittedly ... very large body.

"But that's not the point." The energy drained out of me, and my shoulders slumped. "You could have died. And I felt like I was dying right along with you. Don't ever do that to me again."

I fixed him with one last meaningful look before grabbing my delicious latte and walking out of the pool house. With nowhere else to go, I wandered to the edge of the pool, watching the bright sun glistening on the blue surface of the water, taking a few cleansing breaths before finishing the last drops of my coffee.

After a few moments, Ethan came to stand at my elbow.

"I heard you, Eve. I get it. This is going to be an adjustment for all three of us, but I promise I will never willfully do anything that might hurt you ever again. It's impossible now that I know you're my Vital, now that my ability has recognized your Light. I'm sorry last night was such a mess. I'm OK now."

I released a heavy breath and looked up at him. There was nothing but sincerity in his eyes.

I nodded, giving him a small smile. There really wasn't much else he could say or I could ask for. This was new territory for all of us, and we would just have to do our best to navigate it together.

I was rewarded with one of his big, infectious grins.

We moved toward each other, naturally wanting to hug it out, but we never got the chance. Three frantic voices of protest piped up behind us, and we snapped away from each other, sticking our arms to our sides like naughty children caught in the act of trying to steal a cookie out of the jar.

"No hugging!" Alec shouted, stalking toward us and emphatically cutting through the air with both arms. "For fuck's sake! No touching at all. Eve has no idea how to control the amount of Light she releases, and Ethan has never had practice controlling higher levels of his ability."

He was right. We had no idea how dangerous it could be. We could end up lighting all of Bradford Hills on fire.

And yet I *wanted* to see what Ethan could do with the extra power from me. My brain was itching to learn everything about our connection, to explore it hands-on. Instead of looking appropriately chastised, I couldn't contain the excited smile pulling at the corners of my mouth.

There was nothing I loved more than a good experiment, and here was a big, muscly, dimpled one standing right in front of me.

TWELVE

When I was living a quiet, pretend life in Nampa, if someone had told me I was a Vital and would one day be standing by a massive pool on the grounds of a mansion in Bradford Hills, about to test the limits of my power, I would have suggested they get psychiatric help. But there I was, the calm blue water glistening in the bright sunshine as I stood next to *my* Bonded Variant with a rare and powerful fire ability, getting excited to see what we could do together.

Ethan had the same look on his face as I assumed I did, just as enthusiastic to find out what this connection really meant. He was even bouncing a little on his feet.

"No. Don't even think about it. What did I *just* say?" Alec's voice was beginning to sound more like a growl.

"We really must be cautious with this. It would be best to explore your connection in a safe, *controlled* environment." Tyler looked all kinds of wary.

Josh was standing back slightly from our tense group, looking amused, his hands in his pockets. I could tell the exact moment when the idea hit him: his eyebrows raised, and his head tilted slowly, eyes drifting to the water. "We do have a—"

"Pool!" I shouted over the top of him, unable to contain my excitement. He laughed, a little surprised at my outburst.

I spun to face Alec and Tyler, who were standing shoulder to shoulder, both with their arms crossed, both wearing disapproving expressions.

"It's a perfect controlled environment," I reasoned, hoping to appeal to Tyler's academic curiosity. "What could contain fire better than a large pool of water? Plus this is probably the best time to try this safely. We're both still kind of weak from last night, so neither one of us will be firing on all cylinders. Right? Pleeease!" I pressed my hands together in supplication.

Tyler dropped his arms, his resolve wavering.

Behind me, a giant splash spattered my calves. At Tyler's first sign of weakness, Ethan had jumped in the pool.

Alec was still glaring at everyone. "This is a bad idea."

"Maybe." Tyler sounded wary again. "But we have to try it sometime. And she does make some good points. Might as well get it over with while there's no one home." He looked down at his watch, checking the time.

"Yes!" I fist-pumped and spun around, running toward the water before he could change his mind.

I dropped the borrowed shorts from my hips and stepped into the pool, opting to take the steps instead of jumping in. Ethan was standing in the middle, water dripping off his wet hair and down his broad chest. The water only reached a few inches below his sternum, which was moving up and down rhythmically as he breathed, slightly winded from his dive. His eyes were trained on the spot where the water met my body, following it up as I waded farther in.

While he watched my progress, I took in his tattoo. I'd noticed the little match on his left arm peeking out from under his T-shirt a few times, and I'd been vaguely aware last night—and when I'd seen him shirtless in the bedroom—that the ink covered a much larger area, but my full focus had been elsewhere. Now, I was paying attention. Coming off the little wooden match was a massive flame, the fire licking up Ethan's arm and over his shoulder in vivid reds and oranges that seamlessly blended into one another. It was beautiful and suited him perfectly.

Behind me, everyone else had gone silent too. The sudden hush gave me a twinge of nervousness. As Alec had pointed out, I had no idea what I was doing.

Thankfully, Ethan took the lead.

"Come here." He held a hand out, beckoning me forward.

"The Light transfer is triggered most easily if her emotions are running high—a physiological reaction will stir it naturally." I knew Josh was thinking about our kiss as he spoke. I was too.

"Perhaps that's not the best way to go forward though." Tyler sounded a little uncomfortable. "Maybe we should try a more controlled transference, a smaller dose, if you will."

Alec sighed loudly. He was not on board with this, but he was clearly outnumbered, and outranked by Tyler.

"All right. Let's start slow then." Ethan held out his other arm in invitation. "See if you can feel the Light and push it through your hands. OK?"

I nodded as I closed the distance between us. The water was just below my shoulders as I stood in front of Ethan and reached my hands out, placing them in his. We watched each other, curiosity mixing with excitement, and prepared ourselves.

Except I had no idea what I was supposed to be feeling.

Obviously I had channeled the Light before. Obviously I had access to it.

I had pushed enough of it to both Ethan and Josh to know that it was there, coursing through our connection. But I hadn't done those things on purpose. They'd just happened. *How was I supposed to replicate that now?*

That familiar soft, tingling feeling flitted over my skin where our hands met. Was that what it was? Should I be trying to increase that somehow? And where did the Light come from? Should I try to . . . get more of it from somewhere?

I was no longer meeting Ethan's eyes. I was staring at our joined hands, my view of them distorted by the water, a frown of concentration on my face. Why was this so difficult? It had come easily the last few times.

I looked to the side of the pool, searching for guidance from the person who always seemed to be ready with knowledge.

Tyler stood with his hands in his pockets, a thoughtful expression on his face. Next to him, Alec was crouching down, his face level with mine and his disapproval written all over it. His body was poised to jump into action, as if he was expecting the worst.

"She's overthinking it," Josh said from behind me. He didn't sound worried or frustrated. He was just stating the fact—as he had when I couldn't remember what I was doing in bed with Ethan.

I didn't have a chance to ponder how he'd figured me out so quickly, because Ethan was apparently in agreement with him.

"Stop overthinking it." He tugged on my hands and pulled me closer.

For the millionth time in the past twenty-four hours, I found myself in Ethan Paul's arms. His right arm banded around the middle of my back, pulling me up and firmly against him, my feet leaving the bottom of the pool. My hands instinctively went to his shoulders, and our proximity demanded that I meet his eyes again. They still held excitement, the amber almost dancing, the sun reflected off the water making them light and free.

He lifted his right hand out of the water, and his fingers gently caressed the back of my neck, making their way up into my hair. He leaned his head forward as though to kiss me, and—though I briefly considered the fact that we had an audience—my body reacted immediately. My breathing shallowed, my heart pattered inside my chest. I felt lost in his eyes and found in his arms. My lips had parted of their own volition, my brain remembering the last kiss we'd shared.

I wanted more.

But he didn't kiss me. He lowered his head until our foreheads were touching, and then he told me what I needed to hear.

"You can do this, Eve." He whispered it so softly that I don't think the others even heard, but I felt it inside of me as surely as I felt his breath on my face.

That's when I felt the Light.

I didn't have a name for it before, but now that I knew what it was, I was *sure* that was the unbridled power I was feeling. Every spot on my body where we touched—my hands, my forearms, the front of my thighs, my forehead— was tingling pleasantly, as it always had when we'd made contact, but now it was so much more than a tingle. The energy was almost audible, like a *buzz*.

I could *feel* the power coursing through me and flowing into him, and it felt *incredible!*

Ethan's eyes went wide. He pulled his head away and looked at me in astonishment. He'd never felt it before. The last time I'd pushed any Light at him, he'd been passed out, nearly dead. Neither one of us had known or been able to really appreciate what had been happening.

But he was feeling it now, and by the look of pure serenity on his face, it felt just as good to be on the other side. He lifted his head toward the sky and closed his eyes.

That pure look on his face tugged on some invisible string within me. Even though we were pressed against each other, I wanted to be closer. I needed more of him. It was easy to lift my legs in the water and wrap them around his middle. I used my hands to pull myself higher, wrapping my arms around his neck.

That's when things got really hot. Literally.

Ethan's arm around my waist stiffened, and his eyes snapped open. There was heat in his stare now, a new intensity.

Our moment was interrupted by panicked shouting and a lot of obscene language coming from outside the pool. The water was on fire.

The water was on fire!

All around us were flames, flicking twelve, thirteen feet into the air, blocking the other guys from view. I couldn't see the bottom of the pool. I couldn't see the water at all.

I shrieked and pulled myself impossibly closer to Ethan, lifting my body even higher onto his and burying my head in his shoulder.

He chuckled and playfully squeezed my sides. "It can't hurt you, Eve."

Now that he mentioned it, it wasn't actually hurting me. It looked mean and scary, but I was not being burned alive in the pool.

I slowly extracted my face from the safety of Ethan's neck and looked around. The flames were dying down already. Ethan was reeling them back in, a focused expression on his face.

As the flames disappeared completely, Tyler and Alec came back into view. Both were crouching by the edge of the pool, wearing matching horrified expressions.

Josh stood behind them, grinning. "Told you she was fine. It can't hurt her. It can't hurt me either, now that we're both in her Bond," he drawled, rolling his eyes.

"Why can't it hurt me?" I directed the question to the fire fiend between my legs. I wasn't quite ready to let go.

"It's a self-preservation thing. I'm able to do what I do because of the power you provide. We're connected now. Your Light and my ability know each other. They recognize each other. My fire couldn't hurt its power source if it wanted to. Same goes for Josh's telekinesis. We can't harm each other with our abilities anymore because that would cause you pain."

"Cool!" I'd have to delve into the theory of that later. Right now I had the practical application in front of me, and I wasn't about to waste this opportunity. "Show me."

I adjusted my grip so I was more on the side of Ethan's body, my right arm slung around his neck. I lifted my left arm in front of our faces, wiggling my fingers in a demonstration of what I wanted him to do.

He flashed me his brilliant grin and lifted his hand up beside mine. Just as I'd seen him do when showing off for his friends, he formed his hand into a loose claw, then flexed his fingers, opening his palm flat. But what emerged this time was *not* a little magic trick fireball.

It was a flamethrower. The fire whooshed from his hand and climbed into the air, fast and intense, the center of the blaze a dangerous blue.

"Whoa!" Ethan's look of surprise morphed into a focused expression once again as he reined in the inferno.

When the giant flamethrower had shrunk to a moderate-sized flamethrower, I tentatively reached my hand out. Logically speaking, sticking your hand into a raging fire was a reckless thing to do, but there was no longer any apprehension in me. In fact, I felt a strange kind of affection for that fire.

The complete lack of any sensation as the flames engulfed my hand was mind-blowing. There wasn't even any heat as I touched my palm to Ethan's, pressing each of my fingers against his much bigger ones.

I have no idea how long we were in that pool, both of us staring, transfixed, at our hands pressed together and enveloped in flames. But eventually I felt a gentle touch on my shoulder, and then someone was extracting me from Ethan's grip. For a second, Ethan's hold on me tightened possessively, but when we both realized it was Josh in the pool with us, he came back to himself and released me.

Josh pulled me back against his chest, both arms looped around my front, and dragged me through the water a few steps away from Ethan and the fire that was still flying off his fingers. He held me against him as we both watched Ethan slowly contain the flames.

Only then did Josh release a heavy breath and let me go. Apparently everyone had decided it was time to pull us apart before we lit something up that wasn't impervious to it as I was. Since Josh was immune to Ethan's ability too, the task of breaking us out of our trance had fallen to him. Although, as I turned around, I saw Alec had his shirt off and looked ready to jump into the water. I knew he would do anything to protect his cousin, but I questioned his self-preservation instincts, even as I took in the many tattoos covering his chest and arms.

Tyler was standing a bit farther back, but his posture was radiating tension as well. Our little fire show must have been as anxiety-inducing for them as it had been mesmerizing for us.

I cleared my throat, praying it didn't sound as awkward as I was suddenly feeling. "I'm going to go dry off."

Murmured agreements chorused around me as I moved to get out of the pool, avoiding eye contact with all of them. Alec cursed under his breath, pulling his shirt back on.

"You guys go ahead." Ethan's voice drew my eyes away from their intense examination of the pavers around the pool. "I need a minute."

I turned my head just in time to see him disappear under the water. Alec cursed again and stalked off toward the house.

I marched in my underwear and white tank top, which was definitely see-through by now, into the pool house in search of towels.

I found some in a bathroom and dried off, putting my remaining dry clothing back on. Testing my connection to Ethan had been exhilarating, but the events of the past few hours were beginning to catch up to me. A lot had happened, a lot of information had been dumped on me, yet there was so much I still didn't know. It couldn't have been more than an hour or two since I'd woken up in Ethan's arms, but I was exhausted.

I was ready for a break and some proper clothing; it was time to head back to my res hall and rejoin the real world.

I felt more than a little uncomfortable walking out of the pool house in just a cardigan and oversized T-shirt, pulling the hem down constantly because I'd decided not to keep my wet underwear on. Of course, the person I least wanted to see me naked in this scenario was the one waiting for me outside.

The others had disappeared and left Tyler to deal with me.

THIRTEEN

Tyler was sitting on the edge of one of the loungers, his head bent over his phone, typing rapidly. He must have changed at the same time I did, and he was now in jeans and a T-shirt. It was the first time I'd seen him dressed in anything other than slacks and a button-down.

He was easily one of the most intelligent people I'd ever met, and I genuinely looked forward to speaking to him whenever I had the chance. After last night, though, things were going to be different between us. How could they not be? I had just become permanently, supernaturally glued to two people he considered family, right after one of them nearly died. Those kinds of events forced a certain intimacy between people.

I didn't necessarily mind the idea of being closer to Tyler; I *had* been developing a serious crush on him since we first met. I just hoped it didn't ruin the relationship we already had.

On the other hand, I didn't even want to think about what it meant that I was still crushing on him despite having an attraction to both Ethan and Josh—an attraction that was more than just the Light-fueled connection between us. How did this work in Variant Bonds with more than one Variant involved? I would need to broaden my research to include Variant-specific sociology and psychology instead of just focusing on the hard science.

As I approached him tentatively, he looked up, swiping his messy hair out of his eyes, and gave me a wide and genuine smile.

"You did exceptionally well, Eve."

"Thank you." I ducked my head as I replied. I wasn't a blusher—my cutaneous blood vessels happened to be deeper in the skin, so when I got embarrassed, my cheeks didn't get red—but if I was, I would have been blushing. Why was his praise making me shy? He had praised me before, and I hadn't felt embarrassed.

"I was just texting the others to let them know I would drop you back at the Institute. I think we've all had enough excitement for the day. Plus, I don't want to risk Beth coming back here and making a scene. We need to keep a low profile." He stood, and we started walking back toward the house.

"Oh shit! Beth!" I had completely forgotten about my new friend and how she'd followed my crazy ass all the way here last night. She'd stuck with me, and I'd *completely forgotten* about her. I was a terrible friend!

"It's all right. We covered for you. We managed to convince her you were safe with us for the night, but she's going to have questions. That girl can be . . . forceful." He chuckled, as amused with Beth's strong protective instincts as I was touched by them.

As we spoke, Tyler led the way through a side door off the house's massive entrance hall, down some stairs, and into a cavernous garage with at least half a dozen cars.

"I'm sure she'll understand when I explain it all to her. She's one of the nicest people I've ever met."

"I'm glad you're making friends, but Eve, you can't tell her anything." He stopped and faced me fully, making sure I could see the seriousness on his face.

"I don't understand." Why would he want me to keep my newfound Vital status from my new friend—one of my only friends? "I thought this was a good thing. You were all so excited this morning. I've read up a little on American Variant history. I haven't come across anything that indicates it's bad to be a Vital."

"No. It's not a bad thing. And we *are* happy. I'm happy that Ethan and Josh have found you. You're incredible to have the Light necessary to sustain not one but *two* such strong abilities. But there are things at play here you don't understand."

He sighed and got into the driver's side of a black sedan that looked more expensive than the commercial plane I'd flown in to get here from Nampa. I followed suit and strapped myself into the passenger side, careful to pull the long T-shirt over my thighs and maintain some semblance of modesty.

It wasn't sitting well with me that he was being secretive. He had always encouraged my curiosity. "Don't do that. Don't be vague and evasive. That's Alec's thing."

"Please don't take Alec's behavior personally. He's had a lot of pain in his life. No pun intended." He laughed a little, but it was half-hearted. "We all have."

I didn't know what to say to that, but Tyler must have taken my silence as an invitation to continue, and I hung on every word.

"We all lost our parents at a young age. They were close, and as a result, we kids were too. They all died in a big accident . . . Ethan was only nine when it happened and Josh was ten. I was fifteen and Alec was seventeen. Alec and I thought we were grown up until, all of a sudden, we had no parents to turn to. But we grew up pretty fast after that—Ethan and Josh needed us to."

I swallowed around the lump in my throat, doing my best to keep my voice even. "I'm so sorry that happened to you."

He smiled weakly. "The point is, Alec is not always the best at expressing how he feels, but he's very protective of those two. Now that we know you're their Vital, he's going to be protective of you too. We both are. We're going to do all we can to guide you through this, Eve. To keep you all safe."

"And to make sure we don't burn Bradford Hills to the ground? Secretly though, because no one can know what I am, right?" I was trying to lighten the mood.

It worked, managing to get a smile out of him as he pulled out of the garage. "I'm not being intentionally evasive. There's just so much you don't know, and it only takes five minutes to drive back to the Institute. I can't possibly cover it all, but if I don't get you back there soon, it's going to raise even more questions."

"I don't understand." I looked out my window, watching the beautiful trees whiz past as we drove down their massive driveway.

"I know. I'm sorry. Look, the Vital power is revered in our community, yes, but it's also coveted, and that makes it dangerous for you. Haven't you noticed that every high-profile Vital you see in the news is surrounded by security? But it's not just that. This could be dangerous for Ethan and Josh too. There are things happening on a bigger level—bigger than all of us—that could make them targets if it became known they've found their Vital."

Ethan and Josh could be in danger. Now that he'd said that, I was no longer annoyed by his being vague. I just wanted to know who was trying to hurt my guys. I tried not to dwell on the fact that I was suddenly thinking of them as *my guys* as I tried to push the irrational murderous rage aside. "OK."

"OK?" There was a tiny hint of surprise in Tyler's voice. He hadn't been expecting me to cave in so easily. "I promise I'll explain everything. Just not today. I'm going to set it up so we're having regular one-on-one sessions—

I'll say it's intensive tutoring to bring you up to speed with your Variant studies. Your test results will be enough of an explanation. There's no hiding those now. I will arm you with all the information you need to navigate this clusterfuck as best you can. I promise."

So much had happened that his cursing didn't even surprise me. I was beyond being fazed by language from an authority figure.

"I need you keep this to yourself. You can't even tell anyone about your test results. Not until after our next meeting, which is when I'm meant to officially tell you. Can you do that, Eve? Do you trust me?"

We were pulling into the main gates of the Institute, and his eyes were focused on the path ahead, but all his other senses were focused on my reaction.

"No. I hardly even know you. Why would I trust you?" I crossed my arms over my chest, staring straight ahead just as he was.

Out of the corner of my eye, I saw his lips twitch into an involuntary smile. "Liar."

"Dammit!" I dropped my arms and turned on him. Stupid lie detector ability. "No fair."

With some of the seriousness of the moment dispelled, I flopped back in my seat, unable to pretend I was still mistrustful and suspicious. Curious and a bit worried, yes, but nothing they'd done so far indicated they were shady in any way. I did trust them, and Tyler probably would have known it even without his ability.

"Great! Now that we've established that you trust me, can we establish an official meeting so I can pretend to tell you for the first time that your blood test came back positive for Variant DNA? I have a slot at 9 a.m. on Thursday."

"Fine. Thursday it is. I'll wait for my answers—many, many detailed answers. But what am I supposed to tell Beth? And Zara, come to think of it, because there is no way Beth didn't fill her in."

"Right. About that." We came to a stop near the back entrance of my residence hall, and he angled his body toward mine but didn't meet my eyes. "Obviously, we couldn't tell her what was really going on. There was no covering up the burned-out car, and she's a smart girl, so she knew it had something to do with Ethan's ability. We kept it as close to the truth as we could. We told her he had overused his ability, that he was in trouble . . ."

Taking a deep breath, he told me the rest in a rush. "We told her you and Ethan were secretly seeing each other and that's why you were so upset, and that we called you when he collapsed because we knew you would want to be there for him."

I blinked in astonishment, my eyebrows slowly rising as Tyler finally met my gaze. At least he had the decency to look sheepish about it.

"You what?!" How was I supposed to convince the Reds I was dating Ethan Paul—notorious womanizer and destroyer of scholarships—when I'd shown nothing more than a fascination with his ability and a passing interest in the guy wielding it?

"I know. I'm sorry, but it's done now. We panicked. We had no idea what was happening, and we had to do something to cover it up. When Josh blurted out that Ethan was your boyfriend, we all just ran with it."

"Unbelievable . . ." I muttered to myself, but the idea of being with Ethan *did* intrigue me. We had kissed, after all, and there was no denying we were drawn to each other. I just couldn't be sure how much of that was mutual attraction and how much was driven by the Light coursing through my body.

Once again, I didn't have the luxury of space and time to figure it out for myself. I would have to pretend to be in a relationship with a boy whom I'd only known a few weeks—and whom I now liked more than I cared to admit. Throwing the "boyfriend" label into the mix seemed like an unnecessary complication. *Ugh! What a mess!*

"Eve?" Tyler snapped me back to the present. "We can't keep sitting here. Someone will notice."

"Right. Fine. I'll pretend to have the hots for Ethan. How hard can it be?" Probably harder than I expected. I was an exceptional liar when it came to handing over a fake passport or using my fake name, but I didn't know if I could lie to the two girls who had fast become my friends. I didn't know if I wanted to.

I got out of the car, slamming the door just a little bit harder than necessary, and trudged into the building.

When I made it upstairs, I peeked my head in the room and, finding it completely silent, breathed a sigh of relief as I pushed inside.

My phone was still charging by my bed, where I'd left it in my rush to get to Ethan. I had a few missed calls from Zara and Beth, but they must have found my phone in my room and given up quickly. There were also a few messages in our group chat.

Zara: We're heading out to catch up with some friends but when we get back . . . questions. So many questions!
Beth: What she said. Hope you're OK. xo

I winced, not looking forward to that particular conversation. Then I smiled in spite of myself. It was nice having friends who cared enough about me to demand explanations for strange behavior.

It made me feel even worse that I would have to lie to them.

I typed out a quick response—*Home now and I'm fine. No need to rush back!*—and dropped my phone back on the nightstand.

I wanted to throw myself onto the bed next to it. I was wrecked; the heaviness of the situation, coupled with the fact that I'd helped Ethan set the damn pool on fire, was getting to me. However, I also smelled like chlorine, so I headed for the bathroom first.

I took a long, hot shower, using the time to think about what I would say to Zara and Beth when they got back, but my brain was too fried to get very far.

"It's just a casual sex thing. He's hot, and I'm not talking about his fire ability." I couldn't even get to the end of that one without cringing.

"We have a lot in common actually?" That came out as a question.

"It was an accident. I . . . tripped . . ." Ugh. I rolled my eyes at myself.

I gave up. Hopefully the right thing would just come to me.

I dried my hair as quickly as I could, leaving it a big, frizzy mess, and pulled on underwear and a tank top before climbing into bed and falling asleep at two in the afternoon.

I woke up an hour later to Zara jumping on me and yelling, "No sleeping during your interrogation!" at the top of her lungs.

I groaned and tried to push her off, but Beth had already jumped on my legs, and I was pinned down. I started laughing in spite of myself. They released me, Zara moving to perch on my desk chair while Beth just leaned on the wall at the foot of my bed.

"Spill," Zara demanded, and I immediately got super nervous.

I still had no idea what to say but decided sticking as close to the truth as possible was probably the best option.

"Look, I know you warned me off him, but he's not what I expected." That was true. Ethan had shown me a tender, vulnerable side I had a feeling few people ever saw. "Beth, you've said he can be a nice guy if you get to know him. I didn't tell you guys, because it's all so new, and, I mean, we've only kissed, so it's not even that serious."

Their frowns of confusion made me realize my mistake—if it wasn't that serious, why had I been a hysterical mess last night?

"That is to say"—I scrambled for an explanation—"it wasn't really that serious until last night. I don't know, I guess knowing he might be in danger kind of made me realize how much I care about him." Also true. I just left out that my intense interest in his well-being had more to do with our supernatural connection.

"So, you're saying that you haven't even slept with him?" Zara sounded incredulous.

Technically I had, but I knew she wasn't referring to the actual sleeping we had done. At least this was one thing I could be truthful about. "No. Yes. That is to say, you are correct—we have not had sex." I looked down at my hands clasped in my lap, a little embarrassed.

"Oh god, are you a virgin? This just gets better and better. Ethan Paul is not the guy you want to lose your V-card to."

"I don't know," Beth piped in from the foot of the bed. "Doing it with someone who's more experienced might be good. They know what to do and all that."

"Um, girls? Not a virgin. I had a boyfriend when I was living in Australia, and I dated a bit while I was living in Idaho."

"Ooh, the plot thickens." Zara awkwardly pulled herself over on the wheelie chair and rested her elbows on the bed beside me, dropping her chin into her hands. "Tell us about the Aussie."

"Wait, weren't you in the middle of interrogating me about Ethan?"

"Aww, it's 'Ethan' now. I guess 'Kid' is too casual a nickname for a beau," Beth cooed.

"Beau?" Zara and I both laughed.

"Who says *beau* anymore? It's not 1956, Mary Sue," Zara teased, then turned back to me. "Look, we were worried, but you seem to really like him, and honestly, I've never heard of him actually dating someone. Like putting actual time and effort into getting to know a girl. So that's promising. Just be careful and know that we're here if it ends in tears."

"What she said," added Beth, smiling warmly, "except the Mary Sue bit. That was just mean. I am a modern woman. Hear me roar!"

I leaned back against my pillow, relieved the conversation hadn't been as difficult as I thought it was going to be.

We spent the rest of the afternoon lounging around the living room, eating junk food and talking about exes. I didn't have too much to contribute after my Harvey story was relayed, but it felt so good to be doing normal girl things with people I could actually call my girlfriends.

An afternoon spent relaxing, followed by a good night's sleep, did wonders for my energy levels and outlook on the whole situation.

The Reds had promised—at my insistence—not to tell anyone about me and Ethan. Considering his reputation, they were happy to keep it to themselves.

The girls weren't upset with me, the boys would be glad our secret was safe, and I was excited. I had so much to learn about this world I was apparently a part of, and I couldn't wait.

The Reds and I walked toward the Variant studies building together, me with much more pep in my step than was normal for anyone on a Monday morning. Ethan and Josh were in my first lecture for the day—Variant History—and I was looking forward to seeing them.

As we approached the front of the building, I spotted my boys immediately, chatting together as people streamed past them through the front doors. They turned in my direction at the same time and smiled in greeting. I couldn't help the grin that spread across my face in response, my eyes flicking from one to the other.

Thankfully, we were far enough away that the girls thought I had eyes only for Ethan. Beth grabbed my arm and bounced up and down excitedly before remembering it was supposed to be a secret and making a visible effort to calm herself. Zara just rolled her eyes and walked off toward the humanities building, waving goodbye as she dragged Beth along with her.

Ethan laughed as I walked up to them, no idea how I was supposed to act. "Should I just ignore you? Should we pretend like . . ." I spoke quietly, unsure how to end that sentence. We were pretending so many things already.

"Good morning, Eve. Why, yes, I'm doing just fine, thanks." Ethan chuckled before slinging an arm over my shoulders and moving us off toward class.

I froze up, worried we were about to burn down the science building. "What are you doing?" I hissed in Ethan's ear.

"Chill," he stage-whispered back. "As long as we avoid skin contact, we should be fine. Only over clothes." He winked at me, managing to make the comment both informative and suggestive. I rolled my eyes at him but found myself fighting laughter.

Josh snickered, stepping up on my other side. He handed me a latte and smiled a secret smile.

He'd brought it from the only café in town that made a decent latte; I was touched. "Thanks."

Ethan chose seats near the back of the lecture hall, and I found myself seated between him and Josh. A few people stopped by to say hi to Ethan, but I kept my eyes glued to my notebook, pretending to revise my notes.

As Ethan chatted with a guy on the football team about some upcoming game, I felt Josh's hand land gently on my leg under the little foldout table—

over the fabric of my tights and nowhere near any exposed skin. He squeezed gently and spoke very low, so only I could hear. "You're doing fine, Eve. Just try to relax. Everything will be OK."

And then he pulled away. When I glanced over at him, his head was buried in a book, and he looked so unassuming that I wondered if I'd imagined the entire moment.

Once again, Josh had picked up on what was going on inside my head and given me the encouragement I needed. I hadn't even realized how nervous I was until he reminded me to relax.

The rest of class passed by uneventfully, and the lecture managed to interest me enough that I forgot about the two boys on either side of me and all that sat between us—at least for one hour.

I had no more classes with the guys that morning, but at the end of my second class, I noticed Josh *happened* to be sitting on a bench outside and *happened* to leave just as I left, heading in the same direction.

As I emerged from my third class, with Zara, they were both there, chatting with Tyler. I didn't even need to look back to know they were following Zara and I as we headed to the cafeteria. I guess the stalking thing wasn't about to let up now that we knew we were in a Bond. If anything, I had a sneaking suspicion it was about to intensify.

Pretending to the world I was someone different was not new to me. I had been doing it my whole life. The new part was constantly having to resist the urge to go to them. Now that I knew who they were, *what* they were to me, all I wanted was to be close to them, talk to them, walk with them, touch them. It was infuriating to have to pretend we were nothing to each other.

By the end of the day, I was over being vigilant. As I finally collapsed into bed, looking forward to a good sleep and a break from it all, I realized I would be denied even that simple luxury.

My arms and legs were itchy in that now all too familiar way. I kicked the covers off—they suddenly felt as if they were made of raw wool.

Now that I thought about it, I had been scratching absentmindedly all day. I had been so distracted by Ethan and Josh and our situation I hadn't noticed the tickle beginning at my wrists and ankles.

With a sigh of frustration, I got out of bed, any semblance of fatigue gone, and prepared myself for another sleepless night.

FOURTEEN

The following three days were torture.

Ethan, Josh, and I were avoiding being seen together too much outside of class, but that meant we couldn't talk about our situation, and the longer I waited to get the full story, the more questions I had. It was driving me mental.

To make matters worse, my insane levels of energy were back. I hadn't slept at all the past three nights. As an upside, I was now ahead in all my coursework. In my extra time, I was devouring anything I could get my hands on to satiate my thirst for Variant-related knowledge, whether that was Variant studies journal articles or trashy tabloids about high-profile Variant people.

From a gossip website, I learned all about Senator Christine Anderson's Variant ability to understand and speak any language, her passion for purebred poodles, and her determination to have Variant interests represented on a national level. When I clicked through to an article about a Variant actress whose ability was to slightly alter her physical appearance, I drew the line and tried to read something from the business pages.

The name Zacarias caught my attention. It was an article about Alec and Ethan's mysterious uncle—Lucian Zacarias, head of Melior Group—and Davis Damari, another rich Variant who ran a pharmaceutical company. The two had struck some big deal to start a revolutionary new venture together. When it started talking about "mergers" and "dividends," I got bored and gave up.

There was very little about Lucian Zacarias on the Internet—the perks of being in charge of an international spy agency, I guess. There was, however, a lot on Davis Damari. Most interesting was that he hadn't manifested an ability until his thirties, unheard of in the Variant world, as most people presented with an ability by age twenty. His story had given many twenty-something Variants hope. I made a mental note to ask Tyler about it, then got sucked down another gossip website hole.

I had gone for 5 a.m. runs and done countless sit-ups and push-ups, but the energy was not abating. By the time Thursday came around, I was still bouncing off the walls, and the itchiness was coming and going more often. This worried me; the itchiness usually subsided as soon as I exhausted myself. The buzzing energy took a bit longer, but it usually went not long after.

Maybe it was something related to my Vital nature and Tyler would have some insight. I was glad our appointment was for first thing in the morning—I didn't think I could wait any longer.

I arrived twenty minutes early and paced the corridor outside Tyler's locked office, trying not to scratch, failing miserably, and garnering a few strange looks from other staff making their way to their offices.

At ten to nine, he arrived.

"Finally!" I groaned as he came around the corner.

He paused briefly in surprise before an amused look crossed his face.

"Sorry," I said. That was rude. "I didn't mean to jump down your throat.

I'm just . . ."

"Eager?" he supplied, unlocking the door and stepping inside. "Enthusiastic? Frustrated? Slightly crazed?"

"Yes. All of the above." I laughed nervously, closing the door behind us and sitting down in one of his tub chairs.

He deposited his messenger bag on his desk and sat next to me, as he had on the first day. "OK. Let's dive right in then. Perhaps you might like to ask some questions?"

I nodded emphatically and opened my mouth to start firing them off, but . . . nothing came out. I had been thinking about this for three days straight. There were so many things vying for my attention—the Light, the Variant-Vital relationship, my blood tests—I couldn't get my mind to focus on just one.

What did come out surprised me, although it shouldn't have; it was the only thing I couldn't research. "Why do we have to keep this a secret?"

Tyler blew out a heavy breath. "Right to the hard stuff, huh?"

"I just don't understand." I looked down at my hands. "I know that being a Vital is a big deal—that they're a cherished and respected part of Variant culture. So why do Josh and Ethan not want anyone to know I'm theirs? Is it because it's . . . me? Because I wasn't raised Variant and I have no idea what I'm doing? I don't want to embarrass them, but—"

Tyler cut me off midsentence, placing a gentle hand on my arm. "Eve. No."

I hadn't realized I was feeling so insecure about my new Vital status and my connection to the boys, but now that I was saying it, I realized it had been in the back of my mind since Tyler dropped me off, imploring me to lie to my friends.

"It's not like that at all," Tyler said. "Ethan and Josh are ecstatic to have found you. When a Variant finds their Vital, it's like a piece of the puzzle they didn't know was missing falls into place. No one could ever resent that. They couldn't care less what anyone, human or Variant, thinks about your Bond."

"Then what is it?"

"This is such a precarious issue . . ." he muttered, almost to himself. Then he turned his eyes back to me with a determined expression. "OK. I promise this is all related."

I nodded and shifted in my seat to face him more fully. His hand slipped off my arm as he began to speak, and I immediately missed his comforting touch.

"Throughout history, the balance of power has shifted between Variants and humans. At times, Variants, thinking our abilities made us superior, have enslaved and demeaned the humans for our own gain. At other times, the humans, considering us too great a threat, have imprisoned and segregated us, treating us like mutants, abominations, and defective versions of themselves. It has swung back and forth throughout history and from region to region. Sometimes religion was used to justify the segregation, sometimes politics, and sometimes a simple survival need—more land for farming and crops available to *us* at the exclusion of *them*. It's all bullshit, of course."

He was obviously passionate about this. He'd begun to gesture with his hands, his voice rising.

"Two Variant parents are just as likely to produce a human child as two human parents. There is no discernible reason why some people are born with the Variant gene and others aren't. It's not hereditary and it's not contagious. We have isolated a protein that, when present, indicates the individual is Variant, but we have no idea what causes it. And even when it is present, that doesn't guarantee the child will ever present with abilities or Vital access to Light—they could just have a dormant gene. This hatred of one another has nothing to do with actual differences. It's a basic psychological phenomenon of self-identification; the 'us versus them' theory. We are better able to quantify to ourselves who we *are* by identifying who we're *not*. Are you following?"

"Yep. We've been slaughtering one another since the dawn of time, and we like to join clubs to give ourselves some illusion of belonging. Go on."

I knew all this. It was basic history and psychology. I needed to know how it related to my present situation.

Tyler smiled at me indulgently and continued. "In a nutshell, in the last fifty years or so, we have enjoyed relative peace between humans and Variants, at least in the Western world. We've worked hard to create unity, understanding, and equality. We have laws that prevent discrimination, we work side by side, and mixed marriages are no longer as taboo as they used to be, although those are only possible for Variants without a Vital. But that's a whole other thing I won't get into right now."

He was alluding to the fact that most Variant-Vital connections that weren't between blood relations resulted in romantic relationships. I'd done a little research into this during my sleepless nights, but when the journal articles that came up had headings like "Polyamorous Relationships in Variant Bonds and the Associated Social Implications for Wider Communities: A Longitudinal Study," I quickly moved on to other things. I was definitely attracted to both Ethan and Josh, and I was about 80 percent sure the feeling was mutual, but I wasn't ready to deal with the idea of dating them both. *At the same time.*

I avoided meeting Tyler's eye and waited for him to continue.

"Over the last few years, cracks have appeared in our current harmonious coexistence. There are radical groups on both sides arguing for the dominance and superiority of one group over another. Variant Valor are Variant elitists who think a genetic fluke makes them better than 'average' humans. These are the type of people who use the word *Dimes* proudly. The Human

Empowerment Network are fearmongering nuts who think Variant abilities are an abomination and need to be controlled if not entirely purged. They are loud and outrageous, and at the moment they're seen mostly as radicals on the fringe, but they are gaining support at alarming rates. The Melior Group is keeping a very close eye on the situation while making considerable efforts to maintain positive relations with the mostly human government. It's one of the things Alec is involved in."

The information about Alec had me sitting up straighter. The kind gesture with the latte notwithstanding, he was still avoiding me like the plague, and I still hadn't managed to deliver my thanks to him, let alone question him about the night my mother died. Any insight was precious.

Tyler saw my enthusiasm and held up a hand. "I can't tell you much more than that, so don't even ask. The point is, the government and Variant organizations like Bradford Hills and Melior Group are on edge at the moment. The reason we wish to keep this secret is twofold."

He twisted to face me fully, and a weary expression crossed his face. "Firstly, if Melior Group found out Ethan and Josh had found their Vital, they would be recruited. Their abilities are rare and powerful, and in dangerous times, having power like that . . . well, let's just say they wouldn't have a choice. I don't want either of them being forced to fight, and they don't want it either."

Ethan was only one year older than me, and Josh was two. We were college kids—they couldn't go around waving guns and abilities, getting in life-threatening situations, any more than I could. My heart did a little jump in my chest at the thought of them in danger, but Tyler was still speaking, so I did my best to focus on him.

"Secondly, it's dangerous for you. We've managed to suppress this in the press to avoid panic in the Variant community, but there have been a series of abductions in the last six months all over the world. All of them Vitals, none of them found yet. If it became known you were a Vital, your very life could be in danger. We may not be able to contain this information much longer—Variants like to gossip more than a bunch of sixteen-year-old girls—but regardless, it's better that no one learns your true nature."

I slumped back in my chair and stared off into space, scratching my left wrist absentmindedly. All three of us were in danger—the guys from being recruited into a life of violence, and me from potentially getting kidnapped by some lunatic terrorist organization.

Some of the guilt about lying to the Reds lessened. This was so much bigger than gossip-filled confidences between roomies.

How had my life changed this much in a few short weeks? What did we do now? Just avoid each other and hope that the connection went away? From my reading, I knew that was impossible. Once the Bond was formed, it was for life. But just as I was avoiding thinking about how being in a relationship with more than one guy would work, I was trying not to think about how *permanent* the Bond was.

This situation was overwhelming on every level—from the global-extremist-group one right down to the personal-relationship one.

"What do we do now?" I turned my slightly panicky question to the only person who had a chance at making me feel better about this situation.

"We train." Tyler declared with a firm nod.

"Right." I nodded too, much more spasmodically. "We train." I took my sweater off. The itch had spread to my elbows, and the sleeves had begun irritating my arms. But I couldn't focus on that. Tyler was speaking again, and he was the man with the plan.

"It's too late to suppress your blood test results now. The Institute will know you have Variant DNA, but we can use that to our advantage. It gives us an excuse for you to have more one-on-one sessions with me."

"Right. Good excuse." I stood up and paced, my energy levels refusing to be ignored any longer. I did my best to concentrate on what Tyler was saying as I gave in and started scratching my arms from wrist to shoulder.

"The official story will be that you're getting extra tutoring in your Variant studies, and you will, but we'll also use the time to teach you how to get a handle on your Light. With practice, you will be able to control how much you channel and how much of that you funnel into Ethan and Josh. Eventually you'll be able to touch them without Light transferring automatically, and you'll be able to choose to push larger amounts to them without having to get . . . ah . . . so close."

"Learn how to transfer Light without sucking face. Got it." My breathing had begun to speed up, and I moved on to scratching my neck.

Tyler laughed and then looked at me quizzically. "Eve, are you all right?"

"Yeah, yeah. Just a little jittery. Lots to consider. Lots to do. Is it hot in here?" I moved over to the window and yanked it up. "It feels hot in here."

"Oh . . . kay . . ."

"So what do I tell people when they ask about my new Variant status?"

"The truth. Your blood tests came back positive, but it's news to you. You've never had any hint of an ability. Leave it at that. It means you'll be forced to attend some Variant events that get put on from time to time to facilitate Variants meeting one another, but we can handle that. The guys and I have been going to those things since I can remember."

"Cool, cool. Keep it vague and go to some parties." I laughed nervously; the notion of going to some exclusive Variant dating event suddenly seemed hilarious. "I don't think I have anything to wear to a nice party. Oh man!"

The itching was becoming unbearable as it spread farther. I was alternating between scratching my arms and the top of my chest, right down into my cleavage.

Tyler stood up, eyebrows raised, his attention fixed on my hand down my top.

I couldn't worry about him though; my T-shirt was starting to feel like a cotton torture device. I grabbed the bottom of it with both hands, ready to yank it over my head.

"Eve! No!" Tyler took a step toward me, his right hand raised in a "stop" motion in front of my torso. "What the hell are you doing?"

Through the fog of insane energy and unbearable itchiness, I managed to stop myself from stripping in front of my new tutor, but I was still really uncomfortable. Why wasn't it going away? I had gone for a two hour run just that morning after staying up all night and studying. I felt as if I was going to explode!

I grunted through gritted teeth and shook my hands next to my sides while jumping up and down, trying to *literally* shake some of the intense energy out of my body. I looked at Tyler pleadingly. "I don't know what to do. It's *so* itchy. And it's everywhere, and I feel like I could run a marathon and still have extra . . . help me!" I didn't know what I expected him to do. I had no idea what to do myself, but I felt scared. It had never been this intense before.

Realization crossed his features, and he ran one hand through his messy brown hair, breathing out a curse. "This is happening sooner than anticipated," he said, more to himself.

Another growl of frustration from me and I had his full attention again.

"It's going to be OK, Eve," he said. "This is just an overflow of Light. It knows now that you have two very powerful abilities to feed, and it's flowing freely into you to get to them. It just needs to be released. And you're going to release it all into me."

He took another step toward me and held his hands out in invitation.

"What? How?" Was he saying he was going to kiss me?

"Transference comes much more instinctively with members of your Bond, but it is possible for a Vital to release Light to any Variant. It doesn't feel as natural or as good, but it can be done quite easily by most Vitals. And you're already worked up—your heart is beating like crazy, your breaths are shallow and erratic, and your emotions are all over the place. The floodgates are open. We just need to give it something to pour into."

He punctuated his statement with a flick of both wrists, emphasizing that he wanted me to take his hands.

So he wasn't going to kiss me after all.

Trusting that he knew what he was talking about, I stepped forward and placed my hands in his. As soon as our skin made contact, I could feel the excess energy draining out of me. The sense of relief was so intense that my eyes rolled back, and I may have made an embarrassing sound of pleasure.

My shoulders relaxed, the tension easing out of the taut muscles all over my body. My breathing evened out, and the itchiness disappeared, draining out of me right along with the Light.

Within minutes, I was calmer, more relaxed, more myself. I was surprised at how easily I was able to transfer the Light to Tyler after what he'd said about it being more unnatural with people who weren't in my Bond. I didn't know what it was supposed to feel like, but it felt good. *Exquisite.* As good as when it had happened with . . .

My eyes snapped open.

Tyler was staring, transfixed, at our joined hands, his mouth open slightly, his breathing heavy and deep.

He looked up and met my gaze. For a few moments we just stood there, holding hands and looking at each other, the realization that had dawned on us both hanging heavy in the air.

"That," he said softly, and swallowed hard, "felt fucking . . ."

"Amazing," I finished, my voice as soft and breathy as his, and my hands squeezed his reflexively.

He responded by gently tugging me toward himself. Our eyes were still locked on each other, and I could see the gray in his almost alive with movement. Just as Ethan's had been in the pool.

Inch by inch we drifted toward each other. It felt like that first day when we'd sat side by side in this very office, chatting and drawing closer without realizing it. Only it was way more intense, and now I knew why we were drifting.

Tyler, just like Ethan and Josh, was *mine*. He was in my Bond.

"How is this possible?" he whispered, echoing my train of thought.

"I don't . . . I . . . I'm . . ." I had no idea what I was trying to say. All I knew was that his lips were mere inches from mine, and I wanted to close the distance.

It didn't matter that he was about to be my tutor, that I'd been trying really hard to stop myself from developing a crush on him, that I knew this urge was driven by my Vital instincts—a Light-driven reaction, pushing me to solidify my connection to another member of my Bond. All I could think about was how his lips would feel on mine.

I flicked my eyes down to those very lips, but that's what seemed to break the spell for him. He stepped away from me and dropped my hands. The sudden movement startled me, and I couldn't mask the disappointment that fell over my face.

"Oh, Eve." The pity in his eyes made me feel foolish. Like another one of those females on campus harboring fantasies for the hot guy on the staff. Which is exactly what I was—a girl with a crush. Of course he wouldn't want this. I too would resent being stuck by an uncontrollable supernatural force to someone seven years my junior.

I went to turn away from him, to try to cover up my childish disappointment, but with a firm hand on my forearm, he stopped me. He pulled me toward him and enveloped me in a hug. It was not the kiss I was hoping for, but it was still contact, some semblance of the intimacy that the Light inside me was pacified by, even if my girlish emotions weren't.

I wrapped my arms around his middle and dropped my head on his shoulder.

"It's not that I don't . . ." He sighed. I guess he was struggling with how to process this as well. "We're in such a delicate situation already. We can't have the ethics committee sticking their noses in too because it looks like I'm getting too close to one of the students. It's better if we keep it platonic."

He squeezed me a little bit tighter before releasing me.

I couldn't help feeling the sting of rejection. I knew he had a point about raising suspicion with the Bradford Hills staff, but I wondered if that was also a convenient excuse for not jumping at the chance to deepen our Bond as enthusiastically as Ethan and Josh had—or as romantically.

With some effort, I pushed away the self-conscious thoughts; we had bigger things to deal with. I'd hardly had a chance to figure out what was happening between me, Ethan, and Josh in the first place, and now a massive curveball had been thrown at us in the form of Tyler being part of my Bond.

I gave him my best "I'm OK" smile. He looked relieved, moving to sit behind his wide, heavy desk in a deliberate effort to put some distance between us.

It was probably best to get the conversation going again. We only had half an hour left of our session, and we had so much to cover. "Well, that was unexpected, but I guess it doesn't change much. I still need to train. Learn."

"Yes." He nodded definitively. "It certainly was unexpected. I never thought I would have a Vital. It's less common with passive abilities like mine. Active, physical abilities like Ethan and Josh's tend to need more Light to sustain them. And the fact that you have two people connected to your Light already . . . three is not unheard of, but it is rare."

We spent the remaining half an hour going over my vigorous new schedule. Some of my class commitments had been pulled back, including all my Variant studies. I would now be doing all Variant learning in daily sessions with Tyler. One of the things he wanted me to focus on was meditation. Apparently finding inner Zen was the key to fully controlling my Light. If I could control how much I took into myself, then I could avoid the itchy, sleepless ball of energy situation I'd found myself in the past few days. And if I could control how much I transferred, I wouldn't be slamming the guys with it every time we touched, making them dangerous to any living (or inanimate) thing in their general vicinity.

Tyler told me that all four of them had been practicing meditation from an early age. It wasn't as important for Tyler, considering the benign nature of his ability, but it was crucial for the other three. Apparently Alec had worked very hard for many years, doing daily mindfulness practice, to gain the kind of control he had. Ethan and Josh had some control over theirs already, but the amounts of Light I gave them access to put things on a whole other level. We all had work to do.

Until we were certain things wouldn't get out of control, I was to avoid skin contact with Ethan and Josh at all costs and come to Tyler if my Light became unbearable again. It was the only way to avoid suspicion and minimize the chances of a disaster. In the meantime, we would train at their house as often as possible. The privacy of their massive, secure, isolated estate made it the only safe place for me to transfer Light to Ethan and Josh. Having the Reds think I was in a relationship with Ethan would help with that.

He handed me my new, far busier, schedule at the end of the hour and ushered me toward the door, where he asked me to keep another secret.

"If you see Ethan and Josh today, don't tell them about the . . . us," he finished uncertainly. "Let me tell them later, at home. I don't want to chance their reactions in public."

"Oh. OK." I wondered what kind of reaction he was worried about, but before I had a chance to ask, his phone rang, and he hustled me out the door before rushing to answer it.

Naturally, I bumped into Ethan and Josh as soon as I stepped foot outside the building.

FIFTEEN

"Hey, babe!" Ethan flashed me his dimpled grin while Josh waved from behind him. I froze. *Busted.* I hadn't had a chance to prepare for this. And what was with the pet name?

"Oh, h-hey, um, sweetie. What's up? What's going on? Why . . . uh. What, whatcha doin' here?" I ended that eloquent outburst with a stilted laugh and a shuffle of my feet, crossing my arms over my chest before immediately propping them on my hips. *Smooth.*

Why was it that lying to government officials about my identity was so easy, but trying to lie to Ethan and Josh was making me feel like the most awkward person on earth?

They exchanged a look, chuckling but confused.

"We just thought we would come and see how your meeting with Gabe went." Ethan said. "Maybe grab some coffee?"

"Are you OK?" Josh interjected. *Crap!* Not Josh. Josh knew things just by looking at me. Stupid, observant, sexy . . . no! *Focus, dammit!*

I couldn't look at him, so I addressed his shoulder. "Mmmhmm. Yep. Fine. How are you?"

"Fine." He cocked his head to the side, trying to make eye contact. I could practically see the curiosity wafting off him.

I needed to get things moving before they started asking questions.

"Sweet. So yeah, gotta get lunch! I'm starving." I marched off toward the cafeteria, hoping they wouldn't follow me or notice I had just suggested lunch at 10 a.m.

Of course they followed me. They had been following me around for the last several weeks; why would they stop now?

Josh caught up to me first and stepped up on my right. Ethan surprised me by coming up on my left and draping a strong arm over my shoulders. I jumped a little but managed to keep walking. After days of avoiding even speaking too much in public, we were suddenly at the casual touching stage?

"What are you doing?" I stage-whispered to him out of the corner of my mouth. "Aren't we supposed to be keeping things secret?" People were already throwing us curious glances, murmuring to one another.

"Yeah, but only about the Bond," he whispered into my ear. I could feel his warm breath in my hair. It made me lean into him a little more.

"Wh-what?" I had to shake my head to clear it. The Light inside me was practically singing at his close proximity. It was thoroughly enjoying being around my Variant guys, especially since I was still on a high from the intense Light transfer with Tyler only half an hour ago.

"We need to keep our connection a secret, but it's only a matter of time before everyone starts gossiping about why we're spending so much time together. This way we get to have some control over what the gossip is. Plus, it gives me an excuse to touch you in public." As he spoke the last sentence, his hand started to travel down my back toward my ass. I slapped it away and fixed him with a glare.

He laughed out loud, drawing even more attention to us, and returned his arm to my shoulders, dropping a quick kiss to the top of my head.

"This is so not fair," Josh muttered on my other side. His gaze was fixed straight ahead, and a tiny muscle was twitching in his jaw.

We'd made it to the square outside the cafeteria, but instead of heading toward the entrance, Ethan led me to another building. As if they had planned ahead, Josh opened the door so Ethan could hustle me inside.

"I thought we were going to lunch." We were inside what looked like another residence hall. It was deserted.

Neither of them answered me as they walked toward the back of the building. Josh opened another door under the stairway, standing next to it like a butler, and Ethan ushered me into what I now saw was a storage closet. Mops and brooms were stacked on one wall, a shelving unit with cleaning supplies on the other.

"What the hell? What are we doing here?"

Josh closed the door behind him, and Ethan reached up to pull the cord on a little light bulb swinging from the ceiling.

It was a small space, not intended for three people to stand inside. Definitely not intended for someone Ethan's size. We were cramped, and it should have been uncomfortable, but I found myself liking the proximity to both of them.

I was facing Ethan, his broad, white-cotton-clad chest just inches away. Josh stood directly behind me, blocking the door.

"Something is wrong, and you're trying to keep it from us." Ethan crossed his arms over his chest. "Spill." He had that serious look on his face, the one that disappeared the dimples.

"What are you talking about? I'm fine." *More than fine now that I'm alone in a confined space with the two of you.* The Light was apparently not as determined as I was to ignore the whole "getting involved with multiple people" thing. It churned inside me, chomping at the bit to flow into the guys crammed with me in the storage closet. It was making me confuse the supernatural urge for a more basic, physical one.

Or was it? How much of my attraction could be attributed to the Bond connection, and how much was just me?

Josh placed a gentle hand on my shoulder and pulled lightly, trying to get me to turn to him. I knew I should resist, that Josh's way of picking up on unspoken things was freakishly accurate, but I melted into his touch. Behind me, Ethan stepped in a little closer.

I was careful not to meet Josh's eyes. Like a child playing hide and seek, I was trying to convince myself that if I couldn't see him, then he couldn't see me and my secret.

"Eve." His voice was soft but firm. "What happened? We only want to help. It's all we ever want when it comes to you—to help and to protect. I know it has something to do with your session with Tyler this morning."

My eyes snapped up. "How . . . ?" and then I immediately realized my mistake. He smirked, satisfied. I had just confirmed his suspicion.

"No fair!" I half-heartedly slapped his chest, but instead of removing my hand, I left it resting just over his heart, feeling the soft fabric of his mint-green shirt and the warmth of his body under my palm.

"What did he tell you that freaked you out? I'm sure whatever it is, it's perfectly normal . . ."

I chuckled. "Oh, I know it's normal. Or as normal as a paranormal connection can be." My voice had dropped to a mutter, and Josh frowned.

Ethan grunted in frustration behind me, his chest bumping my back. He was having trouble figuring out what we were talking about, and I didn't blame him.

"Eve." Josh narrowed his eyes, but he didn't remove my hand from its position on his chest.

"Look, it's nothing bad. I don't think. Tyler is going to tell you tonight anyway. We really should get to class."

Unsurprisingly, my attempt at deflecting didn't work.

"So there *is* something to tell then," Josh said. "Come on, Eve. What is it?"

I shook my head and pressed my lips together.

"*Eve.*" I wished he would stop saying my name with increasing levels of disapproval in his voice.

"We're not leaving this dirty storage room until you tell us what's going on." Ethan stepped impossibly closer, pressing his body flush with my back.

My brain latched onto his use of the word *dirty*. Logically I knew he was referring to our current location, but coupled with his body heat radiating behind me and the feel of his hard chest pressed into my spine, I was considering all the other connotations of the word.

"Please . . ." I wasn't sure how I'd originally intended that sentence to end, but I collected my thoughts enough to say: "I promised I wouldn't say anything."

I immediately groaned in frustration. I'd given them another clue. I'd also given away the fact that their proximity was directly correlated to how much information I was giving away.

"It's something Tyler wants you to keep from us?" Josh's voice was considerably lower now, his intense green eyes trained on me. "Why?"

Again, I shook my head, refusing to answer. But it was too late. They had figured out my weakness.

Moving in tandem, Ethan placed his hands on my waist just as Josh stepped forward and grabbed my arm, lifting it from his chest to his shoulder. Instinctively I raised my other arm, and Josh grabbed it so he was holding both my wrists. He ran his hands slowly up my arms, stopping at my shoulders, at the very edge of my shirt's collar, careful not to actually touch my skin.

At least some of us had the presence of mind to avoid sudden and violent Light transfer. It certainly wasn't in the forefront of *my* mind.

"Eve." When he whispered my name again, it was more pleading than demanding. Ethan wasn't saying anything, but his chest pressed into my back with each heavy breath he took, the warm air tickling my scalp. His fingers dug into my sides, and I immediately arched into him, inadvertently pressing my chest against Josh, tight as we were against each other.

His sudden intake of breath told me I wasn't the only one affected by our current situation. The hardness pressing into both my backside and low on my belly confirmed it. Josh's hands left my shoulders and replaced Ethan's on my waist as Ethan's warm hands slid down over my T-shirt, stopping on my hips.

Ethan's forehead came to rest on the back of my head, and he cursed softly. "If she doesn't tell us what this is about soon, I'm going to break the 'no skin contact' rule. In a big way."

"Eve. Please." This time Josh actually did plead with me, punctuating it with a squeeze of his hands on my waist.

I was torn. My Light-driven instinct was to please the members of my Bond, to strengthen the connection. But what the hell was I supposed to do when I would end up disappointing one of them regardless? Plus I had no idea how to actually tell them. "This is so hard. You guys have put me in a really tight spot."

Ethan groaned, and they both chuckled. I realized what I had just said and laughed. At least some of the tension was dispelled.

191

"What I mean to say is, I don't want to disappoint you or let you down. It feels painful to think about. But I also don't want to disappoint Tyler or let him down. That's *just as painful.*"

I equally hoped that they would get the idea and that they would be more confused and drop it.

"Holy shit." Of course Josh got it right away.

"What?" Ethan was nuzzling his nose in my hair. I wasn't sure he'd even heard what I said.

"She's his Vital. Tyler is part of our Bond."

"What? Are you sure?"

"Yes." Josh and I answered at the same time.

"I don't know how to feel about this," Ethan said. Josh just stared at me, looking as if he wasn't sure what to make of it either.

And now I understood why Tyler had wanted to tell them himself. Would they be angry? Would they be disappointed in me?

Ethan must have suspected our connection when we first shook hands, and Josh had thought I was his for several weeks, even if I'd had no idea what was going on. A couple days ago they'd had to deal with the fact that they would be sharing me. Now they would be sharing me with Tyler too. Was there enough of me to go around? Could I handle that much Light coursing through me?

And what would this mean for *their* relationship? These guys were like family—in some ways more than family. I didn't want to be the thing that came between them. Josh was already bothered that Ethan had an excuse to touch me in public when he couldn't. That didn't sit well with me either; I wanted to give them equal attention, equal Light.

How would that work with Tyler in the mix? Considering our current position—the guys pressed up against me, all of us breathing hard, using every ounce of self-control to avoid the skin contact we knew was unsafe—it was clear they were interested in a romantic and physical relationship. And while I needed some time to get my head around being with more than one person, I wanted them too. How was I supposed to keep things even when Tyler had made it clear he wanted our relationship to be platonic?

The tight proximity of two warm bodies I'd craved moments ago suddenly felt stifling, and I swallowed hard and pushed on Josh's chest. He backed away immediately, and I saw he was staring at Ethan over my head. While I'd been having my quiet mental freak out, they'd been having a silent conversation. The look on his face was incomprehensible. How was he able to read me so clearly when I couldn't decipher his feelings at all? It wasn't fair.

"If there had to be another one . . ." Josh looked down at me as he spoke, but it was Ethan who finished the thought.

". . . better him than anyone else." I heard a smile in his voice as he said it.

Predictably, Josh saw the inner turmoil written on my face and gave a confident smile. "It's OK, Eve. I can see why Gabe might have been wary of our reaction, but we're OK with this."

"Really?" I stepped back into his arms, and he wrapped me up in a tight hug.

"Yes. It's going to be an adjustment, but hey, what else is new? And like Ethan said, better Gabe than some random."

"Yeah, don't go fusing any randoms to our Bond," Ethan piped up before stepping forward and encircling us both in his big arms. "Group hug!"

We all laughed, and the heavy weight in my chest lifted a little.

After checking that the coast was clear, we left our hidey-hole and walked off campus to the café where Alec had gotten my latte. We took the morning off, having amazing coffees and then lunch, chatting about lighter things, before heading back for afternoon classes.

As the three of us walked back to campus, I got a message from Dot asking where I was. I shot her a quick reply, telling her I was on my way back and would see her in our biology lecture, but as we came through the front gates of the Institute, she came marching up to us with an amused grin on her face.

She was wearing black-and-silver boots that looked as if they were part of a video game character's armor, and she'd paired them with a pinafore dress—with a massive matching bow in her hair—and a studded choker. She looked like a toddler assassin, and the look on my face was just as amused as hers. I was amused by her outfit; I had no idea why *she* was amused.

"So, suddenly you're a Variant and you're dating my cousin. Someone's been busy." She nudged Ethan out of the way and matched our pace as we kept walking to class.

"Dot, I'm sorry I didn't tell you. It's just . . ." I had no idea how to end the sentence.

"It's all good. Gabe told me he would be meeting with you this morning to give you your test results, so I knew before you did. He wanted me to keep an eye on you once the news was out." She giggled, and I laughed nervously along with her. It was better that she thought she found out before I did.

"This one, however"—she turned around to glare at Ethan, who managed to look sheepish and satisfied with himself at the same time—"failed to mention he was boning *my* new friend."

"Look, it's all kind of new and—wait. Boning? Um, that's not . . ."

Ethan's booming voice drowned me out. "*Your* new friend? I saw her first Dot."

"Technically, Gabe saw her first," Josh cut in.

"Gabe doesn't count, bro." Ethan laughed, and the two of them started bickering as Dot looped her arm through mine and spoke in a more serious tone.

"It's all good, Eve. Considering his reputation, I can understand why you weren't telling everyone you guys were seeing each other. And I can totally understand why you would want to go public with it now that the cat's out of the bag about your DNA test."

"Yeah . . . wait. What?" The stuff about Ethan's reputation made sense, but she'd lost me when she started sounding paranoid about my DNA test.

"Yeah, the next few days might be a little . . ." She waved her hand in the air and gave me a pitying look, making me even more worried. "Most students start here at the beginning of semester, and everyone's test results come out at once, resulting in a frenzy of information sharing and speculation, with no one person singled out. You arrived at the end of the year, so your results are going to be the talk of campus for a while. People are going to want to suss you out, so expect some extra attention. It's why Gabe told me your results ahead of time. He was hoping it wouldn't get out for a day or two, but he underestimated the power of gossip. Welcome to my world."

I groaned, hoping she was exaggerating, but even as we approached our lecture, I noticed more eyes on me than I'd ever been comfortable with. With a sinking feeling, it dawned on me that the people staring this morning when Ethan had tucked me under his arm weren't interested only in our relationship—they were interested in my newfound status. I was no longer a Dime, and the whole student population knew it.

That was *exactly* why Ethan had put on the affectionate boyfriend routine—to send the message I was already his. He had outed us before I'd even had a chance to express an opinion on the matter, without asking if I might have one. I was more than a little annoyed at him but decided to deal with one problem at a time. My sudden popularity was a more pressing issue.

By the time I walked out of my last class for the day, I was already over it. Several people I'd never met before had come up to talk to me. Some of them came right out and said they'd heard about my test results and proceeded to tell me about their own abilities or lack thereof. Some of them just acted extra friendly, inviting me to hang out with them and asking if I would be attending some gala happening soon.

All of them made a point of shaking my hand, and it didn't take me long to figure out why. They were making skin contact to check if I was their Vital or Variant—to see if we were connected.

The boys and Dot did their best to run interference, chatting to people who approached and trying to take some of the attention off me. I was grateful they were trying to shield me, but there was only so much they could do. Yes, these people had ulterior motives, but they weren't technically doing anything wrong.

Dot took it all in stride, but Ethan and Josh became more and more agitated as the afternoon wore on. Josh managed to cover it well, keeping a neutral, bored expression on his face, but the tick in his cheek was incessant. Ethan became visibly surly, his usually light and carefree demeanor disappearing behind a frown and crossed arms.

None of my protectors had been in my last class, and I'd had to deal with the vultures on my own. My own arms were crossed over my chest and my head was turned down as I exited the lecture hall. If I avoided eye contact, maybe no one would have an excuse to start a conversation.

I was wrong.

"Eve, right?"

The overly friendly male voice came from close by, and I groaned even as I looked up. Ethan, Josh, and Dot were standing together just a few feet away, but my view of them was blocked by a broad chest as a guy about my age stepped into my path.

"Yeah, hi." I wasn't even trying to hide the disinterest in my voice.

He chuckled. "Long day, huh?"

In answer I just stared at him, waiting for him to get it over with. He had honey-blond hair and looked friendly enough, but I was not in the mood.

"Look, I get it. I just want to introduce myself. I'm Rick, and this is my ability."

He held his hand out, just as I'd seen Ethan do many times, but instead of fire, what appeared between his fingers was electricity, sparking and darting around in a mesmerizing dance. My fatigue with all the unwanted attention warred with my fascination for unique abilities, and I couldn't help a small, amused smile pulling at my lips as I watched the blue bolts moving in jerky movements between his fingers.

My view of Rick's ability was interrupted by a bright ball of fire shooting between us. Rick laughed and dropped his hand, the electricity disappearing, as I jumped, startled.

Ethan stepped up behind me, wrapping a possessive arm over my front and pulling me against him.

"Hey, Rick." He sounded friendly, but I could hear a hint of tension in his voice. "I see you've met my *girlfriend*."

Josh and Dot joined us as Rick answered, still friendly and seemingly oblivious to Ethan's hostility. "Hey, Kid. Yeah, I was just introducing myself." He extended his hand.

I shook it as quickly as I could and pulled my hand back, shrinking into Ethan's warmth. I had been outraged he'd all but staked his claim on me this morning without discussing it with me, but after the afternoon I'd had, I was glad he'd done it. I shuddered to think how much worse my day would have been if I'd had to deal with things on my own.

Of course I felt nothing when I touched Rick's hand, and he wouldn't have either. But apparently he was in the mood to stir some shit.

"Hmm. That was quick. Not sure if I felt a little something or—"

Ethan tensed, but before he could react, before Rick had even finished his sentence, Zara barreled into our little group, Beth hot on her heels.

"Beat it. I need to talk to my friend." She looked kind of mad, speaking over her shoulder to Rick.

Beth kept throwing her furtive glances and only waved at me in hello. I waved back as Rick laughed.

"Excuse me," he said. "We were having a conversation."

"And now it's over. I said leave, you overgrown toaster."

Dot chuckled, and Ethan's big shoulders shook behind me as he tried to contain his own mirth.

"God," Rick said, "you're such a bitch, Zara."

"Thank you." She smiled at him; I was pretty sure she genuinely took it as a compliment.

"Whatever. I have to go anyway. See you around, Eve." Rick winked at me and walked off.

Zara turned on me. "Why didn't you tell us you were a Variant?"

"Zara," Beth soothed, "come on, I'm sure that—"

"She only just found out, you psycho," Dot interrupted. "She got her test results this morning."

Zara rounded on her. "Why are you even here, Dot? What, now that she's officially a Variant, you think she's yours? She might not even have an ability. Are you going to drop her as fast as you did me when you realize she's not special?"

"What? I didn't drop you. You're the one that stopped coming to things or answering my calls. Don't put your identity crisis shit on me. Or Eve for that matter."

They were beginning to raise their voices, and I really didn't want to give the Bradford Hills gossip mill more to talk about. In one day, I'd found out I had not two but *three* Variants in my Bond, been claimed by Ethan, and been accosted by half the student population. Now two of my three friends were about to have a public showdown over old grievances brought up by my current situation.

As someone who had spent her whole childhood pretty much alone, I was not used to this level of attention.

"Enough!" I yelled, stepping out of Ethan's arms to look at them all. "I can't handle this shit. I'm leaving. *Alone*. Can I get, like, two freaking seconds to process? I just . . . Dammit!"

They all stared at me, stunned.

Charlie chose that moment to walk up, oblivious to what was going on. "Hey. What have I missed?"

"Where the hell have you been?" It didn't seem fair that he'd managed to avoid all the drama of the day and was now standing there, casually unaffected by it all.

"I've been in the library all day working on my thesis. What's going on?"

"Eve's test results spread around campus like wildfire, and she's been swatting people away like flies all day. Dot and Zara are finally having it out about why they stopped being friends, and Ethan and Eve are officially a couple," Josh supplied helpfully, giving me an understanding look. I had no doubt he understood what I was feeling—he'd proven himself to be very good at it—and it must have been frustrating for him not to be able to do anything about it in public. Being reminded of another complication in my life only added to my foul mood.

Charlie whistled low, stuffing his hands in his pockets. "A bit then."

"I'm leaving." I didn't wait for a response from anyone. I just walked off toward my res hall, trying to forget the day for just a few minutes and focus on the swaying branches of the trees lining the walkway, and the sound of the rustling leaves.

Charlie caught up to me quickly, matching my pace in silence, giving me space. Which was exactly what I needed.

"How much did you already know?" I asked once I was feeling a bit calmer.

"I've known about your test results as long as Gabe. I do some work for Melior Group in their cyber division—it gives me access to certain . . . information."

He gave me a cheeky smile. The access he was talking about wasn't, I suspected, entirely legal. I shook my head at him but smiled a little despite myself.

"I suspected there was something between you and either Ethan or Josh, but that was only confirmed today."

"Yeah . . ." Ethan *or* Josh. I wanted so badly to tell him it was both, to have at least one thing off my chest, but I kept my mouth shut.

We reached the front of my building, and he turned to face me. "The attention will die down as the novelty does, and Ethan's overprotectiveness will go with it. Dot and Zara will sort their own shit out—that has nothing to do with you and has been a long time coming. And we'll get you through all this new Variant stuff. Everything will be OK, Eve."

"Thanks, Charlie." I gave him a hug. It was exactly what I needed—someone to cut through the shit and remind me that, as overwhelming as this felt now, it would pass.

We said goodbye, and I headed upstairs, locking myself in my room for some much needed alone time.

I went to bed feeling better about the situation but utterly exhausted and a little wary after the crazy day. I was not at all superstitious, putting all my faith in science, but a sense of foreboding still hung over my head as I lay on my bed, staring at nothing. My life at Bradford Hills was about to get more complicated.

So much for focusing on my studies and having a few quiet years while I got my degree.

SIXTEEN

Ethan's face was frozen in shock, his amber eyes wide, his hands out at his sides as if to steady himself. There wasn't much he could do about his current situation though, floating as he was, eight feet off the ground in Josh's bedroom.

"Shit shit shit," Josh muttered, his eyes as wide as Ethan's. He held his arms out toward him, keeping him elevated with his telekinetic ability.

I was standing off to the side with my lower back pressed against the couch, my hands over my mouth. I had done my part for this training session—I had identified the Light inside me, monitored the levels, and transferred a specific amount to Josh through our hands. All I could do now was stay out of the way.

Tyler stepped up to Josh with slow, deliberate movements, but his posture was relaxed and confident. "It's OK. You've got this, Josh."

"What?" Josh sounded much less calm. "It doesn't feel like I've got it, Gabe!"

"You do. You're holding him up. He's safe for now."

"What if I drop him?"

"You won't. You have enough Light, courtesy of our Vital." He flashed me an affectionate smile, and I just stared back, wide eyed. "If you were straining or overusing your ability, Eve would have noticed. She'd be feeling a pull to you. Are you feeling a pull, Eve?"

I dropped my hands to my throat to answer. "Nope! You're doing great, Josh."

"See, you're doing great." Tyler gave Josh an easy smile, and I could see some of the tension in his back release. "Now, take a deep breath and focus."

Tyler encouraged and guided Josh until he gently and precisely lowered Ethan to his bed, unharmed, and we all breathed a massive sigh of relief. Josh rested his hands on his knees and took several deep breaths.

Half my evenings and most of my weekends were now spent at the Zacarias mansion, training with Ethan and Josh. It was the safest place to do so without being discovered, but we still had to be careful. Dot and Charlie were close with the boys and spent a lot of time at the house, not to mention all the gardeners, cleaners, and other staff that were ever present.

Josh's ability appeared to be limited to items he could see, so we were able to close ourselves into a room and practice without fear of him accidentally floating one of the staff out of a window. It was a little more difficult to find time to train with Ethan. Tyler insisted we do it in the pool for safety reasons, but the only time there was no one around was at night. Luckily, he too was getting better at controlling his ability, and I was hoping Tyler would let us practice outside the pool soon. Some nights it was way too cold to be outside in a bikini.

I gave Josh a reassuring pat on the back as he straightened. The fabric of his Green Day T-shirt felt soft under my palm. He was in the comfort of his home, and I'd learned that meant he would be in one of his seemingly endless supply of band Ts.

"I'm so sorry, Kid." Josh still looked a little worried.

"It's all good, bro!" Ethan scooted to the edge of the bed. "But there are healthier ways to express your jealousy over the fact that *I'm* Eve's boyfriend and not you." He flashed us both a cheeky grin.

"You mean *pretend* boyfriend, right? You haven't actually asked me out yet," I reminded him.

"Uh huh. Sure thing, dumpling."

"Come here, dimples, you have a cobweb in your hair."

After Ethan's calling me "babe," the nickname thing had stuck around, and now we were in an ongoing game where we called each other by a different pet name every time. We hadn't run out yet, but they were starting to get more and more inventive.

Tyler told us to take a break while he made a few calls and headed downstairs. The three of us collapsed on Josh's couch and he put some music on while we chatted.

As the boys started bickering about something—it was both their favorite pastime *and* how they showed affection—I slipped out and made my way to the end of the hallway. To Alec's bedroom door.

I had been keeping my eyes open for an opportunity to approach him about the night of the crash again, but he'd started actively avoiding me, so I wasn't having much luck. Tyler had mentioned he was home. I just hoped he wasn't sleeping.

Wringing my hands, I mentally chastised myself for my own nervousness. This whole situation had turned into something way bigger than it ever needed to be. Part of that was his fault for making it so difficult, but part of it was mine for letting it get to me so much.

Steeling my shoulders, I knocked firmly on his door. My heart beat a little faster at the sound of movement on the other side, but I took a deep breath, determined to look calm and confident.

He opened the door in a towel. All the things I was going to say to him, all the words I had practiced for over a year, just flew out of my head, chased away by broad shoulders, corded muscles, countless tattoos, and that towel, slung dangerously low.

"Can I help you?" His voice was low but still devoid of that smooth sweetness I remembered from the night of the crash.

I snapped my eyes up to his face, feeling like an idiot for staring. The eyebrow with the scar quirked just a little in amusement, his lips pulled into a crooked smirk.

"Hey, um . . . sorry, I just . . . uh . . ." Words were eluding me, and now embarrassment was making it even more difficult to get my shit together.

Usually, by this stage, he would have closed the door in my face, but apparently he wanted to watch me squirm.

"Yes? What's up?" The cruel little smirk grew as he leaned one arm on the doorway and grabbed the edge of his towel with the other, pulling it up but then dragging it just a little lower and leaving his thumb tucked into it. Naturally, my eyes were drawn to the newly exposed sliver of skin, and he chuckled.

He was enjoying torturing me.

Just as the outrage was about to overpower my ridiculous stupor, Dana sidled up to him, wearing one of his black T-shirts, her blonde hair all messed up.

What had I been thinking, trying to force my thanks onto him by going to his bedroom?

Dana looked at me with raised eyebrows, as if asking "what?" but Alec's face had gone blank.

When I *still* didn't say anything, frozen to the spot by the shock of Alec's shirtlessness and the sheer awkwardness of the situation, she simply turned her face into his neck, completely ignoring me. Her hand reached for his where it was still holding the towel, and her elegant fingers inched their way under the fabric.

Alec used his free hand to slam the door closed, but it wasn't in my face; I had already turned to leave. The overtly sexual act was apparently all I'd needed to snap me out of it.

Instead of heading back to Josh's room, I went to the stairs, jogging halfway down the first flight and plonking myself down. I needed a moment.

With a low, frustrated growl, I banged the side of my head against the railing a few times. Alec had been a dick about the whole thing, purposely making me more uncomfortable, but Alec was always a dick about everything. And Dana's dismissive attitude had been downright rude, but maybe she just wasn't a morning person.

I had been the one to intrude. *I* was the one who had created the opportunity for the awkwardness and the rudeness.

I was still sitting there, berating myself, when unintelligible shouting came from above. Alec's voice boomed from behind a closed door, then the same door slammed, then footsteps hurried in my direction.

I shot up, not wanting to get caught on the stairs, but before I could make my getaway, Dana bounded past, taking the stairs at breakneck speed and not even slowing down to acknowledge me.

When I heard Ethan calling my name, I headed back to my guys.

A few days later, as I walked toward the front gates of Bradford Hills Institute, I caught another venomous look from a girl with short black hair and long, toned legs. I knew Ethan had a reputation, but the number of girls I was getting dirty looks from surprised me. I hadn't said anything to him, not eager for him to confirm exactly how many women he'd slept with.

According to Dot, Ethan had never stayed with a girl as long as he had with me, and they were wondering what made me so special. Sometimes out loud, as I walked past. If they only knew . . .

I ignored the black-haired girl, keeping my eyes trained ahead and focusing on the feel of the warm sun on my back. I was on my way to the Zacarias mansion to get ready for an exclusive gala dinner. Josh had offered to pick me up, but I had insisted on walking, wanting to enjoy the nice weather.

When I rounded the bend in the path, I saw him leaning on the massive gate. His yellow shirt was perfectly fitted, the sleeves rolled up to the elbows in a way that was unusually casual for him when in public. His dirty blond hair was perfectly set in a neat style, and his head was bent over a small paperback.

I slowed to take him in for a moment before he noticed me, a smile playing on my lips. Of course they would never let me walk to their house alone, unprotected, but I couldn't be mad about getting to catch Josh absorbed in a novel, looking like the promise of summer in his cheerful shirt and black sunglasses.

I walked right past him, keeping my pace steady and fighting the mirth bubbling up inside, threatening to spill over in a fit of giggles.

He caught up to me almost immediately, tucking the novel into his back pocket and flashing a brilliant smile.

"You couldn't wait until I finished the chapter?" He laughed, shoving his hands into his pockets. We still couldn't hold hands, as much as I wanted to.

"Oh, hey, Josh," I said with exaggerated surprise, and that time we both laughed.

We walked in companionable silence for a while and then started chatting about classes and books and what had been happening over the past few weeks.

"How are the Reds?" he asked. "Zara still giving you the cold shoulder"

"Nah, it's all sorted now." Zara had eventually apologized for dragging me into a fight that was between her and Dot. I quickly accepted her apology and told her it wasn't my intention to deceive her; it was a flat out lie and I felt bad about it, but now that I knew my guys could be in danger if our secret came out, my resolve to keep them safe was unwavering.

Once we cleared the air, we had a group hug—instigated by Beth. She could have thrown her hands up and avoided the whole situation—it had even less to do with her than it did with me—but she helped Zara work through her emotions and encouraged us to talk it out. She was a good friend.

Things went back to normal with my roomies, but Zara and Dot's relationship got decidedly more icy. They were both loud, strong, and stubborn, and even Beth couldn't get them to sit down and talk.

"Ethan still at baseball practice?" I asked Josh.

"Football," he corrected, chuckling. "He should be back any minute now, but he can take his time. I like having you to myself."

We shared a loaded look but didn't let it linger. Being this close and not being able to reach out and touch him was torture. Time alone with either of them was rare, but at least I could be affectionate with Ethan in public.

He had attempted to apologize for being an overprotective oaf that day, but I'd stopped him halfway through his awkward speech. His hulking presence had turned out to be a lifesaver, and I could understand why he'd done it.

Josh cleared his throat. "How are your sessions with Gabe going?"

"Yeah, really good. I'm actually starting to like meditating."

The meditation was just one part of my new routine. During the day I attended my science classes and went to my intensive tutoring sessions with Tyler. We were breezing through my Variant studies theory and spent half of each session working on my Light control. Tyler talked me through how to quiet my mind and focus on identifying that low thrum of the Light coursing through me.

It was pure energy, unadulterated power. Now that I knew what I was looking for, I realized it had always been there; it had always been part of me, under the surface, waiting to find the Variants with the abilities it was created to sustain.

I practiced transferring Light to him in controlled, deliberate amounts. It was always through our hands, and he would always pull away as soon as it was done, going to sit behind his desk.

"Do you think your control is improving?" I asked.

"Yeah, I guess. It'll take time."

"I think you're doing great. I mean, you haven't accidentally floated anyone up to the ceiling in days."

He grinned. "Oh, come on! That happened once."

It *had* only happened that one time with an actual person, but it had happened plenty of other times with inanimate objects. Tyler was always there to keep us calm and focused though.

It was fascinating to watch Tyler's natural leadership shine through and the others take his lead. Apparently, he also had serious clout with Bradford Hills Institute, because no one questioned his decision to pull me from half my classes and tutor me himself. Zara, however, did raise it one day over lunch, a suspicious look in her eyes. I shrugged and played it off as the Institute's decision—that because I'd had so little contact with Variants growing up, they wanted me to learn all I could in case my ability manifested.

She grumbled a bit about "Variants digging their claws into me" and "indoctrination," but thankfully, she dropped it.

Beth, on the other hand, was a hopeless romantic, had multiple crushes, and devoured romance novels like I did science journals. She jumped in, gushing about how I got to "spend hours every day locked in a room with Tyler Gabriel."

The conversation had then turned to which guys were single, descending into a gossip session, and I'd breathed an internal sigh of relief. Every time I had to actively lie to them, my heart would race, and I would have to work really hard to make sure I looked calm and casual. It was exhausting.

At least the gossip was no longer about me. Mostly. When it appeared I wasn't Bonded to anyone and there was no sign of me having an ability, the attention had slowly died down.

The current hot topic was tonight's exclusive Variant society event. Bradford Hills Institute, with sponsorship from the Melior Group, was hosting a gala in Manhattan. The black-tie event was a fundraiser for Senator Anderson's upcoming re-election campaign. The New York senator, the woman I had read about online, was one of the only Variants in the Senate and a Bradford Hills Institute alumnus.

As we started walking up their long, tree-lined driveway, Josh raised the event with a visible cringe. "You still dreading tonight?" He already knew the answer. I'd been complaining about it since realizing I would have to go.

Anyone who was anyone in American Variant society would be flashing their cash at this gala, and most Variants my age would be using it as one of those networking events Zara had spoken about with such derision. All my fellow Variant students were excited to meet other young Variants in the hope they might find a Bond.

I already had my Bond, so I had very little interest in the whole thing. Of course, no one knew that, so the guys were insisting I attend in order to avoid suspicion. I'd tried to argue, but Tyler had put his foot down, and since he was in charge of pretty much everything, I had to go.

"Oh, no! I can't wait!" I laid the sarcasm on thick, giving Josh a wide fake smile before rolling my eyes and deadpanning, "I would rather listen to a climate change debate." There was nothing left to debate—the science was solid and definitive.

"Wow. OK." Josh chuckled, "I know you don't want to go, but I'm looking forward to spending some extra time with you. And you'll finally meet Ethan and Alec's uncle."

I had yet to meet the elusive Lucian Zacarias. The boys had told me he would be at the event tonight but was flying in too late to make an appearance at home, instead staying at their apartment in the city—because of course they had an apartment in the city. On the Upper East Side. Where else?

"Yeah, it'll be good to meet him." I gave Josh a genuine smile as we climbed the stairs to the front door. All the guys had a lot of respect and affection for their absent father figure.

"Good." He smiled back, opening the door for me. "Now, can I keep you to myself a little longer before Dot disappears you? What takes all afternoon to get ready?"

I had no idea, but Dot had insisted. I dared not defy her for fear of having a bear carry me in its claws to her tiny, waiting feet.

I did hope, however, that she had a dress I could borrow. Even though Zara had flat out refused to go, she'd given me some details on what to expect. This particular event was one of the big ones. It was not a "jeans and nice top" kind of party.

I had exactly two dresses in my meager wardrobe. One was a T-shirt dress, which was too casual, and the other was my mother's summer dress. One of a few items that had been salvaged from the plane crash, it had big yellow and red poppies on a black background, and the full skirt fanned out if you twirled on the spot. I couldn't bring myself to wear it yet, and even if I could, this event was no more a "summer dress" event than a "jeans and nice top" event. I needed a gown.

"Beats me." I laughed. "But I'm happy to put it off a little longer."

"Come. I have something for you." Excitement sharpened his features as he took off his sunglasses.

"Oh?" My curiosity was piqued.

My sneakers squeaked softly on the polished marble of the entrance hall as I followed him into a room on the right.

It was a formal sitting room. On the opposite wall was a massive fireplace; in front of it, a wide glass coffee table and two velvet upholstered couches facing each other. After a quick glance to either side, Josh shut the doors behind us.

As soon as the doors were securely closed, he took two long strides and wrapped his arms around me. Dropping my bag to the floor, I returned the hug eagerly and pressed my cheek into his shoulder, taking a deep breath. His crisp white shirt smelled like clean laundry warmed by the sun.

In public, Ethan always had an arm slung over my shoulders as we walked, a hand on my knee as we sat together, a palm to my back as we passed through a door; Josh had to suppress his instinct to touch me or even look at me too long. But behind closed doors, it was Josh pulling me back to lean against him as we listened to Tyler explain the next exercise, hugging me tight after a long day, pulling me into his lap as we took a rare break to just hang out and listen to music. As we became closer, the Bond deepening naturally, it was getting more and more frustrating to have to keep a distance.

"I missed you," Josh mumbled into my hair.

"I saw you yesterday in class, you goof." I chuckled, but I knew what he meant. Having to sit side by side and be constantly wary that someone could be paying too much attention was torture. It was almost worse than not seeing each other at all. "I missed you too," I added, because I really had.

We stood like that for a few moments, just holding each other.

My relationship with my Bond was still undefined and confusing, but I couldn't deny that I craved each of their company. I needed Ethan's infectious positivity; Josh's observant, caring attention; Tyler's confident leadership and challenging conversation. The Light was pushing me toward my Variants, but I needed them in ways that had nothing to do with the Light.

With a soft kiss to the corner of my mouth, he released me and reached for a flat, rectangular box—big enough to fit two of my science textbooks—that had been sitting on the coffee table.

"What did you do? What is this?" I wasn't sure how I felt about impromptu gifts from my kind of, not really boyfriend, whom I was definitely attracted to.

"Open it." With the excitement in his face, you would think he was the one who'd just been presented with a surprise gift.

I undid the black silk bow and lifted the silver lid, placing it on the table. Tissue paper—held together by a little round sticker with "Dior" embossed on it—concealed the box's contents.

I hesitated. I may not have had a keen interest in fashion, but even I knew Dior. This was a very expensive gift, probably more than I could guess at. I wasn't sure I could accept something so extravagant.

"Stop." As usual, Josh knew what I was fretting about. "Please don't let something as petty as money ruin this moment. I got it not because it's expensive. I got it because it's beautiful, and I want to see you in it. And also because I figured you would need something to wear tonight. Let me do this for you."

I could have argued. I could have told him it was just too much; there are plenty of beautiful things that don't cost more than an average car. But I didn't want to ruin the moment, so I chose to accept it graciously. Once again, Josh had done something thoughtful for me.

I smiled at him and shook my head, tearing the tissue paper and lifting the dress out. It tumbled down between us in a cascade of soft fabric and delicate beading. It was easily the most beautiful thing I had ever held. The dress was a dark, gunmetal gray, the bottom of it covered in rich emerald-green beading, dense at the bottom and getting sparser toward the middle.

I launched myself at Josh, squishing the garment between us, and he dropped the box to return the hug. Wrapping my arms around his neck, I pressed my mouth to his enthusiastically, and as naturally as I'd initiated, he responded. His arms circled my middle, and he deepened the kiss, sighing with what could not be mistaken for anything other than satisfaction and relief.

It was the first time we'd kissed since the night of the party, but just as it had that night, it felt as if we'd been doing it for years. Our lips moved against each other in perfect rhythm, our bodies pressing together as though they were made to fit.

As I reveled in the moment, thoroughly enjoying the new level of intimacy, I vaguely registered the logical part of my brain reminding me why we hadn't been kissing all this time. The kiss had been spontaneous, and I hadn't made sure my Light flow was locked down.

As the kiss gained a new level of heated intensity, the alarm bells in my head got louder too. The Light was flowing freely and fast out of me and straight into Josh.

He grunted in frustration before pulling away and looking at me, the green in his eyes more vibrant than I'd ever seen it. "You can't go kissing me like that."

He had a point. The coffee table next to us was floating in midair. Josh focused his gaze on it, managing to lower it to the ground gently and without smashing the giant piece of glass that composed the top.

I grinned at him. "No harm done! See? You're getting better at that."

"Mmmhmm," he murmured, no longer listening. Instead he buried his face in my neck, running his lips feather soft up to my ear. "If that's the reaction I get, I'm buying you a dress every damn day."

"Don't you dare." I meant it to sound firm, but it came out on a whisper. Someone had to put a stop to this, or I really would run out of time to get ready. I took a deep breath and nudged his shoulder. "Hey, you're ruining my new dress, you brute."

I felt him smile against my neck, sending another shiver down my spine, and then he backed off.

Before he stepped away completely, I dropped one last chaste kiss on his cheek. "Thank you, Josh. I really do love it."

"You're welcome," he said before moving over to the double doors to make sure the coast was clear.

He took the box with him and disappeared into the back of the house as I gingerly carried my new dress up the stairs. I was smiling to myself, the feeling of Josh's soft lips still present on mine, so I didn't notice until I was halfway up that Dot was standing on the landing, hands on her hips and a deep frown on her face, her damp black hair falling in a mess around her shoulders.

My heart sank. How much had she seen? I was supposed to be Ethan's girlfriend, yet I had just come out of a room with Josh, and if he was having as much trouble containing his smile as I was, we were definitely busted.

SEVENTEEN

"Finally!" Dot huffed, throwing her arms up and letting them flop down at her sides. "Where have you been? We're behind schedule already."

"There's a schedule?"

"Come on. I need you to help me straighten my hair. Do you know what you're wearing?"

She took off, climbing the second set of stairs to the level where all the guys' bedrooms were. I followed, breathing a sigh of relief. Maybe she hadn't seen anything after all.

At the top of the stairs, in answer to her question, I held up my new dress, letting the delicate fabric tumble down between us.

She gasped and took it from me. "I love it! When did you have time to go shopping?"

I shrugged, hoping she wouldn't press me too much on it, and we headed toward one of the spare rooms—the one she used when she stayed the night.

Even though we were "behind schedule," instead of following her in, I found myself gravitating toward Ethan's room.

Josh's room seemed to be where everyone congregated during our rare moments of freedom, but Ethan's room was the same size and had almost as impressive a bookshelf. But where Josh's shelves were crammed with books and music, Ethan's were bursting with cookbooks.

I'd discovered Ethan's love of cooking one night when I came over for training. Ethan was at practice for one of his many sports, so the session had been between only me and Josh, with Tyler supervising. It was around dinnertime when we finished and headed downstairs, the smell of something incredible hitting me before I even entered the kitchen.

Ethan was at the stove, several steaming pots and pans in front of him as he expertly bustled between them, lifting the lid to peer into this one, stirring that one, adding something to a third. He looked completely in his element and was so engrossed he didn't even hear us come in.

"So, my 'boyfriend' cooks!" I used air quotes around the word *boyfriend*. "The plot thickens."

He looked up, flashing me a quick smile but keeping his attention on the food. "I don't think I could get any thicker, babe," he spoke over his shoulder as he grabbed something out of the fridge. "It would just be gratuitous to go any bigger. People would think I was on steroids."

I laughed and took a seat at the bench.

"Ooh, gratuitous! Someone learned a big new word," Josh teased, sitting next to me.

Ethan just flipped him off before dipping a spoon into one of the pots and bringing it to my lips. I let him spoon the sauce into my mouth, immediately closing my eyes and moaning at the taste. It was creamy and rich but not heavy, with an amazing earthy flavor.

I opened my eyes to find them both staring at me with amused smiles.

"Ethan, this is incredible," I declared, already wanting more.

The usually confident guy surprised me with his quiet and sheepish "Thanks."

"You'll stay for dinner then?" Josh asked, and I nodded enthusiastically. Ethan could feed me any damn time he wanted.

He may have been big and naturally talented at sports, but Ethan's real passion was food. I learned more about it over dinner, as he told me all about the dishes we were eating, what he wanted to try to cook next, and what his favorites were.

After dinner he took me to his room to show me all the cookbooks. I couldn't believe how many he had. He told me he had bought some but that most were his mother's. She was a chef before she died, and they used to cook together when he was little. My heart broke over the bittersweet look that came into his eyes, but he didn't speak about his parents very long, changing the conversation to something lighter. I understood that—I didn't like talking about my mother either. I was glad he'd felt comfortable enough to tell me a little bit about his.

I enjoyed learning about each of them as we spent more time together. I learned that Ethan could cook and that he had a sweet side under that bravado. I learned that Josh liked to read with music on—actually, Josh liked to do almost everything with music on. I learned that Tyler was a workaholic, but he loved his job, and that he was a bit of control freak.

The door to Ethan's room swung open just as I reached it, bringing me back into the present. He stood on the other side, barefoot and shirtless, in nothing but jeans, slung low on his hips.

"Hello, dearest." Another new pet name, delivered with a bright smile.

"Hey, sexy," I shot back without even thinking about it, my focus on his broad chest and the way his fire tattoo wrapped around his shoulder. I had seen him shirtless plenty of times, but there was something more intimate about it at the threshold of his bedroom.

At hearing my choice of nickname, his smile widened. "Damn. Now I can't use that one. I was saving it for a special occasion."

He turned, giving me a view of his back, the muscles rippling as he reached for a T-shirt on his bed. I followed him into the room.

"Were you? That's good to know." Even though we joked and flirted all the time, somehow it felt heavier in that moment, less lighthearted.

He took his time pulling the white T-shirt over his head. Then he turned to face me, and, just as with Josh, we seemed to gravitate toward each other.

He pulled me into his arms, and I had to lift up onto my toes to reach his shoulders and return the hug—which wasn't a simple hug for long. Within seconds, his lips were on mine.

I quickly forced myself to pull away, making a conscious effort to bring my Light flow back under control. I couldn't indulge in this kiss as I had with Josh. While Josh's ability could be destructive, Ethan's was downright dangerous.

He tightened his hold on my waist.

"Ethan." I gave him a warning look. I couldn't speak about the danger with Dot so close by.

He frowned, loosening his grip a little. "What's happening?" he whispered, his face still only inches from mine. "Why . . . ?"

He trailed off, but I knew what he was asking. Why were we so drawn to each other so suddenly?

"It might be because I kissed Josh just before," I whispered back. "The Light. It wants to deepen the Bond evenly. I . . ." *I want to deepen the Bond.*

"Did you?" The cheeky smile had returned. He wasn't jealous that I'd kissed his best friend; he was pleased by it. I smiled back, intrigued at his reaction. Maybe it had something to do with the Light fusing us *all* closer together and not just deepening my Bond to each of them individually?

That's how Dot found us—holding each other and whispering.

"For fuck's sake, Eve. Did I not say we were on a schedule? You can make out later."

She marched over, yanked me away from Ethan with a vicelike grip on my forearm, and dragged me into the next room.

Thankfully, instead of teasing me or asking question about our relationship, she just launched into talking about dresses and makeup and asking my opinion on which shoes she should wear.

We put some music on and took our time doing each other's hair and talking about pointless things. Squiggles was curled up on the bed, watching us with a contented look on her furry little face. From time to time Dot would look at her with concentration, and Squiggles would spring into action, retrieving a tissue from the bathroom or digging a tube of mascara out of a bag across the room. It was adorable and handy at the same time.

As I was halfway through straightening Dot's silky black hair, Charlie wandered past the room and stuck his head in.

"Charles!" Dot yelled before he'd even had a chance to say "hello." "Come!"

"Dorothy." He glared at her but walked toward us anyway. "What do you want?"

She glared back at him through the mirror as he gave me a kiss on the cheek in greeting. "Juice me up. I'm feeling a little drained, and I still need Squiggles to fetch things for me."

"You could just get off your lazy ass and fetch things yourself."

"And you could stop *being* an ass and fulfill your birth-given duty to be my living battery."

"Whatever." He slapped a hand half over Dot's face, and the half that I could see smiled a little at the pleasant sensation of the Light coursing into her.

"You're lucky I haven't started my makeup yet."

Charlie ignored her and turned to me. "How are you, Eve? Excited for tonight?"

My eyes were glued to his hand on his sister's face. I burned to ask him more about how the Vital-Variant connection worked between siblings, what it felt like to expel Light, how he managed to control the flow, if he too had experienced the crazy itching and energy that came with overflow. But they didn't know I was a Vital, so I had to keep my mouth shut and focus on the conversation. What was he asking about?

"Oh, I guess. Yeah?" I didn't sound convincing at all, and they both chuckled.

Charlie released his sister's face, and I went back to straightening her hair as he chatted with me about what to expect that evening, trying to give me all the facts so I wouldn't be so nervous.

Not that snooty social events were complicated, but he was—just like Tyler—really good at explaining complicated things in simple language. Charlie was writing his thesis in the Variant studies field, so he had joined a few of my study sessions with Tyler, helping to advance my knowledge where he could. I appreciated his insights and company, despite his presence meaning I couldn't transfer Light to Tyler or practice controlling my Light flow.

It was also a bit ironic that the knowledge I most craved was about the biggest thing we had in common.

"Just stick with one of us during the night and you'll be fine," he finished, and I nodded, hoping he hadn't noticed I'd barely heard a word. "Anyway I'll leave you girls to . . . whatever this is."

He waved a hand in our general direction, already walking backward toward the door.

"You're welcome to join us." I smiled at him.

"Thanks, but no thanks. I may be gay, but I'm still a man and won't need more than half an hour to get ready. I've got better things to do with my time."

He was teasing us, a wicked grin falling over his face as he turned and ran for the door. Dot grabbed the first thing her fingers found on the vanity, and so did I, the lipstick and comb landing lamely in the spot Charlie had just dashed away from.

His laughter echoed in the hall as he disappeared down the stairs, and Dot and I couldn't help the laughter that bubbled forth in his wake.

By the afternoon, my hair and makeup were done. All I had left to do was put on the amazing dress Josh had given me, but my stomach was grumbling, and I decided it would be safer to have a snack without it on.

I left Dot to finish her own makeup—she had been drawing on and repeatedly wiping away something she called a "dramatic brow"—and headed downstairs to the kitchen.

Some of the bread Ethan had baked *from scratch* the other day was still left over, wrapped up in the pantry. I did a fist pump; it was just enough for two thick slices with butter and jam—also homemade by Ethan.

I was just putting the jam back in the fridge when Alec stormed into the kitchen. He never just walked anywhere—he stormed in, radiating hostility, or stalked, unseen, startling you when you finally spotted him.

His features immediately hardened upon seeing me. I was having that effect on him a lot. The nice gesture with the latte after I'd saved Ethan's life was the first and last time he'd shown me any kindness since the plane crash. As the weeks wore on, he avoided me more and more.

I knew he was helping Ethan and Josh gain better control of their abilities, sharing all he had learned over years of striving to master his own. They talked about it often—Alec's tips on meditation, his patience when they messed up, the laughs they shared when some mishap inevitably happened.

Those conversations made me feel a little left out. While Tyler was being incredibly attentive with my own training, Alec was never around during our group sessions. I'd briefly mentioned this to Tyler once, and he'd said something about Alec not wanting to intrude when we were all together as a Bond. Then he'd quickly changed the subject. I caught how his brow furrowed though, making me suspect there was more to the story.

"Is that the last of Ethan's bread?" the man in question asked me in the kitchen.

"Yeah . . ." I was about to offer some to him, then realized there wasn't enough, and if I went back upstairs without food, I was pretty sure Dot would sic Squiggles on me. Or a bear.

He huffed, mumbled something about me "taking his brothers *and* his bread," and stormed back out of the kitchen. I rolled my eyes at his retreating form. His behavior was beginning to border on juvenile.

As I trudged back up the two flights of stairs, plate of delicious bread in hand, I tried to put Alec out of my mind. He was just so frustrating!

"Earth to Eve!" Dot snapped me out of it before I could start obsessing again. She grabbed one of the slices of bread off the plate.

"Sorry. How did it go with the brows?" I bit into the other slice, reveling in the deliciousness of homemade bread *and* jam.

In answer she wiggled the brows in question and smiled around her mouthful of bread. They were perfectly symmetrical and, I had to admit, dramatic.

I gave her an appreciative look and a thumbs-up.

"What's got you all distracted?"

"Nothing." I rolled my eyes. "Just Alec being . . . Alec."

"What's he done now?" She chuckled, pushing various clothes and bits of makeup off the bed so she could sit down. Squiggles scampered into her lap and intently watched her eat.

"I just don't know what his problem is. He can't even stand to be in the same room as me. What have I ever done to him?" I joined her on the bed, leaning back but being careful not to ruin my hair. Dot had expertly put it up into a smooth low bun.

"Don't stress. He's just worried you're going to take away his family since you're their Vital. He'll get over it once he realizes how awesome you are."

I sighed and nodded. I had figured the same thing. Those boys were really close, and Alec didn't seem to have many other people in his life due to his ability. Now all of a sudden here I was—Bonded to all three of them and changing the dynamics.

"Wait! What?" I snapped my head up, nearly choking on my last bite of bread. She grinned at me wickedly.

How did she know we were Bonded? I hadn't told a soul, and I was certain the boys hadn't either.

"Oh, come on, Eve." She rolled her eyes. "You three might be fooling everyone else, but I can see how attached Ethan is to you, and I can see the secret looks you share with Josh when you think no one is paying attention. Ethan doesn't get close to anyone outside his family, and he's telling you about his parents and his cooking after a few weeks? And Josh used to lock himself in his room for days on end, his head buried in books, but now he's constantly hanging out with you, noticing things even Ethan, your *boyfriend*, doesn't? It's kind of obvious, really."

"Well . . . shit." How could we be failing so badly at keeping our secret? At least she didn't seem to know about Tyler. Maybe that connection wasn't as obvious because he was keeping the kind of distance between us that Josh and Ethan wouldn't or couldn't.

"Is it really so obvious?" I asked on a desperate whisper, fighting the urge to track my guys down to make sure they were OK. If Dot knew, maybe everyone knew, and what if they were in danger?

"Chill." Dot chuckled.

I'd started to get up, and she grabbed my arm and pulled me back down to the bed. It reminded me of the first time we'd met and she'd done the same thing as I went to chase after Alec. Those were simpler times . . .

"It's not that obvious. I only know because I know *them* and I'm smart and I notice stuff. Also Squiggles saw you guys training in the pool one night, and she told me all about it. She is such a gossip!" She was talking about Squiggles as if she were a person and not a ferret, and for a second I questioned her sanity, but when I looked down at the elongated ball of fur, the look on her little face was *guilty*.

"You used your ability and your ferret to spy on us? Dot!" I was no longer paranoid about our safety, but I couldn't believe she'd done that.

"Spy is such a negative word. I . . . inquired . . . surreptitiously."

I gave her a look that made it clear I wasn't buying it. "Who else knows?"

"Charlie."

"Dammit, Dot!"

"I'm sorry! But he's my Vital, not just my brother. Could you keep anything from someone in your Bond?"

She had a point; I couldn't imagine lying to any of them. My time in the storage closet with Ethan and Josh had proven that—although I was pretty sure that wasn't how Dot and Charlie got information out of each other.

"He already suspected anyway, and I haven't told anyone else. Squiggles might be a gossip, but I'm not. You're lucky she can only talk to me."

"Dot, this is serious. You guys can't tell anyone."

"I know." She put her serious face on. "Charlie went on about the dangers of the situation for, like, an hour after I told him. We don't want to put any of you in danger. We just want to help."

I nodded, uneasy that the circle of people who knew of our secret was widening, but at this point, there was no option but to trust them.

"Come on. Time to get dressed." Dot pulled me off the bed and handed me the dress Josh had given me.

I allowed myself a smile as I caressed the soft fabric. At least now I wouldn't have to be evasive with her about where I got it. Maybe sharing this new part of my life with Dot would actually make things easier.

EIGHTEEN

As I stood in front of the mirror, it became clear how observant Josh truly was. The dress fit me perfectly, the bottom of it floating just above the ground.

It clung in all the right places, accentuating my figure and only slightly fanning out from about mid-thigh. There was no beading whatsoever at the top; the soft fabric was cut high in the front and glided over my breasts delicately. You could say it was conservative, except that the back was completely nonexistent, consisting of nothing more than two slim strips of fabric draping over my shoulders.

It was more out there than I would have chosen for myself, but neither my cleavage nor my legs were on display, and as a result, I felt comfortable. Sexy even. I wanted to let my hair down to cover my back a little, but Dot insisted on showing off the stunning lines of the dress and made me leave it up.

We kept my makeup understated—I would have felt uncomfortable in anything remotely as heavy as her everyday look—and she lent me a pair of actual emerald earrings, which matched the dress perfectly. I was paranoid about losing them and tried to refuse, but she insisted.

"I just need to get dressed and I'll be right down," she shouted over her shoulder as she walked into the bathroom.

I grabbed a small black clutch—also borrowed from Dot—and made my way downstairs. I kept my hand on the banister and went carefully, still getting used to walking in something so long, but the dress was surprisingly forgiving and nowhere near as constricting as it looked.

As I neared the bottom, I looked up and stopped in my tracks.

All three of my guys, plus Alec and Charlie, were standing near the front door, waiting for us.

Ethan and Josh were chatting quietly with Alec, who had his back to me, and Charlie was standing off to the side with Tyler, who had his face in his phone, as always.

Josh was following my descent down the stairs, and it was meeting his gaze that stopped me.

He was wearing a black suit with a white shirt and, in a subtle nod to the beading on my dress, a green bow tie. His blond hair was slicked back, and he was smiling at me with so much warmth in his face I almost forgot the others were there.

Ethan was in black pants, a white jacket, and a blood-red tie and matching pocket square, hinting at his fire ability. He looked up and stopped speaking, his eyes rapidly flying up and down my body to take in my sophisticated new look.

Tyler was the next to look up, at first distractedly, obviously in the middle of something important on his phone, but then with his full attention on me. He was in navy blue, and his gunmetal gray tie was almost as close a match to the top part of my dress as Josh's bow tie was to the bottom. I wondered briefly if he'd had a part in choosing the dress too, but judging by how his hand slowly lowered his phone and his lips parted slightly in shock, he had no idea.

He took a small step toward me, his free hand lifting as if to reach for me, but he pulled up short and looked away, brow furrowing. Did he feel as drawn to me as I did to him in that moment? My grip on the banister tightened as images of the kisses I'd shared with Josh and then Ethan earlier in the day flashed through my mind. What would it feel like to kiss Tyler too?

No one was speaking. Josh put his left hand in his pocket and lifted his right, drawing my attention to him. With his finger pointed to the ceiling, he twisted it in a circle, silently asking me to show him the back.

I looked down, slightly embarrassed, but the dress was making me feel confident, so I slowly pivoted on the spot until I could place both hands on the banister, giving them only a partial view of my exposed back and looking over my shoulder.

Alec turned just as I did. Because his back was to the others, I was the only one who could see his face.

He was in all black, as usual, his suit clearly tailor-made and hugging his tall form perfectly, but he wore no tie. "I have to go to your stupid event, but I refuse to wear a tie," it seemed to say. His outfit was grudging and uncompromising, just like its wearer.

Where Ethan's eyes had flown all over my body, not knowing where to look first, Alec took his time.

With a deliberate intensity I could scarcely understand, Alec drew his eyes over my face, down the curve of my neck, and over my shoulder, sliding them down the naked expanse of my back all the way to my ass, where they lingered.

I felt exposed. I could almost physically feel his stare caressing my body.

I should have felt uncomfortable, outraged even, that he was looking at me so . . . so *lasciviously*. He was Ethan's older cousin, he was dangerous, he was frustrating, and he clearly wanted nothing to do with me.

Yet there he stood, practically licking my body with his eyes. And there I stood, *enjoying it.*

Not taking his eyes off my ass, he spoke. "If you guys are done drooling, we should probably get going."

His voice didn't betray even a hint of the perplexing intensity in his stare. He dragged his eyes back up, stopping just before making eye contact with me, then turned and walked to the front door. He opened it and leaned on the frame.

"We have to wait for Dot." Josh stepped forward and extended his hand.

I descended the last few steps and placed my palm gently in his, making sure my Light was in check.

"You look stunning." He spoke low, but his voice carried through the marble foyer clearly. "As I knew you would. Thank you for wearing it."

"You look smokin'!" Ethan's voice boomed in comparison to Josh's, and everyone chuckled.

"I don't know what you two were doing in there for four hours, but you do look lovely, Eve." There was a hint of amusement in Charlie's voice as he walked past, going to stand by the door with Alec.

Apparently the guys had all forgotten he was there too.

Josh's eyes widened, and he dropped my hand. We'd been standing at the foot of the stairs hand in hand for way longer than was appropriate if I was supposed to be Ethan's girlfriend.

Charlie laughed at Josh's abrupt shift, and knowing he knew our secret, I couldn't help laughing too. The wide-eyed, worried looks on all three of my guys' faces only made me laugh harder.

"Oh, relax. We know." Dot came down the stairs in a pair of the very high, very dangerous-looking heels I had refused to wear. They were sparkling black, matching her perfectly straight, shiny black hair. In contrast, her full-skirted, calf-length dress was white with some kind of subtle, textured pattern. It was only when you got up close that you could see the pattern consisted of little skulls.

"What do you mean, you know?" Tyler was all business as he stepped forward, half blocking me from Dot with his body. *From Dot.* I'm not sure if he even realized how protective the move was, but it surprised me, finally quieting the giggles I was struggling to control.

"Oh, come on, Gabe, did you really think you could keep the fact that Ethan and Josh had found their Vital from me and Charlie?" Dot breezed past him, patting him on the shoulder as she went, not fazed at all.

"Car's here," Alec announced, walking out without waiting for anyone else.

Tyler pressed his lips together, as if biting something back, and glared at Dot as we all made our way outside.

The "car" was a sleek stretch limo with a driver who was on a first-name basis with all of them. We piled inside, careful not to ruffle our clean-cut appearance.

Even with the privacy screen up, Tyler wasn't willing to talk about my Vital status out loud. He opted to say whatever he had to say via text, having a heated conversation with Dot and Charlie, their fingers flying across their screens as they threw each other loaded glances and I looked on, amused.

"Gabe! We know. We've got their backs, man," Charlie finally said aloud, giving Tyler a pointed look and ending the conversation.

We arrived in Manhattan about an hour later, our limo pulling up outside a very fancy-looking hotel. There was even a red carpet leading to the entrance and a horde of people behind velvet ropes.

I groaned. "Can't we go through the back or something?" I hadn't even wanted to go to this thing, and now I had to deal with … *are those paparazzi?*

Alec surprised me by being the one to answer. "I think that's the first time you and I have agreed on anything." He gave me a small crooked smile, rendering me completely speechless.

"I'm a representative of Melior Group, and Alec and Ethan are nephews of the managing director. We have to be seen," Tyler explained.

"I don't have to be seen by anyone," Josh piped up. "I could take her through the back."

"No," Tyler, Ethan, and Alec replied immediately, surprising me once again.

Dot and Charlie were falling over each other laughing. I didn't think it was that funny, but then Josh groaned, dragging a hand down his face. "That's not—"

"You said it. It's out there now!" Dot cut him off, reaching for the door. "Come on, Charles, let's be seen."

Shaking his head, Charlie followed her out.

As the door clicked shut behind them, the double entendre of Josh's words dawned on me. I should have been mortified, but for some reason, my first reaction was to snort-laugh.

As if they'd been waiting for my reaction, the others laughed too. Hesitant chuckles gave way to unrestrained laughter and ended in full-bellied, uncontrolled guffaws. It was the first time I'd heard Alec laugh. I liked the sound. He seemed to be in a much better mood than usual.

As we finally calmed down, Tyler wiped the tears from the corners of his eyes. "Let's get this over with."

He straightened his tie and stepped out of the car. Immediately, the flashing lights intensified, and people started shouting. I could have sworn that some of the voices sounded angry and aggressive, but I couldn't dwell on it, because Ethan had stepped out too and was offering me his hand.

I checked my Light, making sure it was locked down, before placing my hand in his and letting him help me out. His fingers flexed around mine, and he quickly placed my hand in the crook of his elbow; I must not have done a very good job of stopping the Light from transferring.

As Josh appeared on my other side, Tyler set a brisk pace down the length of the red carpet. I glanced behind us and was almost startled by how close Alec was to my back. They had pretty much boxed me in, shielding me from the worst of the crowd.

As the grand doors closed behind us, one malicious voice rose over all the others.

"Fucking elitist pigs!"

I turned around, stunned. Alec was still close behind me, and my sudden stop caused him to pull up short, his hand landing on my shoulder just as a bright camera flash blinded me through the window.

Alec nudged me, dropping his hand quickly, and Ethan pulled me away from the entrance.

"What was that about?" I asked no one in particular.

"That was the Human Empowerment Network getting louder and more obnoxious," Tyler explained. "They've been kicking up a fuss for decades, but in the last few years, there are more and more of them. They show up with picket signs at Variant events, disrupt businesses owned by Variants, send hate mail to prominent Variant persons. I've never seen a crowd this large though."

He looked a little worried, his eyes on the tinted windows and the throng outside. Now that I knew what I was looking for, I could see at least a hundred people behind the photographers, shouting and waving handwritten signs.

They looked *so* angry. "Are they dangerous?"

"Don't worry, Eve." Tyler turned his attention back to me, fixing me with a relaxed smile. "You're safe."

I returned his smile, but I was still worried. *That wasn't what I'd asked.*

Tyler quickly excused himself to go stand in a corner of the room, where he was soon in conversation with a man wearing a simple black suit and a serious, commanding expression. Taking a look around, I noticed several other men dressed identically to the one Tyler was speaking to. They were positioned at the edges of the room, keeping a watchful eye on everything, the bulges under their jackets hinting at the weapons they carried. It didn't take a genius to figure out that Tyler was demanding information from his Melior Group minions and ordering them around appropriately.

"Don't worry, beautiful. I'll protect you." Ethan gave me one of his brilliant, dimpled smiles.

"My hero," I teased, rolling my eyes, but I was secretly thankful for the comforting feel of his strong arm under my hand.

I didn't get the chance to dwell on my worries for long. Alec had disappeared into the crowd, but Ethan and Josh guided me through the impressive, lavish lobby and into the ballroom.

To call the room opulent would have been an understatement. The ballroom was softly lit by chandeliers, expensive linen draping the tables at the edges of the room, thousands of candles and fresh flowers covering every flat surface.

"Wow," I breathed, and they both smiled at me.

"It's got nothing on you in that dress," Josh whispered close to my ear, and I couldn't stop the wide smile from pulling at my mouth.

Women in stunning dresses and men in perfectly tailored suits milled about, only adding to the extravagance, and the next hour was a blur of new faces and names as the boys introduced me to people. I met some of their friends who didn't go to Bradford Hills, some of Tyler's work colleagues, and a few "acquaintances" they told me they had to be nice to for the sake of Ethan's uncle and his business dealings.

"At least we don't have to deal with Davis," Josh muttered.

"Ugh!" A frown crossed Ethan's perfect face. "Thank god. I can't stand that guy."

I looked between them. "Who?"

Josh leaned in to answer. "Davis Damari. One of Uncle Lucian's business acquaintances. Can't put my finger on why, but he gives me the creeps."

Of course. I remembered reading about Damari on the Internet. As another couple approached us, I made a mental note to avoid him. If Josh had a bad feeling about Damari, there was almost certainly a reason for it.

Later in the evening, Dot introduced me to her parents. Both she and Charlie clearly took after their father, getting their black hair and green eyes from him. Their mother was a natural blonde, but I could see her delicate features and petite form reflected in Dot.

"So this is the infamous Eve my daughter keeps telling me about." Her mother smiled warmly and shook my hand. "I hope you know you won't be able to get rid of her now. You've got a friend for life in Dot."

Instead of getting embarrassed by her mother's comments, Dot just smiled and nodded.

"I certainly hope so." I chuckled. I'd only known Dot for a few weeks, but she'd claimed me as her friend from day one, and I wasn't complaining.

We chatted for a little while, and then they excused themselves to go speak to some of their friends.

Dot grabbed us two glasses of champagne from a tray as it floated past on a waiter's hand. No one even tried to stop her. Several people our age, or even younger, were sipping on alcoholic drinks. I guess legal drinking age didn't apply when you had this much money and influence.

The bubbly drink was delicious. It was better than any wine or champagne I'd ever tried, and I shuddered to think how much it must have cost to supply an event this large with champagne that good.

We helped ourselves to canapés as we chatted. The bite-sized morsels of pure deliciousness rivaled even Ethan's skill with food, and I smiled affectionately as he tasted each one, his face getting all serious while his mouth dissected the nuance of flavor in each piece.

As we stood around, my friends pointed out other people from the constant stream of glamorous attendees filtering through the room. There were many celebrities, which explained the paparazzi, as well as several high-profile billionaires (with a *b*!) and politicians.

Dot and Ethan were doing most of the talking, and it didn't take long for it to turn into a game. One of them would point out a person in the crowd, and the other would have to state their name; their ability, if they had one; and an interesting fact about them.

As they went back and forth, forgetting that the point was to get me up to speed on who was who, I stopped paying attention. I only tuned back in when Dot pointed toward the grand entrance at a couple who had just arrived.

"Those are Zara's parents," Ethan answered immediately, his competitive streak shining bright, "Con and Francine Adams. Neither of them has a Vital, but interestingly, they both have the same ability—enhanced speed. Mrs. Adams used to head up research and development for one of our uncle's tech companies. She was fired, but that's not widely known." He looked at Dot with a satisfied smile, way too proud of himself.

I was beginning to understand why Zara hadn't wanted to come. Her parents looked harsh and unpleasant even from across the room, smiling even less than Alec. They weren't speaking to anyone, although they stood out in the crowd; they were both tall, and Mrs. Adams had Zara's bright red hair. Mr. Adams was surveying the room intently as he sipped on his champagne.

Someone stepped in front of me, obstructing my view. The man was wearing a black pinstripe suit and looked as though he was in his mid-forties. He was tall and broad in the shoulders, with dark hair and intense eyes—like

Alec's, but not as bright blue, and surrounded by more laugh lines. When he smiled politely, I saw a hint of Ethan's dimples as well.

"Uncle Lucian!" Ethan confirmed my suspicion, stepping forward and giving his uncle a warm hug, complete with the enthusiastic, affectionate thumps on the back that men seemed to always inflict on one another. The more love between the men, the louder and more violent the thumps.

Lucian Zacarias greeted Josh, Dot, and Charlie just as warmly, and then his full attention was on me.

"Uncle, this is Eve Blackburn. My girlfriend," Ethan introduced me, his arm wrapping around my middle as he smiled widely. He had been introducing me to people as his "girlfriend" all evening, but those interactions had been tinged with the same lightheartedness that was always present when we were pretending we were an item.

When he introduced me to his uncle, his chest puffed out, his arm around me flexed possessively, his smile was genuine and warm. Ethan clearly cared for his uncle and craved his approval. Knowing that approval, in that moment, rested on what he thought of me made me a little nervous.

"Is she?" was Lucian's perplexing response. His face was still relaxed, a small smile playing on his lips, but he was studying me intently, eyes flying over my features, from my eyes to my lips to my hair.

His examination was making me feel self-conscious, so I looked down at his very shiny black shoes as I extended my hand, hoping he didn't notice the little shake in it. "It's a pleasure to meet you, sir."

I managed to look up and make eye contact again as he gently took my hand and shook it.

"The pleasure is all mine, I assure you." He sounded sincere, and some of my nerves melted away.

He released my hand just as the guest of honor arrived. We all turned to see Senator Christine Anderson, resplendent in a stunning gold gown, make her entrance. People crowded around her immediately.

She's much shorter than I expected, I thought as she disappeared, buried in a sea of suits, dresses, and jewels. *Not as short as Dot, but nearly.*

"Duty calls, I'm afraid. I'll catch up with you kids later. Enjoy your evening, Eve." Lucian gave me an amused smile, and I frowned—what did he find so amusing about me?—but he'd already turned away, pushing through the crowd toward the senator.

Before long we were sitting down to a six-course meal while a string quartet played onstage at the back of the room. Tyler was seated at the senator's table with Lucian, while the rest of us were on one of the many tables filled with young Variants eager to mingle. I'd caught only glimpses of Alec since we'd arrived, but I couldn't spot where he was sitting. I wondered if he was at a table with Dana—I had seen him speaking to her—but pushed the thought aside.

The organizers had arranged the seating plan so that no one would be next to someone they already knew, facilitating the process of finding the members of your Bond, if you had one. Ethan blatantly switched the name cards around so that I was seated between him and Josh.

The food was exquisite, and even getting to know the other people at our table wasn't too bad. The champagne continued to flow freely, and it wasn't long before I was busting for the toilet. Halfway through dessert, I excused myself and headed toward the bathrooms.

"...Eve Blackburn. You certainly haven't mentioned her in your updates."

The sound of my name pulled me up just short of the corridor leading to the bathrooms. I pulled back and tried to look casual while straining to hear what was being said.

"Eve? Why would I mention her? Our calls would be unnecessarily long and boring if I briefed you on every one of Ethan's playthings."

Lucian Zacarias was the one who had spoken my name, and it was Alec's voice answering, reducing my connection with Ethan to something cheap and dirty. I swallowed hard, my brow furrowing. I knew he was just trying to throw his uncle off, protecting our secret, but it still hurt to be referred to as one of Ethan's "playthings."

There was a long pause, and I leaned in to hear better.

"Alec, you and I both know she's much more."

"Not here," Alec replied immediately, lowering his voice.

"No, certainly not."

It sounded as if the conversation was over before it had really begun; they would be coming around that corner any second. In a panic, I decided to beat them to it.

I rushed into the corridor, nearly barreling into Alec.

"Oh, hello!" I said a little too loudly. "Sorry, got to go. I'm busting! Too much champagne."

Laughing nervously, I speed-walked to the ladies room, hoping they would attribute my odd behavior to too much alcohol.

I was equally impressed and disturbed by how calm they'd both looked when I'd appeared, even though they had *just* been talking about me. I guess it came with the territory when you, respectively, ran and worked for an agency like the Melior Group.

In the bathroom, once my bladder was empty, I looked at myself in the mirror and practiced my neutral, polite face. Had something in my expression given our secret away? I knew Lucian Zacarias wasn't a mind reader, so it couldn't have been that. The boys had told me he was a shield—similar to Dana, but where her ability blocked all others from working around her, Lucian's blocked them from affecting *him* specifically. I wasn't sure how he'd figured out his nephews weren't presenting the whole truth about me, but I had a feeling I would need a better poker face with Variant high society.

As I walked back to our table, I scratched absentmindedly at my forearm, gradually becoming aware that my ankles were a little itchy too.

Shit.

I cursed myself for getting distracted by all the glitz and glamour, the cloak and dagger, and the politics and gossip of the evening—for letting my concentration slip. I had to get my Light under control.

Because there was no way we could explain me transferring Light to any one of my guys when I wasn't even supposed to be a Vital.

NINETEEN

With dinner over, people moved out of their seats, mingling about the room, going to the bar. Ethan and Josh got stuck talking to a dignified, elderly gentleman with a cane. As she dragged me away, Dot explained that he used to be the dean of Bradford Hills Institute and took every opportunity to talk the ears off current students, regaling them with stories that began with "when I was dean" or "back in the sixties."

Dot introduced me to a couple of her other girlfriends, and I promptly forgot their names—I had met so many people that night, my brain was refusing to retain any more information. Not that it mattered—I got separated from Dot soon after.

While the frenzy of people introducing themselves had died down on campus, there were plenty of people at the gala who were enthusiastic to meet me. I got swept up in a dizzying game of musical chairs, except I was the chair and everyone wanted to sit on me. One of the guys was always nearby, keeping an eye on me, but I had to make pleasant conversation with all the new Variants without them as buffer.

".. . noticed the increased security?" a young guy with glasses and platinum-blond hair continued, drawing my attention away from the itch at my elbow. "There's a Melior Group guard in every corner."

"It's because of the Dimes out front," his tall, skinny friend replied, rolling his eyes. "Not that they're any kind of threat against a room full of Variants."

They both laughed, their noses in the air. Were their derisive comments and casual use of slurs supposed to impress me?

I frowned at them, but my attention was pulled away again. The itchiness on my arms had spread, and now it was around my neck and chest. I took a sip of my champagne and tried, surreptitiously, to scratch my collarbone. Suddenly I was wishing the dress had a plunging neckline.

"I have to go," I rudely declared, cutting the blond off midsentence. I turned on my heel and walked away, scratching with my free arm as I finished off my champagne and scanned the room.

Looking for Ethan was probably the best bet; he was the tallest. Alec was nearly as tall, but not quite. But Alec wasn't relevant—why was I even thinking about him?

Ethan's booming laugh came from somewhere to my right, and I headed in that direction, depositing my empty champagne flute on a side table. I found him surrounded by a crowd of bimbos and had to push my way through to get to him.

The girl with short black hair who had glared at me as I left campus that morning had her hand on his bicep, laughing with her head thrown back. I wanted to tear her arm out of its socket, but I settled for shoving her out of the way and taking her place by Ethan's side.

"What's up, buttercup?" He smiled wide at me, all but ignoring his growing harem.

"Yeah, hi," I said hurriedly as I again tried to scratch my chest through the fabric of my dress. I was in no mood to play our nickname game. "I need your help."

He nodded.

"Um, excuse me." One of the chicks behind me was not happy to see me monopolizing Ethan's attention. "Ethan was in the middle of telling us a story."

I completely ignored her and leaned up to whisper in Ethan's ear, very careful not make skin contact. "I need you to help me scratch an itch."

I gave him a pointed look. He wasn't always the best with hints. My big guy was all about direct communication.

I could almost see his mind going into the gutter as his lips curved into a naughty grin, but he got there in the end, realization wiping the cheeky look off his face. "Oh. Right." And then louder, for the benefit of his audience. "Yes, we have to go speak to that guy. About that thing."

He barreled through the small crowd of disappointed girls, all of them giving me dirty looks as we passed.

"Real smooth," I said dryly, rubbing my arm against the beading on the side of my dress, trying to find relief.

"Haha! You put me on the spot. It was the best I could do. There's Josh." He pointed to a back corner near the bar, where Josh was speaking to some people I didn't recognize.

As we approached, he looked up, saw me writhing in my own skin, deduced the situation immediately, and extracted himself from the conversation before we even got to him.

"Ethan, stay here with her. I'll find Gabe."

Ethan nodded and somehow managed to usher me to the end of the bar without actually touching me.

The dress that had felt like smooth butter gliding over my skin just a few hours ago was beginning to feel like coarse wool. Tearing it off my body in strips seemed like a perfectly reasonable idea.

Thankfully, Josh and Tyler returned quickly, managing to look casual while still moving through the crowd as fast as they dared.

Tyler positioned himself next to me, our backs to the wall at the end of the bar, and Josh and Ethan stood facing us, blocking most of my body from view. Ethan had ordered drinks while we waited, and he handed them out, leaning one elbow on the bar counter. To any casual observer, we would have looked as if we were simply chatting.

I didn't know what to do next, terrified of making a scene, so I kept my eyes trained ahead of me, on a spot in the middle distance between Josh and Ethan's heads. The itching was becoming unbearable.

"Eve." Tyler spoke without looking directly at me. "Take a few deep breaths. Remember your meditation practice. You're going to have to do this discreetly."

"Here? In front of everyone?" Couldn't we go find a private room somewhere?

"My agents are under strict instructions to keep the three of you in sight, but even if I call them off, there are eyes and ears everywhere. It would look too suspicious for us to slink off into a bathroom stall together. Now, focus."

I wanted to argue, but we were running out of time. Instead I did as Tyler said, focusing on the cool air as I breathed in through my nose and the warm air as I breathed out. The amount of Light coursing through my veins, demanding to be released, made the mindfulness technique frustratingly difficult.

"Good girl. Now, place your hand in mine and try to release it slowly."

My hand found his, and our fingers laced together instinctively. I tried to release the Light gradually, but once it knew it had an outlet, it just rushed out.

Tyler grunted, and Josh covered the sound up by coughing. Ethan clapped him on the back animatedly, drawing away any unwanted attention.

I took a deep breath, sighing in relief as the nervous energy drained out of me along with the excess Light, the itchiness disappearing completely, my breathing returning to normal. Next to me, Tyler was taking slow, measured breaths.

He squeezed my hand in reassurance, and I squeezed back, whispering a sincere "Thank you."

He nodded, still not looking directly at me, and released my hand. We'd managed to pull it off without anyone noticing; that was what I needed to focus on—not the fact that I'd let it get to that stage in the first place. I'd have plenty of time for crippling self-doubt later.

At the other end of the room, on the stage, someone was trying to get the crowd's attention. The music had stopped, and people were halting their conversations to face the speaker.

"Good evening, ladies and gentlemen." The young woman at the lectern wore a simple black gown, her hands clasped around a clipboard. "Welcome to the Variant Party Fundraising Gala. It is my great pleasure to introduce to you the reason we are all here, the most influential Variant voice in politics, Senator Christine Anderson."

Ethan and Josh turned around but stayed in front of Tyler and me, shielding us from anyone who happened to turn our way. Not that it mattered anymore—we were out of the woods, and everyone's eyes were trained on the senator, her gold dress shimmering in the candlelight as she made her way onstage.

As she began to speak, Tyler's hand reached up behind me, the very tips of his fingers landing at the base of my neck. I gasped, my lips parting and eyes widening just a fraction. After weeks of him building up very clear boundaries, only touching me on the hands during Light transfer, the sudden physical contact was unexpected.

He tilted his head in my direction but kept his eyes forward, speaking very softly. "You look stunning tonight. I'm sorry I didn't get a chance to tell you sooner."

It was a simple compliment, but it was undoing all the hard work I'd put in to even out my breathing.

He didn't say anything else, but his fingers trailed a feather-soft path down the length of my spine, stopping where the fabric started. Then he placed his palm, firmly and confidently, just above the curve of my ass. It felt as if his hand were on fire—as if Ethan were touching me with his fire hands—but the delicate, deliberate movements were so Tyler.

My "thank you" died in my throat, and I swallowed hard, trying not to look affected. What was he doing? What if someone saw? Did I want him to stop? No. *I definitely didn't.*

After only a few moments of exquisite torture—the spot where his palm connected with my bare skin tingling in a way that had nothing to do with the Light—he removed his hand and took a step away.

Everyone was clapping; Senator Anderson had said something impressive. I guess I would never know what it was.

I didn't hear a word of the rest of the speech, focusing instead on controlling my breathing. There was something deeply intimate about the way Tyler had touched me.

I craved more.

What did this mean for the strictly platonic tutor-student approach he'd been adamant about maintaining?

When the speech finished, the music kicked back up, and the people in the room were on the move again—dancing, getting back into conversations, making their way to the bar for more drinks. I excused myself and said I had to find the bathroom. I didn't actually need to go, but I did need a moment to myself.

As I stepped out of the ballroom, I glimpsed Alec turning down the corridor to the bathrooms. I stopped, unsure about my next move.

The smart thing would be to continue into the ladies' room and avoid him altogether. But I needed a distraction from the confusing feelings Tyler had stirred up by keeping me at arm's length for weeks and then touching me *like that*.

And I still *needed* to say my piece to Alec. His dogged avoidance of me had turned my simple wish into a mission I refused to fail; the more he resisted, the more determined I became that he would hear it. Plus, I was convinced he knew more about how and why my mother died. I wasn't sure how much of it was "classified," but I had to at least ask those questions. I had to try.

I had never seen Alec in a better mood. People were more forthcoming with information when in a good mood. *Right?* The release of excess Light had made me calmer, and I may have been a little emboldened by the three glasses of champagne I'd had. So I waited.

He came out of the bathroom a few minutes later, pausing halfway up the corridor when he spotted me blocking his way.

"My, what a determined look you have on your face, Eve." He narrowed his eyes, but there was some humor in his smirk. For once it wasn't all menace. "You wouldn't be trying to ruin this perfectly lovely evening, now, would you?"

"Look." I held one hand out, pleading. "Just give me five minutes. I *need* to get this off my chest. You don't even have to speak, just listen. And then I promise I will never bother you again."

"Highly doubt that," he muttered before stalking forward slowly. "You know I can easily overpower you. You're not actually blocking my way."

"Yes. I am aware of your scary pain ability." I waved my hands in his general direction. "Everyone keeps reminding me. But I don't think you would actually use it on me."

He just watched me, but he wasn't making a run for it, so I drove my case home in the most pathetic way I knew how.

"Pleeease." I drew out the word as only someone who was slightly drunk could.

He rolled his eyes, and I knew I had him. "Fine."

"Oh my god." Excitedly I shook my hands in front of me, shifting from one foot to the other.

But before I had a chance to start, a group of girls came laughing and stumbling down the corridor. They jostled past me but quieted when they saw Alec, skirting the walls to avoid contact with him. In his usual unyielding fashion, he stared them down, not moving an inch to get out of their way.

Once they were gone, he stepped past me and I deflated, thinking he had changed his mind. But then I heard a door open, and he declared in an impatient tone: "I don't have all night."

I spun around, stunned, and didn't waste any time, walking through the door into what I realized was the cloakroom. There was no one inside and it was very dim, the only light coming from the serving window in the wall to my left. It was just enough to see by.

He followed me in, closing the door behind him, and stood in the middle of the small room, arms crossed, feet wide, surrounded by coats and furs. I took a deep breath and gathered my thoughts, moving in front of the door to block his exit.

Facing him fully, I looked straight in his ice-blue eyes and said what I had been waiting to say for over a year.

"I don't think you understand how much it meant to me what you did. And I'm not just talking about pulling me out of the water and getting me medical attention. I don't know what happened to you to make you think that you don't deserve thanks, but you do."

He tightened his arms across his chest but averted his eyes, looking uncomfortable.

I kept going, determined to get it all out before he bolted. "You saved my life by doing your job, and maybe it was just part of your job, but you and your team still deserve my gratitude for doing that. So, thank you."

I paused, wanting to make sure I got the next bit right. "But what you did in the hospital after—*that's* what meant the world to me. *That's* what had me trying to track you down for a year."

He finally looked at me again, his brow creasing.

"You were there for me in the lowest moment of my entire existence. I felt more alone and adrift when I woke up in that hospital bed than I ever did floating by myself in the middle of the Pacific. I don't know what made you stay with me, or what made you comfort me when I realized that my . . ." *mother died.* I still couldn't bring myself to say it. "What you did for me in the hospital is what truly saved me. I may have been too destroyed by grief at the time, but after, I realized you had given me hope—a hint of the idea that I didn't have to be alone in the world. And for that I am truly grateful."

His arms slowly dropped to his sides as I spoke, an incomprehensible expression falling over his face, so intense that I almost withered beneath it. Almost.

"Alec Zacarias, *thank you*." Finally, I had said it. *Finally*, he had heard it.

"I had no idea . . ." His voice was softer than I'd heard it since I first saw him in the square months ago. That smooth honey quality—the one I lived to hear—was back. "If it really meant that much to you, I accept your thanks. You're more welcome than you know."

With a sigh of relief, I leaned back against the door and closed my eyes;

he had taken me seriously, and he'd accepted my thanks. I'd been so focused on delivering it, I hadn't realized how much I'd been dreading his response.

I tried to focus on how to phrase my next question—how to bring up the night of the crash. I hoped the moment we'd just had would soften him up enough to give me the answers I needed.

But I never got a chance to say anything else.

I heard him step forward, and when I opened my eyes, he was right in front of me, his eyes searching my face. I was reminded of how he'd looked at me on the stairs at the start of the evening, and a warm shiver ran down my spine.

His eyes flicked down to my lips, making his intention very clear.

I had no idea how I'd found myself in this situation, but apparently I wasn't interested in getting out of it, because I didn't say anything or move away. Instead, I tilted my face up, and my lips parted of their own volition.

"Put your hands behind your back. Don't touch," he whispered.

His tone wasn't forceful or demanding, but my body obeyed immediately. Some small part of my functioning brain briefly registered that this was a bad idea, considering his ability to deliver excruciating pain regardless of whether I was touching him or not, but I didn't care. If anything, the potential danger made it more exciting.

He placed his hands on either side of my head, against the door, and leaned in, kissing me with all the demanding force that had been missing from his voice a moment ago. I moaned into his mouth, surprising myself. He didn't press his body into mine. Nowhere did we touch except our lips.

He pulled away after only a few dizzying seconds.

And for the first time since I'd met him, it was I who ran from him.

My head spinning, I turned around, yanked the door open, and ran to the ladies' room. I shut myself into a stall and took several deep breaths.

What the hell was I doing? Why had I been so willing to do as he asked? So eager for him to kiss me?

This was wrong. I knew it was wrong. *But it had felt so right.*

I was on the verge of panic. I felt as though I'd betrayed not only the three amazing guys I was connected to but also myself.

Yes, Tyler was reluctant and cautious, doing everything in his power to keep things between us platonic, but he was still a part of my Bond. Ethan and Josh clearly wanted to be with me, but we were forced to take it slow. My relationship with them was ambiguous and restrained, but I was their Vital, and they were my Variants. They were *mine*.

Even just being attracted to Alec made me feel awful. I had three, *three*, guys that I knew without a shadow of a doubt were mine in one way or another, and I still wasn't satisfied. *What the hell was wrong with me?*

A few women came into the bathroom, chatting, and I did my best to calm myself, straightening my dress and taking another breath before flushing the unused toilet and stepping out. Smiling at them politely, I washed my hands, checked my reflection, and went back outside.

Alec was nowhere to be seen.

I made my way back to the ballroom and hunted down a waiter, snagging a champagne from his tray and downing it in three big gulps. Because adding more alcohol to the mix after doing something stupid was always a good idea, right?

With the formal proceedings of the evening over, the lights were dimmed and the music turned up. Everyone appeared to relax. Both the dance floor and the bar became more and more crowded as the night wore on. I spent the rest of the gala avoiding the guys as much as I could and dancing with Dot, distracting myself as best I could from my own poor choices. She threw me a couple of questioning glances but thankfully didn't prod me for an explanation.

By the end of the evening, my hair had completely come loose from the bun, and I shuddered to think what my makeup looked like. As all the beautiful people in their shiny eveningwear streamed out of the ballroom, I realized I was drunk.

At least I wasn't the only one. Dot was a giggly mess, and Tyler's eyes had a distinct glassiness to them, although he held his liquor much better than I did. Ethan and Josh had had a few drinks, but neither of them was messy. I suppose they couldn't afford to really lose control with the kinds of abilities they had. Charlie was the only one who hadn't had anything to drink. He'd glued himself to Dot and me, declaring that "someone has to take care of your drunk asses."

I hadn't seen Alec since the . . . incident in the cloakroom. I was hoping he had done his disappearing act and I wouldn't have to see him again for a few days.

"Man, Alec is such a jerk." The alcohol in my system had significantly thinned the filter between my brain and my mouth, and everyone laughed as our group spilled onto the street. All the paparazzi were gone, as was the angry crowd with the signs, but I did notice a few of Tyler's men hovering close by.

Dot slung an arm over my shoulders. "Did"—she hiccupped—"did you try to thank him again, and he ran away again?"

"No." I leaned into her, overbalancing, but Josh was on my other side and pulled us up straight. "I mean, yes. I mean, I made him listen to . . . and it was a really good thanks, you know? Like, I put a lot of effort into how I was . . . how I worded it. And then he listened. He *listened*, Dot!" She nodded sagely. "And I was so happy. And then that . . . that jerk face, douche canoe ruined it."

Everyone else laughed at my choice of words, but Dot sounded outraged. "No!"

"Yep." I was still with it enough to stop myself from elaborating on *how* exactly he'd ruined it, which was a miracle, because it would have made the next five minutes even more awkward than they were.

We decided not to wait for the limo to be pulled around, walking up the street to where it was parked

"I've texted the driver. He's on his way," Tyler told us as he pulled open the door.

The limo's interior light came on, and the mystery of Alec's whereabouts was solved.

He was seated in the middle of the back seat, legs stretched out in front of him, his shirt unbuttoned and half off his shoulders. Straddling his lap was Dana, one of the straps of her dress hanging down. Their hands were all over each other.

For a beat everyone just stared, and then Dot shrieked, "EEW!" and covered her eyes with her hands.

Alec's head whipped up, and his eyes went straight to mine. They widened in pure horror just as Tyler slammed the door shut.

Bile rose in the back of my throat, and tears burned my eyes. I turned, shoving past Ethan and Josh, and managed to make it to some trashcans by an alleyway before I doubled over and vomited.

Dot was at my side in an instant, my messiness sobering her up. She expertly pulled back my hair while shouting at the boys, "Stay back, this is strictly a girlfriend job!"

I was so grateful to Dot in that moment. It was bad enough that I was vomiting Dom Perignon all over a dirty alley, getting it on the beautiful green beading at the bottom of my dress. I really didn't need my guys seeing this shit up close.

When my stomach was empty, Dot handed me a napkin, and someone produced a bottle of water. For once I wished I could blush, if only so they could all see how embarrassed I was without me having to speak.

"I'm so sorry," I said, my voice low and hoarse—just like my feelings. "That was so gross." I wasn't sure if I meant what we'd all witnessed in the limo or my vomiting. And I wasn't sure if the vomiting was due to the alcohol or the fact that Alec had kissed me and then promptly forgot about it, running straight to that . . . woman.

"It's OK, Eve," Tyler said as I avoided eye contact with everyone. "Let's get you home. Alec and Dana took a cab." He opened the door of the limo once again, but I cringed away.

"Nope!" I said a little too loudly. "I am not getting in that car. Nyet. Nein. Non. No way."

"She's got a point," Dot, my hero for the night, piped in. "I don't want to catch any diseases. We'll walk. It's only four blocks."

Charlie said he'd walk with us, and Ethan wrapped a comforting arm around my shoulders. "I'll go too. My cocoa puff could probably use a walk to sober up."

"Thanks, muffin." I tried to inject the usual playfulness into my voice, but it just came out flat. I was confused, tired, guilty, and still a little drunk; I smelled like vomit; my feet hurt; and I had been humiliated twice over. I was so ready for bed.

TWENTY

The next morning I woke up in an unfamiliar room, the light streaming through the window sending a searing jolt of pain through my skull. I really had to stop making this "waking up in strange beds" thing a habit.

Wherever I was looked like a high-end hotel room. The walls were a muted gray, the half-drawn curtains a rich teal color. I rolled away from the light to face the wardrobe, leaving plenty of room on either side of me on the king-sized bed.

At least this time there was no one in bed with me. I lifted the covers to check the situation anyway; I had on my underwear and a very large white T-shirt. A vague memory of comforting arms steadying me as I stumbled into a bathroom, said T-shirt in hand, drifted back to me.

Once one thing wormed its way into my fragile mind, so did the rest.

Like a disaster comedy played in reverse, I remembered the walk to Ethan's uncle's apartment, where we'd planned to stay, Ethan draping his jacket over my shoulders as I started to cry. He had asked me quietly what was wrong, and I'd snuggled into his side and refused to answer. He hadn't prodded me, instead just holding me close as we walked.

Before that had been the vomiting. As I remembered the rank smell of the trashcans and everyone's eyes on me, I groaned and lifted the soft sheet over my head.

Before that had been Alec and *her* in the limo.

Before that had been champagne and dancing.

And before that had been Alec. In the cloakroom. Kissing me.

As that particular memory assaulted me, I threw the covers off and sat bolt upright in bed.

Alec had kissed me!

I'd let him. I enjoyed it. I wanted more. *What the fuck was wrong with me?* My chest tightened, all the awful feelings from the previous night returning and riding another wave of nausea.

I was an awful, selfish, treacherous *harlot*.

And Alec was a man-whore. Who kisses a girl and then does *that* in the back of a car with another girl on the same night? Dirty car sex is dirty car sex—I don't care how fancy the car happens to be.

I couldn't think about any of this clearly; the pounding in my head wouldn't stop. And I was too guilty and angry and hurt. And just so damn confused.

I groaned and dropped my throbbing head into my hands.

The door opened, softly scraping the carpet under it.

"Look who's up!" Ethan was way too loud. "Hey, drunky."

The mirth in his voice made my stomach knot. Did he know what Alec and I had done in the cloakroom? Is that why he was enjoying seeing me in pain?

I snapped my eyes open to look at him, ignoring the stabbing in my head, but he didn't seem upset. He was smiling at me with his trademark dimpled smile, nothing but affection in his eyes.

It made me feel like shit.

"I feel like shit." Apparently the filter between my brain and my mouth was still flimsy.

"Yeah, I bet. Hopefully this will help." He lifted his arms, a paper bag in one hand and a tray with coffee in the other. He made his way over me, awkwardly stepping over something on the ground.

I leaned over the edge of the bed to see what it was; a pillow and blankets were lying there in a heap. "You slept on the floor?"

"Yeah." He sat down on the edge of the mattress and handed me the coffees. He was dressed in shorts and a tank top, a light sheen of sweat covering his forehead. He had been for a run. "Dot and Charlie might know our secret, but my uncle stayed here last night too. It would have been weird if we didn't sleep in the same room. But I wasn't going to take advantage of a crying drunk girl. Even if we are in a *pretend* relationship."

He fixed me with a rare serious look. The intensity of it surprised me.

"Pretend . . ." I let the word hang in the air. We may have been forced to pretend for the outside world, but we both knew there was something between us.

And I'd just ruined it by kissing his cousin!

To cover the guilty look on my face, I took a sip of the coffee. The latte was good, and a genuine smile of pleasure crossed my features. "Yum."

He beamed at me, opening the paper bag. The smell of bacon made me realize how desperate my empty stomach was for food. "Bacon and egg bagels. Dig in, my drunk little bagel."

I snatched the bagel out of his hand and ripped into it with a satisfied moan.

Ethan chuckled as he bit into his own. "God, I love feeding you."

I looked away, suddenly self-conscious. "Thanks?"

He ignored my awkwardness and finished his breakfast in three big bites. "I'm going to grab a shower. We're leaving in half an hour, so you might want to think about getting dressed." He casually leaned forward to wipe a stray crumb off my cheek, planted a kiss on the top of my head, and headed toward the door.

"Ethan."

At the sound of my voice, he stopped.

I took a deep breath. I still hadn't had a chance to unravel my thoughts and feelings, but there was no way I could keep the events of last night from any of them.

"About last night. I'm sorry . . ." I didn't know how to finish the sentence. I'm sorry I kissed your cousin? I'm sorry I'm such a mess? I'm sorry I'm a failure at being a Vital and a pretend, but not-really-pretend, girlfriend?

"Don't worry about it, bagel baby. It happens to the best of us. And you didn't do anything *that* embarrassing." He gave me a reassuring smile and walked out of the room.

I sighed and took another bite of the delicious bagel I didn't deserve. It was probably better to tell them all at once anyway.

Lucian had left for the airport by the time I dragged my aching body out of bed, so I didn't get to see him again. I had no memory of getting back to the apartment the night before, and I had almost no chance to check it out before we made our exit, so even as we pulled out of the parking garage, I still had no idea what it really looked like.

The seven of us were driven back to Bradford Hills in the same limo, and I made sure to sit as far away as I could from the end where we'd caught Alec mid-coitus the previous night. He was back to his brooding self, the glimpse of a relaxed nature from last night gone.

And he was back to ignoring me.

The drive back was subdued. I wasn't the only one with a hangover. Dot, Josh, and Tyler were all quiet and looked about as fresh as I felt. Tyler spent most of the ride tapping away at his phone, and Josh produced a book.

I chanced a look at Alec, not sure what I was even looking for. Some kind of acknowledgment of what we'd done? Some semblance of caring about the people we'd hurt?

He was staring out the window, sitting in the same spot where he'd had his encounter with Dana last night. The images of his hands all over her assaulted my mind again, and I couldn't help the disgusted expression that came over my face.

He looked up just in time to see it, our gazes locking across the car, and his eyes narrowed. Was he pissed off at *me*?

Then, before I could be sure I'd seen it, a hurt look crossed his features, and he turned away, back to the city zipping past.

Did he think I was disgusted by him? Was I? I guess I was, but only because of what he'd done in the limo. Did he think I was disgusted by our kiss? Wasn't I? If I was being honest with myself, I wasn't. I'd enjoyed it and wanted more.

Maybe I was just disgusted with myself. I had no idea about anything anymore. I'd hoped to use the ride back to clear my head, think about how I would broach the subject with the guys, but it was just getting more confusing.

I huffed and rolled my eyes at myself, and they landed on Josh. He was still holding his book in front of him, but his piercing green eyes were on me, his head tilted slightly to the side. He slowly turned his head to glance at Alec before turning back to me, fractionally lifting one eyebrow in a silent question.

Of course Josh had noticed. But this was not the time to get into it, all of us crammed into the limo and the driver within earshot. I shook my head almost imperceptibly. After another curious glance at Alec, Josh returned his attention to his book.

After dropping Dot and Charlie off at their house, we arrived back at the Zacarias mansion, and everyone piled out of the limo. Tyler said he would drive me back to my res hall and started to head toward their garage.

I stayed where I was, my overnight bag at my feet, my jeans and loose-fitting sweater feeling constrictive on my body, the bright sunshine bringing on another headache. "Actually, can I come inside?"

Alec was already at the front door, and as I spoke, he paused and turned around.

"I need to speak to the three of you. It can't wait."

"Of course." Tyler smiled gently at me and picked up my bag as he passed. "We can talk in my office."

"Everything OK, babe?" Ethan asked as he followed suit.

"Let's just get inside." There was a waver in my voice. My heart was hammering, and that pressure on my chest was back.

Josh looked between me and Alec and followed Ethan inside.

"You wouldn't," Alec whispered as I passed him.

I paused and looked him dead in the eye, injecting as much steel into my voice as I could. "Watch me."

I didn't wait for his reaction before I walked inside, but I heard him following close behind.

We deposited all our bags at the foot of the stairs and filed into Tyler's office. Tyler leaned on the front of his desk, his hands by his sides. Ethan took a seat next to him on top of the desk, and Josh stood on Tyler's other side, his arms crossed loosely over his chest.

I walked to the couch in the corner and sat down, wringing my hands in my lap. But that put me below their eye level, and having the three of them looking down on me made me even more uncomfortable, so I stood up. But then I thought, *Maybe they should be looking down on me. Maybe that's what I deserve.* So I sat back down. But then I realized that I had no idea how to start, so I stood up again and started pacing the room.

My three guys were all watching me with varying degrees of caution.

"Eve?" Tyler was the first to speak. "You're starting to worry me. What's the matter?"

"I'm sorry. I'm just trying to figure out how to tell you this."

"OK, now I'm getting worried too." Ethan had one of his rare intense looks on his face. "Nothing good ever came out of 'we need to talk.'"

Josh remained silent, his focus drifting between me and something by the door.

I turned slightly to see what he was looking at. Alec had followed us in. Almost. He was leaning against the doorframe, eyes narrowed and following my every movement. Why did he always stand in doorways? Was it his agency training, always putting himself in a spot where he could observe the whole room? Or was it just him, always needing to be in a place that allowed him to escape any situation easily? He was never fully in or out.

If his stare was meant to intimidate me, it failed; all it did was steel my resolve.

"Shut the door. This is a private conversation." I didn't tell him which side of the door I wanted him on—that was up to him—but he was either in this room, this conversation, or not. I refused to let him be half in and half out.

He stepped inside and kicked the door closed with one booted foot, then gestured for me to continue, eyebrows raised, a hint of a smirk on his face. He didn't think I would do it. *Arrogant asshat.*

I turned back to my guys, doing my best to ignore him.

"OK." I took a deep breath and focused on Tyler's crossed feet resting on the dark carpet. "I know we haven't exactly discussed the nature of our relationship yet—like, romantically—but I know enough about Variant Bonds to know where it's likely heading, and . . ." I blew out a big breath, choking on my words.

"What are you saying, Eve?" There was a slight tremor in Ethan's voice. Like a coward, I still couldn't look at him. "You don't want it to go there? Have we done something to make you feel uncomfortable? God, I knew I shouldn't have slept in the same room as you last night. Idiot! I swear to god, nothing happened." He was getting more and more upset as he spoke; it was breaking my heart.

I still couldn't look at him, but I shook my head, hot tears welling up in my eyes.

"It's not that, Kid." Josh—correct, as usual—spoke at last. He too was working at keeping his voice even. "Tell us what you have to tell us, Eve."

"It's not that I don't want you. This. It's that I've done something, and . . . it's that I don't think you'll want me . . ." My words cut out on a sob, and the room fell into silence.

"Eve. Whatever it is, just tell us, and we'll figure it out together." Tyler was the only one who still sounded calm. He had no idea what I was about to say, but his faith that we could work through it was unwavering. Another sob escaped me, and I had to fish a tissue out of my pocket to disgustingly blow my nose before speaking again.

None of them were moving to comfort me, and for that, at least, I was grateful. I wouldn't have been able to do this with them showing me any more of the kindness I no longer deserved.

I knew I had to look them in the eyes when I finally told them, so I lifted my head. Three sets of gorgeous, concerned, loving eyes looked back at me, and I nearly broke down again.

"Alec kissed me."

Three sets of eyes, now shocked and confused, flew to the man standing behind me.

"Last night at the party, he . . . that is to say, *we* kissed. I let it happen. I even . . ." *liked it.* I couldn't get the last two words out.

"What the fuck, man?" I'd never heard so much emotion in Tyler's voice. He pushed off his desk, fists clenched at his sides.

"Why would you do that to us?" Ethan had deflated in his spot on the desk, his shoulders sagging. He sounded so hurt. *Betrayed.*

Josh just glared.

All three of them were directing their hurt and anger at Alec, dismissing my part in it. They assumed I was the victim, the one that needed protecting.

I didn't deserve them.

"Stop!" I yelled, throwing my hands out. My breathing was coming in pants, and tears streamed down my face, unstoppable now that they had started. "We *both* did this. I deserve just as much of your anger as he does."

I wasn't defending him, but I deserved to have them yell at *me*, turn away from *me*, want nothing more to do with *me*. Coming between them was the last thing I wanted. They had been family since birth, and I'd been around for only a few months. Now they were at each other's throats.

Before I could say anything else, Josh held his arm out at his side and, with a motion that was now familiar to me from our training, flung it out. A book from the shelf behind him came hurtling out into the room. At first I thought he was aiming for me, but his gaze was still focused over my shoulder, and the book sailed right past me.

I spun around just in time to see it heading for Alec's face, but instead of whacking him in the nose as it should have, it came within an inch of his head, bounced away, and thudded to the ground. Alec didn't even flinch. He just stood there, arms crossed.

"What the fu—" Josh's confused utterance was interrupted by Ethan jumping into motion. He lifted his hand, fingers curled, and a ball of blue fire appeared. This was not the harmless magic trick he flicked around to impress his friends. This was angry fire, dangerous and lethal.

In the space of a heartbeat, he was hurling it at his older cousin, but just as the book had deflected away from him, the fire curved over Alec's shoulder and sputtered out into nothing, leaving him completely unharmed.

Ethan looked down at his hand as if it were a faulty gadget, his brow creasing.

Alec finally spoke, sounding resigned. "You can't hurt me."

"Holy shit," Tyler and Josh said in tandem from behind me.

My brain had begun to piece things together since the book had bounced off Alec harmlessly, just as all those items had bounced off me in Josh's room when we'd first met. Just as Ethan's fire had curved benignly over my skin in the pool.

I was reeling, but when Alec spoke those words, confirming what my brain was slow to articulate, a deep-seated rage from somewhere deep inside my chest began to fill me. It coiled around my insides, memories fueling it as it grew.

When I first saw him at Bradford Hills, naively hugging him, everyone around us had doubled over in pain, yet I felt nothing. When his hand landed on my bare shoulder as we entered the gala, it had felt pleasant, not painful. When he kissed me, he didn't tell me not to touch him to protect me from his ability; it was to protect himself. To keep me from finding out . . .

The room had gone completely still. The rage was spreading out to my limbs, filling me with explosive energy. This had nothing to do with the Light. This was purely emotional, and it was about to rain down on Alec's head.

"Wait, does this mean that she's *that* . . ." Tyler was struggling to finish a sentence. "I can't believe I didn't see it before . . ."

"Yeah. Look—" Alec began.

But I didn't give him the chance to try to explain himself or justify everything he had done—I cut across him.

"You knew!" The shriek that came out of me was like no other sound I'd ever heard myself make. It was guttural and feral, and it had the desired effect—he stopped talking and regarded me warily. "All this time you knew. From that night in the hospital, you knew we were connected, and you said nothing!"

"Hospital? What hospital?" Tyler asked, confused.

I hadn't told anyone Alec had stayed with me after the crash, but I couldn't stop to explain now. I barreled on.

"You knew I was completely alone in the world. I'd just lost my mother, and I thought I would never belong anywhere again for the rest of my life. And you knew I belonged with you, and you said nothing! Instead you actively avoided me, blocking my attempts to find you. For a whole fucking year! Why were you so determined to make me miserable? *What did I do to you?*"

The last question came out on a sob, but I didn't let him answer, a new wave of rage edging me on.

"The last few months, you haven't been staying away from me because you though I didn't need to thank you. You weren't avoiding touching me because of your pain ability. Your ability could never hurt me. You've been avoiding me like the bubonic fucking plague because you didn't want me to realize I'm your Vital. Because if I touched you, I would have known."

I was breathing hard, the words pouring out of me as fast as they were coming into my mind, frenzied and laced with hurt.

"And last night. It was perfectly natural for us to be attracted to each other. It was natural for me to want it, to like it. But I didn't know that. I thought I was an awful person for having those feelings for you, for going outside my Bond. I felt like the scum of the earth for what we did, when in reality, there was a reason it felt right. And *you knew.* You let me feel like shit about it when you knew, this whole time, that I was your Vital. You . . . you *fucking asshole!*"

I screamed the last part into his face, my fists tightly clenched, completely giving in to the rage.

He stared back at me with intense, stormy eyes, his own breathing getting faster, his shoulders tense under his shirt. He kept his mouth shut, but an all too familiar tension entered his stance.

I knew this look. I'd seen it over and over every time he'd bolted out of a room to avoid me. He was about to run. I was done letting him.

"NO!" I declared with more finality in my voice than I knew I was capable of. "You don't get to leave. You don't get to run away from me anymore. You don't get to avoid this clusterfuck you've created. I'm the one that's going to leave now, and you're going to stay here and sort this shit out with the three people who have been your closest family since day one. You owe them that much."

I took a deep breath and walked to the door. With one hand on the handle, I said in a much softer voice, "Don't any of you dare follow me."

And then I walked out, purposely slamming the door. As I started climbing the stairs, Tyler's office erupted into a frenzy of voices.

TWENTY ONE

I pushed open the door to Josh's room, stepped inside quickly, and slammed it closed, leaning against it as I tried to catch my breath.

It felt good to slam doors.

I didn't know why I'd chosen Josh's room. Maybe because it was the first door at the top of the stairs. Maybe because this was where we'd been spending the most time together. Or maybe because this was where it had all started—with a kiss and a room full of floating books.

But that wasn't where it had started. Like so many other things, that was a lie. It had really started in the hospital with Alec.

Another wave of anger surged through me, and with a grunt of frustration, I pushed off the door and started pacing the room. I was feeling so many things, I had no idea where to start unpacking them. Anger seemed like the easiest one to latch on to. It was safe and defensive.

He had avoided me for a year. A whole fucking year!

And it wasn't just me he'd hurt. He had deceived the three people closest to him, and in a way, that was even worse. I had only known them for a few short months, but one thing was painfully obvious—they would do anything for one another. Did I factor into that equation now? Logically, considering our Bond, I must, but . . .

I paused to lean against the bookshelf by the fireplace, feeling drained. I had gone from crippling guilt and self-loathing over what I thought was a betrayal to searing rage over Alec's *actual* betrayal in under a minute. It was a lot to handle.

My thoughts started down a dark and twisted path—what exactly did this mean about my Bond, about our connection? If Alec could resist it so easily, that meant Tyler could too. Maybe Josh and Ethan weren't entirely thrilled about it either and were just being nice. After all, they were adamant about keeping it a secret. Maybe they resented my barging into their family, throwing their perfect lives into chaos. Maybe *none* of them really wanted me around.

Hot tears started pouring down my face again as doubt and worry overtook the anger. There was no denying I was already attached to them. Much of that had to do with our supernatural connection, yes, but I would be lying if I said I didn't like it. The Light coursing through me had tethered us together, and for the first time since my mother died, I didn't feel as if I was alone in the world.

But maybe that was an illusion too. If Alec could lie about it, hide it, and keep seeing other women, maybe the strength of our Bond was all in my head. Was I so afraid of being alone that I'd deluded myself into thinking our connection was stronger than it actually was?

I started sobbing, sinking to my knees, a horrible gaping wound opening in my chest. It was that same crushing feeling I'd had in the hospital. And it terrified me.

But something inside wasn't allowing me to fall apart this time. A surge of anger rose up again, and I growled in frustration and lashed out with both arms, knocking the contents of the shelf to the ground. Josh's books, CDs and other random items fell in a mess that closely resembled my current emotions: chaotic and haphazard.

The force of my own blow sent me swinging sideways, and I landed on my hands and knees in among the stuff I'd knocked to the ground. I was breathing hard, my vision blurry from the tears still flowing freely through my rage. I tried to take some deep, calming breaths for the millionth time that morning, wiping the tears from my eyes.

As the mess under me came into focus, my attention snagged on something right under my face. A photo album had fallen open, its pages half-covered by another book. I frowned and leaned my head closer, pushing the book aside.

Someone familiar looked out at me from one of the images—the chocolate hair, the dull blue eyes, the black dress with the yellow and red poppies. The very dress that was hanging in my closet; the one I couldn't bring myself to wear.

I was looking at a photo of my mother.

She was standing outside—smiling, bare feet in the lush grass—in the center of four other young women, their arms around one another's waists. She must have been around my age when this was taken, maybe a little older.

I pulled the photo out of its sleeve and brought it up to my face, absorbing every detail of my mother's youthful image as I sat back on my heels.

I missed her so much. Being reminded of her now, when I was already in such an emotional state, was like a punch in the guts. But my brain, always looking out for me with its logical thinking, reminded me how weird this was.

Why did Josh have a photo of my mother in his room? How did they know her? Or, more accurately, used to know her? Because I would have noticed if they'd been around growing up. That's not something I would have forgotten. *Right?*

Great, now I was questioning my own memory and possibly my sanity.

No. They had definitely not been around when I was growing up. No one had been around when I was growing up. My mother had made damn sure of that.

A sickening thought hit me, sending a chill of fear down my spine.

What if they were what my mother had been running from this whole time?

Obviously my mother had known something serious enough to keep us moving my entire childhood. How much of it had had to do with the four men downstairs—four powerful, dangerous men?

She looked happy in that photo. People don't leave happy lives for no good reason.

I stood up on shaky legs. There had to be an explanation.

I folded the photo and stuffed it into my back pocket, moving toward the door, determined to get some answers. I would march down there, ask why they had a photo of my mother, and make them tell me everything. I was done with being kept in the dark by the people closest to me.

But halfway to the door, I stopped. Uncertainty wrapped around my throat like a vice, making it hard to move or breathe. If they had known who I really was this whole time, that meant they *all* had been lying to me.

My mother's face flashed through my mind. The sensation of her hand slipping out of mine as she disappeared into the darkness . . .

It had been a confusing, overwhelming day, but one thing I could be sure of without a shadow of a doubt? My mother had always had my best interests at heart. She may have kept a lot of secrets, but I never questioned her love for me. As much as I'd struggled with our nomadic lifestyle, I'd always trusted her.

I wasn't about to stop now.

If my mother had given up her life to keep me away from this place, possibly away from these people, then I needed to get out of here. Now.

The balcony was my best bet. I crossed the room, listening for approaching footsteps, and peered through the curtains by the balcony door. The coast was clear.

As quickly and quietly as possible, I made my way outside and over to the stairs leading into the grounds, then rushed down them. The stairs ended at the side of the house. Just around the corner was the winding driveway, the window to Tyler's office, and past that, the grand front doors.

I had to get across the open grass area to reach the cover of the trees lining the driveway. Anyone who happened to look out on that side of the house would see me. I hoped like hell they were all still in the office, too preoccupied with Alec's revelations to look out the window.

I took a deep breath and crossed the grass at a steady pace. If anyone in the house were to look out, it would seem suspicious if I was running like a maniac or sneaking like a cat burglar.

Those twenty seconds were the longest of my life. I didn't dare turn around. The adrenaline pumping through my body was demanding that I break into a run, but I managed to remain in control until I reached the trees.

Then I did break into a run. No one could see me now, and I needed to put as much distance as possible between me and the mansion.

I ran as fast as I could to the front gates, emerging onto the wide, tree-lined street. Once again I had to keep a normal pace. I couldn't chance drawing attention, but I didn't know how long it would be before they noticed I was missing. I settled on a light jog and hoped that if I kept a steady pace, I would just look as if I were out for a run.

Nothing to see here people; just burning some calories.

I made it to campus without incident, but my heart was hammering in my chest. I'd spent the entire time glancing back, expecting to see Tyler's black SUV pulling up behind me, the tinted windows hiding the men inside poised to grab me.

I had been so focused on getting out of the Zacarias mansion and away from the guys that I'd neglected to make any real plan. As I reached the front door of the room I shared with the Reds, I paused, realizing my potentially fatal mistake.

This is the first place they would come looking for me. What other place did I have to go? *Stupid!* How could I have been so predictable? What if they'd already noticed my absence and were on their way? What if they'd called Zara and Beth, and my roomies unknowingly delayed my escape. Or, and here my stomach sank, what if Zara and Beth were in on it? Did they know too?

I was crippled with indecision, my hand poised over the door handle. *Go in or run for it again? Quick! Decide! Your life could depend on it!*

The memory of my mother's voice repeatedly telling me to "never trust anyone" had me pulling my hand back.

I looked up and down the corridor, no idea how much time I had. Doing my best to stop my hands from shaking, I quietly made my way back down the hallway, then ran down the stairs and out the door.

Pausing, I glanced around the corner. I only had a partial view of the lane winding up toward the front gate, but no black SUVs were coming toward me, so I hurried down the stairs.

The sun had retreated behind clouds and taken some of the heat with it. If I wasn't so flushed from the running and the panic, I would have been cold.

I took the walking tracks through campus to a side entrance—the one closest to the center of town and the train station.

Memories of all the times my mom and I had packed up and disappeared kept flashing through my mind. Tears pricked my eyes as panic threatened to take over, but I knew I had to get out of town. *Fast.* It was what she would have done.

The adrenaline was not letting up, making it difficult for me to calm my breathing and formulate some kind of plan. As I walked through town toward the train station, I kept looking over my shoulder, fractured thoughts and half-baked strategies flying through my mind too fast to grasp.

Only one paranoid thought managed to stick—I needed to change my appearance. The image of my mother hacking mercilessly at her hair before dying it some awful yellow-blonde burst across my brain.

I gathered my hair into a ponytail, my eyes scanning the busy street in front of me. Without thinking about it too much, I snagged a hoodie that was slung over the back of a chair in front of a café, its owner probably inside paying their bill. Awkwardly juggling the two pieces of clothing as I hastened my steps, I pulled my loose sweater over my head and dropped it in the trash, pulling on the gray hoodie in its place. It was at least two sizes too big and smelled faintly of smoke.

I thought about getting a taxi into the city, but my mother and I had never taken taxis when we moved. Taxis had cameras and route logs and drivers who made small talk and remembered your face. The anonymity of public transport was a much better way to go.

I made it to the station only to find that the next train to New York wasn't due for another ten minutes. I had no choice. I had to wait. I picked a spot near the exit and pulled my hood low over my face.

Those ten minutes felt like hours. I was jumpy and constantly looking around, expecting them to burst onto the platform at any moment. I probably looked like a paranoid drug addict.

When the train finally pulled into the station, I all but sprinted into it, launched myself into a seat in the far back, then bounced my leg maniacally until the doors closed and we moved off. At last, I took a deep breath and leaned back.

I was so on edge that when my phone rang in my back pocket, it startled me so badly that I shot out of my seat, gaining me some strange looks, including one from a guy in a bright pink leotard and Santa hat. Even the weirdos on the train thought I was a weirdo.

The incoming call was from Tyler. I waited for it to ring out, then unlocked the screen. I had sixteen text messages and twelve missed calls. How had I not heard it going off before? I had been so focused on my surroundings, so worried I was about to get caught, that I'd forgotten it was even in my pocket.

The messages were from Ethan and Josh—text after text asking where I was and if I was OK, and saying that they wanted to talk. The last few said how worried they were.

There was one from Zara too:

You OK? Your boyfriend and his 3 pseudo brothers showed up here looking for you. What did you do? LOL

And then another one straight after.

What did THEY do? I don't care what kind of scary abilities they have, I will fuck them up.

Shit. They knew I was on the run.

It took an hour to get into the city, and I watched the doors with trepidation at every stop, waiting for one of them to step inside and haul me off. Past getting out of Bradford Hills, I had no plan whatsoever. Knowing they knew I was gone, I would have to find which train was leaving first and just go there. I would literally be getting on a train going anywhere, just like that stupid Journey song.

Which made me think of how Josh loved his music and how frantic Ethan's last text was and how Tyler had tried to call me *twelve* times. A little lump in my throat formed as I thought of them.

But I had to be strong. Something was not right here. This was exactly the kind of thing my mom had been warning me about my whole life. They had lured me in—these feelings were not real. It was the opposite of emotional blackmail. It was emotional entrapment. Was that a thing? I'd have to look it up in one of the psych books. If it wasn't a thing, I was making it thing. I gave myself props for coining a term while under duress and on the run.

It was a good distraction for about three seconds.

I turned my phone off and focused on not getting upset—my life depended on it. As soon as the train pulled into Grand Central, I would beeline for the ticket counter.

I was beginning to get hot and uncomfortable in the hoodie, so I took it off as the train pulled into the station. It was probably good to change my appearance again anyway. I was now in just jeans and a black tank top, the hoodie tied around my waist.

Stepping off the train and into the crowd, I looked around. The ticket counters would probably be in the main section, and following the crowd off the platform was my best bet for avoiding attention. Everyone was heading toward a staircase leading up, so I joined the flow of bodies and tried to keep pace.

At the bottom of the stairs, one hand on the railing, I looked up to see where I was going, and my eyes locked with a pair of ice-blue ones.

My stomach dropped.

Alec was standing with his legs apart and his arms crossed over his black-clad chest. He was staring right at me, eyes narrowed, but he was too far away for me to see his expression. Was it angry? Annoyed? Murderous?

None of the others were anywhere in sight, and I wasn't sure if that was a good or bad thing. Regardless, I was caught.

I had tried my best to do as my mother would have wanted, and I had failed.

TWENTY TWO

Alec's intense stare pinned me to the spot. Panic rose inside me again, my palms getting sweaty and my breathing becoming erratic. He couldn't hurt me with his ability, but there was more than one way to inflict pain, and I had a feeling Alec was intimately acquainted with all of them.

I looked over my shoulder, searching for another way out. There was nothing other than the edge of the platform and the dark tunnel into which the train was disappearing. I briefly considered taking my chances with the tunnel, but I knew the limits of the human body and I had a better chance of surviving an altercation with Alec than I did with a moving train, so I turned back to him.

He flopped his arms by his sides and rolled his eyes. "Can we just talk?" His voice echoed off the concrete walls.

The platform had cleared. It was just me and him. He started down the stairs, and I immediately backed away, matching him step for step.

Halfway down, he slowed to a stop, his brow creasing as he watched me retreat. "Are you . . . *scared?* Evelyn, you know I can't hurt you with my ability. I would never do that, even if I could."

"How do you know my name?" I gritted out between clenched teeth. His use of my real name had confirmed my suspicions. I no longer believed he would give me the truth about anything, but I couldn't help asking the question.

"That's what we need to talk about. I handled this so badly . . . but when the boys went to look for you, you were gone, and . . ." He looked uncertain, his eyebrows drawn together in confusion, but he wasn't making any sense.

I had nothing left to lose. I reached into my back pocket and pulled out the photo from Josh's room.

"I know." I thrust the photo toward him, my voice shaky but loud in the cavernous space. "What . . . ? Why . . . ?" I wasn't sure what I was accusing him of. My mother had never actually told me why she kept us moving, but it *had* to have something to do with Bradford Hills. It was too much of a coincidence.

He finished his descent and stood before me, reaching for the photo. As soon as he grabbed it, I stepped back, putting more distance between us.

With a soft curse, he pulled his phone out of his pocket, tapped at it, then put it away again.

"I don't know what's going on in that head of yours, but you don't know the full story." He held the photo out so I could see it. "What do you think this proves? Obviously it has you spooked enough to run away." I didn't move to retrieve the photo—it felt like a trap.

Why did he sound as if he only now realized I was making a run for it? Wasn't that the whole reason he was here? To kidnap me back to Bradford Hills and . . . and . . .

It was becoming more difficult to think clearly. I let out a grunt of frustration, turning away from him and tugging at my hair.

When I spun back around, realizing I'd given my back to the enemy, he was in the exact same spot he was in before, arms crossed over his broad chest, watching me with those intense blue eyes.

When he'd raked his gaze over my body the night of the gala, it had felt exciting and sensual. Now his gaze just made my skin crawl.

"What are we waiting for?" I wanted him to make a move. Maybe if we got off this platform, I could try to get away from him. "Why aren't you gagging me and throwing me into the back of a van?"

He threw his head back and laughed, a hollow, humorless sound. "You are so far off the mark it's hilarious. And we're waiting for reinforcements."

So that's what he'd done on his phone. *Shit!* I might have been able to slip away from Alec in the crowd, but there was no way I could get away from an entire team of trained special agents. My shoulders sagged in defeat, and I wrapped my arms around myself, my nails digging into my sides.

Itchiness crept up my arms—maybe some of my fidgety energy had nothing to do with adrenaline.

Just as I'd realized my control of my Light had slipped in my mad escape attempt, the "reinforcements" came barreling down the stairs.

It was not a Melior Group Special Forces team, as I had imagined. It was Tyler, Josh, and Ethan, all wearing matching looks of concern. Taking two steps at a time, Ethan made it onto the platform first and headed straight for me.

A cold jolt of fear went straight through my body, and I backed away, arms raised. He stopped in his tracks, the concern on his face replaced with shock.

"Eve?" He looked so broken and vulnerable. His big shoulders sagged, one muscled arm stretched out to me, his fire tattoo peeking out from his T-shirt sleeve. It made me remember how good it felt to be held in those big arms, and I longed to step into them.

I scratched at my arms frantically, trying somehow to discern how much of my nervous energy could be attributed to the excess Light coursing through me and how much was due to my instincts.

Tyler and Josh took a more measured approach. Josh stepped up next to Ethan and placed a hand on his shoulder, watching me warily. Tyler, as usual, took charge of the situation. He moved forward slowly, his arms held up in front of him, as if he were approaching a wild animal. I suppose I might have looked like one, my wide eyes darting between them, still looking for an escape route, while my fingernails raked frenziedly at various parts of my body. The itching was getting worse.

Alec, true to form, was hanging back and leaning on the railing of the staircase, letting everyone else clean up the mess he'd made. Typical. He was always ready to run away. How dare he? I was supposed to be the one running away today. *Dick!*

As Tyler regarded me cautiously, Alec filled them in, his voice dripping mocking amusement. "She was actually trying to run away. She thinks we're here to kidnap her and stuff her into a—what was it? The back of a van? She thinks we've been keeping something from her."

"You *have* been keeping something from her. From all of us!" Ethan responded, eyes still locked on me.

I was getting confused. Why were they fighting among one another? It seemed like Ethan was even on my side. But he had been keeping things from me too. Hadn't he?

Unaffected by his younger cousin's reprimand, Alec handed the photo to Josh. The amusement had left his now hard voice. "She found a photo of Joyce with our moms. She's convinced herself that it's proof of something shady and underhanded."

Josh examined the photo before passing it to Ethan, the looks on their faces indecipherable.

Tyler, on the other hand, didn't take his eyes off me, but neither did he try to get closer. "Eve, I can understand how you might have come to some frightening conclusions, considering all that has happened over the last few weeks. But your Light is out of control, and it could get dangerous if you don't get a handle on it."

"Stay away from me!" I was scared he would try to grab me under the pretense of helping me expel the Light. At the same time, I was craving his contact just as much, the Light inside me begging to be released. My hands were now under my tank top, scratching at my belly; I was seriously considering ripping the thin fabric off.

"I'm not going to do anything until you say so. Neither are the others. Eve. Look at me."

I couldn't help myself; I looked into his face. He wore a neutral expression, but his gray eyes were overflowing with intensity. It was a little mesmerizing.

"Good. Now, just try to take some deep breaths." He took an exaggerated inhale, and I mimicked him, both of us exhaling together. Some of my mindfulness practice came back to me, and I focused on calming my breathing.

"Good." He was speaking in the gentle, encouraging voice he always used in our tutoring sessions. "That's good. OK, now, I know you're scared, so I'm not going to argue with you, but I am going to ask you to consider the facts." He was appealing to my natural affinity for learning, for logic, for the scientific process. "What are the facts, Eve? What is the observable truth? What is the simplest explanation? Ockham's Razor, Eve."

I continued to take deep breaths as I thought about it. What did I *know*?

I knew that that the unbridled power coursing through me was verging on unbearable. The Light was *demanding* to be released.

I knew I was connected to the four men standing on the platform with me. I'd learned enough about the nature of Variant Bonds and physiology to be able to recognize this for what it was.

I knew Tyler always encouraged me to ask questions and learn more, just as he was doing now. He had never been evasive with me.

I knew Josh was so observant and in tune with my body language and facial expressions that he sometimes knew what I was thinking before I did.

I knew Ethan had done all he could to make it clear I was his to all the other Variants at Bradford Hills, without actually giving away that we were connected.

I knew Alec was a total douche bag—but that wasn't really relevant at the moment.

I knew they were somehow connected to my mother—to my past before I had any memories of it. The photo I'd found, and that Alec had used my real name, was evidence of that.

I knew my mother had kept us running my whole life to keep us from something dangerous. But . . .

I never knew what that was exactly. I had no concrete evidence to suggest it had anything to do with my guys.

My guys.

My Bond. The men that I was connected to by a tether stronger than anything on this physical plane.

I knew they couldn't harm me if they wanted to. I had stuck my hand in Ethan's fire enough times to know it was harmless to me. Josh's telekinesis had items bouncing off me as if I was surrounded by a force field, and Alec . . . Alec had hurt me badly but not with his ability.

As I puzzled these things out, I was trying, and failing, to get a handle on my Light, but at least my fear was subsiding. When I'd found that photo, I'd assumed the worst, my body going into fight or flight mode and choosing what I'd spent my entire childhood perfecting—flight. My suspicion wasn't completely gone, but perhaps my fear was unwarranted.

Someone was calling my name.

"Eve!" Alec's almost panicked voice crashed into my consciousness. "Evie!"

I snapped out of my thoughts and looked at him. He had used my childhood nickname, the name my mother used to call me. No one had called me that since before the plane crash.

But why was he so desperate to get my attention?

I looked over to the other three. They were all staring intently at my face. Ethan's eyes, almost of their own accord, flicked down to my body, then back up to my eyes.

The infuriating itch had spread to every part of my body, and I was frantically running my nails over my skin, from my arms to my shoulders to my belly to my legs. My bare legs . . . *Why wasn't I wearing pants?*

I looked down at myself. Without even being conscious of it, I had stripped down to my underwear, the Light raging through me so uncomfortable that I had removed the constrictive fabric. But that wasn't the most shocking thing.

I was glowing!

Every inch of my body had a soft white luminescence to it. Like a nightlight or a Christmas tree or *fucking plutonium!*

Any semblance of trying to get my Light under control went out the window, and I went into full panic mode.

"What the fuck?" I screeched, my eyes darting around the platform in a futile search for a solution.

"Eve, please let me help you." Tyler sounded desperate. He was breathing hard, his messy hair hanging loose over one side of his forehead, his eyes wide.

"Yes! Make it go away!"

He was in front of me before I even finished speaking, holding his hands out in the familiar way. I squeezed my eyes shut and grabbed him around the wrists, needing something to hold on to.

As soon as we made skin contact, the Light poured out of me. But unlike our usual transfer sessions, it didn't channel through my hands and into Tyler at the points where we touched. It burst out of me everywhere, as if every part of my body, every pore on my skin, was releasing Light as freely as any river.

It was a force of nature.

"Whoa! You feel that?" Ethan's voice came from somewhere behind Tyler, followed by the heavy thud of booted feet running up the concrete steps.

"Yeah . . ." Josh sounded unsure of his answer, which was odd for him.

"Back up, you two," Tyler said from right in front of me.

I was reveling in the relief from the frenetic energy, but I forced myself to open my eyes. Tyler was looked as shocked as he had been the first time we'd done this. He released my arms and placed one hand on my neck. The other he laid flat against the exposed skin on my back.

I could feel the Light transferring through the spots where Tyler was touching me. It was the first time I'd transferred Light through someplace other than my hands (unless you counted the times I'd done it while kissing), and if the fractured conversation I'd just heard was anything to go by, apparently I didn't even need the contact.

But that was impossible according to every bit of research I'd read about how Light transfer works. What the hell was wrong with me? Not only was I releasing Light without skin contact, I was *glowing*.

I reached out, still needing something to keep me grounded, and grabbed a fistful of Tyler's shirt in each hand. With my hands in front of my face, I was beyond relieved to see I was no longer glowing.

"Incredible." Tyler's breath washed over my face. He was holding me close. On a train platform. In one of the busiest terminals in the world. And I was in my underwear!

I looked around nervously. By some miracle, the platform was completely empty of people. Josh came up behind me and draped my discarded, stolen hoodie over my shoulders.

I pressed myself a little closer to Tyler and said, with as much conviction as I could, "Thank you."

He smiled in relief and gently kissed my forehead in place of a "you're welcome." Then he released me into Josh's arms.

Josh spun me around and pulled me into a bone-crushing hug, and I wrapped my arms around his waist and held on tight. I'd only been on the run for a few hours, but it felt so good to be back with them. How could I have ever felt unsafe with my guys?

With one final squeeze that expelled all the air from my lungs, Josh released me. He held the hoodie out so I could pull my arms into the sleeves, then darted his eyes around the platform before kissing me quickly on the lips.

I turned away from Josh to find Ethan still standing in the same spot, arms by his sides, his expression guarded. He'd looked so hurt and rejected when I'd moved away from him in fear, and it was killing me to see the uncertainty still in his eyes.

I rushed over and launched myself at him, wrapping my arms around his shoulders and my legs around his middle. He caught me effortlessly, holding me much more gently than Josh had, considering his size. I buried my head in his neck, and he mirrored me, breathing deeply. For a few moments, he rocked us side to side, then lifted his head.

Unlike Josh, he didn't bother to look around the platform before kissing me. He just mashed his lips to mine, pouring all his feelings into that fierce kiss. I returned it just as enthusiastically, knowing he needed the reassurance and comfort.

Just as our tongues met, the kiss deepening naturally, Tyler cleared his throat.

"We're running out of time. Alec is keeping the crowd off the platform, but there isn't much he can do about the train that's about to roll in."

As if to prove his point, the distinctive *whirr* and *clack* of an approaching train issued from the darkness of the tunnel. I pushed against Ethan's shoulders, and after a moment of reluctance, he released me. Once again, Josh was there with clothing, handing me my jeans and shoes.

I hurried to pull on the pants, and Josh zipped the hoodie up over my bra just as the train rolled into the platform. Tyler shoved my discarded tank top into his pocket and led our group to the stairs, Ethan with his fingers laced through mine and Josh close behind us.

I had tried and failed to do as my mother would have—to run. I hadn't even made it out of the state, but I had succeeded at something I'd never even seen her attempt.

I'd found someone to trust.

Ethan Paul, Joshua Mason, Tyler Gabriel, and even Alec Zacarias had—through the Light-fueled, supernaturally intense connection we shared—become a part of my life.

Despite the many complicated issues we had to work through, they were as much a part of me as I was of them. If I couldn't trust my Bond, whom could I trust?

TWENTY THREE

Like a sentinel, Alec stood at the top of the stairs with his feet planted wide, his arms crossed. He had pulled the sleeves of his black top up to his elbows, and the tight muscles in his forearms were on full display. There was obvious tension in his shoulders.

In front of him, a disgruntled mob of New Yorkers was getting increasingly impatient. Many were muttering and throwing pissed-off sideways glances in Alec's direction. He wasn't using his ability—no one was doubled over in pain—so I had no idea how he'd managed to keep them all at bay, but none of them were even trying to get past.

Tyler reached the top first and whispered something to Alec before pushing through the crowd. Alec nodded once, and just as Ethan and I made it to the top, he dropped his arms by his sides. His hand landed right next to mine, and he wrapped his warm, calloused fingers around it.

When our hands connected, he didn't even turn his head to look at me. He just held on and took the lead, dragging me along behind him. The intense Light transfer I'd just experienced on the platform was keeping the energy satiated for the time being—I felt only a light tingling where we touched, a tiny amount of Light passing from me to him.

Still, the Light was pulling us toward each other like magnets. I'd just had an intense couple of days, punctuated by the most overwhelming Light overflow I'd experienced to date—I mean, I fucking glowed!—and the Light was demanding closeness to my Bond. I'd melted into my guys on the platform like chocolate left in the sun. Each of them, in their unique way, made me feel as if that was exactly where I belonged—in their arms.

Now the Light was pushing me to bring Alec into that fold too. At least, I was pretty sure I was experiencing an instinctual reaction to our connection. Why else would my traitor hand grab on to Alec's and hold on? I was still pretty pissed off at him, and the logical side of my mind was reminding me he was still a massive jerk.

But there we were, hand in hand, pushing through the grumbling crowd. With Ethan still holding firmly on to my other hand, we made a short human chain as we rushed toward the exit.

Tyler's black SUV came to a screeching halt in front of us just as we stepped out onto the street. Josh took shotgun, and I found myself squished into the middle between Alec and Ethan.

As soon as all the doors were shut, Tyler took off as if we were in a high-speed car chase. Ethan draped an arm over my shoulders and held me so tight I wasn't sure I even needed my seatbelt, but Alec made me put it on anyway, holding the clip out at my side silently while dialing a number on his phone.

He made several efficient calls, speaking softly but firmly and saying things like "contain the situation," "pacify the civilians," and "acquire CCTV footage." I tried to listen in, but the motion of the car and the softness of Ethan's embrace lulled me. Other than Alec's few phone calls, the car was silent.

A few minutes after his last call, Alec's hand landed on my thigh. I opened my eyes to look at him, but he had his face angled toward the window.

He took a deep breath and squeezed my leg firmly, his quiet voice carrying in the silent car. "Don't ever do that again, Evelyn."

Next to me, Ethan tensed. All of my sleepiness vanished, replaced by more of the rage that had coursed through me in Tyler's study. I sat up straight, shrugging Ethan's arm off.

"Do what?" I demanded through gritted teeth. "Lie? Evade? Keep secrets?"

He snapped his head around, and for the first time since I'd come face to face with him on the platform, I looked properly into his vibrant ice-blue eyes. Pain flickered across his face before that familiar emotionless mask fell into place.

Before he had a chance to reply, Tyler raised his voice from the front seat. "Enough! We will discuss this like adults, or we won't discuss it at all."

Alec clamped his mouth shut and glowered at me, but I wasn't willing to back down. I clenched my hands into fists.

"The hell we won't! I deserve answers!" Of course, taking my anger at Alec out on Tyler wasn't fair, but the frustration was growing fast.

"Yes, you do," Tyler answered in a level voice, fixing me with a look in the rearview mirror. "But can we try to do it without everyone getting so worked up? Or do you want to go another round of glow-in-the-dark, Eve?"

That sobered me up, and I checked in with my body. Sure enough, my elevated emotions had caused my control to slip again, and I was surprised to find Light coursing through me so soon after I'd expelled it into Tyler. I took a few deep breaths and slammed the mental door shut, preventing it from getting out of hand.

I had forgotten Alec's hand still resting on my leg, so I was startled when he suddenly whipped it away, pressing himself to the car door and as far away from me as possible. I looked over, giving him my best "what the fuck" look. His reaction was confusing, considering how drawn the other three were to my Light, their abilities pushing them to instinctively seek me out.

I didn't have time to dwell on it though. I had so many other questions.

"OK, fine," I said in a much calmer voice. "I'll behave. But can someone please start speaking?"

Surprisingly, it was Josh who answered, leaving Tyler to concentrate on the road. At the speed he was maintaining, we would be back in Bradford Hills in record time.

"The photo you found, of your mother—the other women in it are our mothers. They were all friends a long time ago. For the first five years of your life, Eve, we were like family. Our parents were close, and we spent almost every day together. Then one day, your mother and you just disappeared. I was only seven at the time, so I don't remember much, but I remember everyone being really upset about it. They refused to answer any of our questions. I think they knew more than they told us, but I guess now we'll never know."

He leaned his head on the window, seemingly lost in thought.

Ethan spoke next, but instead of picking up where Josh had left off, he knocked the breath out of me with his soft, insecure voice. "Why did you run?"

I took his big hand in both of mine and squeezed tightly, swallowing around the lump in my throat. I hated that I'd hurt him.

Before I had a chance to explain myself, Tyler did it for me. "She thought her mother had kept them on the run all those years because she was trying to keep her from us."

Shocked, I looked to the front of the car, but he didn't meet my eyes.

"She saw the photo of her mother, she was already in a highly emotional state, she panicked. She was reeling from Alec's revelation, and she wondered what else we could be keeping from her. She spent her childhood running from place to place, her mother keeping them constantly on the move to evade an unexplained threat. It came naturally to her to run."

The car descended into silence, all of us staring at him in astonishment.

"How . . . ?" I was positive I hadn't told Tyler anything about my mother keeping us on the run, not even how much I'd moved around as a child. I *knew* I hadn't told any of them how panicked I was when I found the photo, although I guess that would be a logical conclusion.

He cleared his throat and glanced at me in the mirror. "I've been noticing some . . . enhancements to my ability with all the extra Light I've been receiving. With a particularly large dose, like just now, not only can I tell when someone is being untruthful, I can tell what they are being untruthful about and what the basic truth behind the situation is."

After another beat of silence, the car erupted into animated noise, all of us shouting over one another. Ethan was asking if that would apply to all their abilities and what enhancements he might experience, Josh was outraged that Tyler had not told us all about this sooner, Alec was demanding to know what else Tyler "knew to be the truth," and I wanted to know more about how it worked. How much Light was needed to kick this into action? How long did it last?

Unfortunately, none of us got any answers. We pulled into the parking garage at the mansion, and Tyler shut off the engine. Turning in his seat, he silenced us all with a stern look.

"Look, this is pretty new, and I'm still figuring it out, but in the interest of transparency"—he looked pointedly at Alec—"I wanted to share it with you all. Going forward, I think we need to be more honest with one another, and I'm trying to lead by example. Now, I don't know about any of you, but it's nearly dinner time, and I haven't eaten since breakfast. I'm still hungover, and I need food."

Without waiting for a response, he got out of the car and went inside.

As soon as Tyler mentioned food, my stomach grumbled. I too hadn't eaten since my breakfast bagel. *Was that only this morning?* Not to mention that intense, unbridled Light transference had left me feeling depleted in every way, just as it had on the night Ethan nearly died.

An unspoken agreement settled between us, to put the heavy conversation on hold until our bellies were full. We sat in companionable silence around the big kitchen island, wolfing down leftovers.

Ethan situated himself next to me and ate one-handed, his other hand resting on my knee. He'd refused to leave my side since the train station. I hated seeing the larger-than-life, boisterous show-off acting so insecure. I hadn't seen a hint of the dimples since that morning.

Alec was the first to finish eating. Sitting at the head of the bench, he was resting his chin on his clasped hands and watching me intently.

Done with being intimidated by him, I returned his gaze. All our interactions over the last few months whirred through my brain, every conversation, every look falling under a new light. Knowing he was part of my Bond had made certain things click into place—his tenderness at the hospital and his willingness to help keep an eye on me once we found out I was connected to Josh and Ethan—but it raised more questions than it answered.

"Why did your ability hurt Tyler?" It was just one of a million questions that had been running through my head when I'd opened my mouth to speak.

At his confused look, I elaborated. "When I first saw you at Bradford Hills, remember? I ran up and hugged you, and everyone freaked out because they thought you would hurt me." I chuckled, knowing now how impossible that was, and the others laughed with me. Even Alec dropped his hands to the bench and smirked. "You got all worked up and lost control of your ability, and everyone got a headache. If Tyler is in my Bond, why was he affected?"

Tyler hummed thoughtfully around his last bite of stir-fry. "We weren't connected yet."

I gave him a questioning look. "I was under the impression that Bonds were a preordained kind of deal. You can't choose who you connect with— you just hope to find the people the Light has fused you to already."

"Well, yes. The connection is a force of nature we have little control over, but it still needs to be formed, strengthened, developed. When you first saw Alec in the square, our connection hadn't formed yet. We hadn't touched, you hadn't transferred Light to me. It was an inevitability now that we were in such close proximity, but it still wasn't an actuality at that point."

I nodded. The Light inside me had still needed to get to know him.

"Oh shit!" Josh laughed out loud from the end of the bench. "Finally, the field is leveled."

"Yes!" Tyler and Ethan exclaimed at the same time, turning to high-five him over my head.

"What am I missing here?" I grinned, totally lost but overjoyed at the reappearance of Ethan's dimples.

"Every year, at Thanksgiving, we play a game of football," Ethan explained, returning his possessive hand to my knee, "and every year Alec cheats by using his ability. Now he can't do it anymore!" He bounced a little in his seat as he finished.

Alec leaned back, his arms crossed loosely over his chest. He was staring daggers at the other three, but there was amusement in his face too. "I do no such thing. You know my ability leaks out when I get excited. It's a total accident."

A chorus of skeptical remarks and teasing was thrown his way.

"This is why I didn't tell any of you I was part of your stupid Bond! You're just going to use it against me!" He said it jokingly, but it had a sobering effect, and everyone fell quiet again.

"Wait a minute." Something wasn't making sense to me. Actually, a lot wasn't making sense to me; this just happened to pop into my mind first. "I was in the hospital. They did tests. How come they didn't pick up that I had Variant DNA?"

Everyone turned to Alec.

"Uh, yeah. I took care of that."

"Elaborate, please!"

"I had the tests intercepted and the results of the Variant screening falsified." No hint of remorse. Not even a scrap of sheepishness on his face.

Overlooking the disturbing fact that this had been easy for him to do, I asked the obvious question. "Why?"

It was a heavy, loaded "why," encompassing more than just the falsified records. It was the question I had been struggling with since the moment I realized we were connected and he had been lying for over a year.

He sighed and stood up, leaning on the counter. The posture put his head just under one of the pendant lights hanging over the island, and it cast his face into shadow.

"Look, the reasons why I did what I did are complicated, but I want you to know one thing, Evie. Your safety was always the primary concern. I suspected, from the moment I wrapped my arms around your frozen, soaking body, that you were mine. When I got a good look at your face, when I couldn't find it in me to leave your hospital bedside, I knew who you really were. I took the necessary measures to ensure that your status as a Variant—a Vital, no less—would remain secret. To keep you from this world, to keep you *safe*. I know you feel betrayed, and—"

I shot out of my seat. "You have no idea how I feel. How dare you presume to know what I'm thinking or feeling when you've kept me at arm's length for this long? You have no clue who I am as a person."

"I know you better than you might think!" The declaration was heavy with bitterness, and he'd raised his voice to match mine. "What I'm trying to say is, I stayed away from you for a year and I thwarted your attempts to find me, but I didn't abandon you. I kept tabs, I watched your grades, I vetted your foster parents, I had agents tail you when necessary. The only reason I didn't realize you had ended up back here was because the agents were only instructed to alert me of anything dangerous or suspicious. I would have stepped in without a second thought had you needed me."

A part of me was outraged and disturbed to know I'd been practically stalked for the past year, but a much bigger part of me latched on to his last statement: that he would have been there had I needed him. Hot tears welled up in my eyes.

"I needed you." It came out sounding weak and vulnerable. I was so sick of crying. I swatted away the tears on my cheeks in frustration.

I heard him walk over to me, but I couldn't look at him. All our conversations were ending in shouting or tears or both, and I just couldn't do it anymore. After a moment, he walked away, muttering about needing a shower.

As soon as things had become difficult, once again, Alec had run.

I dropped my hands and sighed in defeat. The others all stood from their seats, but it was Tyler who pulled me into a hug. I pressed my cheek against his chest and wrapped my arms around his middle. It was unnerving how comforting his touch was, especially considering he'd kept a careful boundary between us when it came to showing affection.

I felt better, safer, and more alive with one of them near me. I positively hummed when one of them touched me. No wonder I'd descended more and more into paranoid hysteria the farther I ran away from them; I needed them as much as they needed me.

He held me for a long time, and I listened to the boys cleaning up in the kitchen, putting containers back in the fridge, doing the dishes.

After a while, he nudged my chin up until I met his gaze. His gray eyes held warmth and tenderness, but they were tired and bloodshot. Another pang of guilt shot through me for putting them through this.

"I want you to feel safe with us," he stated firmly as his hand massaged the back of my neck, "and not just because your Light-driven instincts tell you that you belong with us. I want you to feel safe on every level, including the highly logical, questioning one you're so good at. I know that Alec's lies have tested your trust, but please believe me when I say we had no idea about any of this. So—"

"Wait," I cut him off, "I need to know. When you say you had no idea, what does that mean?" How much had they all lied to me?

"It means we didn't know you were really Evelyn Maynard." There was a hint of bewilderment in his eyes. "I was twelve when you and your mom disappeared, and it's not like I looked at pictures of her every day for the past decade. There was something familiar about you when we first met, but I couldn't put my finger on it. Later, when we found out we were Bonded, I put the feeling down to our connection and dismissed it. Ethan and Josh just thought they had found their Vital—it never even crossed any of our minds that you were anyone other than who you said you were."

"So you haven't been keeping it from me this whole time?" I needed to hear him say it again.

"Eve, no. I promise. It didn't fall into place until this afternoon, when Josh's book bounced off Alec and I realized he was in our Bond too. That's when I knew who you must be—because we always suspected you were his. He's been keeping this from us too. But no more secrets, OK? If you want to know something, ask. If something makes you uncomfortable or unsure or worried, just tell us. I'm never letting you out of my sight again, so let's make sure you're comfortable where you are, OK?"

He smiled—tired but genuine—and it was infectious, pulling my own lips up at the corners.

"Bunch of stalkers," I whispered and leaned in without thinking.

He closed the distance but, instead of kissing me, squeezed me to his chest one more time. His words had soothed my most pressing anxiety—I believed he hadn't been lying to me. I couldn't see him being very good at it anyway. He held truth above all else as a virtue.

"Stay the night," he said, letting me go and turning toward the door. "I have to go deal with the lying one before I crash."

No sooner had Tyler released me than Ethan stepped up and threaded his fingers through mine. "You'll stay, won't you?" he asked softly.

"Yes. I don't want to be anywhere else right now."

"You can take my room," Josh piped up from the sink, where he'd just finished with the dishes.

Ethan cleared his throat. "Is it OK if I sleep in there with you? I'll take the couch, of course. I just . . . I can't have you out of my sight right now."

"Of course, big guy." I punctuated that with a wide yawn.

Turning out the lights, Josh led the way to his room, and then they left me alone to get ready for bed.

I was wrecked. The day's events had taken a massive toll on my body. Glancing at the clock, I couldn't believe it was only eight. After rushing through my bedtime routine, I pulled my phone out and texted the Reds.

Staying at Ethan's tonight. See you guys tomorrow?

The reply was instant.

Zara: what? What was with them all showing up here earlier? You can't just not explain that.
Beth: you ok?
Me: I'm fine. I promise! It was just a misunderstanding.

Understatement of the century. How was I going to explain that one?

Zara: I smell a story . . .
Beth: you can tell us all about it tomorrow. Cant's wait to hear all about the party too! I guess it was good if it's still going ;)
Zara: Gross . . . But you better at least be getting some if you're ditching us again.
Me: haha!
Beth: They're having that Variant alumni event on campus tomorrow because of the senator being in town. Maybe we could crash that and try to score some free hors d'oeuvres?
Zara: You get free food at the cafeteria every day you fruit-loop!
Beth: So? This is fancy free food.
Me: Sounds great! See you guys tomorrow. Xo
Zara: xo
Beth: *a series of sexually suggestive emojis.*

I had just snuggled in under the dark blue covers of Josh's ridiculously big bed when there was a quiet knock at the door.
"Come in."

Ethan walked inside, wearing nothing but boxers, with Josh hot on his heels in underwear and a tank top, both of them carrying bundles of bedding. I tried not to stare, but judging by Ethan's dimpled smirk, I failed.

"I hope you don't mind," Josh said as he came to stand by the bed, "but I'm going to sleep in here too. It is my room, after all. I'll take the floor. Can I borrow a pillow?"

Ethan was setting up on the couch by the fireplace. It occurred to me how silly it was for Josh to be asking to borrow one of his own pillows, and I laughed.

His green eyes sparkled. "So, that's a 'no' on the pillow? Harsh."

It was ridiculous for them both to sleep uncomfortably when the king-size bed could easily accommodate us all. We were all exhausted, and if I was being honest, I was craving their touch. I had expelled so much Light earlier and made such a concentrated effort to stem its flow afterward that there couldn't possibly be any danger of levitating the bed or setting it on fire.

"Actually, no, you can't take this pillow," I teased, flopping back onto the item in question. "But you can still use it," I finished quietly and flipped the corner of the blanket down in invitation.

Slowly his eyebrows rose in surprise. "You sure?"

"Yep. Get in here. I need cuddles."

His makeshift bedding forgotten on the floor, he climbed in on my left and gave me a brilliant smile.

I hadn't forgotten Ethan. Lifting myself up onto my elbows, I saw him standing by the couch, awkward and uncertain. One of his arms hung by his side, and he was rubbing it with the other, his eyes darting all about the room before finally meeting my gaze.

I gave him a big smile and lifted the other corner. That was all the invitation he needed. Sprinting across the room, he launched himself at the bed and landed half across me, his face buried in my hair.

After our giggles subsided, he gave me the softest kiss on the cheek, whispered "good night," and rolled off me. I turned onto my side, toward Josh, and Ethan draped his arm over my middle, snuggling into my back. He was asleep in minutes.

Josh turned the lamp off and lay back down. The only light was moonlight streaming in through the windows, and it took my eyes a few minutes to adjust. I brushed a stray lock of blond hair off his forehead, and he captured my hand, pressing a warm kiss to my palm before resting our joined hands on the bed between us.

"Do you think Ethan's going to be OK?" I whispered.

"Yeah." Josh whispered back, a sad smile playing on his lips. "He just has some . . . abandonment issues. He was only nine when our parents were killed. He puts on a cocky façade, but deep down, he's still that kid, crying for his parents. Finding you—and now, discovering who you are—it's like finding a family all over again. To have that in his hands and then for it to slip away so suddenly . . . it just brought a lot of memories back. He'll be fine once he wakes up and sees you're still here."

"I'm so sorry." I could tell by the end he wasn't talking only about Ethan. Josh had gone through the same things; he just wasn't as expressive about it.

"It's OK. I get it." He squeezed my hand for emphasis. Of course Josh got it. Josh got everything.

"I was scared and I panicked, but I know I hurt you all by running off like that. Well, maybe not Alec. I think Alec would have preferred for me to go away." I let that hang in the darkness between us.

Josh sighed. "He cares. Trust me. It might not seem like it, but what the four of us went through—we're closer than family. We have no secrets. The fact that he kept this from us for so long tells me that he puts your safety even above our friendship. I believe that in his own messed-up way, he was convinced he was doing the right thing. He couldn't have known you would be connected to all of us. We always suspected that you and Alec were, but not us. That's why we didn't realize who you were from the start."

"So why is he still being . . . him, now that it's all out in the open? He's still acting like he wants nothing to do with me."

"Eve, he chased you down to New York just like we did. He helped bring you back here, where you belong. He's just . . . We all have our issues. Alec is no exception."

He paused, pain written all over his face. I gave his hand a squeeze, just as he had mine, and he smiled sadly.

Storing the information on Alec away for another time, I leaned forward on the pillow and pressed my forehead to Josh's, running my fingers through his dirty blond hair.

"I never even got to say goodbye," he whispered so softly I almost didn't hear him.

I knew exactly how he felt. "I never got to say goodbye to my mother either."

It had been one hell of a rollercoaster of a day, and I just had no tears left. I pressed my lips to his gently, then hesitated. I didn't want him to think I was kissing him to shut him up. But he responded immediately, placing his hand on my hip and scooting forward to deepen the kiss. I leaned into him, but as soon as I moved, Ethan's grip on my waist tightened, pinning me to his chest.

I chuckled against Josh's lips. "I think someone's not quite ready to let me go."

He pressed another desperate kiss to my lips before pulling away. "I don't think he ever will be. I don't think any of us will. So don't bother trying to leave. We'll just keep coming after you."

I smiled and let sleep finally take me.

At some point in the dead of night, the door creaked open, and I pushed my face farther into the pillow to shield my eyes from the light. The brightness disappeared quickly, but in its place were two hushed voices, one firm and sure, the other smooth like honey. I could have sworn they were talking about me, but I was half-asleep and couldn't be sure I wasn't dreaming.

Josh snuggled in closer to my front, and Ethan sighed into my hair. I felt cocooned and safe, surrounded by my Bond, and my breathing evened out again, matching theirs.

TWENTY FOUR

The next morning, I woke up when Ethan jostled me. I was pressed into his side, my head resting on his shoulder, with Josh spooning me. Ethan carefully eased himself out of bed, his movements slow and measured, but I was a light sleeper. I kept my eyes closed and pretended I was still asleep as he got up.

He dropped a kiss onto my head, shuffled around in the bathroom for a few minutes, and then left, probably to go for a run. That boy had more energy than I did when I had Light overflow.

As soon as the door closed, Josh nuzzled into me tighter. Apparently I wasn't the only one pretending to be asleep. A secret smile spread over my face, but I kept my eyes closed. That is until I felt him—all of him—pressing into my ass. I don't think he meant to do it, because he exhaled loudly and rolled away.

Biting my lip, I kept pretending to be asleep to avoid an awkward situation. With a deep sigh he got out of bed, kissed me in the same spot Ethan had, and left the room.

I stayed in bed a while longer, drifting in and out of sleep, until my two bedroom companions burst into the room.

"Morning, my little panini!" Ethan was carrying a plate containing not a panini but homemade French toast.

"Morning . . . coffee." My voice was still croaky from sleep, and whatever new nickname I'd been about to call him was forgotten as soon as I saw the little takeaway cup in Josh's hand.

They sat on the end of the bed, watching me enjoy my French toast and latte and nursing massive cups of their own. I didn't hold back on the moans and compliments. I was feeling spoiled. This was the second morning in a row I'd woken up to breakfast and good coffee, delivered by my boyfriend. Boyfriends? Bondmates? Ugh! It was too early to get into all that.

We didn't talk about the previous day, just enjoying a light and easy morning together. Before long it was time for me to head back to campus. Ethan said he would wait for me downstairs, and Josh said he had "a date with pain and a yoga mat" and left soon after.

On my way to the bathroom, I paused, noticing the bundles of bedding the boys had abandoned were now spread out on Josh's couch and the soft rug next to the fireplace. Had my hazy dream of someone talking last night been real after all?

I could understand Tyler coming in to check on us and deciding to sleep on the couch. I was still his Vital, and after what I had pulled, wanting to stay as close to me as possible was a natural reaction. But the second lot of bedding, the one that suggested Alec had stayed too, had me scratching my head.

Maybe what Josh had been hinting at during our whispered pillow talk wasn't so far from the truth. Maybe Alec really did care, but he was too messed up to know how to deal with it.

I wanted to hunt him down—I was pretty sure he would be doing yoga with Josh somewhere—and sort this mess out, but I knew better than most that when it came to running away from things, especially emotional things, explaining it, or even understanding it, was rarely easy. I'd spent my whole life running with my mother, and I still didn't know why.

Which was another thing I hoped the guys could shed some light on, considering they had known her. Us. I couldn't believe we had known one another when we were kids! I was having trouble imagining it. I had so many questions.

But first, I needed a shower, a change of clothes, and to check in with my roomies.

The plan was for Tyler to drive me back to campus, but Ethan volunteered to come along too, obviously not ready to be away from me.

It was a quiet ride, the pattering rain and rhythmic back and forth of the windshield wipers lulling me into a contemplative silence. We hadn't even made it out of the driveway when Ethan reached over from the back seat to caress the back of my neck, leaving his fingers there for the duration of the ride. After asking how I'd slept, Tyler didn't speak much, lost in his own thoughts. He looked as if he wasn't nearly as well rested as me.

What had he and Alec talked about last night?

Too soon, we were pulling up behind my building, and it was time to say goodbye.

Tyler grabbed my hand tenderly. "I'm glad you're back where you belong, and I hope we can gain your trust." The rain and his quiet tone made me feel cocooned in the car.

"You already have. It's just Alec . . ." He smiled warmly, waiting for me to finish, but I didn't know how. My feelings were all over the place. "I just don't know how I'm supposed to believe anything he says."

A heavy, thoughtful look fell over Tyler's features, and he turned to watch the rain hitting the windshield. "My ability is more passive than the others. It can't hurt them no matter how much I use it, so they're not ever going to be immune to it. I can't speak for the others, but *I* promise to always be truthful with you, Eve."

He gave me a meaningful look, his gray eyes serious. He hadn't said it in so many words, but I was pretty sure he was telling me that if I asked, he would share whatever his ability allowed him to learn.

I nodded, and he smiled again, looking back to the front. I was starting to realize the burden Tyler must carry—it couldn't be easy to know so many secrets and have no one to share them with. Maybe, eventually, I could be that for him. He could ease my worry, and I could share his burden—if he let some of his walls down, that is.

With one last squeeze of my hand and a satisfied nod, he released me.

Ethan jumped out of the back seat and opened the door for me, wrapping me up in a massive hug as soon as I got out. "I don't want to let you go, baby cakes," he muttered into my hair after we'd been standing in the rain for far too long.

I chuckled. The silly nicknames were back in full force, and the mood between us was getting lighter again. "Come on, you big teddy bear. I'll see you tomorrow. I'm getting soaked."

When he still didn't let go, I pulled away slightly, gently grabbing his face between my hands and forcing him to look at me. "I'm going inside to hang out with the Reds. I'm *not* leaving. I'll be right here, and you can check in with me on the phone anytime. OK? I'm not leaving. I promise."

He nodded and leaned down to kiss me. I wanted to deepen it, but the rain was making me pretty cold. Luckily, I didn't have to choose; Tyler barked at us to hurry up, and with matching wide smiles, we pulled apart, Ethan taking my place in the front seat and me running for the cover of the entrance.

I took the stairs instead of the elevator, needing the few extra minutes to set my thoughts straight. I would need to speak to the guys about letting the Reds in on the secret. Charlie and Dot already knew some of it, so why couldn't the Reds? I trusted them, and I really hated lying.

When I entered our little living area, they were both on the couch, mugs of coffee in their hands and some morning show on the TV.

"Well, well. Look who finally decided to grace us with her presence." Zara gave me a mocking grin.

"Hey, Eve. Want some coffee?" Beth did her best not to laugh while taking a sip of her own. They both knew very well how I felt about their "coffee." Beth had taken to amusing herself by offering me a cup every chance she got.

Scrunching up my nose in disgust, I shook my head. "How was your weekend?" I asked, dropping my bag and plonking myself on the couch between them. I wanted to get them talking and keep the attention off me. Naturally, it didn't work.

"Um, no." Zara poked me in the ribs. "How was *your* weekend?"

"Yes, I want to know all about the gala. And where did you get that dress? Dot posted a photo of you guys, and you looked freaking incredible." Beth started firing a litany of questions.

But before I had a chance to answer any of them, the door to our room burst open, startling us all and causing Beth to slosh a good portion of her coffee all over the place.

Tyler and Ethan barged in, slamming the door closed and locking it.

"Hey!" Zara jumped to her feet. "What the fu—"

"Get away from the windows!" Tyler's authoritative voice cut across her, and we all obeyed immediately, jumping up from the couch to go stand by

Ethan, who was trying to make a call by the door.

Tyler took two long strides to the window and peered outside before drawing the curtains half-closed over it.

"They've jammed the signal." Ethan cursed under his breath, tucking the phone into his back pocket and reaching for me.

I let him pull me against his side, watching Tyler closely.

Zara tried again. "What the fuck is going on?"

"Someone is invading the campus," Tyler answered, keeping an eye on the window. "We saw vehicles and heavily armed people setting up positions at the east gate. It looks like the Human Empowerment Network, but that doesn't make sense . . ."

"Oh my god." Beth sounded panicked. Zara had her phone out, but she put it away quickly after confirming with a huff that Ethan was right about the cell service. The two of them held hands and looked to Tyler. He was the adult in the room, the person with authority, the Bradford Hills staff.

My breathing had become quick and shallow. Every horror story I'd seen on the news about American mass shootings and lax attitudes toward gun control came flooding back. Statistics assaulted my brain.

It is estimated that there are between 270 and 310 million guns in America—almost one for every person. There were more than fifteen thousand gun-related deaths in America in 2017, and that was just *deaths*— it didn't even include the more than thirty-one thousand *injuries*.

I held on to Ethan a little tighter. The muscles under his damp T-shirt were taut with tension.

"I don't think the staff know what's happening yet." Tyler was still looking through the window. "They haven't advanced past the gates. I think they're securing the perimeter. It's too organized for a renegade group of humans. What the hell is this?"

He was trying to assess the situation, but he didn't have all the facts. I knew how incredibly frustrating that was.

Then it hit me—we had a way of getting more information without even leaving this room. He'd told us about it just last night in the car.

I straightened and gasped. Everyone turned to look at me.

"Ty, we need more info." I didn't wait for a response, extracting myself from Ethan's protective hold and walking over to him. As I placed my hand in his, understanding fell over his features, and he gave me one decisive nod.

I closed my eyes, took a deep breath, and dropped any attempt at stemming the flow of Light. He pivoted to face me and grabbed my other hand as the Light flowed freely into him. After only a few moments, I opened my eyes and gave him a questioning look.

"Let's find out," he murmured, dropping one of my hands to pull the curtain back slightly.

Ethan stepped up behind me and placed his hands on my shoulders, both of us waiting with bated breath to see if it would work.

"Oh my gosh!" Beth breathed at the same time Zara said, "Holy fuck!"

I turned to them in surprise, having almost forgotten they were in the room. I guess my secret was out.

"They're going after the alumni event. They're waiting until all the exits are blocked before moving in. But this isn't just the humans. Variant Valor is here too. Are they working together?" he asked in disbelief, speaking more to himself than any of us.

"No," he continued. "Variant Valor is just using the chaos to ... it's unclear. The bulk of the force is going to come up through here." He pointed to the main avenue winding up from the east gate and toward the admin building, behind which the event was to be held. "At least a hundred Human Empowerment Network and a much smaller force of Variant Valor assailants. There are a lot of angry people down there. This is going to get violent very fast."

"We have to do something." I couldn't wrap my brain around why the human extremists were allowing themselves to be manipulated by the Variant extremists, or why the Variant extremists were trying to get Variants killed. Politics and strategy were not my strong suits, but even I knew people were about to die needlessly. "We might be the only people who know about this."

"We need a distraction," Ethan growled from behind me. "Something to take them off track. Buy us a little time. Maybe we could somehow alert . . . the authorities." He was talking about Melior Group. The local law enforcement would be severely out of their depth.

"If you can cause a distraction, I can make it down to the event and warn everyone," Beth said with determination, but when I spun around to face her, there was fear in her eyes.

Zara looked as shocked as I did. Then she rolled her eyes and put her hands on her hips. "Fuck! *We*. We can warn everyone."

"No." Tyler was using his adult voice. "It's too dangerous."

I couldn't let him talk us out of it. We *had* to do something.

"The chemistry lab!" I blurted, and they all looked at me as if the stress had broken my capacity for thought. "It's just south of here, and it's close enough to the avenue to draw them away from the admin building for at least a little while. I can think of six ways to cause a massive explosion just off the top of my head. That should be distracting enough, right?"

Tyler still looked skeptical. "Well, yeah, but . . ."

"We don't have time for this!" I got in his face. "I know you want to protect me, but people are going to die. We have to do something."

A resolute look crossed his features, and he dropped my hand, reaching behind his back. "Right. You two," he addressed the Reds, "come down to the ground floor and wait for the explosion. Then—*only* then—run for it. Raise the alarm and then hide. That's it. Don't go off script."

They both nodded emphatically, eyes wide.

He turned to me and pulled a gun out from behind his back, cocking it and holding it by his side. "Eve, juice him up." He nodded in Ethan's direction.

"Is that a gun?" It was a stupid question, but in my defense, I had never seen a gun before. All of a sudden, the gravity of the situation hit me. "Why do you have a gun? Oh my god!"

"He said juice me up, babe. No time for freak-outs over firearms." Ethan spun me around and planted his lips on mine.

It was what I needed to snap me out of it. I plastered myself to him and let the Light flow freely. Then, as quickly as he'd initiated the kiss, Ethan pulled away and dragged me toward the door, where Tyler was waiting with one hand on the knob.

"Stay close to me and do exactly as I say." Tyler didn't wait for a response. He cracked the door open and peered down the corridor, then made for the stairs. We all followed, much more noisily.

At the back door, he again checked that the coast was clear before nodding once to the Reds and darting outside.

I squeezed Zara's hand in goodbye and reached out to Beth, but Ethan was already pulling me through the door and my fingers only just scraped hers. She gave me a shooing motion before pulling the door closed.

My heart was hammering in my chest as I scrambled to keep up with Tyler, keeping my eyes peeled for danger.

We rushed over to the next building and huddled in its entranceway. The solid door was locked, and the chemistry building was on the other side, so we would have to go around.

Before we could keep moving, however, two people came around the corner. I was so startled I jumped on the spot, my heart leaping into my throat. Tyler raised his gun but lowered it immediately when he saw it was Dot and Charlie.

"Charlie!" he hissed in their direction.

Charlie looked over, registered the gun in Tyler's hand, and immediately grabbed Dot by the elbow, dragging her over to us.

"Hey! What . . ." She was slower to pick up on the situation, but once she saw us, her heavily lined eyes widened in panic.

Tyler gave them the rundown. "Campus surrounded. Comms down. At least thirty armed at east gate. More at other entry points, plus heavy vehicles. It's humans, but there is more at play here. They're going after the Variants at the event."

"Where do you want us?" A hard mask had fallen over Charlie's face.

"We're on our way to create a distraction and delay them, but we need backup."

"I can do that," Dot piped up. I'd never heard the confident girl sound so quiet and unsure. "Write a note on something."

Moving with the kind of ease that comes from having done something your entire life, Dot and Charlie held hands, and I could almost *smell* the Light Charlie was pushing to his sister. Before he was even done transferring, Dot's face tightened into a look of concentration. Next to me, Ethan pulled a scrap of paper out of his wallet and started scribbling a note on the back.

By the time he finished writing, Squiggles was scampering up Dot's leg and onto her shoulder. Tyler passed Dot the note, and no sooner had she handed it to the ferret than Squiggles was off again, the paper held gingerly in her teeth.

Tyler gave Dot a nod of thanks. "Stay out of sight. Go up to Eve's room and hide."

Dot's brow creased in defiance, but Tyler didn't give her a chance to argue. The boys were already on the move again.

TWENTY FIVE

A few tense minutes later, we made it to the science building—which was locked.

"Dammit!" I cursed, but apparently Ethan had run out of patience for locked doors. He picked up a rock and smashed it through the glass by the old-fashioned doorknob, reaching through and unlocking it from the inside.

With Tyler in front, we scaled the two flights of stairs and ran down the corridor to the chemistry lab. As we came to a screeching halt at the door, it swung inward, a very surprised professor in a lab coat standing at the threshold.

"Gabe? What is this?" His eyes flicked down to the gun, and he stepped back.

"Peter, the school is being invaded by armed gunmen. We need access to the lab."

"What?" The older mad looked terrified. "Why?"

"There's no time for explanations." Tyler's tone brooked no arguments. "Go down to the basement level, lock yourself into a storage room, and stay there."

The man nodded and rushed past, heading for the stairs. We were lucky to have run into him. The labs had secure doors, and you needed a key card or a code to enter.

We burst into the room and Tyler ran to the window, yelling, "Do your thing!" over his shoulder. "We don't have much time."

I needed something that we could explode *fast*. I considered dragging the hydrogen tanks downstairs and having Tyler shoot them from a distance, but they were bulky and awkward, and it would take ages. Then I toyed with the idea of combining nitric acid with an organic solvent in a closed container of some sort, but I would need massive amounts of both for the kind of explosion we needed, and again, it would take time to set up. In the end, I decided the simplest solution was the most effective.

Running to the back corner of the room, I checked the gas tanks and started turning the knobs, letting the methane flow freely. Ethan didn't ask what I was doing, simply taking my lead and turning the other knobs until all five tanks were releasing the highly flammable gas into the air.

I did a quick calculation. The room was approximately seventy by fifty feet with seven-foot-high ceilings, meaning it had a volume capacity of 24,500 cubic feet. With all five tanks flowing, it wouldn't take longer than two minutes to fill the room with enough methane to cause a pretty big explosion.

"Close that window! Let's go!" I yelled. Tyler obeyed immediately, pulling the small window shut and leading the way out of the room.

The building was deserted, and I prayed that it stayed that way.

When we made it outside, I pointed to a building across the avenue.

Tyler shook his head. "Too exposed. We can't go running across their path."

"We need to be farther away when it goes boom," I explained. Without waiting for a response, I dashed across the wide avenue, forcing myself not to look toward the south gate, where I knew there were many people with loaded guns.

The guys were hot on my heels as we rounded the corner of the building opposite the chemistry lab. Tyler looked back to where we had come from, then whirled on me. "I said you do exactly as I say. What the hell were you thinking?"

Ignoring him, I reached out to give Ethan another quick zap of Light, then pointed up at a window on the second floor. "I need you to throw a fireball through that window. One of the blue ones."

"What?" His face twisted in panic. "This whole plan hinges on me? I've never thrown a fireball that far!"

"You've never had me. You can do this." I checked my watch. It had been four minutes. It was more than ready to go.

"They're on the move." Tyler cursed profusely. His ability was still coming in useful. "Ethan. Now!"

Narrowing his eyes and squaring his shoulders, my big guy stepped out from behind the corner and rolled his neck. After another moment of hesitation, he lifted his arm by his side, and an angry blue ball of fire appeared in his grasp. He leaned back, lifting his front leg, and pitched it like a baseball. It arched through the air magnificently and smashed, dead center, through the window I had pointed out.

There was a split second of silence and then a *BOOM*, louder than anything I'd ever heard. The burst of heat that followed was so intense it was hard to inhale. Ethan pivoted, shielding my body with his, as Tyler pulled me back behind the safety of the wall. A shard of glass still managed to make it to my face, slicing a fine line across my right cheek. It stung like a bitch but didn't feel too serious.

With the immediate danger over, Ethan backed away from me, and Tyler leaned in.

"You OK?" He raked his eyes over my face and body, looking for injuries more serious than the cut on my face.

"I'm good." I nodded as he ran his thumb under the cut gently, his brows furrowing. I pulled a tissue out of my pocket and pressed it to the cut, giving him a reassuring smile.

All three of us peered out from our hiding spot. One corner of the science building was on fire, flames licking the sides of the walls, and all the windows of the second-floor lab had been blown to pieces. The explosion had been visually impressive and probably loud enough to be heard miles away. If Squiggles hadn't made it to Alec, this would have gotten his attention.

It had certainly gotten the attention of the gun-wielding people, now inching toward the charred building.

"It worked." Tyler pulled us back behind the wall. "But it won't last long."

"What do we do now?" Ethan was breathing as hard as me, fire flickering down the length of his arms. With all the danger, coupled with the extra Light I had pushed into him, he was having trouble controlling his ability.

"You two do nothing. Find a way into this building and hide. Ethan, you fry anything that moves in your direction. I'm going to go check if Zara and Beth managed to warn the others."

"No!" Ethan and I protested at the same time.

I folded my arms. "We are not separating right now. I refuse."

"I agree. We should stick together." Ethan matched my stance, backing me.

Tyler's gaze flicked between us, exasperation leaking into his features. He dragged a hand down his face, growling. "Fine! But this time you do *exactly* as I say. No running off. Am I understood?"

"Yes, sir," I agreed readily as Ethan nodded. I was more than happy to take his lead. I had no idea what I was doing.

315

"They're everywhere. We'll have to go around this building and come around the back of the admin building to get to where they've set up the marquee for the event." He walked past us and away from the carnage we'd just caused, setting a rapid pace.

We circled around the building, sticking close to the walls, then darted across a clearing and into some trees. The woods at the periphery of campus provided decent cover as we looped around the massive admin building. The morning's rain had made the ground soft and muddy, and we made a mess of our clothing as we trudged through the undergrowth.

Tyler made us stop at the edge of the trees. The lawn where the event was to take place was clearly visible. It had stopped raining, but the heavy clouds were still casting a dull grayness over the whole scene.

Everyone had heard the explosion, but they didn't know what to make of it. People were milling about, talking to one another hastily, some of them walking away.

Finally I spotted the Reds near the entrance to the admin building, speaking with a man and a woman both dressed in suits. Beth was gesturing wildly behind her while Zara stood next to her, nodding.

"There!" I pointed. It looked as if they were having trouble convincing the staff to evacuate.

We were running out of time to get people to safety. Maybe we should go up there. Surely Tyler could convince them.

Just as I was about to suggest it, I heard movement in the brush behind us.

Tyler and Ethan had kept me behind them, peering between their shoulders to get a look at the lawn, so when we all turned, I ended up in front. Before us stood two people, bandanas over their noses and multiple weapons strapped to their bodies. They wore matching black clothing and had identical semiautomatic pistols in their hands.

We all froze.

A little machine in one of the gunmen's hands bleeped. He looked down at it in surprise, then lifted his gun to point at us. "We got one. Grab her."

They both moved forward, weapons raised.

The sound of gunfire from both sides was deafening. Tyler stepped up on my left and let off three quick shots, aiming at the gunman with the little machine.

The first two bullets thudded against his chest, knocking him back but not penetrating the Kevlar he was wearing. The last one went straight through his forehead. Blood gushed down his face as he crumpled to the ground, a spurt landing on Tyler's expensive shirt. The bright red was a stark contrast to the crisp white.

At the same time, Ethan came up on my other side, pushing me behind him with one strong arm and throwing his other arm forward. A blast of fire shot out of his hand, intense and angry, and hit the other gunman. The impact threw the man onto his back, enveloping him in fire immediately.

The man screamed—an animalistic, terrifying sound—and I found myself screaming too. The blood and the fire; the death and the pain—it was all happening too fast.

Tyler pulled me into him one-handed, his other hand still holding his gun at the ready, and blocked my view of the burning man. I clutched his shirt as if my life depended on it and screwed my eyes shut, my screams collapsing into long shuddering breaths.

After a moment, I forced myself to open my eyes. There were armed maniacs on the loose, and I needed to be aware of my surroundings.

I looked over to the two forms on the ground. Ethan was standing above the burned man, who was smoking and moaning on the ground. As I watched, the man stopped moving and lay still.

Panic rose in me again. "Is he . . ." My voice was shaky.

Ethan came over to stand with us, his eyes wide. "No. He just passed out from the pain. The other guy though . . ."

The other guy had a bullet in his brain. You didn't need to be a doctor to know he was dead.

Tyler had killed someone.

My hands were shaking, but his were steady, his hold on the gun firm.

That's when I realized the flames that had been licking up and down Ethan's arm had been replaced with streaks of crimson.

"Holy Thomas Edison!" I yelled.

Ethan's left bicep was red and glistening, macabre streams of blood trickling down his arm. A single drop from the tip of his middle finger fell to the forest floor.

I pushed out of Tyler's arms and rushed over to him. My hands hovered over Ethan's skin, unsure, panic beginning to set in. I couldn't figure out how badly he was hurt.

He pulled me into his embrace one-handed, as Tyler had. "Shh. It's OK. It only grazed my shoulder. I'm fine." He was the one that had been *shot*, and he was comforting me.

Before I had a chance to reply, a piercing woman's scream drew our attention back to the lawn. Tyler swung his gun in that direction as we all turned to look.

The field had erupted into chaos. Gunmen had swarmed the main area and begun shooting. This group, however, didn't look like the two assailants we'd just encountered. They appeared less organized, without the matching black clothing, their weapons a mishmash of handguns, shotguns, and automatic rifles.

The rain had started up again, and most people had gathered under the marquee to stay dry. They were easy targets. Bodies fell to the ground like ragdolls as terrified, guttural screams mingled with the menacing sound of bullets cutting through the air.

There was blood everywhere.

Just as Tyler had predicted, the Variants were not taking this lying down. While some people were running away in abject terror—many falling down lifeless in midstride—others were fighting back.

A man in a blue suit, one of the sleeves ripped, was standing in front of a group of huddled students. He had his hands up in front, feet wide apart. He must have had some kind of defensive ability, because there were several gunmen firing directly at them and the bullets were bouncing off, inches away from hitting him.

A girl about my age was standing in the thick of it all, holding hands with a boy, her Vital. She was using her ability to form the rain into icicles, their deathly sharp points embedding themselves in gunmen's chests. The pair took down three of the assailants before two attacked them from the back.

The two men who approached the Variant and her Vital looked identical to the ones who had attacked us in the woods, uniformly dressed and carrying identical weapons. The gunmen hit the boy and girl in the back of their heads, their bodies crumpling to the ground. Then they dragged the boy away, leaving the Variant girl lying lifeless in the rain.

Another young man was running through the crowd throwing bright bolts of lightning from his hands. I recognized Rick—the friend of Ethan who had introduced himself and his electric ability to me.

As Rick charged the bulk of the gunmen, Zara and Beth ran out from the cover of the admin building's entryway, trying to get away from a scuffle there. Their red hair was like a beacon, and I watched them run, terrified, into the crowd, straight into Rick's path.

I could see what was about to happen, but I was too far away to stop it.

With a panicked "NO!" I burst past Ethan and Tyler and ran straight for them.

Rick threw another bolt of angry electricity just as the Reds ran into his path. It hit Beth directly in the chest. She flew back several feet, her hand wrenched out of Zara's grasp, and flopped to the ground behind a row of chairs. The force of Beth getting blasted away knocked Zara to the ground too.

Neither one of them was getting up.

I pumped my legs faster, desperate to get to my friends, but I was no match for Ethan's athleticism. He caught up to me just as some of the gunmen noticed us, wrapping his big arm around me and twisting us sideways as bullets sailed past our heads. Tyler was right behind him and started returning fire.

We were out in the open and definitely outgunned.

An engine roared in my ears, and a motorcycle came to a screeching halt in front of us, blocking us from the gunmen. Alec climbed off the bike with grace and speed, turning his attention to our assailants, and Josh pulled up on his bike only a second later. They were soaked from riding in the rain, and they must have come straight from yoga, because they were both in shorts and tank tops.

I had a momentary spark of annoyance that they hadn't worn protective gear on their bikes, then nearly let loose a frantic giggle at the absurdity of that thought. Just as it had during the plane crash, my brain always seemed to throw useless information at me in moments when everything was falling apart. Was it some desperate bid for control? An attempt to feel better by focusing on the mundane—facts, statistics, the importance of wearing helmets?

People began moaning in pain. Everyone—human or Variant, crazed gunman or Bradford Hills student—was doubled over. Alec wasn't targeting specific people; he'd just unleashed the pain and let it incapacitate everyone. As soon as the bullets stopped flying, Josh flicked his hands up, and a shotgun flew over his head, landing somewhere behind us.

They were working as effectively and in tune with each other as Ethan and Tyler had in the woods. One by one, firearms sailed past as Josh pushed his ability to the edge.

I watched them for a few moments, transfixed by their abilities, and then remembered I could help. I pushed against Ethan's chest, trying to get to Josh, but he held me firmly.

"I need to juice him up!" I yelled, and Ethan let me go.

I ran to Josh and wrapped my arms around his middle, pressing my face into the cool wet skin at the back of his neck. He jumped in surprise, his muscles tensing, but relaxed as soon as he realized it was me. I pushed his tank top up and placed my palms flat on his stomach, letting the Light flow freely.

He rolled his shoulders, standing taller, more confident, more energized. I craned my neck to see around him as he lifted both arms, every remaining gun flying up into the air.

With a sharp motion, Josh brought his hands down, and the guns landed on the backs of the assailant's heads, all the Human Empowerment Network gunmen falling to the ground unconscious in perfect synchronicity. Then, with another gesture from Josh, the weaponry stacked itself into a menacing pile of metal behind us.

Alec took a shaky breath, and his shoulders sagged. The remaining people in the clearing stopped moaning and straightened, looking a little dazed.

Josh turned in my arms and crushed me to him. His breathing was erratic, the staccato rhythm only matching mine in its unevenness. He placed several firm kisses on my forehead and cheeks as he pulled away slowly. Then he held me by the shoulders at arm's length, his eyes raking over my body methodically, lingering on the cut on my cheek.

"I'm OK. I'm OK. I'm OK," I kept repeating in a quiet voice, my hands gripping his wrists until it sunk in. His green eyes finally looked into mine, and he breathed a sigh of relief.

"I'm OK." I said it once more, nodding for good measure. I needed to convince *myself* of the fact as much as I needed to convince him.

I was dirty from the mud in the woods, wet from having run around in the rain, and tense in every muscle. There was blood on me, but most of it wasn't mine. All the bullets had missed me, and thanks to the guys, none of the gunmen had gotten close enough to lay a hand on me.

"More are coming." Tyler stood a few steps away, looking in the opposite direction of where the first group had come from. He pushed a wet strand of hair off his forehead. The rain had settled into a steady patter, and we were all getting soaked.

"What?" Josh went to stand by him. "How do you know?"

"My ability. I'm able to see the truth of the situation, to an extent. At the moment, the most pertinent information is where the threat is, so that's what's most clear in my mind. They were holding this group back for something ... I'm not sure. The extra Light Eve transferred is wearing off. But I know they're sending more in."

"Shit. How far out?"

"Two minutes. Maybe three. Alec."

Alec was still standing next to me in the same position, shoulders sagging, head bent.

"ETA on reinforcements?"

Without moving or even looking up, he answered, "At least nine minutes."

All three of them cursed profusely, and then Ethan piped in. "We need to get these people somewhere safe, and then we need to get Eve the hell out of Dodge." He was breathing hard, the white T-shirt stretched across his heaving chest nearly transparent from being so wet.

"Right." Tyler turned back to us, his face grim. A dark splatter of mud had joined the blood on his shirt. He directed the others to start maneuvering the crowd to safety, and he, Ethan, and Josh shouted at people to go hide, that there were more gunmen coming, that it wasn't over.

I kept my eyes on Alec. He was still staring at the ground.

I didn't understand it. Alec was the one who worked for the Melior Group in the field. Tyler outranked him and was a natural leader, so it made sense that he was taking charge of the situation, but Alec had the most combat experience. Shouldn't he be in his element here? Not standing there as if he had no clue what to do with himself?

He was breathing hard, his shoulders bunching with tension, each ripple of muscle making the visible tattoos under his tank top dance. His hands were clenching and unclenching at his sides, and his eyes were flicking around almost wildly, calculating, looking for the best course of action.

Around us, the others weren't having much success with steering people into hiding. Some had heeded the warning and taken off for the comparable safety of the buildings, but others, mostly Variants with active abilities, were insisting on staying and fighting. Rick was being very vocal about it, getting in Ethan's face and yelling about defending our people.

I wasn't allowing myself to wonder how seriously Beth and Zara were hurt. Many people had already died. Many more probably would.

And then realization dawned on me.

Alec wasn't trying to figure out the best course of action. He was trying to steel himself for it.

Ethan called my name, having abandoned his argument with Rick. He was saying we needed to go. I could see Tyler over Alec's shoulder, reloading his gun as he shouted something, and I could hear Josh somewhere behind me, still yelling at people to run.

But I focused on Alec. I knew just as well as he did what we had to do, and we were running out of time.

"Alec!" My voice was steadier than it should have been, considering the mess of emotions and fear writhing inside me. His eyes snapped up to mine, the blue more intense and yet brighter than I'd ever seen it, and I briefly wondered how eyes so light could hold so much darkness.

He held my gaze, but the overwhelming anger radiating off him nearly made me shrink away. He turned toward the sky and let the rain fall onto his face, teeth grinding, then took a deep breath and looked back at me with cold determination.

He gave one firm nod, and I launched myself at him.

I wrapped my arms around his neck and pressed my lips to his almost violently, our teeth knocking. He immediately pushed his tongue into my mouth, and his strong hands grabbed me under my ass, lifting me so I could wrap my legs around his waist. He grunted when the Light started to flow between us, and his fingers dug roughly into my thighs.

Even after all my practice transferring Light through my hands, this was still the quickest and most efficient way, and we were out of time. I could already hear the pop of gunfire in the background, the first line of more assailants coming upon us.

I pressed myself impossibly farther into him and let the Light flow completely free, focusing on the lines of his hard body pressed to mine, his hands gripping me all over. I moaned into his mouth, acutely aware how fucked up it was to be turned on at a time like this but consoling myself with the fact that the arousal would only make the Light flow faster and more intense.

A loud *bang* near us made my eyes fly open. I was glowing again; my arms, still wrapped around Alec's shoulders, were luminescent. He broke the kiss and looked at me with wide eyes, both of us breathing hard.

He began to shake lightly, and then, with me still wrapped around him, he dropped to his knees. His grip tightened around my flesh, then slackened, a little vein popping at his forehead.

Why wasn't he using his ability? Had the Light transfer not worked?

And then it hit me.

"Why are you holding it back?" I yelled into his face.

Anger fell over his features again, his head shaking a little with strain.

"Alec!" I was beginning to sound frantic.

He released me, sitting back on his heels and throwing his arms out wide, flicking droplets of rain off his fingers. I held on, planting my knees on the ground and using his shoulders to balance. He lifted his head to the sky and roared like a wild animal.

A massive burst of energy flooded out of him in all directions, like a sonic boom. His ability couldn't harm me, but I could feel the sheer power as it poured out of him.

I pressed my face into his neck. I wasn't going to let him do this on his own. I focused on the feel of the cool rain dripping down my neck and his body under mine, muscles rock hard with effort.

After only a few seconds, he went quiet and dropped his arms by his sides, his whole body sagging. I still held on. Chest to chest, heart to heart, we took shuddering breaths together.

Around us, everything had gone still.

When the body experiences too much pain, the brain shuts down as a self-preservation mechanism, resulting in unconsciousness. With my Light to power it, the blast of Alec's pain ability had been enough to knock everyone out cold. Only Tyler, Josh, and Ethan were still standing, watching us with varying degrees of shock on their faces.

As usual, Tyler was the first to take charge. "You guys can't be here when they arrive. They'll take one look at this and know about Eve and our Bond."

Alec moved to stand, and I untangled myself from him and stood up too. I wondered if he felt as drained as I did. He draped one heavy arm around my shoulders and held me to him but didn't meet my gaze.

The world dipped sideways and I lost my balance, but big warm hands steadied me. Ethan.

I vaguely registered them talking around me, discussing what to do, what to tell the authorities. Then somehow I was in the back of Tyler's car, my body cradled in Alec's arms and my legs resting across Ethan.

Then we were climbing the stairs of the mansion, a heavy silence weighing down our steps, making us all slow.

Then Alec was collapsing in the foyer. Ethan and Josh carried him into Tyler's study and deposited him on the couch, taking his soaking tank top off.

The pulling, urgent pain was in my chest again—just like the night Ethan had nearly died—and I took my soggy, blood-soaked, mud-splattered T-shirt off too. Josh and Ethan protested, saying I was too weak myself, but I shrugged them off and approached Alec on shaky legs. I had to try. The Light was demanding contact, and I didn't have the strength to resist it.

Josh supported me as I staggered over to the couch, the pain in my chest beginning to feel like tearing. Alec had given it all he had out there—he had unleashed the full, terrifying force of his ability, and it had taken a toll.

I draped myself over his body, the Light humming on my skin where we touched, my eyes already drooping closed. I could hear the guys bustling around the room, lighting a fire in the fireplace, bringing in extra space heaters. Someone draped a blanket over us, and then I was out.

TWENTY SIX

I woke up a few hours later, but this time it was not slow and languid, as it had been when I'd awakened in Ethan's arms. I shot up on the couch, Alec groaning in protest next to me. Ethan was at Tyler's desk, his head resting on his forearms, and he jerked up in his seat at my sudden movement.

"Shit! The Reds!" Everything my overloaded brain had been incapable of processing earlier was flooding back, and I sprang to my feet. "I have to make sure they're OK."

Ethan rushed around the desk. He looked as awful as I felt—his clothing rumpled and dirty, his eyes bloodshot. It was lucky he moved so fast, because as soon as I stood, my knees buckled.

"Whoa," Ethan said as he caught me. "Take it easy. Just sit back down, baby."

He guided me back to the couch, where Alec was now sitting up. He looked like shit too. Dark circles under his eyes stood out against his otherwise pale face. He was probably out of the woods, but the Light inside me was still pushing me toward him; I reached over to squeeze his hand, sighing softly as the distinctive tingle of Light flow soothed us both.

"What happened?" My body may have been screaming at me to curl up next to Alec and embrace unconsciousness, but my brain was demanding answers. "I don't remember much after the . . . Are they OK?"

Ethan crouched in front of me, his warm hands on my knees. His left shoulder was bandaged, and the sight of the clean white gauze, stark against his tanned skin, reminded me of the blood dripping down his arm . . . the men pointing guns at us.

I broke contact with Alec to pull Ethan closer, pushing up the sleeve of his T-shirt so I could inspect the bandage. His hands on my knees flexed, and he swallowed hard, his gaze focused on the ground.

"Ethan?" I grabbed his face, forcing him to look at me. He had tears in his eyes.

"Zara's in the hospital. She's going to be OK," he whispered as one tear slid down his cheek.

My own eyes began to sting. Next to me Alec sat up straighter, shifting closer to me.

"And Beth?" I whispered back.

Ethan looked down, shaking his head sadly, and whispered into my lap, "I'm so sorry."

"No," I croaked, the tears spilling over.

"They said she died instantly. Before she even hit the ground. She took a direct hit at close range, and her fragile human body just couldn't . . ." He looked up at me, the amber in his eyes almost molten with emotion.

Beth was dead.

One of the only people I had ever referred to as a friend—sweet, thoughtful, kind Beth—was dead. The bandage on Ethan's shoulder was a sharp reminder that it could just as easily have been him. It could have been any one of us.

It felt like a stab in the guts. I doubled over, sobbing uncontrollably.

For a split second, I wasn't sure where I was. Was I sitting on the couch, crying over the death of my friend? Or was I in the hospital, crying over the death of my mother?

Ethan was running his hands through my hair, whispering calming things, but I couldn't hear him over my own grief. My body folded in on itself, trying to cover the hollow feeling in my stomach, just like in the hospital.

And just like that night, Alec wrapped his strong body around my weak one and held me together. He positioned himself behind me on the couch, one leg on either side of my sobbing, shaking form, and wrapped his arms around me firmly, his chest pressed to my back.

"You are not alone," he said. The same words he'd said to me that night in the hospital.

I had lost another person.

I had lost her after spending a year feeling as if I'd never find another soul to share my life with. I'd found Zara and Beth, Dot and Charlie, and my guys. These people had made me feel as though I had a place in the world.

Now one of them had been taken from me. It had hit me so hard I was thrown right back into that hopeless despair I'd felt in the hospital, staring down the barrel of a solitary existence.

And once again, my honey-voiced man was there.

He moved his head so his lips were right at my ear and whispered it again. "Evie, you are not alone."

My frantic crying calmed a little, the nightmare of my memories fading away. I took shuddering breaths as silent tears continued to stream down my cheeks, the falling drops mingling with the hair on Alec's forearms and sliding away.

He and Ethan spoke in hushed voices, and then Ethan left, shutting the door softly. Alec pitched his body to the side and gently laid us back down. He held me, just as he had in the hospital, and I drifted back to sleep.

When I woke up again some time later, it was much more slowly and gently. We had shifted positions in our sleep. Alec was on his back, stretched along the length of the couch, and I was tucked into his side, my head resting on his shoulder and my leg hitched over his thighs.

The heavy drapes in Tyler's office were drawn over the window, but a sliver of golden afternoon light cut across our waists. I could see tiny particles of dust floating in it.

Alec's chest was rising and lowering gently as he breathed, but I somehow knew he wasn't asleep either. The tattoos on his back curved over his shoulders and around his ribs, and now that my face was on his skin, I could see the scars that intermingled with the ink. The tattoos weren't placed carefully to cover the scars; they were just there. Unapologetic. Just like him.

Slowly I lifted my hand and dragged my fingers through the light spattering of hair on his chest, stopping at a ragged scar just under his shoulder.

"What happened here?" I whispered into his skin.

"I was stabbed," he whispered back, his voice quiet. Passive. The honey was gone.

My hand continued its exploration of the history of his pain, trailing a path over his shoulder and stopping just above his bicep. There was a smaller, circular scar there. "And here?"

"I was shot."

I drew my fingers down the length of his arm and ghosted them back over to his stomach. At his hip, disappearing below the waistband of his shorts, was a raised, uneven, pinkish scar. Some of it was covered by a tattoo. "And here?"

"Ethan. He was still getting the hang of it."

I let my finger trace the edge of the fabric before moving up. Under his ribs were three parallel jagged scars, raised and curving around his waist, disappearing where his side was pressed against mine. I ran my hand over each one. "And here?"

"Claws."

I paused. Did he mean it was an animal attack? But it seemed I'd have to wonder about that forever; Alec was done talking about it.

"I hate you," he whispered in the same detached tone he'd used to tell me about his scars.

I lifted my head to look at him, letting my confusion and hurt show.

"For what you made me do." His face was as detached and passive as his voice, his eyes half-closed. "I hate you for making me use my ability like that."

"Making you?" Anger rushed in to replace the hurt and confusion. It was easier to get angry than to deal with the pain of hearing my Bond member tell me he hates me. "I'm a hundred-and-thirty-pound science nerd. You're two hundred and fifty pounds of pure muscle. I couldn't *make* you do shit if I tried."

I lifted myself over him as I spoke, my hands on either side of his head. My hair fell in a messy heap over one shoulder. His eyes opened wider as he watched me, his anger rising to meet mine.

"You don't fucking understand anything, *Eve*." He sneered at me, spitting my name out as if it left a bad taste in his mouth. I was no longer Evie—my honey-voiced stranger was gone.

"No, I don't," I barked back at him. "I don't understand at all what your fucking problem is. We saved people's lives. I refuse to feel bad about that."

"Regardless of what it does to me, right? Regardless of the fact that it makes me into an even bigger *monster* than I already am? You've got three other guys foaming at the mouth to get into your pants and at your Light. What's one less?"

"What the fuck are you talking about?"

"Forget about it," he growled, his face twisted by anger and some other baffling emotion. He tried to raise himself up, but I had gotten really good at recognizing when he was about to run away, and I wouldn't let him.

I planted my hands on his shoulders and shoved him back down. My movement took him off guard, and he fell back, fixing me with a murderous expression as his hands flew to my hips as if to throw me off.

But he paused.

My body had shifted when I shoved him, and my leg had moved farther over his thighs, higher up. I could feel him getting hard under me. In complete contrast to his harsh words and angry looks, his erection was pressing into my thigh. Very high on my thigh. Just short of where I actually wanted it.

Feeling the undeniable evidence of his arousal had liquid heat pooling between my legs, and suddenly anger was no longer the only cause of my quickening pulse.

For a beat we stared daggers at each other, breathing hard, and then he bucked his hips slightly, rubbing his erection against my leg. The movement was subtle yet deliberate—it was a challenge, and I was not about to back down. Not one bit of me wanted to.

I didn't know who was more fucked up. We both had been turned on twice today—a day several people had lost their lives. But was he worse for thrusting into me, or was I worse for liking it and responding?

Purposely, I rolled my hips, grinding against him, and his mouth fell open in shock. He hadn't been expecting me to meet his challenge.

We leaned into each other, our lips crashing together as ferociously at they had hours before in the rain, our tongues fighting for dominance. His strong hands shoved my hips so that I was exactly where I wanted to be, and I moaned into his mouth. He met my moan with a guttural growl of his own.

We were frantic, our hands all over each other, grabbing, pulling, tugging, our hips finding a frenzied rhythm. He pulled away from my lips, yanking the left strap of my bra down and leaning forward to wrap his hot mouth over my nipple. His other hand remained on my ass, guiding me.

He groped my breast, holding it to his mouth, and sucked on my nipple with the perfect amount of pressure, eliciting another moan from me.

I wanted to taste him again.

I pulled away, causing us both to sit up, and mashed my mouth to his swollen lips. He continued to knead my breast, running his thumb over my nipple.

My skin felt as if it were on fire, and I opened one eye, momentarily paranoid that I'd gone nuclear again. Satisfied that my skin wasn't glowing, I reached one arm over his shoulder and raked my nails up his back. I was not gentle.

He grunted and bucked into me almost violently, sucking on my bottom lip, taking it between his teeth. He was not gentle either.

I wanted more. I wanted to chase whatever this frenzied feeling was—to forget about all the shit that had happened today.

I was only wearing leggings, and he was still in his thin workout shorts, so there wasn't a lot of fabric between us, but I wanted there to be less. None. I wanted to feel all of him.

I shoved him back down onto the couch and started kissing and biting his neck, trailing my hand over his incredible body and down to the waistband of his shorts. I had just lifted my hips and was about to slip my hand down between us when he slapped it away. I didn't have a chance to be confused though; in the next moment, he flipped us over, pushing one knee between my legs and pinning me to the couch with his body.

He started kissing me again as he did to me what I'd just tried to do to him. He dragged his hand over my breasts and down my front before pushing his hand into my pants.

He didn't tease me or try to build me up. He knew I was turned on and ready for it. He groaned when he felt how wet I was, and then he pushed two fingers straight inside and started moving them.

The suddenness of his fingers inside me, stretching me, made me inhale sharply, and he pulled away, kissing and licking down my throat. The way he touched me was nothing like the few high school boys I had been with in the past, who had been as unsure of what I would like as I had been.

Alec was a man who knew exactly what he was doing. He touched me deliberately, with confidence in every movement.

It felt fucking incredible.

I moaned again, throwing back my head and arching my back. My breath was getting more shallow and erratic, and I clawed at his shoulder as if I was trying to bring him closer. As if I was scared he would stop what he was doing to me and leave.

But he wasn't stopping. He set a steady, punishing rhythm, barely pulling his fingers out before driving them back in. The heel of his hand was grinding into my clit, and I couldn't stop my hips from rolling into his movements.

I bit down on his shoulder as my abdominal muscles tensed and other, internal muscles pulsed around Alec's fingers. An intense, almost savage orgasm spread from my core, sending waves of heat throughout my body and making me go still under his expert hands.

He kissed me roughly as I moaned my release into his mouth, stroking me a few more times as I came down off my high. Then he extracted his hand from my pants and rested his forehead on my shoulder, both of us panting.

It took me a few moments to calm down, to stop gasping as if I'd just been on a run. But when I did, I reached for his waistband again, eager to return the favor, to wrap my hand around his warm, hard . . .

But he slapped my arm away *again* and lifted himself onto his hands.

Our positions had reversed. Now he was the one balanced above me, looking down into my flushed face. I frowned, but that impassive look had fallen over his face again.

"Don't worry about it," he said in answer to my silent question. "I don't want *anything* from you."

He pushed himself up to stand next to the couch, his back to me, and stretched his arms over his head. The muscles in his back lengthened, his tattoos dancing with the movement, and I raked my eyes down his impressive form, lingering on his ass. My treacherous body wanted more.

What the fuck was wrong with me?

"What . . ." I breathed, still a little winded, and raised myself onto my elbows. Anger was bubbling up again, and his sudden disappearance from on top of me had left my flushed body cold.

He half turned toward me, adjusted his very prominent erection, and smirked, raising the eyebrow with the scar through it. Then he walked over to the door.

He smirked. He fucking *smirked* at me.

"You are such a fucking asshole!" I yelled after him as he disappeared through the door.

I reached over to the side table, picked up the first thing my hand landed on, and hurled it in his general direction. It shattered into a million pieces against the wall; whatever it was had been glass.

I growled, this time in frustration, as I flopped back onto the couch and threaded my fingers into my hair.

Footsteps echoed through the foyer—someone running, probably to investigate the yelling and the smashing. In some vain attempt to preserve my dignity, I scrambled for the blanket that had fallen to the ground.

Tyler came bursting through the door, sliding to a stop in his socks on the marble. He was in a baggy T-shirt and sweats, his brown hair even messier than usual.

His frantic eyes took in the glass littering the floor and me sitting on the couch, the blanket held up to cover my front, my hair disheveled, my lips swollen. It wouldn't have taken a genius to figure out what Alec and I had just been up to.

"Oh my god, Eve. Are you OK? What did he do?"

I averted my eyes and sat straighter on the couch, pulling my bra strap back into place and tucking the blanket securely under my arms.

"Nothing I didn't want him to," I murmured, the humiliation settling heavily over me. "I'm sorry about the . . . um, whatever that used to be. I'll replace it."

Tyler stepped gingerly over the glass and swept his messy brown hair off his forehead, coming to sit next to me on the couch. "It was just an ugly paperweight. Don't worry about it."

"OK. I'll clean up my mess." I made to get up, but Tyler placed a firm hand on my shoulder.

"Eve." He leveled a stern look at me.

"Don't," I whispered into my lap. "Please, Ty. I just can't . . . I can only handle so much, and I need to table this particular mess for now."

He sighed. "As long as you're OK."

"I'm OK. I promise. This can wait." I was so *not* OK, but I was really not ready to talk about it.

"Well, OK then." He gave me a weak smile. He knew I was lying, obviously, but something in my face must have told him not to press me. "If you want me to kick his ass, you just tell me. I'll get Josh to hold him down with his ability."

I chuckled, but it was weak. I couldn't find it in me to laugh, but I appreciated him trying to ease the tension. "What time is it? Is it too late to go see Zara in the hospital?"

"It's just after five. I'm sure we can make it before visiting hours end."

"OK. Can I use your bathroom? I really need a shower first."

"Of course." He stood and then paused. "There's something else . . ."

"What?" I stood too, my senses on alert. What now? Hadn't the past twenty-four hours been shitty enough?

He must have read the trepidation on my face, because he turned and walked out, speaking over his shoulder. "Never mind. Shower first. Ten minutes won't change anything."

"OK." I didn't have the will to argue.

He led the way upstairs and into the room across the hall from Josh's. I had never been in his room before. It was the mirror image of the one opposite—bed on the left, sitting area with fireplace on the right. It was decorated in a lighter, more neutral palette—the sheets were crisp white and made with military precision, the heavy drapes a cream color.

I followed him straight to the bathroom door, and he held it open for me. "Help yourself to anything."

He made to leave, but I stopped him with a soft touch on his forearm.

"Thank you, Tyler." Before thinking about it too much, I leaned up, holding the blanket in place with one hand, and placed a chaste kiss on his cheek.

He cleared his throat and rubbed the back of his head. "It's just a bathroom." He chuckled but paused, his gray eyes returning my serious look.

We both knew I wasn't talking about the shower. He had shot a man to protect me—Tyler had literally killed for me. He had been my protector and defender through and through. I needed him to know I wasn't taking it for granted.

"What you did today . . ." I swallowed around the lump in my throat. "There are no words to express—"

"You're welcome," he whispered back, cutting off my rambling before it could even begin.

With a promise to hunt down some clothes for me, he backed away and left me to shower.

TWENTY
SEVEN

Fifteen minutes later I almost felt human again.

I used Tyler's shampoo and conditioner to get the knots and filth out of my hair. When I came out, wrapped in a towel, a ladies tank top and yoga pants were laid out on the bed, as well as a large, definitely not ladies hoodie.

Trying not to think too much about why a house full of men had women's clothes on hand, I dressed quickly and made my way downstairs, slipping the hoodie on as I went. A faint hint of expensive cologne and the scent of fresh air that lingered when clothing was dried outside in the sun wrapped around me. I paused halfway down and took a long inhale, bringing the fabric up to my nose and thinking of Josh.

I found them all sitting around the large dining table off the kitchen. Even Alec had reappeared—he was in fresh clothing and his hair was damp, apparently having showered himself. He was hunched over a laptop and didn't even spare me a glance.

"Hey." I smiled weakly at the other three boys, all of whom looked up when I entered, and I stared daggers at Alec's impassive face before sitting down between Tyler and Ethan. Ethan's hand went straight to my knee.

"How are you feeling?" Tyler asked, leaning back in his chair and giving me a warm smile.

"The shower helped. Thanks." His question was loaded. It could have been referring to what had happened between Alec and me in the study, all the violence we had witnessed and been a part of that day, or the fact that one of my friends was dead. But I chose to keep it simple and focus on the physical. I felt like shit, but physically, the shower had made me feel better.

Josh's foot nudged mine under the table, and I looked up into his intense stare. Those intelligent green eyes read exactly what I'd left unsaid; he knew I wasn't OK, but I was hoping he wouldn't push me to admit it. I stretched my legs farther and let them entwine with his as I gave him a pleading look.

A sad little smile played at his lips for a moment before he spoke. "Nice hoodie."

It was the perfect thing to say, and it even made me smile a little. I wrapped my arms around myself and inhaled exaggeratedly. "Thanks. It's a bit big, but I think I might keep it. I like how it smells." I said the last part softly, almost to myself, but everyone heard.

Alec finally lifted his head from his screen, glancing between Josh and me and frowning before going back to ignoring us.

I chose to ignore him too, focusing my attention on Josh's feet playing with mine under the table; Ethan's warm hand on my knee, rubbing gentle circles with his thumb; and Tyler's watchful gaze. At that moment, their unspoken support made me feel much better than talking about my confused feelings would have.

"All right," I said with a sigh, planting my elbows on the table. "Lay it on me."

Three sets of eyes averted their gaze.

"Shit. Guys, what is it?"

That little tingle of panic was welling up again. I sat up a little straighter, my senses on alert.

As usual, Tyler took the lead. "Charlie was taken."

"What? What do you mean *taken?*" But even as I asked, my mind rehashed the encounter in the woods—the weird beeping machine, the two black-clad, armed men stepping toward me menacingly.

Grab her.

Then I remembered the Variant girl forming icicles from the rain and the boy, her Vital, being dragged away by another two assailants.

Tyler explained even as my mind connected the dots. "It seems that causing chaos and baiting the Variants into a reaction wasn't the only aim of the attack. In all the confusion, a total of twenty-seven Vitals were abducted. Charlie was one of them. Unnervingly, they knew exactly which people had the Light and were very efficient in capturing them before the bulk of the violence even got to its peak."

He pointed to a familiar device, black and sleek with a small handle, sitting on the table in among some other stuff and papers.

"Whomever they were working with or for has developed a technology that is capable of identifying a Vital. It's how they were able to home in on them so fast."

"Shit." The breath rushed out of me, and I stared at the black device on the table. I knew this could potentially have some very serious ramifications for me and my guys, but all I could think about was Dot.

Charlie was her brother *and* her Vital. I had no siblings and had never been close enough to anyone growing up to know what that was like, but I did have a Bond of my own. In a way, that was a kind of family.

A sharp pain pierced my chest at the thought of one of my guys being taken from me. Even Alec. As much as he railed against it, as much as he'd been a total asshole to me only half an hour ago, he was still mine. He was part of my Bond. I was his Vital, and the Light inside me was not OK with the idea of him being taken away.

Then I remembered how the girl with the icicles and her Vital had been taken out, and I began to panic for Dot's well-being. I couldn't lose another friend today.

I pressed a hand to my chest, my breaths getting shallower, and looked frantically around the table from one somber expression to the next. "Dot . . ."

"She's OK," Tyler hurriedly said, reaching a hand out to me. I breathed a sigh of relief and took it gratefully, finding comfort in his touch. "She was knocked out, but she's fine. They're just keeping her in the hospital in case she has a concussion."

I squeezed Tyler's hand, then released it to run my hands through my hair. Taking a deep breath to calm myself, I leaned on the table again, trying to decide which question to ask first. "So, this was all about abducting Vitals?"

"No." Tyler shook his head sadly. "I was updated by the agents still on the scene about fifteen minutes ago. We were in the thick of it, but assailants were attacking people all over campus. There are a hundred and eighteen confirmed fatalities and one hundred and ninety-two people hospitalized. But they're still counting."

"Holy shit," Ethan breathed. Across from me, Josh was shaking his head in disbelief, his eyes wide. Alec just continued to tap away at his computer, unaffected—he would have received the same updates.

"If this was just about abducting Vitals, they would have done it more quietly," Tyler continued. "It just doesn't make tactical sense to kill that many people when they were clearly well trained and highly organized. They used the carnage as a cover, but that wasn't the only reason for it."

"Then what? Who did this? Why?" Frustration was leaking into my voice. I couldn't fathom what could possibly motivate someone to do this.

"The massacre—all those people running around with guns, shooting anything that moved—that was the Human Empowerment Network. They weren't as well organized as the guys in black or as well armed, but they were united in their hate for Variants. They released a video about an hour ago taking responsibility for it. It's just their leader, someone they're calling Mr. X, in a mask spewing ignorant, hateful things at the camera, but the message is clear. The Human Empowerment Network is growing, and they're becoming militant. They're a much bigger threat than we realized."

"And the Vital abductions?"

"That was Variant Valor." Tyler ran his own hand through his hair. I took a closer look at him—he was in sweats and a T-shirt, his hair messier than usual, and big circles drooped under his eyes. He had been home long enough to shower but not long enough to sleep. While Alec and I were in each other's arms, letting the Light restore us, Tyler had been working his ass off to figure out what had happened, to keep us safe. He was spent.

"They haven't made any dramatic public statements about being involved," he went on. "That would defy the point of using the chaos to cover up the abductions. But we have intelligence that suggests it was Variant Valor." He shared a look with Alec, and I knew he wouldn't be saying much more on that front—clearly that information was classified.

"I can't go into details," he confirmed. "But the fact they were so well organized and armed—that alone points to Variant Valor. Plus I had an inkling of it while I still had excess Light." He pointed to his head. He couldn't share classified information, but we were his Bond, and he was willing to bend the rules to share what he'd learned through his ability.

Josh asked the most important question. "What do they want with the Vitals, Gabe?"

"We don't know." Tyler sighed. "We've been trying to figure that out since we noticed a pattern a year ago. There are a few theories, but we're not any closer to finding an answer. They've never been this brazen about it though. They've taken twenty-seven Vitals at once. Rumors have been flying around about the strange Vital disappearances around the world, but this won't go unnoticed. Whatever it is they're doing, they're gearing up for something big."

"Are you sure it's Variant Valor doing this?" I asked. Why would Variants abduct Vitals? Why would we do this to ourselves? It wasn't adding up.

Tyler and Alec shared another look before Ty answered, "That's classified."

So they *were* sure it was Variant Valor, but he technically wasn't allowed to tell us that, or how they knew.

"So, what?" Ethan was frowning at the table in front of him, his hand still firmly on my knee. "The human psychos and the Variant psychos are working together now?"

"No, we don't think so. Variant Valor probably just learned what the humans were planning and used it to their advantage, to cover up what they wanted to do. Look"—Tyler's voice became very firm—"I can't really tell you three much more. I've already said too much, but that's only because I want you to understand the gravity of the situation. The stakes have been raised, and people are really scared. This is only the beginning."

None of us were willing to push for more information now that Tyler had put his foot down, although, judging by Ethan and Josh's questions, they knew as little as I did. That made me feel somewhat better. I didn't want to be the only one out of the loop—especially in *my* Bond.

My mind was racing, struggling to make sense of it all while new questions constantly popped up. Both the Human Empowerment Network and Variant Valor had proven themselves to be very real threats. While the boys' initial insistence that we keep our Bond a secret had seemed overly dramatic and unnecessary at the time, after everything I had seen and experienced that day—and everything Tyler had told us—I completely understood it now.

I would take the secret of our Bond to the grave if it meant keeping us safe—if it meant protecting my Variants.

The table had gone quiet, everyone left to their own morbid thoughts. The soft sound of Alec tapping away on his laptop was the only sound in the room.

Josh broke the silence. "How did you explain all the unconscious people on campus?"

"I didn't." Tyler smirked. "I pulled rank and told them it was classified while putting on my authoritarian voice and ordering our operatives to do what needed to be done—helping the injured, gathering evidence, and so on."

"What about security cameras? Surely something would have recorded me transferring Light to you all." I clasped my hands in front of me, anxiety wrapping around my throat. It was only a matter of time . . .

"That's one thing that worked in our favor," Tyler answered. "They didn't just block the cell signal. All electronics were down—anything with a chip or a power cord was useless. I suspect they had a Variant with an ability to manipulate electronics."

"Won't all the people who passed out have some questions?" Ethan asked.

"Of course, but no one saw anything in the chaos, and then all they could focus on was the pain. The only people I need to answer to weren't present, and Lucian should be able to take care of them anyway."

"You told Uncle Lucian?" Ethan sounded shocked.

All of us snapped our heads up to look at Tyler, even Alec. It was a little disconcerting to know another person had learned our secret so soon after realizing why it was so important to keep it hidden.

Tyler nodded, fixing us each with a meaningful look but holding Alec's gaze the longest. "He already knew. He was giving us space, waiting for us to come to him when we were ready."

"Shit," Josh cursed softly.

"I trust him." Tyler shrugged.

They all murmured their agreement. They weren't worried about Lucian Zacarias betraying us; they were just surprised Tyler had told him.

It had been good to get some more information, but I'd spent the whole conversation keeping an eye on the time. I had to make sure I made it to the hospital before visiting hours were over.

I stood from my seat. "I need to see Zara and Dot. Can we continue this later?"

Ethan and Josh got up at the same time.

"Of course," Tyler said with a yawn. "I really need to get some sleep anyway. The boys will take you."

"While the men do the important things," Alec cut in, speaking for the first time since I'd entered the room.

"What is up your ass, man?" Ethan frowned. "You're even more surly than usual."

Josh just leaned in the doorway, watching everything as he usually did, not looking even slightly put off by his manhood being questioned.

Alec scoffed and tried to go back to ignoring us all, but if he was going to drop passive aggressive comments like that, I wasn't going to just let it go.

I leaned my palms on the table and spoke directly at him. "You may not think that other people are important, but some of us are actually capable of normal human connections. And *you* may not want anything from me"—I threw his words back at him—"but there are others who do."

He fixed me with an angry glare, but I didn't wait for him to respond, turning around and walking toward the door. The boys followed, as I knew they would.

Tyler called after us, "Kid, if anyone so much as looks at her funny, you fry them to a crisp and get the hell out of there."

"Goes without saying, Gabe," Ethan called back, overtaking me and leading the way into the garage.

Josh kept pace with me. "What was that about? And don't try to tell me it was nothing. You don't usually let him bait you like that."

I didn't say anything, hoping he would drop it, but he gently grabbed my hand so I couldn't run away. I mentally checked that my Light was under control, but it was out of habit more than anything. I'd expelled all I had to get Alec recharged—now was the safest time for them to touch me, and they weren't being shy about it.

"Something happened between you two in Tyler's study."

So much for him dropping it. Of course he'd figured out something more was up, but even Josh wasn't omniscient. He knew something big had happened, but he didn't know what.

"Josh, I don't want to talk about it. Please." It was bad enough that Tyler had seen the aftermath. I didn't need Josh and Ethan knowing how a member of my own Bond had hurt me in the most humiliating way.

I fixed him with a firm look, trying to pull my hand out of his, but he held on and pulled me back to his side. He watched me with concern in his eyes for a moment. Then he kissed me gently, sighing against my lips.

TWENTY EIGHT

The drive to the hospital was quiet. They'd tried again to ask me what was going on with Alec as soon as we were on the road, but I shut it down, crossing my arms stubbornly and staring out the window.

It was hard to stay even a little mad at them though. Especially when they were touching me. They seemed to instinctively know there wasn't as much danger from my Light. Josh wrapped his hand around mine, prying it away from my chest, and Ethan leaned on the back of my seat, running his fingers through my hair.

As we reached the hospital though, they dropped it, and I was glad they did. I needed to focus on Zara and Dot. My personal shit wasn't going to get in the way of me being there for my friends.

We were a little surprised when the receptionist told us they were in the same room. I cringed, hoping they weren't making this whole situation worse on themselves by bickering, as they usually did.

Josh thanked her and took the lead down the hall. Now that we were in public, he was making sure to keep his hands off me. The events of the last twenty-four hours had been sobering—we had to be more careful. Ethan wrapped his arm around my waist, and I returned the side hug as we followed Josh into the elevators.

On the third floor, we walked together down the corridor, my guys flanking me like silent sentinels, but before we reached the door, I paused, wringing my hands.

Ethan draped an arm over my shoulder, but it was Josh who spoke from my other side.

"You got this, Eve."

He knew I was nervous. I had been keen to get to my friends to make sure they were OK, but now that I was actually here, I had no idea what I was supposed to do. I had no experience with having friends, let alone comforting them during a difficult time.

"Just be there," Ethan added.

I nodded and took a breath, squaring my shoulders. I could do this. If I could deal with Alec, I could deal with this.

With one final reminder to myself to put that asshole out of my mind, I raised my arm to knock on the door, but it swung open in front of me.

Dot and Charlie's mom stepped through it. Her face was streaked with tears, the mascara running down her cheeks, and her messy hair looked as if she'd run her hands through it a million times. Shoulders hunched, she looked up at me—or rather, *through* me—and blinked a few times.

"I'm getting coffee," she said in a detached voice.

"Mrs. Vanderford?" I placed a gentle hand on her shoulder.

She seemed to snap out of it, shaking her head lightly, some amount of clarity returning to her eyes.

"Oh, Eve." She drew me into a tight hug. "I'm glad you're here. They could both use a friend right now." Her voice broke on the last word, but she pulled away, making a visible effort to compose herself.

"I wouldn't be anywhere else. I just can't believe . . . Charlie . . ." My own voice was breaking as I struggled to find the words.

"How are you, Olivia?" Josh asked, saving me from having to find a way to finish.

"Is there anything we can do?" Ethan piped in.

"You're doing plenty by just being here," she replied in her shaky voice. "And we're holding up as well as can be expected. Lucian has already been in touch. He's furious, and he's promised to throw the full force of Melior Group at this. Knowing that something is already being done about it is helping. Henry is on the phone with him in the waiting room around the corner. I was just on my way to get us some coffee."

"Uncle Lucian won't rest until we find him, Aunt Olivia." Ethan stepped forward and wrapped his aunt up in one of his massive hugs.

"I know, sweetie." She sniffled. "I'll let you go see the girls. They shouldn't be alone."

She squeezed Josh's hand as she went past, her heels clicking on the gray floor.

I turned back to the door, taking a deep breath and wiping my eyes before pushing inside.

There were two beds in the sterile room, pushed up against the right wall, but I was surprised to find one of them empty. Zara and Dot were both in the bed closest to the window. Zara was lying under the covers, tubes sticking out of her arms, and Dot was sitting next to her, her knees pulled up.

They both looked in my direction, and I tried my best to hide my shocked expression. Not that I needed to.

As soon as she saw me, Dot flew off the bed and ran into my arms. We hugged tightly, just standing there, trying to find comfort in the embrace. Her delicate shoulders bobbed up and down softly as she cried. I'd been around her plenty of times without her massive heels on and knew just how short she was, but standing in the hospital room hugging her, she truly felt tiny in my arms—more fragile than I'd ever imagined my confident friend could be.

She pulled away slightly without letting go, and I saw she wasn't wearing any makeup either. Another first. Her bare face was splotchy and covered in tears.

"Charlie—" she croaked.

"I know," I cut in, saving her having to repeat it. "I'm so sorry, Dot. I can't even imagine."

Her face got a faraway look, and I guided her by the shoulders back to Zara's bed.

Zara watched us, silent tears soaking her pillow. With one last squeeze, I released Dot and slowly climbed onto the bed. I enfolded Zara in a much gentler hug, wary of hurting her, but she wrapped her arms around my neck tightly, and my own tears finally overflowed.

We held each other and cried for Beth—our beautiful friend who hadn't deserved this. An innocent, sweet girl who'd been dragged into a conflict that had nothing to do with her. She'd been there only because she was brave and wanted to warn people, and she'd ended up as collateral damage. Just another Dime that got in the way.

I pulled away and wiped my tears with the sleeve of Josh's hoodie.

"We're going to find out who did this," I said quietly, but the steel in my voice surprised even me.

Zara sighed and looked down. She didn't believe me, but she had no energy for a sarcastic reply.

Dot reclaimed her spot next to Zara, and I ended up sitting in the middle with my legs tucked under me, facing them. They were both staring into space, lost in thoughts of loved ones ripped away from them. I knew all too well how that felt.

"I'm a Vital," I blurted, and they both looked at me, a little confused.

I was trying to distract them, but I was also sick of secrets. If today had taught me anything, it was that life was precious and could be taken away at any moment. I'd lived my whole life lonely. Now I had two friends sitting in front of me, and I wanted them to know me. All of me.

"I know you guys already know that," I went on. Dot had figured it out ages ago, and Zara had put it together when I'd transferred Light to Tyler earlier that day. "But it feels good to say it. Do you want to know who's in my Bond?"

"Ethan," they both replied at the same time, but Zara added, "And Tyler Gabriel."

Dot looked at her in shock. "No, it's *Josh* as well as Ethan." Her eyes darted between Zara and me in confusion, the conviction in Zara's voice tripping her up.

"No," Zara replied. "It's *Tyler* and Ethan."

"You're both right," I piped in, stopping an argument before it started.

Zara gasped, lifting the hand not hooked up to an IV to cover her mouth in shock. "Ethan, Tyler, *and* Josh?"

I nodded, pressing my lips together and bugging my eyes out.

"Holy shit," Dot breathed. "Three Variants? That's so rare."

Sheepishly I raised my hand, holding up four fingers.

"*Four?!*" They spoke at the same time again, and I briefly wondered how they could be so hostile to each other. They were much more similar than they thought.

I nodded as they stared at me, mouths hanging slightly open. Having three Variants in a Bond was rare; four was almost unheard of.

"No, please, take your time in telling us who the fourth is. It's not like we're on the edge of our seats or anything." Zara managed to cock an eyebrow, and I smiled, glad to see some of her spunk back. I'd made the right decision in telling them, even if it made them forget for only a few minutes.

Dot gasped dramatically before I could speak. "In the square that day. You didn't get a headache."

She'd figured it out. I smiled at her and nodded. "Alec."

"As in Zacarias?" Zara asked for confirmation. "Kid's cousin. Brooding. Always wears black and scowls at people. Master of Pain. *That* Alec?"

"That's the one."

"Shut the fuck up. I don't believe you."

"I do," Dot cut in. "His power didn't affect her. I saw it with my own eyes. I can't believe I didn't put two and two together! Such an idiot! It's so obvious."

"Uh, no." Zara crossed her arms over her chest. "It's not. I've been living with this lying bitch for the last few months, and I had no clue she was even a Vital until today. It's like you've been living a double life."

"I'm so sorry for lying to you." I looked at her uneasily, feeling guilty. "It was not easy. And I felt like you could see straight through me every time I did. I was so awkward!"

She shrugged it off. "It's OK. I get why you're all keeping it on the down low. Especially considering . . ." She glanced over at Dot.

Dot began to cry again, her shoulders quivering, and I wrapped her hand in mine. Zara surprised me by grabbing her other hand.

Before I had a chance to say anything, though, Josh and Ethan walked in and announced that visiting hours were over. A stern-looking nurse was kicking people out, and they wanted to be gone before she set her sights on us.

Dot and Zara stared at them, my revelations heavy in their gazes. The guys shared a look.

Ethan crossed his muscled arms over his chest and frowned. "What?"

Instead of answering him, Zara looked at me. "You're going to have your hands full, girl. I don't know if I'm worried about your reputation or just jealous."

"Eew." Dot whacked her, but very gently. "You know I'm related to two of them, right?"

"What the hell are they talking about?" Ethan demanded, but instead of answering him, Dot climbed off the bed and gave him a hug. Ethan hugged his cousin gently, his big frame making her appear even smaller in his arms.

Josh made his way over to Zara's bed and spoke quietly to her. I heard them talking about her parents—they'd been in Canada at the time of the attack but had started heading to Bradford Hills as soon as they heard their daughter was in the hospital.

After a few moments, the boys swapped. Josh gave Dot a comforting hug while Ethan surprised me by propping himself on the edge of Zara's bed and leaning down to gently embrace her as well.

They'd had their differences in the past, but none of that petty shit mattered anymore. Not when Charlie was missing. Not when Beth was dead.

The stern nurse bustled in not long after and insisted we clear out, also ordering Dot back into her own bed. I gave the girls another tight hug each and, with a promise to come back the next day, left with my guys.

As soon as we were in the car, Josh turned to me. "You told them?"

"Told who what?" Ethan asked from the back seat.

"*Whom*," Josh corrected, keeping his eyes on me.

"Man, screw you and your grammatical shit," Ethan griped but with humor in his voice. "Tell me!"

I bit my bottom lip, worried I was in trouble for spilling our secret. It was done now, though, and I couldn't find it in me to feel bad. I'd shared something real about myself with my friends. Friends whom I cared enough about to feel their pain over what had happened to them today. Friends who cared enough about *me* to want to know this about me.

So I just nodded at him and turned away, strapping myself in.

"Eve told Zara and Dot about us. Our Bond," Josh filled Ethan in as he pulled out of the parking spot.

Ethan whistled from the back seat but didn't say anything.

"They already knew most of it anyway. Dot's known for ages, and Zara saw me with you and Ty today. I only filled in the gaps." I shrugged. "I trust them."

"It's OK. We were never going to be able to keep it secret forever." Josh reached over the center console to hold my hand as he drove.

"Yeah, I want everyone to know you're mine anyway." Ethan stuck his head in between our seats to give me a wink and a flash of his dimples. Of course, we all knew we needed to keep our Bond secret from "everyone" for as long as possible, but I still appreciated the sentiment.

"*Ours*," Josh corrected him for the second time in five minutes. "And everyone already thinks you're dating."

"Bro, it's not the same."

As they bickered lightheartedly over the semantics, I settled back into the seat and smiled to myself. I'd just come from seeing two people I could truly call my friends. I was a Vital with *four* guys in my Bond—four people I'd apparently known from birth.

It had been a bumpy couple of months, but I'd somehow found myself surrounded by people who cared about me, who knew me. I was beginning to learn what it felt like to have a family.

I belonged.

For the first time in my life, I was realizing that feeling as though you belong somewhere has nothing to do with geography. It didn't matter how many times my mother and I had moved, or that I'd never felt sentimental attachment to a family home. Belonging has nothing to do with that and everything to do with the people who make you *feel* as though you belong with them.

I had found my people.

Everything was still fucked up. Beth was dead. Charlie was missing. There was scary new tech that could out me as a Vital. There was a terrifying web of manipulation and ulterior motives, players I didn't have a scrap of knowledge about pulling strings behind stages I didn't even know existed.

And don't get me started on the most frustrating, worrisome, annoying asshole problem of all—Alec.

Yes, everything was a mess, but I had found where I *belonged*, and I refused to not be pleased about it.

EPILOGUE

The room was sparse but clean, the walls white, the two metal cots bolted to the floor. There was a toilet and a small sink in one corner. Three times per day, two black-clad men pushed a trolley down the hallway and one of them slid a tray of bland food through a slot in the door.

Two times per day, two black-clad men accompanied another man or woman wearing a lab coat and carrying a clipboard. The lab coats peered into the room, pressed buttons on the panel next to the door, took notes, and moved away.

Five times per day Charlie tried to get answers from his regular visitors. As soon as he heard movement, he sprang off his thin mattress and rushed forward to the long, thin pane of glass set into the heavy door.

Charlie pleaded and asked questions, yelled and demanded answers. He had tried every way of speaking to them. He was always ignored.

He'd been in his white prison for three full days. He had no idea how long he'd been unconscious before that. A few days at least, judging by the amount of Light coursing through him. His arms and legs were almost constantly itchy, and it was spreading to his torso. Wandering around the bare room nude was beginning to seem like a good idea.

The mechanical clank of the door unlocking startled him, and he sat up. It wasn't time for food, and the last lab coat had come past only twenty-eight minutes and forty seconds ago.

For the first time since Charlie was dragged inside the cell half-conscious, the door opened. Charlie stood, unsure what to do. Should he dash forward, try to escape, or should he back away from the men with the large guns now entering the room?

At least the guns weren't pointed at him—they were slung over the shoulders of the two men half carrying, half dragging another man into the room. The new prisoner was wearing the same shapeless gray pants and top that Charlie had woken up in.

The two men dumped the unconscious form onto the bed and left the room without even acknowledging Charlie's presence. He rushed to the door and watched as the guards retreated down the empty hallway.

Moving back to the other bed, Charlie immediately started checking his new roommate. He knew just enough first aid to determine if the injuries were life threatening. After rolling the unconscious young man onto his back, Charlie checked his air passage and heartbeat. He was alive. With careful fingers, Charlie started checking for broken bones, moving the gray fabric out of the way to look for bruising. There weren't any obvious injuries, but there was no way to check for internal bleeding.

Even though the young man didn't look beaten or tortured, he hadn't regained consciousness, and his light brown hair was a mess, his skin clammy.

What the hell did they do to you? Charlie thought, running his hands through his own hair in frustration.

The sound of voices drew his attention back to the door. He stood facing it, putting himself between whatever was on the other side and the unconscious man on the bed.

"... shouldn't even be here!" a woman's voice carried clearly. "If I'm seen anywhere near this—"

"Why did you come then?" a deep man's voice interrupted her, sounding completely unfazed.

"Because you weren't taking my calls!" she yelled, frustration building in her voice by the second. "It's been over a week since that mess at Bradford Hills. I didn't agree to that many casualties. I *certainly* didn't agree to the Vital kidnappings."

A week? His family would be worried sick. Dot would be beside herself. At the thought of his sister, his Variant, Charlie's chest ached. It wasn't the consuming pain that came when she overused her ability and he needed to get to her. It was a longing—a need to be home.

He had no way of knowing if she was OK. All he remembered was trying to get to one of the residence hall buildings that was under construction, close to where they'd separated from Gabe, Ethan, and Eve. It would have been empty, a good place to hide. But halfway there, Dot crumpled to the ground next to him, her hand slipping out of his. Charlie had turned just in time to see the butt of a rifle coming at his face.

He knew now he'd spent the next few days unconscious and been moved to wherever this hellhole was. But he had no way of knowing what had happened to Dot. He was trying not to think about it.

He forced himself to focus on the voices in the corridor. He was getting more information from this one overheard conversation than he had from all the pleading with his impassive guards.

"Come now, Christine, you didn't think I would expend those kinds of resources without getting something out of it?" The man chuckled darkly. There was something familiar about his voice.

Charlie inched closer to the door, trying to catch a glimpse of the man's face, but it was the woman he recognized first. She came to a stop right in front of his cell, turning to face her companion.

"You're fucking deranged. What the hell even is this place?" Senator Christine Anderson screeched. She threw her arms up, looking around. The last time Charlie had seen her was the night of the gala as she'd stood on the stage and delivered her speech, waxing eloquent about her personal and professional mission to solidify peace and cooperation between Variants and humans, then announcing her intention to run for president.

"You want the presidency?" The man no longer sounded amused. "Well, nothing motivates voters like fear. Correct me if I'm wrong, but your poll numbers skyrocketed the day after the Bradford Hills invasion and have remained high. The fact that I used the opportunity to collect some assets for *my* interests is of no consequence. You will have the oval office, and I will have your cooperation as the leader of the free world when you do. Everything else is semantics. Now, calm down."

"*Assets.* You say it like you signed a contract for delivery of stock, not like you kidnapped nearly thirty Vitals in one day." Her voice had lowered, but she wasn't backing down. "Davis, you took Bradford Hills staff; children of prominent, influential Variants; a fucking chart-topping singer! People are going to take notice."

"They were already starting to. I need the Vitals. It's done now."

Davis. Just as the familiar voice and the name clicked into place in Charlie's mind, the man stepped forward, giving him a clear view of the dark hair, peppered with gray at the temples, and the broad shoulders draped in a three-thousand-dollar suit.

Davis Damari. Why was Uncle Lucian's business partner doing this?

Charlie had met the man on several occasions, usually at glitzy Variant events, a few times when Davis had been invited to dinner by Charlie's dad or Uncle Lucian. Surely Uncle Lucian didn't know anything about this?

Of course, Melior Group knew how to skirt the lines of legality— Charlie had no illusions about that, having done some slightly shady hacking work for them in the past. *But this . . .*

"What do you need the Vitals for? Stop evading my questions." There was more steel in Christine's voice now.

"Once I succeed, no one will even bat an eye at the methods. What's a couple of abductions and a handful of deaths when at the end of it, the world will be changed? I'm going to fix what science doesn't even understand yet. I'm going to show the world that Variants are meant to *rule* the world."

Charlie gasped and took an involuntary step back, the realization hitting him hard.

He was behind it all. Davis Damari was the one who had been orchestrating the kidnappings of Vitals for over a year. He was the one who'd been stirring up tensions between Variants and humans. He was the leader, maybe even the creator, of Variant Valor.

Charlie's movement caught the pair's attention, and they both turned to look. The senator averted her gaze immediately, recognition and then shame crossing her features.

Davis Damari didn't look at Charlie's face, to try to recognize the *person* in his clutches. He saw only an *asset.* His head cocked to the side slightly as his calculating eyes watched Charlie's twitchy movements. Charlie had been so focused on the conversation he hadn't even realized he was scratching vigorously. One hand was under the ugly gray top, the other trying to get at a spot on his hip.

Davis gestured to someone down the hall, and heavy booted footsteps approached. "This one's ready. Take him up and prep him."

As the sounds of the digital panel and the heavy lock sliding back filled the room once again, Davis turned away. "Come, Senator. We can talk in my office."

Davis Damari continued down the corridor, and Senator Christine Anderson followed him silently, her eyes still averted.

Two guards entered Charlie's room, and all thoughts about what he'd just heard fled his mind. Now, there was only fear.

THE END

ACKNOWLEDGEMENTS

First and foremost, to my husband: 'thank you' doesn't even begin to cover the depth of gratitude I feel for your unwavering support. Through the doubts, the struggles, the exhaustion, the elation and everything in between, you were there every step of the way, doing all you could to help and more. I won't say that I couldn't have written it without you – that was all me – but I certainly couldn't have gotten it edited, published, marketed and out there for everyone else to read if it wasn't for your encouragement and faith in me.

To my friends who read the early versions and had nothing but encouraging things to say, thank you for always having my back. Especially Dina – you were the first one to ever read it. It was a mess in draft two and you still loved it! That was more motivating than you'll ever know.

Thank you to Writers Unite – my writers group crew. Your honest, discerning, invaluable feedback shaped this book into what it is. And your support and encouragement always gave me an extra push to keep going. Please don't ever stop brutally tearing my work to pieces!

Thank you to my beta readers – the first group of people outside my close friends to read this book. I was so nervous to take this step but each and every one of you had so many positive things to say even as you pointed out all the errors and inconsistencies. Your feedback helped me finesse and polish the story and I am grateful to each of you for taking the time to provide it.

I am incredibly grateful to have found the RH community in general. I've never come across a more engaged, enthusiastic, supportive bunch of readers. When I needed beta readers, you put your hands up. When I asked for ARC readers, you responded with overwhelming enthusiasm. Whenever I reached out to a new person, reader or author, I was met with nothing but positivity and support. I've made some genuine friends through this process and I'm so glad I've connected with you all.

Finally, to my fur baby – Daisy. Thank you for refusing to change our strict daily walkie schedule. It got me off the computer, out of the house, and into fresh air, reminding me there was a whole world out there past my keyboard! I can't wait to twist more of that world into stories.

ABOUT THE AUTHOR

Kaydence Snow has lived all over the world but ended up settled in Melbourne, Australia. She lives near the beach with her husband and a beagle that has about as much attitude as her human.

She draws inspiration from her own overthinking, sometimes frightening imagination, and everything that makes life interesting – complicated relationships, unexpected twists, new experiences and good food and coffee. Life is not worth living without good food and coffee!

She believes sarcasm is the highest form of wit and has the vocabulary of a highly educated, well-read sailor. When she's not writing, thinking about writing, planning when she can write next, or reading other people's writing, she loves to travel and learn new things.

To keep up to date with Kaydence's latest news and releases sign up to her newsletter here: kaydencesnow.com

OR FOLLOW HER ON:

Facebook: @KaydenceSnowAuthor
Instagram: @kaydencesnowauthor
Twitter: @Kaydence_Snow
Goodreads: goodreads.com/author/show/18388923.Kaydence_Snow
Amazon: amazon.com/author/kaydencesnow

NOTE FROM THE AUTHOR

Thank you so much for reading my book! It blows my mind that people are interested in reading what I wrote. I really hope you enjoyed Variant Lost and you'll consider leaving a review. And if you didn't like it, that's OK too – I'm always open to feedback.

You can email me any time at hello@kaydencesnow.com

Made in the USA
Columbia, SC
12 February 2019